JENNIFER LEWIS
YVONNE LINDSAY
JOAN HOHL

MILLS

First Published in Great Britain 2016
By Mills & Boon, an imprint of HarperCollins*Publishers*
1 London Bridge Street, London, SE1 9GF

BEDDED BY THE BOSS © 2016 Harlequin Books S. A.

The Boss's Demand, *Something About The Boss. . .*and *Beguiling The Boss* were first published in Great Britain by Harlequin (UK) Limited.

The Boss's Demand © 2007 Jennifer Lewis
Something About The Boss. . . © 2013 Harlequin Books S.A.
Beguiling The Boss © 2013 Joan Hohl

Special thanks and acknowledgement to Yvonne Lindsay for her contribution to the *Texas Cattleman's Club: The Missing Mogul* series.

ISBN: 978-0-263-92065-9

05-0516

Our policy is to use papers that are natural, renewable and recyclable products and made from wood grown in sustainable forests.The logging and manufacturing processes conform to the legal environmental regulations of the country of origin.

Printed and bound in Spain
by CPI, Barcelona

THE BOSS'S DEMAND

BY
JENNIFER LEWIS

Jennifer Lewis has been dreaming up stories for as long as she can remember and is thrilled to be able to share them with readers. She has lived on both sides of the Atlantic and worked in media and the arts before she grew bold enough to put pen to paper. She is happily settled in New York with her family, and she would love to hear from readers at jen@jen-lewis.com.

For Michael, Jordan and Mia,
my favourite people in the world.

Acknowledgements:

Thanks to all the people who read this book at various
stages, including Amanda, Anne, Barb, Betty, Car, Cece,
Cheryel, Kathy, Joanne, Leeanne, Marie and Mish.
Special thanks to Carol and Kelle for your insight into
aspects of the oil industry.

One

"I want her gone."

Elan Al Mansur's low-pitched command shot into her ear as she pressed the intercom button to speak with him. Surprise made Sara catch her breath—he must have someone in his office. She held her tongue, afraid of her new boss though she'd only been there a few hours.

"But Mr. Al Mansur…" Sara recognized the voice of Jill Took from Human Resources. "She has a bachelor's degree in business with a minor in geology, she wrote her honors thesis on the profit potential of alternative mining technologies, and her references are excellent."

They were talking about her.

Her finger quivered on the button as her brain told her to hang up. But she stifled her breathing and kept her finger in place.

"Did I not inform you that I require my assistant to be a *mature* woman?" His voice was almost a growl.

"Yes, but…"

"How old is Miss Daly?"

"Twenty-five, but she seems exceptionally mature. She presented herself…"

"Twenty-five!" Sara heard a dismissive snort. "That's hardly what I would call mature. I've made it quite clear that I prefer my assistant to be a woman with decades of experience, and preferably gray hairs on her head."

Sara's finger twitched on the button as her hackles rose. She took in a measured gulp of air.

"Mr. Al Mansur, I'm afraid we don't receive many applications from senior citizens. I…"

"Is Miss Daly married?"

"No, sir, I don't believe she is. But as you know, sir, that kind of information is not—"

Jill paused and Sara pressed the phone to her ear as she heard a loud creak and some rustling. Elan Al Mansur must have silenced Jill with a gesture.

"Miss Took—" His throaty voice coiled into Sara's ear and fear curled in her stomach at his tone. "I'm a busy man. I don't have time for the whims and fancies of foolish girls. We both know the kinds of problems which have plagued my office of late. Miss Daly must go."

"But Mr. Al Mansur…"

"That's my last word on the matter. *Miss Daly?*"

Sara jumped in her chair as her name assaulted her down the phone line. He must have pressed the intercom button, too.

"Yes," she croaked.

"Please, come in."

"Yes, sir." She hung up the phone gingerly. Adrenaline spiked through her body. *I'm going to be fired.*

She could hear the murmur of their voices on the other side of the heavy mahogany door, no doubt discussing the terms of her severance. Her severance? After one morning? She'd moved a thousand miles from her home in Wisconsin to take this job in Placer, amidst the crumpled peaks and wide valleys of Nevada's high desert. All her cash had gone into the security deposit on her apartment and her car had died and… The horror of the situation bloomed like a thunderhead.

This job was the answer to all her prayers. The high salary was her ticket out from under the crushing load of debt from her college loans and her mother's final illness. It had taken her extra time to get her degree while holding down a full-time job, and finally here was an opportunity to build her career and make her reputation as Executive Assistant and Project Manager at one of the fastest growing players in the oil industry.

Now it would be taken from her because she didn't have any gray in her hair?

It wasn't fair. To work so hard for so long and not even be given a chance to prove herself? *No. Not today, Mr. Al Mansur.* She didn't plan to leave quietly.

Fear and rage fought inside her as she rose from her chair. Buttoning the jacket of the conservative suit she'd bought especially for the job, she strode toward the door. Her hand trembled as she reached for the large brushed-steel handle, and she inhaled sharply as she pressed down the lever.

"But she's a plain little thing, I'm sure she wouldn't be the type to…" Ms. Took's words trailed off and pink flushed her cheeks as Sara made her entrance.

Her boss's focused black gaze hit her like a right hook to the gut. He leaned back in a black leather chair, arms on the armrests, surveying her down the length of his aristocratic nose.

Everything about the man seemed designed to intimidate. From his thick black hair and hard-edged features to his broad muscled frame in its tailored black suit, Elan Al Mansur seethed with power and danger.

Sara's angry protest withered on her tongue as he leaned forward in his chair, narrowed his eyes, and pursed his lips slightly.

"Miss Daly."

"Yes." She was surprised her voice sounded so normal as she gagged on a ferocious cocktail of terror and indignation.

His gaze drifted over her face, disdain plain in his raised eyebrow and slightly curled lip.

Anger simmered inside Sara along with an unfamiliar sensation. An odd tension that tightened her muscles and nerves, wound them taut like the strings of an instrument as a searing note of high-pitched anxiety rose in the air.

His eyes locked on hers. "You're being reassigned to a position in accounting. Your salary and benefits will remain the same. You'll begin your duties immediately."

Accounting? She'd moved here to take a highly visible position as right hand to the CEO, with assurances that her duties would range far beyond administrative tasks. A transfer to accounting was a step backward. A slap in the face.

"But why?" The words shot out before she had a chance to shape them into an intelligent question.

Jill Took shifted awkwardly in her chair, "Er, we believe your skill set and attention to detail will be better employed in, er, other capacities."

Sara tore her eyes from Miss Took and fixed them back on the man who wanted her gone. He didn't even know her and already he despised her.

Instead of shrinking in the face of his distaste, she felt her assertive impulse growing, swelling, threatening to burst its boundaries.

But she had everything to lose and nothing to gain from alienating this man. *Proceed with caution.*

His arrogant features had an unsettling beauty to them. Some women might find him attractive. But to her he was simply a boss.

An ordinary man in a dark suit who just happened to have eyes that tore through flesh and bone with the intensity of their gaze.

She stared at him for a full five seconds and he didn't flinch. A curious expression lit his unblinking eyes. His lips parted slightly but he didn't speak. At last, he leaned forward—his chair let out a violent creak—and reached for a pen on his desk.

"You'll be compensated for your inconvenience, Miss Daly."

"I don't want compensation." At last her repressed ire bubbled over into speech. "I want this job. I'm qualified for this job and I'm a hard worker. I'll be the best assistant you've ever had, I promise you that, Mr. Al Mansur. You will find no fault with me."

She could hardly believe she was begging to keep a job with a man who obviously didn't want her around, but she was damned if she'd let a career opportunity of this magnitude be snatched rudely away.

"That will not be possible, Miss Daly."

His poker face and easy posture threw fresh fuel on the flames of her indignation.

"I overheard your conversation." The words slipped out before she had time to consider the consequences. Good. It was time to lay all her cards on the table.

He raised an eyebrow and a shadow clouded his face. He blinked once, then his fierce eyes tunneled into her again with harrowing intensity.

Sara struggled for breath, for strength to defend herself. "I heard you say I'm not old enough for the position."

"Er, Miss Daly—" Jill Took rose from her chair, but ceased speaking when her boss raised his hand.

"Miss Daly, I'll be frank with you." His voice was deep, his tone casual. He leaned back in his chair—creak!—and crossed his arms over his chest. Sara couldn't help noticing how thick his upper arms were, even through the wool of his suit.

"I've had my fill of flighty girls who are here merely to hunt for a husband. Don't think I flatter myself that I'm the object of their attentions. Frankly, I find them pathetic."

He looked down his slightly aquiline nose at her for a second and the full force of his disgust threatened to knock her off her feet.

"I have a business to run and I will no longer tolerate the foolish behavior of those who have anything other than my business on their mind. For this reason I shall no longer consider young, single women for this position."

He leaned forward again—creak!—and picked up a pen off the desk. As if to sign her death warrant. "That will be all, Miss Daly."

A rush of exasperation propelled Sara to his desk. She placed her fingertips on the polished mahogany and leaned toward him. Close enough to taste his scent—subtle and masculine—the fragrance of a deodorant soap released by warm, active skin.

He leaned back slowly, surveying her, arms crossed over his chest. Listening.

Now she was on the offensive.

"Mr. Al Mansur, I may be a young, single woman, but, believe me, I have no interests beyond performing this job to the best of my abilities. I am an experienced executive assistant."

And a plain little thing. Plain, was she? So much the better. She lifted her chin and fixed her gaze directly on his dark eyes. He narrowed them slightly.

She sucked in a breath. "Your company is the kind of fast-growing, forward-thinking firm I want to work for. You've achieved revenue growth of ten percent a year over the last five years. You're a leader in exploiting new drilling technologies and reducing environmentally harmful emissions at your drilling sites."

She steadied herself, refused to wilt in the heat of his scorching stare. "Your company has won praise for creating a progressive labor-friendly work environment. Praise it may not deserve, given the way I'm being treated. And if you take this job away from me I'll *sue* you for reverse age discrimination."

As her words reverberated off the stark white walls of his office, she sprang back from the desk. She crossed her arms over her chest, mirrored his defensive gesture. Her assertiveness thrilled her—and appalled her. A lawsuit? She couldn't even afford a two-piece suit. She was bluffing, but what the heck, she didn't have much to lose.

Well, except the position in accounting. Which did still have the same excellent salary and benefits. Recrimination snaked in her gut. She was playing pretty high-stakes poker with her life right now.

His face tightened as he watched her. His black eyes burned with intensity that sent an icy shiver up her spine. If looks could kill… Perhaps looks *could* kill? The one he gave her right now seemed to be sapping her life force in an alarming way.

On second thought, Mr. Al Mansur, perhaps counting a few beans…

"You…" He uttered the single word in a voice so deep it was barely within the human range of hearing.

He paused, then rose from his chair in a single swift motion.

"You…" Rage crackled in his throaty speech and sparked in his eyes. He rested a big hand on the desk, amidst the piles of papers and stacks of files that covered its surface. Awareness of his threatening physique cowed her as he leaned across the desk, a muscle working in his jaw. "*You*—will sue *me?*"

"It's not fair. You haven't given me a chance. You're firing me for something someone else has done." She sounded calm and rational, though she felt anything but. "Let me prove to you I can do this job. If you aren't happy with my performance, then you can transfer me or fire me outright and I won't complain."

He considered her for a moment, brow furrowed. Then he drew himself up and crossed his arms over his chest. He shot a glance at Jill Took, then looked back at Sara with one eyebrow raised.

"All right, Miss Daly. You shall have one month."

She sagged with glorious relief.

"One month to prove that you can keep your mind focused on your duties."

"You won't be disappointed, sir." She resisted the urge to add a military salute.

Her shoulders locked with sudden anxiety as he strode around his desk. Disobeying the instinct to shrink from his approach, she forced herself to stand steady. She took his offered hand and shook it with what she hoped was authoritative firmness. Big and warm, his hand gripped hers for a mere instant.

And in that instant she realized the magnitude of the challenge before her.

An invisible shudder rocked her as his skin touched hers. His dark eyes seemed to see right through her, their piercing gaze penetrating to the core of her being. Everything in her pricked up—ears, hair, goose bumps—agonizingly aware of the danger-ously male life force before her.

When she drew her hand back it tingled slightly. Her body flushed with sudden heat that belied the air-conditioned chill of the office. If not for the stiff fabric of her new suit, her newly tightened nipples would be clearly visible.

What on earth?

Chemistry? Sara stepped backward, blinking, afraid of the strange sensations surging through her. How could a man she didn't know—a man she didn't like at all—have this kind of effect on her?

Oh, dear.

She cleared her throat, desperate to get control of her errant body and mind and demonstrate the focused professionalism she'd promised.

"Will that be all, sir?" She sounded like a movie character. Right now she needed a script.

She needed to get out of there.

ASAP.

Her boss had turned away to rifle through the mess of papers sprawled over his huge desk.

"Hmph," he grunted, without looking up. Then he nodded dismissively to the two women. "Thank you."

Jill Took rose from her chair and bolted for the door. Sara scurried behind her like a startled rabbit.

Outside in the spacious annex that held Sara's desk, Jill turned to her.

"Sara, what I was saying when you came in, about you being a plain little thing…" Her cheeks turned pink again. "You know I was just trying anything I could think of to get Mr. Al Mansur to change his mind."

"Of course." Sara nodded vigorously, wondering why Jill's cheeks were so pink if she wasn't fibbing. "And I appreciate you standing up for me. I won't let you down."

"I know you won't. I hired you, remember?"

Sara laughed a little, glad to release some tension.

Jill lowered her voice. "He's all right really. It's just that, well, he's right, quite honestly. I hired his last two assistants. They appeared to be perfectly capable, suitable employees, very polished and efficient, but they… I don't know how to explain it. They went gaga over him." Jill widened her eyes comically.

Sara blinked and swallowed. She'd tasted a sip of gaga and was still tipsy from it.

"I mean, he's a good-looking guy and all," Jill continued quietly, with a quick glance at the closed door. "But he has some kind of bizarre effect on women that makes them throw themselves at him in the most embarrassing way. I could tell you weren't that sort at all."

Since you're such a plain little thing.

The unspoken words hung in the air between them. Sara shrank like Alice in Wonderland before the immaculately attired thirty-something blonde in her designer suit and high heels. Apparently Jill was impervious to whatever strange curse of irresistibility hung over the head of poor Elan. Sara felt thoroughly humbled.

"Not at all," she managed. "I need this job and I mean to keep it."

"You'll do great," Jill said, giving her a reassuring squeeze on the arm.

Sara nodded resolutely. "You bet I will."

Sue him for reverse age discrimination, would she? Elan raised his eyebrows. That was a first. She obviously knew little about discrimination law, but it stung that she'd thought to accuse him of bias.

He had nothing against female employees. He'd even hire them out in the oil fields if they wanted the work.

But he wanted nothing more to do with simpering maidens who draped themselves across his desk and fluttered their eyelashes over his morning coffee. They exhausted him with their intrigues and flirtations. And none of them could even make a decent cup of coffee. Weak—the coffee and the women.

He looked up at a knock on the door. "Come in."

Sara entered with a report he'd asked her to prepare and placed the file on his desk.

"Can I get you anything?" Her voice rang in his silent office like a bell. She waited quietly. A strand of pale hair had come loose from her bun and fluttered near her chin, which lifted in a gesture of defiance.

"I could use a cup of coffee." He cocked his head.

"I don't know how to make coffee." She stared at him, her attitude almost insolent. He leaned forward in his chair, struck by her refusal.

"I suspect you have the aptitude to figure it out," he said slowly. "But never mind. Too much caffeine rattles the nerves."

He saw a slight smile tug at the corners of her mouth, but she quickly gained control of her features and regarded him once again with a stony expression.

He'd felt the sharp edge of her attitude and he had to admit he liked it. She stood her ground admirably.

She leaned over to replace the cap on a pen lying open on his desk. The loose strand of hair hung momentarily in her eyes and she raised a hand to brush it aside. As she tucked the lock behind her ear she looked up at him, caught off guard, and their eyes met.

A mute challenge.

Suddenly his office seemed uncomfortably warm.

She turned and left without another word. A good sign. She wouldn't bend his ear with idle chitchat.

He'd give her the chance she asked for. That she'd demanded. He'd seen the fire that flared in her eyes. Eyes the color of rare jade, cool and flecked with gold. Fringed with pale lashes that had blinked in anger as she'd stared him down.

A plain little thing? What an expression. He was amused by the way some people defined beauty in terms of how loudly it shouted at you. For him, true beauty was a quality that shone from within, that brightened and strengthened, like the morning sun rising behind dark mountains. A force that could be dangerous to its beholder.

But Sara's quiet beauty had no effect on him. He'd grown used to enjoying the more obvious kind of feminine attributes. When in Rome… Fast cars, fast women and the comfort and ease of being alone in his bed at the end of the day.

No ties, no responsibilities, no commitments. Something that would be unheard of, horrifying even, to the people he'd left behind in Oman.

But he had everything he needed here, including freedom from the crippling bonds of traditions that had no place in the modern world.

* * *

Sara spent much of the afternoon rearranging the files in her desk. Her predecessor's organizational system baffled her. But then it didn't sound like she'd been there long. Nor had the woman before her or the one before that.

Had they all fallen victim to the dangerous charms of a boss who wanted nothing more than an efficient worker?

She smoothed the last of her newly printed labels on her neatly rearranged file folders and eased the drawer shut.

Her boss emerged from his office and walked past her desk without saying a word or even looking in her direction. He strode across the floor with the powerful gait of a predator.

As the tall mahogany door to the elevator lobby closed behind him, Sara reflected that Elan himself must be the reason this job came with hardship pay. She could already see he worked like a demon and expected his employees to do the same.

Oh, she could be a demon all right.

She felt a little circumspect about entering his office when he was away, but he hadn't actually told her to keep out. She planned to organize it in a such a way that he'd wonder how he ever survived without her.

She pushed open the door and stepped into the hushed space. No paintings or statues, not a single photograph ornamented his desk. Elan was clearly all business all the time.

She'd felt it necessary to establish that she was not the coffee waitress, but now she was keen to prove she'd do everything in her power to make Elan's day run smoothly. With brisk efficiency, she sorted and rearranged the disarray of papers on his desk, labeling them with sticky notes if they required action. She sharpened his pencils and tested his pens, threw away any dry ones.

She'd rustled up a can of WD-40 to rid his chair of its infuriating squeak. Proud to be a roll-up-the-sleeves type of person, she was on her hands and knees under the chair when the door opened.

"What on earth…?" Her boss's deep voice rumbled across the silent office. From her vantage point under the desk she could see two shiny black brogues, and the crisp cuffs of his pinstriped suit.

A fist of apprehension seized her gut and she obeyed the instinctive urge to leap to her feet.

"Ouch!" She banged her head hard on the underside of the chair.

The brogues took a step forward and Sara swallowed hard. She maneuvered out from under the massive chair and clambered to her feet with as much dignity as her fitted skirt would allow.

The sunset streaming through the wall of windows made her blink. As did the sight of Elan, his broad shoulders silhouetted in the doorway. His suit jacket was unbuttoned and his tie loosened, revealing a glimpse of dark throat that beckoned her eyes.

The harsh features of his face gleamed like rare metal in the copper rays of the lowering sun as he stared at her, dark brows lowered over narrowed eyes.

He looked down at the shining mahogany surface that had previously been covered by papers, then at her, and the can in her hand.

"What are you doing?"

She cleared her throat. "Your chair creaks."

One black brow raised.

"Didn't you notice? It's been driving me crazy. Let's see if I got it." She jumped down into the seat of the enormous leather chair and was pleased to hear absolutely nothing. "I think I nailed it."

He hadn't moved a muscle. "What have you done to my desk?" He wrenched his eyes from hers to the newly uncluttered expanse of mahogany.

"I sorted your papers into relevant categories. I didn't throw anything away, but the pile on the left can go, I think."

He frowned at her. His face darkened and suspicion clouded his eyes. "How could you possibly know enough about my work to organize my papers on your first day?"

"Instinct."

But all instinct fled as her skin began to sizzle under Elan's searing gaze.

"Please rise from my chair." He spoke slowly, as if attempting to communicate with someone with a poor command of the language.

She jolted to her feet. She'd been so transfixed by him she'd forgotten she was lounging in his personal throne.

His dark pupils tracked her with laser-beam intensity. "What made you think you could enter my office and handle my effects without permission?"

She struggled to regain her professional demeanor. "I consider keeping your desk organized to be one of my responsibilities."

He lowered his head slightly, scrutinizing her. "How do I know you weren't placing a bug there?"

"A bug?"

"To record my conversations."

Indignation stung her. "Are you saying anything worth recording?"

She immediately regretted her childish pique.

Elan stared at her. His brow furrowed as he digested her insolence. But his reply was measured, calm.

"To my business rivals, yes." He strode across the room and maneuvered around her. He quickly crouched down and reached a hand under the seat of the chair.

Sara found her eyes resting on his neck, on the strip of tan skin between the starched collar of his white shirt and the close-cropped black hair at the base of his skull. His small, delicate ear was at odds with the massive, powerful build of his body.

He knelt on the floor and reached an arm under his desk. The roping muscles of his back, visible even though the dark fabric of his suit, captured her attention. It took a few seconds before she realized he was feeling the underside of the desk, searching for electronic devices.

Anger at his suspicion pricked her. She'd never been accused of criminal activity before, and distrust didn't sit well with her. She'd worked at one job or another since age fourteen, and the admiration and satisfaction of her boss had always been something she could count on.

Elan leaned further under the desk. His suit jacket lifted, revealing the curve of his rear. Good Lord, the man was built like a decathlete.

She took a step backward, trying to regain control as a sudden swell of heat made her body uncomfortable inside the stiff fabric of her suit.

He backed slowly out from under the desk while she tried to look anywhere except at his well-muscled backside. Elan avoided looking at her, too, as he pulled himself awkwardly back up to his feet.

"Still think I'm a mole?" She cocked her head, daring him to extend his accusation.

He ran a hand through his thick hair. "Your previous job was with an electronics firm, no?"

"Yes, Bates Electronics. I worked there for two years. They have no relationship to the oil industry that I know of and no reason to engage in industrial espionage. I am not a spy."

"Couldn't you have alerted building maintenance to the fact that my chair creaks?"

"Sure, but by the time I'd called them, explained the problem and demonstrated the squeak, I could have fixed it myself. There's nothing highly specialized about spraying lubricant."

He looked at her. The word *lubricant* hung in the air between them. An innocent word, related to the greasing of cogs, the oiling of hinges, the wetting of pistons. Images which sent Sara's mind spinning in all sorts of forbidden directions.

She remembered his warnings against showing any prurient interest in him. The thought triggered a rash impulse to test

Elan's sense of humor by asking if she could be fired for saying the word *lubricant* in his presence.

Mercifully she held her tongue. She dug her fingernails into her palms, tried to control the craziness goading her. Why on earth would she want to provoke and irritate her new boss?

She had an almost irresistible urge to see what lay behind the highly polished granite facade Elan Al Mansur presented to the world.

He drew himself up, took off his suit jacket and hung it over the back of his chair. Unhooked his gold cuff links, dropped them on the desk and rolled up his sleeves. His forearms were muscled, brown and dusted with black hair.

The thought of those forearms closing around her waist, holding her tight, swept through her mind like a gale-force wind.

She stepped backward and smoothed the front of her suit with a hand, trying to brush away the bizarre physical sensation assailing her.

Elan pushed his shirtsleeves up above his elbows as he settled into his chair. Sara suspected her face was blazing as she struggled to keep her eyes off his arms. An arm, for crying out loud! What on earth was wrong with her?

The watch on that arm probably cost more than her mother's last round of chemo treatments. It was gold, the white face covered with dials. Probably a Rolex. She suspected nothing but the best was good enough for Elan Al Mansur.

"You have no work to do, Sara?" He looked up from his papers, fixing her with a slit-eyed stare. She jumped inwardly.

"I wasn't sure if you needed anything."

"If I want something, I'll let you know." One broad finger rested on the page, marking his place. "In the meantime, I'll expect you to provide your own entertainment."

He'd been aware of her eyes on him, studying him, appraising him. Enjoying him. Humiliation clenched her gut. She turned swiftly away as she felt a renewed blush darken her cheeks.

"Would you like me to change the water in that vase of roses?" From one of his legions of tormented admirers, no doubt.

He looked at her for a moment.

"No." He glanced back to his papers. "Perhaps you could take them home? I don't like flowers."

"I can't take them home, I ride a bike to work. But I'll put them on my desk. They'll brighten the place up a bit. Thanks."

She paused to bury her face in the yellow blooms. The soothing scent of rose petals filled her senses, relaxed her.

"They're lovely."

"Not to me. They'll be dead in a day or two. I don't wish to watch them die."

"I'll enjoy their swan song. If you don't need anything else, I'll take off for the day."

He glanced quickly at his expensive watch. "Fine." He went back to shuffling a concertina of papers between his powerful fingers. She lifted the vase and moved toward the door, opened it with her hip.

"Good night." She turned to him.

Lowered in concentration, his face was hidden from her until he raised it. "You ride a bike to work?"

"Yes." She paused, waiting for his disapproval.

"I see." He looked at her for a moment, stony features unreadable. Then he turned back to his papers, opened his pen, and etched a dramatic signature into the crisp white document on his desk.

Sara slipped out through the door with a silent sigh of relief and heard it close softly behind her.

Elan placed the signed papers in his out-box and rose slowly from his chair. He stood in front of the floor-to-ceiling window that looked over the parking lot toward the desert and the distant mountain range beyond.

The sun hung low in the sky, glinting off geometric rows of cars baking in the late-afternoon sun. Many employees had already left. The rest were striding across the parking lot, climbing into their cars and driving out through the gates in an orderly fashion like so many instinctive ants.

A lone figure broke from the orderly procession of cars, darting among them, zigzagging across the parking lot on a bicycle.

Sara.

He narrowed his eyes, straining to get a better look at her. She'd changed out of her beige suit. Of course, who would ride a bicycle in a tight skirt? Well, not tight, but fitted, hugging the curve of her hips gently, as he recalled rather too clearly.

She'd put on shorts. Bicycle shorts, the stretchy kind. He blinked. Swallowed. Her legs were lean, muscled, powerful. Her tawny hair was tied back in a ponytail. Shouldn't she be wearing a helmet?

He tracked her movements across the parking lot as she made a diagonal path to the exit while the long line of cars wound patiently around the edge of the lot. She stood on her pedals as she went over a speed bump, lifted her backside into the air.

He coughed and turned away. Experienced a sudden rush of uncomfortable sensation. Something stirred inside him that surprised and annoyed him. His pulse pounded and he opened his mouth to breathe.

He moved away from the window and undid another button on his shirt to loosen it. The powerful visual of Sara's raised hips taunted him.

A plain little thing? Not so. She merely plied her feminine charms in a more calculated fashion than the girls in miniskirts and high heels.

But already he could see she was no different from the others.

Two

"You may call me Elan."

The rumble of his voice echoed in a previously undiscovered part of her anatomy. She swallowed hard.

"All right, Elan."

His name, spoken in her voice, sounded strangely intimate. The intimacy was a gift to cherish, a reward for her successful first week on the job. She knew he was pleased with her performance. Twice he'd sent her to meetings in his place, and he'd even allowed her to negotiate a new contract with a pipe supplier.

She'd hoped the allure of his masculine charms would fade with time and overexposure. That, unfortunately, had not yet happened.

"Sara, here's my speech for the conference next week. Please proof it and give me your opinion."

He lifted a sheaf of handwritten papers. She noted with chagrin that even his writing was sexy. Bold, thick cursive flowed black from his solid-gold fountain pen.

"I'd be glad to." She took the papers and forced herself not to linger on the seductive thickness of his muscled neck as he bent his head to the stack of contracts she'd handed him.

Elan threw himself into his job with the intensity of a competitive athlete. At the end of the day he looked so tense that she longed to move behind his chair and massage the hard ridges of his shoulders. Longed to hear him sigh with relief as her fingers eased the knots beneath his skin, soothing his tension. Longed to lose her fingertips in the snowy cotton of his shirt, the thick darkness of his hair.

She fought these urges like the beckoning calls to madness they were. A foolish schoolgirl crush that undermined her competence. No possible good could come from sighing over a man who'd made it clear he despised the attentions of female employees. This was the man who held the key to her future in his hands.

Broad, capable hands that haunted her imagination.

"You can read my speech in here if you wish. You won't be disturbed by your ringing phone." He indicated a plum-colored leather chair tucked in a corner of his vast office.

"Great, thanks." Another honor she probably didn't deserve. She settled herself in the soft leather and propped the papers up in front of her eyes, the better to block out any distracting view of her boss.

The more they worked together, the more she was bedeviled by the urge to touch him. Electricity crackled in the air when she came within inches of him, which was often as she worked closely with him throughout the day. But the tiny distance between them was an unbridgeable chasm whose howling depths threatened to engulf her if she were foolish enough to act.

Perhaps a little touch would be enough, a casual brush of the hand.

She couldn't jump off that cliff. This job was too important. And not just for the badly needed money it provided; Elan was giving her a chance to prove herself in the business world, to build a career that would be the foundation for a secure life.

With a successful career she'd never be stuck depending on a man to support her. She'd never have to suffer the way her mother had, trapped in a loveless marriage because she had too many hungry mouths to feed.

But something about the ridge of Elan's cheekbone made her long to bite it gently. Something about his ear called her to trace its delicate curve with a soft fingertip and suck the tender, unpierced lobe. Something about his mouth made her want to part his unsmiling lips with her tongue and plunge into the warm depths.

"What are you looking at?"

She jumped in her seat, totally busted as Elan stared at her, one eyebrow slightly lifted. She blinked, eyelids darting over her lust-dilated pupils. He'd seen her gawking at him over the top of his speech, desire written all over her face.

"I'm sorry, just thinking."

"I can see that." He settled back against the black leather of his chair. His eyes narrowed slightly and the barest shadow of a smile played over his lips.

He knew she wanted him. Just like all those other women had wanted him. She struggled to hold his black gaze, trying not to flinch as he stared, unblinking, taunting her with her own unspoken desires.

He raised one hand, extended a single long finger and brought it slowly to his lips. A thoughtful, deliberate, unbearably sensual gesture. A surge of warmth heated Sara's body, pleasurable and uncomfortable at the same time.

Her suit felt tight, constricting, holding in a body that longed to break free, to give rein to all the crazy impulses jarring her nerves and sending suggestions to her muscles that made her strain to hold her limbs still.

A knock on the door startled her, and she leaped to her feet, dropping Elan's speech unceremoniously in the chair.

"You're jumpy," he murmured.

"Come in," she said sharply, trying to regain the air of prim efficiency she used to pride herself on.

"I've got the samples you requested from the Davis field." Dora entered, her coral mouth pursed in a polite smile. The office gossip, she took far too much pleasure in regaling Sara with tales of her predecessors' downfall.

Dora carried a rectangular metal basket filled with vials of a black substance.

"I'll take them." Sara, lifted the heavy basket by its handles. She looked at Elan for instructions.

"On the desk."

She lowered the basket and put it right on top of the scattered papers as he'd indicated. He picked up one of the vials.

"Thank you, Dora." Elan dismissed her with a nod. She exited with a slight smirk on her face that made Sara's insides twist with affront. Could Dora see into her mind? Know she was tempted down the same path to self-destruction that had tripped up so many women before her?

"Do you know what this is?" He swirled it and the dark liquid clung to the sides of the glass, viscous, slightly metallic.

"Oil?"

"Yes. The reason we're all here." He watched the liquid settle back down into the bottom of the vial. "Black gold."

He removed the lid and lifted the vial to his nostrils. He held it under his nose for a moment, then let out a little grunt of satisfaction. "I never grow tired of this smell." He rose and moved around the desk toward her. "Have you ever handled crude oil?"

"Can't say I have," said Sara. Awareness of his physical presence made her palms tingle.

Elan dipped one of his long fingers into the neck of the jar, plunged it into the thin, black liquid and withdrew it. "Here." He extended his finger under her nose, invited her to sample its bouquet. She wrinkled her nose and suppressed a sudden urge to laugh. The strong crude-oil smell assaulted her senses, a little intoxicating.

Elan lifted his finger to his own nose. On errant impulse, she reached up and pushed his finger gently, so the oil smudged on his upper lip. She'd touched him! She drew her hand back, horrified, her finger quivering. He looked at her in astonishment.

A roiling mass of emotions bubbled up into laughter. "You look like Charlie Chaplin."

His eyes narrowed as he studied her face, and her stomach tightened.

"Perhaps I'm his famous character, the Great Dictator?"

A glint of humor sparked in his eyes and his mouth threatened to curve into a smile. The idea of Elan smiling caused a strange sensation deep in her belly, and she groped mentally for a quick comeback.

"You're a benevolent dictator." She gave him a mocking salute and, slowly, a grin lit his face like the sun bursting out above the horizon.

"I consider that a compliment." The sensual curve of his lips revealed rows of perfectly straight white teeth. His eyes twinkled with amusement as he studied her. The warmth of his smile and the intensity of his gaze combined to seriously undermine her sanity.

"Let me get a tissue for you."

She retrieved one from the box on his desk and raised it to wipe the black smudge from his upper lip. Her fingertips brushed against the skin of his cheek—not rough, yet not soft, either—as she pressed the tissue to his mouth. For a moment she thought she might close her eyes in shameful bliss at finally fulfilling her fantasies of touching Elan.

She bit her lip hard, tried to distract herself from the unsettling physical sensations coursing through her body.

He watched her curiously as she wiped the oil from his lip. It didn't come off particularly easily and she managed to accidentally smudge more of it on his cheek with the dirty tissue.

"Hold on, let me get another." Her heart pounded as she got to touch him again, cleaning the last trace from the crease of his smile.

Deliberate throat-clearing drew their attention as Dora re-entered with a second tray of samples. Her face twisted into an expression of amusement concealed with considerable effort. Sara realized it might well look as if she was wiping her own lipstick from the lips and cheek of her boss.

What a thought.

She shoved the oily tissue into her pocket and snatched the second tray of samples. She half expected Elan to make it brusquely clear that nothing had happened. Nothing *had* happened. But he stood, languid in the center of the room, challenging his employee to make what she would of the scene.

Sara made a fuss of rearranging the papers on the desk to make room for the second basket. "Thank you, Dora." The woman nodded and turned for the door, lips primly pressed together.

The door closed behind Dora. Sara turned to Elan and saw a smile glittering in his eyes.

"She believes we were kissing," he said. The throaty rumble of his voice, and the suggestion in his words, made her body tremble slightly. She was perilously close to the edge of the cliff.

"No danger of that," she replied quickly. "Would you like a tissue to clean your finger?"

"Thanks."

She retrieved the tissue, but as she went to hand it to him he merely extended his finger. His gaze met hers and she read a challenge in it.

She wrapped the tissue around his finger, then took hold of his wrist in her other hand to hold it steady. Currents of dangerous energy snaked up her arm from where her fingers circled around his pulse point.

She wiped until his finger was clean, but she was reluctant to let go. Touching Elan was a sweet thrill she wanted to prolong. She dabbed at his skin again as the fingers of her other hand curved under his to support the firm flesh of his palm.

Stop it, Sara! You're playing with fire. Flammable liquids and flammable emotions are not a good combination.

She pulled her hands away and threw the tissues into the wastebasket. Elan remained silent and she sneaked a glance at him. He watched her with an odd expression in his dark eyes.

"I'll read your speech at my desk," she said, gathering the scattered papers. He nodded. She hurried out of the room and closed the door softly behind her, her heart hammering and her mind whirling.

Wanting Elan was taboo. Touching him forbidden. He was unavailable, off-limits. They had a contract, clearly stated. So why was it so easy to imagine his warm breath on her throat, the pressure of his palms on the curve of her waist?

She had a career to build and she wanted to take on more responsibilities. She wanted more influence in the company, and she knew it was hers for the taking.

And she wanted Elan.

The two impulses were opposing, one canceled out the other. To act on her feelings for her boss would be to end her career at this company. That had been made perfectly plain to her on her first day at the job.

She was still on trial.

One week down, three to go.

"What on earth is this?" Elan looked at her, one eyebrow raised in astonishment as he surveyed the expensive new black leather bump on his chair.

"A lumbar support cushion. It helps to keep your back in a comfortable position. I notice you stretch your spine a lot and I thought this might help prevent it getting kinked up in the first place."

Because frankly, I can't watch you stretch and flex like that even one more time and keep the last shreds of my tattered sanity.

He reached out and prodded it with his long, powerful fingers as if it might have a life of its own. "Hmph."

"It's on trial. It goes back if you don't like it. I didn't file the expense report yet." She turned and took the watering can to the row of shiny, dark green plants she'd bought to soften the austere atmosphere of his office.

She hadn't expected him to be thrilled. Surprise and confusion were the emotions she seemed to conjure in Elan with her little extracurricular gestures, though he did a fair job of hiding it.

Maybe she was trying too hard. She'd spent half her Saturday at the gadget store looking at products designed to ease executive stress. She had other ideas for things he might like, but she didn't want to overdo it.

She heard him settle into the leather chair and couldn't resist turning around to catch his reaction. She was annoyed to find herself pathetically hoping to see him smile. He approached the day with grim determination that only tickled her irrational instinct to say or do something totally inappropriate—so she could watch his stony facade crack and catch a glimpse of what lay beneath.

Not so smart. That wasn't what she was here for.

Turned, she saw him sitting uncomfortably in the newly altered chair, brows arched, eyes fixed on her feet.

Uh-oh, no shoes. "Sorry, my shoes were killing me. I'll go put them on."

Elan cleared his throat. "There's no need. It's the end of the day and only you and I are here. You may dress as you wish."

She mentally spanked herself for finding even the most innocent words suggestive when they emerged from Elan's wide, sensual mouth. "Thanks." She forced a polite smile to her lips.

He shifted in the chair as if negotiating a large pea under his mattress.

"You hate it, don't you?"

"I don't hate it, I'm merely unaccustomed to it." He sat up straight and squared his broad shoulders against the chair in a way that made Sara's stomach quiver.

She wrenched her eyes back to the plants and poured water onto the decorative gravel she'd used to cover the soil. The glossy leaves brought life to the room. It was almost cheerful now, especially since she'd convinced him to let her move in a couple of stunning abstract paintings that had languished in a little-used conference room.

"Sara."

Her breath caught—as always—at the sound of her name in his low, husky voice. "Yes?" She continued watering, resisting the urge to turn and look at him.

"It's not your job to water plants in my office, or to make my chair more comfortable." The odd tone of his voice made her look up.

"I know, I just…" She didn't really know exactly what she was doing. Going the extra mile or something.

"Just as I don't expect you to make my coffee, I don't expect you to concern yourself with such trivialities. It's late and you have a home to go to."

She flinched at the stab of pain she felt at his rejection of her efforts. She had only herself to blame. He hadn't asked for any of it.

"I'm sorry. I guess I'm annoying you with all this…stuff." She gestured around the room at the paintings, the plants, the new coffee machine for the viciously strong coffee he brewed. Her heart sank a little. Okay, so she was overdoing it.

"On the contrary. You've made my office very pleasant." He said it quietly, gave her an unexpected, cautious look that squeezed her heart a little.

"To be honest, I enjoy this sort of stuff, you know, cheering things up." She hugged the watering can to her chest. "I have a lot of time on my hands when I'm not here. I'm not used to being on my own. I have a big family back home—four sisters and three brothers." The words tumbled out and the pitch of her voice rose. "My mom was sick for a long time and I took care of her. I'm used to being busy, looking after things, looking after people, you know. I'm not used to going home all alone, I…"

Shut up Sara!

What on earth was she doing running off at the mouth about how pathetically lonely she'd been lately? That wasn't his problem. It had been her decision to move here. To cook for one. To have conversations with herself over the tiny counter in her kitchen. To move the furniture around in her cramped apartment because she had nothing better to do.

To harass her boss with misplaced nurturing instincts. She felt a flush creep above her blouse as she realized what she'd been doing.

His body motionless, Elan spoke softly. "I appreciate the trouble you've taken. It's a gift to understand the needs of others without being asked." He held her gaze, a guarded expression shadowing his hard features. "Your thoughtfulness is a complement to your excellent work."

She blinked and bit her lip as a rush of emotion sprang from something raw inside her. His devastating seriousness and the gravity of such a huge compliment—his first—nearly unhinged her. The urge to cry warred with the urge to explode into raucous laughter.

"Thank you," she managed.

He immediately turned away and began sorting through some papers. Had his dark complexion darkened yet further? She dismissed the thought. He cleared his throat and loosened his necktie with a long finger.

She inhaled a deep breath and accidentally splashed herself with water from the can as she wheeled around to face the door.

"Good night," she muttered as she hustled toward it, feet silent on the carpet.

"Good night, Sara." Low and slightly strangled, as if his tie was still too tight, his words followed her out to her desk, down in the elevator, across the parking lot and home to her silent apartment.

Elan leaned back in his chair and watched as Sara gave a sales pitch to potential clients from Canada. Her trial month was nearly up and she'd proved beyond a shadow of a doubt she was more than worthy of her position.

"As I've demonstrated, our technology is capable of reducing the amount of sediment in the crude oil to well below the required level. The new techniques we have developed allow previously unprofitable fields to be exploited productively. We provide a complete package of services, from drilling to refining, that allow our customers to take advantage of cutting-edge technology and expertise without investing in their own infrastructure."

Her sharp mind and talent for incisive analysis impressed him. They were intriguingly at odds with a soft, warm side of her that caught him off guard with caring gestures. For someone so young she seemed unusually wise, her intelligence matched and even outmeasured by a natural compassion that rather awed him. And those little flashes of humor she surprised him with, well…

The late-afternoon sun shone through the window, glazing her delicate features with gold and sparking fiery highlights in her hair. Her hair looked so soft. He wondered how it would feel between his fingers, under his palms as he cupped her head, tipping it back to claim her mouth in a kiss.

Perish the thought. He would *never* become involved with an employee. Such an action would be an inexcusable abuse of his authority.

He had *never* kissed one of his assistants. Though not through any lack of effort on their part. A woman who would throw herself at a man in a professional environment could *never* command his respect or his affection.

He could not quite understand the appeal he held for them. He did not think his face held such dazzling beauty as to enslave a fellow human. His body was thick and heavy from his work with the horses, not the kind of elegant male form he imagined women would prefer.

Of course there was his wealth. He'd always been wealthy, even before he'd bought a small drilling company coming off a local oil boom and turned it into the thriving oil services corporation it was today. The oil that ran in his blood had enriched his family and his country before he was born. Was this the irresistible appeal he held for women?

No matter. Sara's predecessors had all departed the company of their own free will, rankling under the low opinion he held of them.

But none of them possessed her talent. Already she performed duties far beyond the role she was hired for. Sara was an asset he would hate to lose. And he wouldn't lose her if he could help it.

He'd arranged to have Sara fly with him to the firm's newest drilling site tomorrow. The trip would broaden her understanding of their work and prepare her to take on greater responsibilities.

The object of his thoughts walked across the conference room to the whiteboard and began to sketch out a formula one of the clients had asked to see. His gaze drifted to her hips, to the lush curve of her backside that shifted beneath her suit as she strained to reach the top of the board.

Suddenly his slacks felt a trifle snug. Perhaps he should send his tailor in London some new measurements? He shifted in his chair, tugged at his tie, which now closed too tightly around his neck, constricted his breathing.

Sara dropped her pen. As she bent forward to retrieve it, her skirt strained tightly over the firm length of her thighs and cupped her buttocks. Elan jolted forward in his chair, as a thunderbolt of sensation rammed through him.

He cleared his throat and grabbed hold of his pen, scribbled some meaningless notes on his papers as he struggled to get his errant body back under control.

Her suit was too revealing.

It was indecent and undignified to display so much of one's physique in a business environment. He would have Jill Took from Human Resources address the matter with her.

Slowly he lifted his eyes again as Sara cheerfully explained the calculations involved in an aspect of the refining process. He surveyed the offending suit with an eye to detailed critique, and was chagrined that on closer examination he could not find fault with it. It was not close-fitting. The skirt came well below the knee. It was demure in cut and color.

The problem lay *within* the suit. And within *him*.

Three

"Seventy-six bottles of beer on the wall, seventy-six bottles of beer…" Her voice was cracking, her throat clenched with terror.

"You've survived, Sara, open your eyes." Elan's words penetrated her shattered consciousness.

"Oh, God." Her whole body was rigid. Her eyelids squeezed tight as she struggled to shut out reality.

"We're above the clouds now. There's no danger." His low voice rose over the mellow drone of the jet engines.

Gingerly she opened her eyes, and the bright light gleaming through the row of tiny oval windows threatened to blind her. Silhouetted against it was Elan's face, features creased with concern.

She realized she was clutching both his hands in a death grip. But she couldn't let go. Desire had nothing to do with it. She clung to him out of sheer terror.

"See, it's not so bad. The plane cruises along. You can't even see the ground from up here."

"Oh, God." The thought of the ground miles and miles below made her stomach drop.

"Are you going to be ill?"

Oh, God, please don't let me throw up. "I don't think so."

"Good."

"I'm sorry I'm such a …" *Wimp? Wuss? Weak woman?*

"Don't apologize, Sara. Many people are afraid of flying." He gave her hands a quick reassuring squeeze.

She took a deep breath, and another. They were airborne. Oh, God.

"You've never flown before?" His look of tender concern caused a swell of emotion to rise to her throat. She swallowed hard.

"No."

"I thought Americans flew everywhere."

"Some do, I guess. Not me." She still couldn't believe they were *above the clouds*. At the thought a fresh surge of horror seized her gut. She saw her anxiety reflected in Elan's pained expression.

He wrenched one of his big hands free from her rigor-mortis clench. As Sara shuddered with—fear?—he unbuckled his seat belt in one swift motion and slid his arm around her shoulder.

The warmth of his sturdy arm encircling her shivering torso soothed her as she leaned into it. She took a deep breath. Maybe she could survive this after all.

"Your family didn't fly abroad on vacation?"

She let out a snort of laughter. A nervous explosion. "No, we rarely left the city limits. My family's finances were strictly hand to mouth."

"They were poor?"

"Very."

"Oh." His lips pursed as he appeared to consider the information. Would it make him think less of her? Surely not. It was hardly her fault. Though she didn't plan to be poor again if she could help it.

"But you're from Wisconsin, aren't you? How did you come to Nevada?"

"By road."

"On your bicycle?" His eyebrows shot up.

She laughed again. The release of laughter and the comfort of his reassuring embrace steadied her nerves.

"No, I drove a car. An old clunker. It died as soon as I got here. That's why I ride a bike now."

He smiled. "I'm relieved to hear it. But you'll buy another car, no?"

"Eventually."

As soon as I pay off tens of thousands of dollars in debt. She didn't really want him to know about that. Her personal burdens were nobody's business.

"The color is returning to your cheeks." He spoke softly. The deep, mellow tone of his voice was intimate, assuring. She gradually became conscious of the way their bodies were entwined. Elan still leaned into her airplane seat, his strength wrapped around her.

His broad chest pushed into her shoulder. The firm surface of his pectorals rubbed against her, heating her through the thin fabric of their clothes. The vibrations from the jet's engine hummed through them both, causing little shock waves of sensation to surge through her, heating and arousing her from head to toe.

The color returned to her cheeks in a blaze of glory.

She tore her eyes from him. As her fear ebbed it was being replaced by an entirely different sensation.

Lust.

His hand rested on her waist just below her right breast. A curl of heat rose in her belly as she became aware of the pad of each long, dexterous finger pushing gently against her skin, warming her through her blouse. Her breast stirred beneath her shirt. Her nipple hardened, craving his touch.

And she was conscious of the scent of him—earthy, musky, with an exotic note of fragrance that wound itself through the air around her.

Elan.

Secret fantasies were coming to life. Dreams stalking the daylight. Her most humiliating craven longing fulfilled in the touch of this man.

Her boss.

As her body tingled with the sensation of sheer physical excitement, her mind struggled with the knowledge that his embrace was purely a gesture of compassion. If he knew what was going on in her body, in her mind, he'd recoil in horror.

But she couldn't help wanting to prolong the illicit pleasure, the dangerous high of being held in the arms of the man whose allure was the torment of her days and the solace of her lonely nights.

Yes, she dreamed about him—waking dreams, as well as sleeping dreams. Fantasies, the shame-laced release of all the pent-up emotion bottled inside her at the end of a long day spent in close proximity to him.

But never as close as this.

On impulse she looked at him and her heart seized as she read the expression in his narrowed eyes.

I want you.

His irises were nearly black, indistinguishable from his pupils, fathomless depths, wells that drew from a dark, secretive soul. But at that moment she knew exactly what was on his mind.

Just as he knew exactly what was on hers.

In a sudden flurry of activity they disentangled themselves. She cleared her throat and smoothed the front of her blouse. He snatched up his *Wall Street Journal* and arranged it in his lap with a good deal of rustling.

He fiddled with his tie. Ran his fingers through his hair.

Unhooked his cuff links and rolled up his sleeves. He shuffled his paper, appearing to scan the columns with keen interest.

Avoiding her glance.

Sara leaned stiffly back into her seat. She had no idea where her briefcase was. In the paralytic terror that had accompanied her onto the aircraft she'd been aware of nothing but an urge to run screaming back down the ramp to the safety of terra firma.

Oddly, though, she wasn't afraid anymore.

Fear seemed a paltry emotion after the intense, primal madness that seized and shook her as Elan held her.

She cleared her throat. "Um, I can't seem to remember where I put my briefcase."

He gave her a quick look of alarm and pointed to where it lay at her feet.

"Thank you." She rifled inside it, bending forward and letting her hair hang down to conceal her crimson face. She pulled out a report she wanted to proofread and made a big show of finding her place and uncapping her pen.

She sneaked a glance at him. His expression was stony as he read his paper. He snapped the big pages open and scrutinized the tiny print with focused intensity. She attempted to concentrate on the dense scientific text in front of her, but her mind couldn't make sense of the words.

"I'm sorry." The words formed on her lips of their own accord. *I'm sorry I can't stop wanting you in just the way you despise.*

"For what?" He didn't look up from his paper.

"For being a gibbering idiot. I had no idea I was going to react like that. I guess I'm officially a white-knuckle flier." She bit her lip. It was humiliating to see how little control she'd displayed in the face of fear.

"It's no matter," he said brusquely, without glancing up from the text. He snapped open another page, appeared to study it for a moment, then looked up. "There's no shame in showing fear of flying through the clouds."

His stony features softened as he looked at her. Sara swallowed hard as a strange surge of emotion threatened to overflow its boundaries. Fear, embarrassment and forbidden lust all roiled inside her, her poor nerve-racked body a fragile vessel for so much unfamiliar torment.

Poor Sara! He could see how greatly she suffered. She'd not betrayed even a moment of hesitation, had not mentioned her lack of flying experience until her fears overcame her as they boarded the aircraft.

Her obvious terror filled him with a powerful protective instinct that shook him to the core. He wanted nothing more than to put his arms around her and comfort her.

And the protective urge frightened him far more than any of the transient sexual thoughts that bedeviled him in her presence.

He'd left his home and his cruel father behind to build his own life, free of ties and obligations he had no use for. He needed no one and no one needed him—until he saw the fear that racked her delicate body and brought tears to her pale jade eyes. He couldn't sit and watch her suffer. And holding her was a pleasure beyond imagining. At his touch she softened and relaxed. Her shivering eased and her flesh warmed. She leaned into his embrace, welcomed his touch. Welcomed him.

Desire had seized him. Desire to offer her far more than comfort, to take far more than the satisfaction of soothing her fears.

He wanted to experience the sweet agony of her soft body pressed against his. To sink his fingertips into her lush curves. To fill her with the joy that swept through him each time she flashed her lovely smile in his direction.

And she was his for the taking. He could see that.

That knowledge alone should extinguish his desire.

"I bet you were a kid the first time you flew in a plane." Her voice startled him out of his tortured contemplation and forced him to refocus on the paper he'd been pretending to read.

"Yes, age eleven." He didn't dare look up. Those wide eyes cast a spell on him that right now he had no power to resist.

"Were you taking a vacation with your parents?"

A vacation? Did the concept even exist in his country? "No."

"Well?" Her lips twitched in a half smile as she waited for him to expand. Soft, delicate lips, thin and mobile.

That begged his mouth to close over them.

He struggled to wrench his mind back to her question about his first plane ride. And the memory it conjured dampened his feelings of pleasure.

"I left my home in Oman for the first time to fly to boarding school in England."

That day he'd left everything he knew, everyone he held dear, to find himself alone and afraid in a strange, cold country where no one understood his speech and customs. It had been a journey from which he would never truly return.

"Were you frightened?"

"Yes. Though perhaps not as you might imagine. I enjoyed the flight. Young boys take pleasure in the power of big machines." He forced what he hoped looked like a natural smile.

"Why did your parents send you away to school?"

Why indeed? Not so he could receive an excellent education, though that had been a result. Not so he could become familiar with the ways of western culture, though in time he had.

So his father could punish his mother. Rip her favorite child from her arms and banish him to a far land. Simply to show her that he could.

Anger still burned in his gut at the memory of his mother weeping as his father's aides dragged her screaming son away from her for the last time. Elan never saw her again. Her health was already frail—a neurological ailment—and after he was sent away her decline was swift, her death sudden.

And he could never forgive his father for taking her life as surely as if he'd slashed a knife at her throat.

He realized Sara was waiting for an answer to her question. "They thought it would turn me into a man."

That, too, was true. His father had reviled his close relationship with his mother. Abhorred how when he was little he'd liked to crawl into her bed to seek comfort from his nightmares, how he followed her on her daily rounds, laughing with her and the women, enjoying her gentle humor and loving caresses.

No son of mine will hide himself in the skirts of a woman! His father's words still rang in his ears.

"Leaving home so young must have been hard." Sara's voice trembled a little as she said the words softly. He realized she must be responding to emotion on his face. A twinge of embarrassment warred with an urge to tell her more.

"Yes. I spoke little English. I'd rarely been to the nearest city, let alone out of the country. I'd spent every day in the bosom of my family, and suddenly I was torn from all I'd ever known. Strange people, strange language, strange food and the English weather…"

Words poured from his tongue unbidden as Sara's kind eyes watched him. "I missed the bright sun of my home almost as much as I missed my family."

"I've heard the weather in England is a bit grim." She smiled tentatively.

"My horses were as surprised as I was. They couldn't understand why the sun had vanished and water kept falling from the skies. They at least enjoyed lush green grass."

"You took horses with you to boarding school?" Her eyes twinkled with curiosity and interest that only fired Elan's impulse to share memories he'd kept locked away for so long.

"Yes. I brought my two favorite stallions with me. The school insisted on gelding them. They said stallions couldn't run with the other horses."

The painful memory of his close companions being deprived of their manhood stung him. It seemed so symbolic at the time. The three of them together were humbled aliens in a strange land, stripped of their former power and position and all they knew. But together they'd found a way to survive. They'd learned a new language, figured out the rules and learned to play by them.

That long, hard exile from his country and from everyone he'd ever loved had made him into the man he was today.

"Aren't stallions supposed to be dangerous?" The innocent awe in Sara's eyes lifted the gloom descending on him.

"They must be handled with care. But a man who's ridden a stallion can never truly be satisfied with any other horse. To harness the feral power of the herd leader and to move with him as one is an experience like no other."

A delicate flush spread up across Sara's chin and cheeks. At first he was surprised, then he realized his words must have triggered a rather different image than the one he intended.

Perhaps she imagined how it would feel to ride *him*.

A smile tugged at the corner of his mouth as Sara's blush darkened a shade further.

To be sure, the image intrigued him, too.

The thought of her slim thighs squeezing him, her long, delicate fingers wound into his hair, her hips moving against him, urging him on—

Elan quickly rearranged his paper to cover his lap. His breathing was in danger of becoming audible and he struggled to focus his mind on something that would douse his desire.

Sara's lips parted as she wrenched her eyes from his face and rifled through her briefcase. Her skin flushed crimson right down to her blouse. Fair skin could be a terrible disadvantage. Her thoughts were literally written all over her face.

But he couldn't help wondering what other parts of her body might redden in response to his presence. Nipples blushing like ripe berries. The delicate flower of her sex a pink rose inviting him to taste its nectar, beckoning him to bury his face in its soft petals—

He cleared his throat loudly and rustled his newspaper. "Pardon me. Something in my throat." Mercifully his dark skin did not betray the sudden flush of heat surging though his body.

He was rock-hard, straining painfully against the zipper of his pants. He regretted removing his jacket, but if he rose to retrieve it from the seats on the other side of the aircraft, his situation would be very evident. Only the *Wall Street Journal* prevented his lust from being clearly visible to its instigator.

Why on earth did this woman have such an appalling effect on him? He felt like a man who'd wandered lost in the desert for months without water then stumbled across a glittering oasis. He gasped with hunger and thirst that had nothing to do with food and drink.

He'd not been celibate for the past decade. Women flung themselves at him on a regular basis, and sometimes he took what they offered. They had their needs, he had his. The enjoyment was mutual, the parting inevitable. Some of them sought a rich beau to pamper them, some of them an exotic lover to walk on the wild side with.

He could give them what they wanted without giving up anything of himself.

None of them saw the man inside. The simple man humbled by the poverty of his spirit. The lonely soul who had learned at the hands of his father that love and affection were crimes to be met with harsh and lasting punishment.

He was no longer capable of love and the knowledge did not even pain him anymore.

Well. That little train of thought had taken care of his erection nicely.

He flipped the page of his newspaper and sneaked a sidelong glance at Sara.

She'd fallen asleep?

Good.

He felt genuine relief for her. It would be far better for her to sleep quietly through their return to earth. The jolt of the landing would be a rude enough awakening.

Some of the client sites they visited had runways that tested the skill of the most experienced pilots. The site they were traveling to was remote, a new field, the runway probably still dusted with freshly turned soil. Even he sometimes became alarmed at the sight of rocky, uneven terrain rising up to meet the plane at high speed.

Quietly, he laid his newspaper aside. He didn't want its crinkling to rouse her from her peaceful slumber.

And she did look peaceful. Her delicate lashes rested against her cheeks. She did not wear mascara and her lashes were a soft, dark gold color, like the soil of his homeland.

Her cheeks were still flushed with pink, and her lips parted, moist, as if she'd just licked them.

And maybe she had.

What dreams danced in her head that caused her face to shimmer with a secret smile? A smile that didn't play upon her lips or sparkle in her closed eyes, but that lit her features with an inner radiance and made them glow with enchantment.

He didn't feel anything so mundane as lust for her at this moment. Her loveliness was a balm to his spirit.

And he respected her business acumen. She displayed an astonishing knack for putting clients at ease, for explaining complicated concepts without blinding business people with science, the way he tended to. He knew he often came off as pompous and standoffish. He wondered if she saw him that way. Probably. And she was probably right.

On their relatively short acquaintance he could see that Sara was a remarkable woman in many ways. A woman who deserved to be treated with respect. And as a mark of his respect he would not take advantage of her attraction to him.

Or his attraction to her.

He was a grown man. He could control his base instincts, rein them in the way he reined in the potentially dangerous power of the stallions he rode. She was a valuable employee. And he would do well to remember that when his primal urges threatened to get the better of him.

"Oh, God!" Jolted awake by a loud bang and a sudden jarring sensation, Sara couldn't remember where she was. "Did we crash?"

"No." Elan's eyes were on her as she opened her own. "We've landed. We're on the ground."

The plane shook and rattled, jarring Sara's rigid body as the wheels shuddered along the crude runway.

"Did I fall asleep?" Stupid question. Of course she had. Though how on earth that had happened she couldn't imagine. A response to sensory overload, perhaps? "Don't answer that."

Elan didn't look as if he had any intention of answering. Casual chitchat wasn't his style. An odd memory of singing with him crept into her consciousness. "Ninety-nine bottles of beer on the wall." Must have been a dream. Weird. And in her dream the singing was his idea. Weirder.

In a rush it all came back to her. Her humiliating display of terror as they'd boarded the aircraft. The way she'd practically hyperventilated as they taxied along the runway. How she'd clung to him as if he were a life raft in the open ocean.

She braced against her seat as the plane ground to an abrupt halt.

"Thank you."

She didn't know what else to say.

He merely nodded, folded his newspaper, and placed it in his briefcase.

Noise from the drilling rigs assaulted her ears as their driver parked the Jeep. She strained to hear Elan as he jumped out and beckoned her to follow. He strode toward the drilling site, enthusiasm evident in his energetic movements.

The heady aroma of crude oil filled the air. A phalanx of beam pumps stretched into the distance, rocking in a steady rhythm, pulling the oil from its age-old hiding place beneath the barren soil.

The oil field was a fairly recent discovery and Al Mansur Associates had bid aggressively for the contract to develop it. Sara had jumped at Elan's suggestion that she come see it.

But now as she stood amid the clamor and bustle of the job site, a twinge of apprehension twisted her gut.

She knew the theories behind supply and demand, soil mechanics, flow ratios. She understood drilling from a technical and economic standpoint. But now she wasn't sure she wanted to see exactly how the earth was plundered and forced to give up its secrets and riches.

Elan introduced her to the site foreman and they left their papers and briefcases in his office trailer. They donned safety glasses, hard hats and earplugs before he led them across the sandy soil and up a flimsy metal ladder onto a rig about to begin drilling.

The driller in charge gave Sara a stern list of warnings about where she could and couldn't stand, what to watch out for, the possibilities for injury if a piece of equipment broke or came loose, or the potential for a blowout if they found a shallow pocket of gas beneath the soil. By the time he'd finished, her nerves jangled as if she stood on a massive bomb that might explode at any moment.

She positioned herself as close to the giant drill as she dared. As it revved into action she imagined the dinosaur-like grinding teeth gnawing their way down through the rock below. Elan came and stood beside her, watching her reaction as the platform shook and shuddered with the movements of the machinery.

"This is my favorite part," he said, shouting over the motors.

"Typical male!" she shouted back.

Elan looked confused for a second then a slow smile spread over his face. He leaned toward her, as if to say something, so she removed her earplug, nerves jumping.

"You have a naughty mind." His lips brushed against her skin as he spoke and his voice resounded in the hollow of her ear canal, triggering a responsive rhythm that pulsed down through her body. The touch of Elan's lips on her skin was a sinfully sweet sensation.

Yes, I have a naughty mind. Since she'd come to Al Mansur Associates, her body seemed to have developed a mind of its own that had nothing to do with her intellect.

Elan's smile stayed plastered across his face. She could only begin to imagine what was going on in his mind as he watched the men guide the drill deeper and deeper into the earth.

When the drilling finally stopped, he placed his hand gently in the curve above her hips to guide her to the downward ladder. The simple and practical caress made her feel languid, sensuous.

"Is it a gusher?" she asked, half-joking, once they were back on solid ground.

"Not yet." He smiled. "Once they pump out the drilling mud it will be. But you won't see oil shooting up into the air. We don't like to waste a single barrel."

They spent the rest of the afternoon visiting wells in various stages of drilling and pumping. Elan moved about the job site with the ease and confidence of a man used to being in command. Honored that he'd chosen to groom her for a larger role in the company, Sara resolved to live up to his obviously high expectations of her.

Back on his private jet, he settled into the seat beside her. She wondered why he didn't sit in one of the other seats on the plane. There was no reason for them to sit together since they were the only passengers. Presumably he'd sat beside her on the trip out because she'd been clinging to him like a limpet.

Perhaps he wanted to be close in case she needed reassurance. Did she? Not about the plane. Now that she'd survived her first flight she was relatively relaxed about flying again.

She would like some reassurance that she could work with Elan without wetting his suit with her drool. And that kind of reassurance was not immediately forthcoming. Especially not as he removed his gold cuff links and—once again—rolled his shirtsleeves up over broad, muscled forearms.

Oh, dear. She pressed her fingertips to her eyelids. *Just don't look, okay!*

"Are you tired?"

"What? Er, yes. I suppose I am a little." Tired of the way she couldn't get a grip on her libido. "It was a fascinating day. I really appreciate you bringing me here."

"You're welcome. I've never brought my assistant out to the field with me before, but I can see your abilities are far above average."

"Thank you."

As the jet's engines roared to life, her gut clenched with sudden apprehension. Without a word he placed his hand over hers. But the warmth of his touch proved anything but soothing.

Fear evaporated as a painful lightning bolt of desire ripped through her, leaving a smoking trail of heat in its path. Her body burned with a dangerous and craven longing to become entangled with this man in a way that was entirely unprofessional.

Elan's hands were calloused. The rough texture of his palms made her skin prickle with awareness. His fingers were soft yet firm as they wrapped around hers. The unwelcome thought of those broad, masculine hands moving over her tortured flesh sent shock waves of agonizing arousal shivering through her.

Her feelings for him suddenly seemed like the oil pressurized beneath the earth, waiting to rush up and explode into the clear sky unless she kept them very carefully capped and sealed. And every second in Elan's presence brought her closer to a potentially devastating blowout.

Four

"Oh, I'm totally fine now that I've gotten used to flying," she'd said. "Really, I'm…" She turned to look out the window. "Oh."

She sat back in her seat quickly and pressed a hand to her chest. Elan glanced past her and saw the landing lights through the porthole window as the plane banked steadily to the right.

"Goodness, does it always tip to the side like that?" Her voice shook and she licked her lips anxiously.

"Yes, it's a normal part of the approach."

She pressed a hand to her mouth and slowly turned her head as the trail of lights twisted under the moving plane. Her knuckles whitened as she gripped the seat rest between them and he fought the urge to put his arm around her.

He wanted to warm her, soothe and caress her, soften her and then… *Typical male.* Her words at the site came back to him and he cursed himself. He'd assured her on her first day at the job that he was anything but typical, and he'd live up to that promise if it killed him.

She was seven years younger than him. She knew little of the world, as evidenced by the fact that she'd never been in a plane. He had a responsibility to himself, and to her, to make sure that nothing happened between them. He had a responsibility to Al Mansur Associates, which needed her sharp mind in its offices more than he needed her soft body in his bed.

The plane banked more sharply, turning in preparation for the final approach, and the twin rows of lights on the ground shone brighter and closer in the darkness. A tiny laugh emerged from her tightened throat. "People always see light coming toward them in their final moments, don't they?"

Instinctively he slid his hand over hers as those troubling protective instincts fired his neurons without asking permission. Her poor hand was so cold, her fingers gripping the metal armrest with grim determination.

"Don't worry, I've landed here probably a thousand times. This turn is a normal part of the…" His words trailed off as she slumped in her seat.

He immediately unbuckled himself and supported her head. He held her steady as the plane bumped down on the tarmac.

"Sara." He patted her cheek gently with his fingertips. "Wake up."

Her skin was ghostly pale, her soft lashes lowered, lips slightly parted.

Her breath was sweet on his face as he leaned into her. He allowed his lips to brush her skin as he whispered her name once again. Her cheek was the color and texture of a delicate rose petal. So soft under his lips, cool.

His memory tormented him with the image of Sara drinking in the aroma of the roses he'd given her in his office.

Those roses were nothing but clutter to him until that moment—dying things that mocked him with his own mortality.

But as she enjoyed their subtle perfume and admired their doomed loveliness, he had seen their beauty in a new light.

Lately he could see many things in a new light.

Sara was so unlike any other woman he had met. A bewitching blend of innocence and experience, candor and caution, she knew when to listen and learn, and when to take the reins and go her own way. A plain little thing? If only she were.

She didn't stir.

His arm brushed against her breast as he shifted position. The nipple tightened under her silky shirt in response to his touch. He sucked in a breath.

"Sara."

He stroked a strand of her golden hair away from her forehead, soft as fresh-spun silk. His fingers struggled with the urge to bury themselves in the fall of hair on her neck and his lips pulsed at the sight of hers, slightly parted as if waiting for a kiss.

The kiss of life?

She is breathing, fool. His urge to settle his mouth over hers had nothing to do with medical exigency.

Elan wheeled around as he heard the door to the cabin open.

"I hope the flight was satisfactory, sir. Good Lord, is she asleep?"

"She's fainted."

"But she's breathing?"

Elan nodded as the pilot strode across the cabin and leaned over Sara. His gut tightened as he watched the other man bend low over her body, close enough to enjoy her scent.

"She'll be fine." The aggression in his voice surprised him and caused the pilot to step back. "I shall carry her."

He took perverse pleasure in bumping the pilot roughly out of his path as he reached for her. He shoved his arms underneath her, steeling himself against the pleasure of touching her.

But no steel could withstand the torturous burden of longing that rocked him as her slender body fell against his.

"Sara." He uttered her name as a talisman against the forbidden desire that roiled in his belly. It must be a crime of some magnitude to lust after a woman who wasn't even awake.

Her eyelids fluttered. His heart constricted at the thought of those jade-and-gold eyes opening to meet his. He leaned his face closer to hers, his mouth almost touching the petal softness of her skin. "Wake up," he whispered.

Her lips parted and a rush of emotion and sensation shook him, making him glad his feet were firmly planted on the floor. He hugged her closer, fighting the urge to kiss her back to wakefulness.

"Er, Mr. Al Mansur, perhaps I should call an ambulance." The pilot's voice forced its way into his ears from a million miles away.

"That will not be necessary." Elan spat the words at him, irritated at the interruption. He wanted to watch his sleeping beauty awaken.

Sara's golden lashes fluttered again and her eyes sprang open. He felt his face crease into a broad smile as she looked at him in astonishment.

"What the…?" Suddenly her eyes were wide with fear and she kicked and struggled in his grasp. He wrestled to hold her still, not sure why, but enjoying it all the same.

"Put me down!" She writhed like a tiger cub and a huge chuckle welled up inside him and burst out as he lowered her to her feet.

"Gladly, madam."

She fussed over rearranging her suit and tucking her hair behind her ears. She looked around, obviously trying to get her bearings. "What are you grinning at?" The fire flashed in her eyes.

"I'm glad to see you awakened. And fiery as ever." He chuckled again.

She glanced quickly around the cabin. "We've landed."

"We have indeed," he said with mock gravitas. He could not help but enjoy her confusion. Feet planted apart, she stood poised to take on a host of attackers. He was almost tempted to throw a shadow punch and watch her spring at him like a tigress.

The pilot had opened the exterior door. "Perhaps we should help the young lady down the stairs. She may still be light-headed after her fainting spell."

"Yes, would you please carry our bags?" With one swift step Elan swept Sara off her feet and into his arms. He was unable to suppress another grin as she twisted and wriggled, struggling to free herself from his grip.

"Put me down! I can walk just fine."

"We'll take no chances. Your unconsciousness may have after-effects. I'll carry you to the ground as a safety precaution."

"This is ridiculous!"

Sara bucked against him, trying to loosen his grasp. He half expected her to bite him. He merely tightened his arms around her.

"Don't fight me. I'll put you down when we reach the ground," he reiterated. The throaty rasp of his voice surprised him. She gave him one last jab in the ribs with her elbow, which served only to widen his smile.

She jerked her head back to look him in the face. "Stop smirking!"

"Pardon me. I'm simply glad to see you alive and…kicking again." He bit back another chuckle.

Sara's lovely face creased into a frown. Somehow it tickled his funny bone more that she couldn't see the humor in the situation.

Her breath came in quick gasps and his blood surged along with hers as her heart pounded against his chest. Her eyelashes flickered against the harsh spotlight illuminating their descent to the ground. He knew she was shaken by what had happened, and that only fired the protective instincts tightening his arms around her slender body.

Slender, yet substantial. Muscled, taut, the body of a woman who knew how to fight for what she wanted.

And at that moment he knew far too well what he wanted. He was glad the blackness of the night hid the evidence of his desire.

Why on earth was she struggling in such a childish fashion? She could tell he found her resistance entertaining.

His arms had closed around her like steel bands, lifting her from the ground against her will. The urge to resist was instinctive, but hopeless against the solid mass of muscle that was Elan. How on earth a businessman came to be built like an ancient Olympian, she could not begin to imagine.

As she kicked and wriggled, his arms simply tightened more firmly around her in an embrace that clearly demonstrated his superior strength. Heat gathered low in her belly as the hard muscles of his torso crushed against her. His broad hands supported her with an ease that made her feel ridiculously feminine, and she struggled not to enjoy the odd primal pleasure of being gathered and held by such a powerful man.

At the bottom of the stairs he released her and settled her carefully on her feet. She stumbled back, burning hot, her heart slamming against her ribs, her limbs weak.

She was ready to get down on her knees and kiss the blacktop as she recalled the sudden rush of terror that had deprived her of her senses as the plane plunged toward the dark runway.

"Are you all right?"

"Yes." She forced out the lie.

"Can you walk to the car, or would you like me to carry you?" His throaty voice sounded deeper than usual.

Carry me.

"I can walk." Her voice emerged as a squeak.

She concentrated on putting one wobbly leg in front of the other as Elan took their briefcases from the pilot and strode to his long black sedan. He flung their bags in the back and helped her into the passenger seat before bidding the pilot good-night. Then he settled in behind the wheel and loosened his tie.

"Your address."

"What?"

"Where do you live? I need to drive you home. Unless you plan on walking."

"Oh, of course. Five-fifty Railroad Avenue. You take a right off Main." She wondered what Elan would think of her rather dingy apartment building. The salary he paid could buy her a nice house, but she had other financial obligations. Last week she'd made the first significant payments on her college loans and on her mother's gargantuan hospital bill, and that was a far greater concern than any luxury dwelling.

He drove away from the airport, silent. The dark roads were deserted, the moon dimmed by wispy clouds. Sara gasped as he braked hard.

"A coyote."

She saw the flash of reflective eyes in the headlights as the nocturnal creature studied them for a second before slinking off into the desert.

"Wow. That scared me."

"I'm sure the animal's fear was greater than yours. The twin moons of our headlights sweeping though the desert must be an alarming sight for the night creatures."

"I know how they feel. Apparently I haven't evolved along with the rest of Western civilization because my body didn't take too kindly to flying through the air. I'm sorry to cause such a scene at both ends of the trip."

"Don't worry about it." He turned to her and his warm smile made her suck in an unexpected breath.

Stop it, Sara!

Even the gentle pressure of her seat belt made her recall—

with a harrowing mix of remorse and pleasure—the far more insistent pressure of Elan's arms around her.

He'd removed his jacket to drive and his sleeves were rolled up. One big hand gripped the wheel, holding it steady as they ate up the long, straight road through the empty desert.

"I'm hungry," he announced, as they entered the neon-lit oasis of the town.

"Me, too." *In more ways than one.*

"Let's pick up something to eat. What would you like?"

"I don't know the restaurants. I haven't bought takeout since I've been here." Trying too hard to squirrel away every penny.

"The fried chicken is good. And the food at the Mexican place is always fresh."

Sara turned to look at Elan, who studied the neon signs with keen interest. Somehow it shocked her that he would eat takeout fried chicken like a regular person.

"Whatever you prefer."

"I believe I prefer steak fajitas." He turned to her with a raised eyebrow.

"Sounds good."

Yikes. As he pulled up she could see it was a drive-through. Did this mean she should invite him into her apartment to eat it? Or would he expect to drop her off with her dinner and return home to eat his?

Probably the latter.

He picked up their food at the drive-through window and handed it to Sara. Lord, she was hungry. The zesty aroma of grilled steak and onions filled the car and made her stomach growl. He chuckled.

"Your hunger is getting the better of you."

Don't I know it? She shifted in her seat, suddenly uncomfortable as she watched his broad hand settle over the gear shift and push it into Drive. She resisted the urge to fan herself or turn the air-conditioning on full as they pulled back onto the road.

"We must eat immediately. And I know just the spot." He sped through the town and back out into the desert.

Outside town he took a sharp turn toward the mountains. Shrubs and boulders along the roadside cast eerie shadows in the headlights. The road disintegrated into a dirt track as they climbed up toward the veiled moon and stars.

After only a few minutes he stopped the car and climbed out. Sara gingerly opened the door and lowered a foot onto the sandy ground of the dark desert. A match flared and she followed its glow to Elan. He'd opened the trunk and now lit a small fire a few yards from the car.

"What are you using for kindling?"

"Mesquite wood. I keep some in the trunk. The fire will keep animals from joining us for dinner."

Okay.

He spread a blanket on the ground while Sara retrieved their food and drinks from the car. The night was pleasantly warm and the fresh mountain air invigorated her tired body. The city lights twinkled below them in the wide valley like a carpet of jewels. Sara sighed with pleasure as she kicked off her shoes and settled on the blanket.

She unpacked their food and handed him his soda.

"Do you come here often?"

Oh, like that didn't sound stupid!

He chuckled. "I do."

"By yourself?"

Sara! Shove some food in your mouth to stop it flapping!

"Sometimes." His dark eyes flashed at her in the flickering firelight. The suggestion she read in them made her gut kick like a gun recoil.

It's all in your imagination!

Quickly she unwrapped her fajita and took a bite.

Elan sat cross-legged on the blanket. The glint of gold from his watch caught her eye as he unwrapped his own food. The strangeness of the situation struck her. She was seated by a fire in the midst of an empty desert, with a filthy-rich tycoon she had a massive and embarrassing crush on.

If my friends could see me now.

She sneaked a glance at him. He regarded her with a curious expression. Was he laughing at her? He hadn't started eating yet, and she hesitated before taking her next bite.

"After many years in England I like to begin a meal with a toast," he said. The fire flared, illuminating his face, where she read nothing but goodwill. "To you surviving your first plane flight." He lifted his soda cup and held it in the air. "Cheers."

She bumped her cup gently against his. "Cheers." She took a sip of her soda. The cool bubbles tickled her throat. "And my second plane flight. Though I only barely survived that one, didn't I?"

"Your response to the plane's descent was rather unexpected." His eyes twinkled with humor.

"Thank you for taking care of me." Her face heated as she realized she had no idea how she'd gone from being strapped in her seat to awakening in Elan's arms.

His dark eyes remained fixed on hers. "It was my pleasure." His husky voice and challenging stare sent her thoughts tripping over each other as they ran in a number of unseemly directions.

She took another bite of her fajita, trying hard not to think about him bending over her, lips poised mere inches from her own, his hands unbuckling her seat belt, loosening her clothing…

No, her clothing had not been loosened. *Earth to Sara!*

Elan did not seem the least bit preoccupied with thoughts of their rather eventful journey as he ploughed through three entrées with impressive gusto. She nibbled at her food and sipped her soda while she watched with amazement.

At last he looked up at her and wiped his mouth with his napkin. "What?" A smile quirked at the corner of his mouth.

"Nothing."

"Rubbish. Your eyes are smiling. What's so amusing?"

"I've never seen anyone eat so much."

"I'm a man of prodigious appetites." He looked at her steadily, his head cocked.

I can imagine.

His lips twitched slightly, as if anticipating something other than eating. Sara suppressed a little shiver as her imagination started to work overtime.

"And we missed lunch today." His mouth creased into a smile. The flickering firelight danced over his proud features and made Sara's insides churn in a most disturbing way.

"Oh, yes, you're right. No lunch." She hadn't even noticed. Food was the last thing on her mind when Elan was around.

"I've been starving for hours."

Me, too.

He leaned back, braced himself on one powerful arm, and rested a hand on his belly. A belly as firm and flat as the desert floor, hidden by his white shirt. She knew exactly how hard it was since she'd been crushed against it only half an hour ago.

His hand was silhouetted against the pale cloth of his shirt, long fingers splayed. It was a hand that looked as though it could cradle the world in its palm. She could still feel his fingers on her flesh as if the heat of them had seared through her clothing and left a smoking imprint on her skin.

The fire sputtered and dimmed. Elan lifted himself and leaned across the blanket, reached past her to rearrange the mesquite strips. He knelt and rested his weight on one powerful arm—like a tiger ready to pounce—as he tended the blaze with one hand.

She struggled to keep her breathing inaudible as his torso almost brushed against her.

He blew on the flames and they flared. He pulled back and knelt beside her.

"This mesquite does not burn as steadily as camel dung." A wry smile curved his lips as he surveyed her with hooded eyes. She let out a laugh, glad of an excuse for a release.

"I guess it's not easy to find things to burn in the desert."

"You learn to make the most of what's at hand."

"Did you actually grow up in the desert?"

"Yes." He looked back into the fire. "We had a home in Muscat, the capital city, but my father usually went there on business alone."

"Do you miss your country?"

"Sometimes." He looked at her and an odd expression crossed his face. "It's a strange confession for me to admit that."

"Why?"

"I've lived here for many years. I left Oman at age twenty-one under circumstances that made me wish never to return." Hooded eyes gazed at the fire as his quiet, controlled voice mingled with the crackling flames. "I'm accustomed to a life of exile."

"Don't you miss your family?"

"My parents are dead." A flicker of emotion passed over his features and Sara battled the urge to ask more about them. It wasn't her place.

"Do you have siblings?" She couldn't imagine growing up without the companionship of her brothers and sisters. While her parents sniped at each other and tore each other down, her siblings had carried her through. She was the youngest and they'd brought her up to be the woman she was today.

Each of them had given up opportunities to help support the family and raise her after their dad had died. While they all wanted to help, she and her brother Derek were the only ones with enough income to make a serious dent in the debts from their mom's cancer treatments, and Derek had given up so much for Sara already. It was her turn to give back, and she'd better remember that when she was tempted away from the path of reason.

"I have two brothers." Elan glanced up from the fire, his eyes black, unreadable in the darkness. "I barely know them now."

The sadness in his voice clutched at her. He turned his head to look back at the fire and the flames danced over the hard edges of his profile.

"What are their names? Do they still live in Oman?" She wanted to draw him out, to learn more about him. But as his eyes met hers in surprise, her simple questions sounded like unseemly prying. Her stomach tightened. Once again she'd overstepped her bounds.

He looked at her for a moment, an oddly vulnerable expression in his eyes.

"My younger brother Quasar is a financier in New York. He's wild, the baby of the family. He was always getting into scrapes as a kid—challenging me to races on our father's priceless camels, hiding insects in the women's robes to make them scream." A smile flickered across his mouth. "He's still up to his crazy tricks, though now I read about them in the papers." His expression turned wistful, then serious as he leaned forward to tend the fire. "I'd like to see more of him, but we're both busy."

He brushed against her as he reached across the blanket and she sucked in a breath as a shiver of awareness fired her nerves. Sparks leapt as he blew softly on the wood. Sara struggled to pour sand on the sparks that crackled inside her as the tang of his alluringly male scent assaulted her in the night air, an exotic blend of soap, clean sweat, horses and expensive wool.

She wrenched her eyes from the powerful forearm revealed by his rolled-up shirtsleeve. Elan seemed mercifully unaware of the thrall he held her in as he settled back on the blanket.

"My older brother Salim took over from my father when he died."

"In the family business?"

"Yes." He wiped a hand across his mouth and looked out into the darkness. "I suspect he would rather have remained in

America." He glanced at her. "He came here for college—we all did. But he has a strong sense of duty and is not one to shirk his responsibilities. He's a good man, and again, a busy one. I grew used to being away from my family while I was in boarding school."

"Your brothers weren't sent to the same school?"

"No. Quasar went to school in Europe, Salim had a private tutor at home." Once again he leaned forward and blew on the fire, his angular features silhouetted against the halo of orange sparks that pierced the darkness.

As he rested the weight of his body on his strong arms she couldn't help a stray wish that he'd take her and hold her tightly, as he'd done when she fainted.

Get hold of yourself, Sara. You're just lonely—and your boss's arms are not the place to seek comfort.

"Does it take long to get used to being away from your family? I miss mine so much." Her voice cracked. "It's only been a month, I know, but…" She bit her lip, not wanting to cry. She was tired, emotionally overwrought after the long day.

"You've never been away from home before?"

She shook her head. She knew tears shone in her eyes as she looked at him.

The tender look in his eyes almost undid her completely. "I cried every night for a long time," he said softly. "I felt like a page ripped from a favorite story. A jumble of words and images that no longer made sense without its companions. In my country family is everything. We live very close, eat together, sleep together. To be separated from the people I spent all my days and nights with—I don't exaggerate when I say it nearly killed me."

"Oh, gosh." Tears pricked at her eyes and she shook her head, braced against a surge of emotions threatening to engulf her. "I can't even imagine how hard that must have been for you. At least for me it was a choice. I left because I wanted to make my own life."

"I understand." His low voice curled around her like smoke

from the fire, warming her. "I made that choice myself when I left my homeland again as an adult, to settle in America. In some ways it hurts more—you can blame no one but yourself for your isolation."

He shifted slightly, turned his head to gaze again at the flames. The flickering tongues of light danced over his features, obscuring them. "In time, a scab grows over even a self-inflicted wound."

But the haunted expression in his eyes belied his words. And in that moment she could see Elan's loneliness was a torment that would likely never leave him.

On instinct she reached out and touched his forearm. He jerked as if stung and she pulled her hand back but he deftly grabbed it and held it firm.

His eyes burned dark fire as he looked into hers. "Loneliness is the curse of man. Once he leaves his mother's womb he's doomed to wander the earth, seeking that comfort he once enjoyed."

He raised his fingers to her face and she gasped as he cupped her cheek with his hand.

"There is no comfort to be found, only solace." He said it slowly, his voice hushed.

She parted her lips to reply but no words formed on them. Her thoughts tangled and scattered to the desert wind as Elan's hot, urgent mouth closed over hers.

Her head tipped back as he leaned into her and seized her in his arms. Her moan escaped into his mouth as her hands flew to his neck.

His arms circled her torso, strong and hard as steel, vibrating with dangerous urgency. She shuddered with the intensity of her own longing, and with fear—of wanting too much, wanting more than could ever be given.

But fear evaporated in the desert air as Elan's arms embraced her. In his fierce kiss she lost herself and claimed the primal closeness her body and soul ached for.

Her skin hummed beneath her clothes as his hand burrowed under the jacket of her suit, fingertips pressing into the muscle of her back through her thin blouse.

She arched her back, bending like a willow under the force of his touch. They inched closer on the blanket, their bodies drawing together, meeting in new places as the distance between them diminished to nothing. Shoulders met, hips bumped, knees shuffled into each other as they wound their arms around each other, banishing any space that separated them.

Her fingers groped up into his thick hair, pulled him to her as their kiss deepened. He licked the inside of her lips. His hunger echoed through her and she gasped as he sucked her tongue.

His hand beneath her jacket tugged her shirt free from her skirt and slid underneath it. As his fingers touched her nipple through her flimsy bra, she shuddered at the stinging intensity of the sensation. Every nerve in her body sang a high-pitched note of quivering arousal.

Elan eased back on his haunches and pulled her over him until she sat with her legs wrapped around him, hugging him. His tongue teased her lips, licked and sucked, parted them gently, then pulled back. He eased her skirt up over her hips, roved over the fullness of her thighs with broad palms.

His fingers slipped inside her panties and played over her backside, squeezing and testing. Her body opened up to him, soft and warm and wet, wanting him. She pushed her breasts against his chest, her nipples straining for contact with the hard muscle.

And, oh, how she wanted him. Her skin smoked under his touch, her blood heated, her whole body burned to be consumed in his fire.

He jerked his head back and licked the outside of her lips with exquisite gentleness. Then he shoved his tongue deep into her mouth with deft and daring ease. Her body bucked at the suggestion and a soft groan escaped her.

She buried her face in his neck, inhaled the intoxicating feral scent of his skin. She cupped his face with her hands, let her fingers explore the hard edges of his jaw, enjoy the cut of his cheekbones, rove into the softness of his hair.

Elan.

Elan!

What on earth was she doing?

She yanked her head back and forced her eyes open, her body literally shuddering with desire as she struggled to regain control.

His eyes opened slowly and the flickering firelight danced in their black depths.

"I want you, Sara. And I know our need for each other is mutual." The low rumble of his voice was a distant earthquake that shook her and crumbled any remnants of reason.

"Yes."

Five

She pulled him closer, settling her mouth over his as she surrendered to forces far stronger than good sense. Crackling bursts of electrical energy shot through her as their tongues touched.

She showered his face with kisses. His closed eyelids flickered under her lips as she dusted his skin with their caress. Her lips tingled as she relished the roughness of his cheeks.

Elan's hands were not idle while she tasted the salt of his skin and grazed the hard line of his jaw with her teeth. He tugged down the zipper on her skirt, sucked in a sharp breath as she gently bit his earlobe.

Her breasts quivered under her blouse as he pushed her gently away from him and undid the buttons of her jacket. He eased it off over her shoulders then tackled the buttons of her blouse with the same careful concentration.

The pause gave Sara time to think about what she was doing. Or what she wasn't doing. Shouldn't she be clutching her blouse, leaping to her feet and running for the sanctuary of the car? *What good could come of sleeping with my boss?*

But at that moment she could no longer see Elan as the boss. The long, powerful fingers carefully tugging at her tiny pearl buttons were those of a man—just a man—who wanted to hold her as much as she wanted to be held by him, and who wasn't afraid to say it.

The moon emerged from behind a bank of clouds, and anticipation shone in his dark eyes, reflecting her own.

His breathing hitched as he parted her silk shirt to reveal her breasts. Her cream lace bra lifted and offered them like fruits ripe for plucking.

She watched as he slowly raised his hands to touch them. The soft curves of flesh thrilled as his fingertips neared them. Her nipples tickled under the scratchy lace, begging to be touched. As if her tortured flesh communicated directly with him, Elan softly tugged at the lace edging the cups until her breasts spilled into his hands.

Sara released a sigh as those broad hands settled over her breasts, kneading them gently as he claimed her mouth with a kiss.

Heat flooded her limbs and she pressed herself against him, rubbed her hips against his hard belly, enjoyed the strength of his arousal through his clothes.

She wanted him inside her.

The ache of loneliness that followed her everywhere had transformed into a raging inferno of longing to connect with this man. Knowing that he, too, felt alone, needing someone—needing her—she knew they would fit together like two parts of a broken whole.

She fumbled with his belt, struggling to free the stiff leather from its loops, as his muted groans filled her ear. His tongue teased her earlobe and sent shivers of sensation sizzling up and down her neck as she tugged at the zipper on his pants and pushed them down over his hips.

She pulled at the buttons on his shirt in her urgency to bare his chest. His skin shone dark bronze in the flickering firelight, but unlike hard metal it felt hot and responsive to her touch.

She trailed her fingers over the ridges of muscle as she pushed his shirt back over his shoulders and he shrugged it off.

"I must get protection," he whispered.

Her eyes widened. The idea of protection had not even crossed her mind.

She gasped as he pulled back. It literally hurt to part from him even for a few seconds. He stepped out of his remaining clothes before he headed back to the car. Naked.

His body was magnificent. The full moon bathed the land in pale silver light. Elan looked like a god walking the earth as he strolled barefoot, dusted with moonbeams, over the rough desert soil.

He opened the passenger door and reached into the glove compartment, then slammed the door and strolled back to her. His easy, rolling gait belied his massive build. Every part of him was big. Big hands, strong arms, thickly muscled torso and powerful legs that carried him back to her in a few long strides.

His arousal was undiminished and hers only intensified by the agonizing separation from his blood-heating presence. She welcomed him back into her arms, gripped him too hard, not wanting to be parted from him again.

She lay back on the blanket and pulled him over her almost roughly. She craved his strength, his steadiness, the raw masculinity of him. Sandwiched between the hard ground of the desert and Elan's hard body, she writhed at the blissful torture. And she wanted to feel his hardness inside her.

He rolled back to rip open the packet and sheath himself. With careful fingers he touched and probed her moist folds and parted them. He eased himself into position over her, teased her painfully aroused flesh with the tip of his penis. Then he entered her.

He sank in, but so slowly she thought she'd go out of her mind with the agonizing pleasure of it. He lowered his body into hers and their skin met as they came together, inside and out, circling each other with arms and legs, mouths meeting and breath mingling in the moment of glorious unity.

Elan sighed softly in her ear as his body settled into hers. A perfect fit.

She could feel him quickening inside her. The sensation made her gasp and laugh and her eyes sprang open and met his steady gaze. His eyes sparkled with joy and a smile teased at the corners of his mouth. His lips parted as if to speak or shout or moan, but he lowered his head and buried his face in her neck, clutching her with his hands.

"I've never felt such desire for a woman," he breathed hot in her ear. She gasped as again she felt him move inside her. "I've never wanted…never needed…" His words were lost in a grunt of pleasure as he moved and shifted, deepening and strengthening the bond between them.

They worked together, hips lifting, bellies rolling over each other, legs and arms hugging and gripping as they moved together toward the ecstasy they craved.

They writhed on the blanket, the solid earth supporting them as she gave herself over to an intensity of sensation, a sheer, wringing pleasure she could never have imagined.

Elan's lovemaking was exquisite. Tender and loving, harsh and demanding, he rode her and fought her, caressed and comforted her, kissed and licked and teased and tormented her. Every inch of her skin, every cell in her body, sang with the clear, mad beauty of love.

Love?

Yes. Surely only love could upend the universe and shake it until stars rained down on them. And that love filled her now until she brimmed with explosive wonder, sheer joy that threatened to burst and shatter her into a thousand pieces.

His hot breath tickled her ear. "Sara, I… I…" She never knew what he struggled to say because at that moment he exploded inside her, shuddering and quaking with the force of his release as her own climax seized her and swept her into a vortex of ago-nizing bliss.

Elan's hand rested gently on her cheek as they lay side by side. They were both spent, exhausted, and Sara's body hummed with calm joy in the aftermath of their lovemaking.

He shifted closer, until his belly pressed against hers. He stroked her hair softly and placed a gentle kiss on her cheek. When his stomach tensed, she expected him to say something, but he didn't. Perhaps he wanted to but couldn't find the words. She certainly had no words for what had happened between them.

She could tell he didn't want to let her go. He didn't want to break the delicate bond that held them together. Maybe he, too, felt whole, warm, safe, blissfully free of rational thoughts and tiresome practicalities. Out there on top of a bluff, with nothing between them and the pale moon, they were the only people on earth.

But the fire had gone completely out and her skin tingled at the thought of all the wild creatures moving around them. Coyotes, bobcats, lizards…rattlesnakes. A rustling in the sand close by made her flinch. They might be the only humans, but they most definitely were not alone.

"We'd better go before something comes and bites us," she said reluctantly.

He nibbled her ear playfully. "You're in great danger of being bitten by me. Anything else that tries to taste your loveliness will have me to answer to."

She wriggled against him. It was easy to imagine Elan taking on any earthly creature. He radiated strength and self-confidence that surely even the most determined scorpion would shrink from.

"But you're right, my beauty. We must go."

They exchanged a last gentle kiss before tearing themselves away from each other to gather up their scattered clothes.

As they climbed back into the car, Sara knew they were leaving the magical world they'd inhabited. The click of the seat belt seemed symbolic of the return to a world of rules and regulations.

Elan's shirt hung unbuttoned over his pants, and she longed to reach over and touch his chest as he drove. But she knew better. The time for carefree touches and playful intimacy was over. Her gut tightened as a surge of apprehension replaced the carefree ease she'd enjoyed only minutes ago.

A dark mood had settled over him. He looked straight ahead as he drove, his face stony in profile. She tried to think of something to say, a casual conversational gambit to break the tension thickening the air, but no words seemed appropriate to the strangeness of the situation.

What could she say? *Thanks, that was fun! Gosh, the desert's lovely at night, isn't it? We'd better get some sleep, we've got an early meeting tomorrow!*

Gulp.

She froze in her seat as the reality of the situation crept over her like icy fingers.

She'd slept with her boss.

No, not true. She hadn't slept with him. She'd clawed his back, howled in ecstasy, pushed her hips against his and ridden him, clung to him and moaned his name in the throes of her orgasm.

Oh, dear.

Perhaps if they were now sitting there chatting about what movie they'd go see on Saturday night it would seem, well, not normal, but okay. But the way he gripped the wheel, his jaw clenched, eyes narrowed, lips pressed together, she could see that tonight was not the first night of an ordinary dating relationship.

As if this kind of night ever could be. What man would want

a girl who "put out" on the first date? And it wasn't even a date. He'd offered her dinner and she'd thrown herself at him.

She was no virgin. She'd had a boyfriend in high school and another in college. But she'd never in her life slept with a man she wasn't "going steady" with. "If you don't respect yourself…" She could hear her oldest sister Nathalie's cheerful voice in her ear. The lecture had been given in a playful tone since no one expected Sara to need it anyway.

Then she'd met Elan. He undid her in a way that was truly frightening. That stripped away the thin layer of civility to reveal her primitive core.

Neon lights flickered on the main drag as they drove back into town. Dawn hovered behind the hills and the purple sky threatened to explode into blazing sunlight at any moment.

"Take a left here."

His big hands slid over the wheel as he turned into her apartment complex.

"Would you like to come up for coffee?" She almost choked on the words but it felt only polite to offer. She would love for him to come up. To talk and break the chill silence that had settled over them like dew on the desert.

"I think we should both get some sleep," he said softly. He pulled the car to a stop outside the front door. For the first time since they'd climbed into the sedan, he turned to look at her.

The faraway look in his dark eyes touched a raw place in her, summoned her. She wanted to touch him. She wanted to close the distance echoing between them even in the cramped space of the car.

She ached to be held in his arms.

He opened his mouth—to speak, or to kiss her?—but he didn't move. And then his mouth closed, full lips settling together, as if they'd already said everything there was to say.

She wanted so badly to kiss him goodbye. To press her lips

against his skin one last time, to feel the heat of his blood warm her mouth. But the rigid set of his shoulders and the high angle of his chin warned her off. No kisses were offered by either party.

"Good night, Sara."

"Good night, Elan." Her voice trembled a little and she thought she saw a flicker of emotion in his eyes. But perhaps it was just a reflection of her own confusion and embarrassment as she fumbled for her briefcase on the floor. She scrambled out of the car, clutching her crumpled clothes around her.

The big sedan didn't move until she'd gone inside, so she never actually heard him drive away. But she suffered his leaving as a limb being torn from her body. If she'd felt alone before, now she felt desolate, destitute. Like Eve banished from Paradise because she couldn't keep her hands off the tempting and dangerous fruit within.

Sara operated on automatic pilot as she parked her bicycle and walked into the office building the next morning. She knew Elan wouldn't be there yet, since she always arrived early enough to change into professional attire and get her desk organized before the day got hectic. He didn't usually come in until around nine.

As nine o'clock drew closer she found it impossible to concentrate on her work. Her blood thundered audibly in her head, her heart banged against her ribs, and she kept catching herself nervously drumming a pen on her desk.

Oh, God. What would they say to each other? *Hi. Good morning. Can I get you anything? Like me, naked on a blanket in the moonlight?*

She cringed inwardly. She was preparing a complicated report with multiple columns of figures and the numbers jumped and buzzed before her eyes like performers in a flea circus.

Each time the doors to the elevator opened she fought an urge to dive beneath her desk like a creature startled to its burrow. Just the mail clerk. The assistant from finance with some new figures. Each arrival sent her into a frenzy of panic.

When a messenger arrived with a small box wrapped in gold paper, Sara's eyes widened. Had Elan sent her something? She leaped out of her chair to receive it, a smile rising to her lips.

"Thanks!"

She ripped open the card with trembling fingers.

"Mr. Al Mansur, thanks for all you've done for us in Alberta. In eager anticipation of another banner year, yours, Tony Leon, Acme Drilling Co."

It wasn't for her. It was for Elan. A corporate gift. Probably another set of gold-plated golf tees.

Sara sagged with misery. How pathetic that she'd so quickly assumed Elan had made a romantic gesture.

Wishful thinking.

She put the box in his office and returned to her chair to resume her anxious vigil.

But he didn't come in.

By noon she was confused and upset. He'd missed an important meeting with a supplier, yet had not asked her to take his place in it. Apparently he'd phoned his regrets to the other attendees.

"When is he coming?" asked first one caller, then another and another.

"I'm not exactly certain," gradually became a mumbled, "I don't know," as Sara's professional demeanor slipped a little further with each admission. She maintained his schedule, made all his appointments and usually knew his movements better than he did.

She was tempted to call his home to see if he was okay. But he'd excused himself from the meeting so he was obviously alive. He'd simply chosen not to come into the office today.

Had chosen not to see her.

"When's Mr. Al Mansur coming back from Turkey?"

"What?" Sara glanced up from her work, anxiety spiking in her gut.

The Assistant VP for Production stood in front of her desk, a pen pressed to her carefully made-up lips. "It's just that I really need him to sign these documents. I had no idea he was leaving for Turkey today."

"Me neither." Despair descended in a heavy fog. He'd left the country without telling her?

"Are you okay?" The other woman's concern wrinkled her smooth brow as she hugged her thick folder of documents to her chest.

"Sure." The word emerged excessively loud as she tried to exude self-confidence she didn't feel. "I'm not sure when he'll be back," she said more quietly. She didn't even know which airline he'd taken. He must have bought his own ticket.

"Is he there to look over the El Barak field? The one where the wells needed deepening?"

"I expect so." She struggled to sound as normal as possible. "I'll let you know as soon as I hear from him."

"You don't look well. Are you sure you're okay?"

"Yes. Just a slight headache, I'll take an aspirin for it."

She rested her head on her desk as the door closed behind her coworker. A woman ten years older than herself and in a position of considerable authority. She was everything Sara hoped to be herself: respected, liked and admired for her quick thinking and effective teamwork.

That could have been her in a few years. *If I hadn't slept with my boss.*

If only she could take an aspirin for heartache.

Elan was gone for four days. She spoke to him twice on the phone and their conversations were entirely professional. He

wanted some documents e-mailed to him. He advised her of his
return flight. She reported the minutes of a meeting he'd missed.

There was no mention, or even suggestion, of what had
happened between them.

Sara was sure she would be terminated as soon as he returned.
After all, she'd promised that if she didn't perform as agreed—
including keeping her eyes and hands off the boss—he could fire
her outright. With that promise she'd slammed the door on any
sexual harassment lawsuit.

She attempted to polish her résumé, but realized she couldn't
even include this job on it if she'd been here only one month. It
would be obvious she'd been fired.

She wondered if she could beg him to keep her on for a few
more months, just until she could find something else. She
wondered if she could brazenly insist on holding her job, as
she'd done on the first day.

It takes two to tango.

Even if she'd been warned from the outset that tangoing with
the boss was strictly not on the agenda at Al Mansur Associates.

"Good afternoon, Sara." Elan swept past her like a gust of
wind, blowing through the doors from the elevator and into his
office. His door slammed behind him before her brain fully reg-
istered his presence.

She hadn't even managed a polite greeting.

Her pulse pounded in her temple as she dragged herself to her
feet. She picked up a big stack of papers and a long series of
messages she'd collected. There was nothing for it but to go in.
Might as well get it over with.

She hesitated, held up her trembling fist for a moment before
rapping on the door. Should she say anything about what had
happened? Attempt a preemptive apology? She'd have to play it
by ear. Ears almost deafened by the blood thundering in her head.

She knocked.

"Come in."

The door swung open to reveal Elan seated in his leather throne. He looked up as if startled, though he must have known it would be her. He sprang to his feet and ran a broad hand through his hair.

"Sara."

She gulped. "Yes."

He looked right at her and she froze, turned to stone. His eyes were narrowed in a penetrating gaze, black and shadowed, his face taut, jaw clenched.

"I feel I must offer my most humble apologies for the events of last week."

Her gut seized and she held her breath.

"You are a valued employee here. I think it's best if we do not mention those events again."

Thoughts rushed her brain and swept around in mini-cyclones—*he isn't firing me.*

He wanted to forget their night together.

The rush of relief at getting to keep her job was undercut by a harsh stab of humiliating disappointment. Had she really expected to continue some kind of intimate relationship with Elan? Even after he disappeared for days, fled to the other side of the world to avoid her?

The ache in her heart told her she had.

"Yes," she whispered. Her voice emerged as a hiss of steam released from an overheated radiator, but she was relieved she could find it at all. "Thank you."

She could almost swear she saw him flinch as she said "thank you." Was he disgusted that she didn't resign on principle? Someone wealthy like him probably couldn't understand how you could need a job more than your pride.

He nodded curtly. She cleared her throat and attempted to give him his messages in as normal a voice as possible.

He listened politely and responded appropriately, but as she talked she could see him looking almost anywhere but at her. A muscle worked in his jaw and his shoulders were rigid with tension. His discomfort in her presence was obvious.

And he had good reason to be uncomfortable. Because even as she spoke, her mind wandered. Wondered. Remembered the feel of his hands on her. Remembered the scent of him as she buried her face in his neck. Remembered the sweet, soothing warmth of being held tightly in his arms.

He studied a document, following the lines with his finger. The finger that had traced a line from her chin, to her belly button, to her agonizingly aroused… She blinked and swallowed hard, trying to shove down the disturbing sensations creeping through her body.

What was it about this man that made her professional demeanor fly out the window? That unhinged her almost to the point of madness?

She tore her eyes from him and tried to focus on the papers on his desk, on the spectacular expanse of clear sky visible through the window, on the spotless gray carpet. But each time her attention drifted back, in imperceptible degrees, to the man who consumed it.

To the way his hair was starting to touch his collar slightly in the back, in need of a cut. To the powerful tanned wrists revealed by the turned-back cuffs of his white shirt. To the way his tie was loosened slightly, accommodating one opened button at the neck of his shirt. Elan always looked a little too confined in clothes, as if he'd like to peel them off and get comfortable.

Or was it just her that wanted to peel them off? The thought made her anything but comfortable. She closed her eyes, attempting to block the sight of him from her vision. To block the image of him from her mind. But his midnight gaze was burned into her retinas.

"Are you…all right?"

"Yes," she said, her voice rather too high-pitched. He might well ask. He'd caught her standing in his office with her eyes closed. Was she all right? *Most definitely not.* She wasn't sure if she'd ever be all right again. "Will that be all?" She managed to plaster on a thin veneer of professionalism, even as she started automatically backing toward the doorway.

"Yes, thank you." Elan had turned away from her and bent over his desk, opening a drawer. She could see his biceps flexed tightly under the cotton of his shirt, his fists almost clenched. The tension in the air was suffocating, a cloying atmosphere of regret and recrimination that tormented them both.

What on earth had she been thinking when she touched Elan, when she kissed him, when she…

She turned on her heel and flew out the door. She accidentally slammed it in her haste to escape. Outside, she gasped a deep gulp of air and bent double as blood rushed to her head.

The only way she could survive this was to pretend it had never happened. To avoid thinking about it. *It.* The elusive *it* that sprang only too readily to the forefront of her consciousness. A night against which all other nights would inevitably be measured for the rest of her life.

Six

"We'd be delighted to do business with you. Thank you so much for coming." Sara shook the last cool hand of the venture capitalist team from New York. She ushered them out of the conference room, professional smile fixed in place.

As the tall mahogany door closed behind them she collapsed into a chair, shaking.

A six-hour meeting. With the CEO, CFO, new business strategist and two administrative staff.

By herself.

"I'm sure you can handle the details," Elan had said, when he announced he had other plans that morning.

Anderson Capital, which planned to invest in small "wildcat" oil-drilling firms and employ El Mansur Associates' technology and expertise to make them more profitable, had the potential to bring millions of dollars of annual revenue to the company. And Elan had handed her the account, to win or lose, all on her own.

He wanted her to fail.

He wanted her to admit defeat. Quit. Leave.

And he wanted that so badly that he didn't mind risking an important account to do it.

She'd already failed once. She'd betrayed his trust, broken her promise that she would not overstep the bounds of her job. This time she was determined not to fail.

Every day her mountain of responsibilities increased. The challenges Elan tossed in her direction grew more complex and demanding. She hadn't slept more than three hours a night lately as she needed every single minute to prepare for the onslaught of meetings, reports and presentations that were now her responsibility in addition to her administrative duties.

Her cell phone vibrated—again—and she thought of the work that must be piling up on her desk right this minute.

She took a deep breath. "Hello."

"Please come to my office." Elan.

A flash of anger warred with the heat his deep voice conjured as it curled into her ear. "I'll be right there." How could he push her this hard?

She hung up the phone, gathered her papers, and shoved out into the hallway.

This is what she wanted, right? A challenging, highly paid position in the exact field of her expertise. Of course she'd never dreamed she'd be performing duties more suited to a senior vice president than to an executive assistant and project manager. She had Elan to thank for that, though thanks was really the last thing on her mind right now.

She stormed out of the elevator on her floor, dropped the sheaf of papers on her desk—which now looked as overloaded and messy as Elan's—and rapped on the door to his office.

"Come in."

She steeled herself against the sight of him.

"How was the meeting?" He lounged back in his chair. His black gaze threatened to steal the breath from her lungs as she groped for a response.

"I believe it went well," she said stiffly. "They were concerned specifically about our ability to scale production quickly in the event a large new field was discovered, and I assured them that would not be a problem."

"Good. I'd like you to prepare a proposal that covers any issues raised during the meeting and provides them with a detailed summary of the services we can offer…"

She nodded, watching his mouth as he rumbled about the chain of production and pipeline capacity.

Was this the same man who had held her that night in the desert?

She'd looked into his eyes and felt a connection deeper than she could have ever imagined. He'd held her so tenderly, so passionately, she was sure she'd found…her soul mate.

She'd been wrong.

She swallowed hard. "I'll have it on your desk first thing tomorrow."

He regarded her steadily for a moment, dark gaze drifting over her face. Could he see she was exhausted? Barely able to function?

Did that give him satisfaction?

She could read nothing in his stern features.

As his fingers wrapped around his gold fountain pen, she couldn't help but remember the way they'd circled her waist, his hands so broad and strong he could lift her as if she weighed no more than a grain of sand.

"Thank you," he said. Her dismissal. He turned back to the report he was reading.

She stood her ground. *You won't break me.*

She stared at him for a moment, daring him to look back up at her. Did she imagine it, or did his fingers tighten around the pen? He paused in his reading, tugged at his collar, then glanced at her.

Their eyes met. "Will that be all?"

Sir.

She wanted him to know she saw the game he was playing.

"Yes, Sara." He said her name slowly, emphatically, his dark eyes unblinking. Her stomach flipped and she held herself steady.

His full lips straightened into a hard line.

Lips that had kissed her with force and tenderness she could never have imagined. Lips that had teased and tempted her into a frenzy of passion.

Lips that held the power to fire her, as she'd invited him to do on her first day.

Yes, she'd failed once, and she wanted him to know it would *never* happen again.

Elan leaned back in his chair and let out a long, hard breath as the door closed behind her. The woman was stubborn as a camel and twice as tough. Any normal person would have thrown in the towel, but Sara?

Nooo.

He couldn't help the smile that sneaked over his lips. This small woman had the courage of ten men. Unfortunately, she had the intelligence and aptitude of ten men, too, so no matter how much work he threw at her, somehow she managed to get it done. He was beginning to wonder if a little man called Rumplestiltskin visited her apartment in the evenings.

No. There was no time for any man in her evenings. He'd seen to that.

He wiped the smile of satisfaction from his face. Her evenings were no concern of his.

He'd made an error of judgment—once.

She'd touched something inside him he'd thought buried and forgotten. Reopened old wounds he was sure had scarred over.

She'd seen past the strength, past the power, past the money—
to the man within.

He'd felt, that night, that he *needed* her.

He rose from his chair, anger flaring in his chest.

He needed *no one,* and he would *never* let that happen again.

Seven

Bent over the sink in the office bathroom, Sara suffered another sudden surge of nausea. She was exhausted, drained, run-down.

And more than three months pregnant.

Until her visit to the doctor that afternoon, the possibility of a pregnancy had never crossed her mind. She'd bled after all, just not as much as usual, and the bleeding never really seemed to go away. She'd felt ill from time to time, but she'd put it down to stress and lack of sleep. After what seemed like a few weeks of intermittent on-and-off period she went to her gynecologist.

Diagnosis: Pregnancy.

The bleeding was abnormal and her doctor's concern showed in her face. Sara had no idea what showed on her own face: astonishment, disbelief, possibly horror.

She was bustled into an ultrasound room and unceremoniously stripped and smeared with gel so the bizarre events taking place inside her could be examined in scientific detail.

All disbelief vanished when she saw it on the ultrasound monitor. *My baby.* Its little heart pumping visibly, its tiny limbs already distinguishable, curved under its big head.

Her panicked gasping had frightened the ultrasound technician. "Don't worry, dear," the nurse said softly. She was soft all over, from her gloved hands to her fluffy blond hair. "The uterine environment looks quite normal. Some people do continue spotting for some weeks with no known cause. There's no apparent danger to your pregnancy."

Her reassuring words penetrated Sara's consciousness, but they only made tears rise in her throat. A turmoil of unfamiliar emotions racked her body. Guilt that she hadn't spared a thought for the "uterine environment." A fearful recoil at the alien life secreted in her belly for so long without her knowledge. And—even more alarming—a fierce tug of intense affection for the tiny person growing inside her.

She stumbled back to the office to prepare a report for a meeting the following morning. It hadn't occurred to her to do otherwise. That was before the reality of the situation sank in. Before she found herself sitting at her desk, unable to focus her eyes, confused thoughts crowding her brain and terror twisting her gut. Before she sprinted into the bathroom, overwhelmed by nausea and the horrifying reality that everything in her life was about to change.

Had already changed.

She couldn't keep working this hard. She was endangering not only her health, but that of her baby. The report for tomorrow's meeting would have to wait. She'd apologize, say she was ill. But she'd sneak out and call in her regrets from home because she just couldn't face Elan right now.

She wasn't sure if she could ever face him again.

All his cruel assumptions about her on her first day had proven horrifyingly accurate. She had lusted after him and seduced him.

She'd risked the career opportunity of a lifetime for a few hours of pleasure.

Gambled with her life for one night in his arms.

And I am carrying Elan's baby.

The thought hit her for the first time like a splash of icy water. Somehow in the terrible excitement of discovering she was pregnant she'd managed not to think about the other person responsible for the life growing inside her.

How would he react? With shock, most likely. With horror, no doubt. Her disgrace was total.

She quickly stripped off her suit and put on her cycling clothes and sneakers, then shoved her suit into her backpack with far less care than usual. It wouldn't fit for much longer anyway.

She splashed her face with water and pulled her hair into a ponytail. Her eyes were red and her skin blotchy with distress. Hopefully she could get away without running into anyone.

She emerged from the bathroom and dashed for the elevator. She hugged herself, struggled to keep her breathing even, to keep tears at bay until she left the office.

But the elevator arrived with Elan inside it.

He strode out, then paused. "Sara, you don't look well."

"Yes." Her voice emerged as a whisper.

Guilt and terror paralyzed her limbs. Her secret swelled inside her, threatening to inflate like a giant blow-up and knock her over.

"Perhaps you're working too hard?" He raised an eyebrow.

"Um…" She couldn't seem to formulate a sentence that didn't contain the words *I'm having your baby.*

I've got to get out of here.

A massive surge of adrenaline flooded her limbs with the urge to shove past him into the elevator and escape. Her heart thundered as she zeroed in on the dimly lit cavern that was her only escape route. If she could just get in there and let those doors close behind her.…

Elan stood barring the way, his brow lowered with concern.

"You're ill. You should not ride your bike. I'll drive you home."

"No!" She spat the word, as images of their last car ride together assaulted her. *Elan, shirt unbuttoned to reveal his hard chest. His broad hand on the wheel.*

His sperm swimming toward her egg.

"I'll be fine. The exercise will do me good. Do you mind if I…" she stammered, able to focus only on the dark emptiness of the elevator that would carry her away from a drama she wasn't ready to take her part in.

He stood aside. Was that relief on his face? "We have no matters that can't wait until tomorrow."

"Thanks." She dove past him. He let go of the elevator door he'd been holding for her. She saw him turn and look at her, his brow furrowed, as the doors closed.

She sagged against the cold metal walls as the elevator hummed into motion.

Oh, I'm not ill. I'm just pregnant with your child.

"You're kidding me," said Erin, after a very long pause. Her sister was the first person she'd called. As a single mother herself, Sara figured Erin would be able to relate.

"Would I kid about something like this?" Sara paced back and forth in her small apartment, trying not to bump her hip on the kitchen countertop or pull the phone off the wall. She couldn't keep still. Too jumpy.

"You're pregnant? By who? You only just moved there and you weren't dating anyone here. Or were you?"

"No. I haven't dated anyone since I broke up with Mike last year." She paused to look out the window. The sun was sinking behind the mountains; soon the town would be plunged into darkness. She swallowed hard, twisted the phone cord in her hands. "I slept with my boss."

"Your boss? I thought your boss was the owner of the company."

"Yes," she rasped. It sounded even worse out loud than it did in her head.

"Isn't he some millionaire oil tycoon?"

"Yes." She closed her eyes.

"Is he, like, fifty years old or something?"

"No, of course not. He's thirty-two." And handsome. And irresistible.

And he despises me.

"So, jeez, is this like, a relationship?"

"No." She tugged at the phone cord, her eyes starting to sting. She bit the inside of her mouth to stem any tears. "It was a one-night thing. A mistake."

She heard Erin blow out a deep breath. "Wow. That's just so…not like you."

"Tell me about it. I've worked my butt off to get this job, and you know how much we need the money. But there was something about him…" Her voice trailed off and she sucked in a breath.

"He must be *hot*. What's his name?"

"Elan." Just saying his name made her face flood with heat. Guilt.

"Wow. Is he married?"

"No! Do you really think I would sleep with a married man?" A rush of indignation made her shove her hand through her hair.

"I didn't think you'd sleep with your boss."

Me neither.

"You haven't told him yet, have you?"

"No. You're the first person I've told. He's not going to be happy, and that's an understatement. After it happened he said we should never mention it again."

"You could sue for sexual harassment." Her sister's voice was low, serious.

"I can't. He actually predicted something like this might happen. He didn't want a young female assistant for that very reason and he tried to get me transferred on my first day. I told him that if my behavior was at all unprofessional—" She sucked in a breath. "He could fire me on the spot."

"Oh, Sara." There was a pause. Sara heard her little nephew say something and his mom whispered a quick reply, then came back on the line. "Don't tell him. Seriously, you don't want to lose your medical insurance at a time like this. Trust me on this one. Been there, done that. I don't know what I would have done without Derek helping me out."

"Derek's going to have a cow, isn't he?" Derek, their oldest brother, had been like a second father to her. More of a father than her real one. He'd worked so hard, taking a second job to help the family through one crisis after another. They'd all been blindsided by Erin's unexpected pregnancy followed by their mother's diagnosis with lymphoma. Sara cringed at the thought of dealing him another blow.

"Derek is a rock. He never said a single negative thing when I got pregnant. He's been there for me every step of the way. We'll all support you. Kristin can look after your baby while you work. She'll be able to have her entire in-home daycare be our kids—it'll be fun. I've missed you so much. You are going to move home, aren't you?"

A question that had zinged around her mind from the moment she learned the news. How could she not move home and be with her family?

But then again, how could she?

"There are no jobs in my field there." She looked out the window at the harsh desert landscape, mountain peaks dark against the shimmering sky. So beautiful.

"Bates Electronics will take you back."

"But I won't make enough to pay down Mom's hospital bills.

I know we're all trying to contribute, but my salary is by far the highest. And then there are my college loans. All of you have your own responsibilities to deal with."

"You don't always have to be a superwoman, you know? It's okay to be human."

No, it's not. I made that mistake one night in the desert.

"I don't think Elan will fire me. If he was going to, he'd have done it already. I promised him on my first day that I wouldn't so much as flirt with him. I guess he has women throwing themselves at him all the time, I just can't believe I turned out to be one of them."

"He sounds like a piece of work. I'd like to get my hands on him."

Erin's gritty threat almost made her laugh. "That's how this whole thing got started, I'm afraid." She took a deep breath. "I'm going to tell him about the pregnancy tomorrow."

"Oh, Sara." Her spirited sister's voice withered. "You know Gavin dumped me when I told him."

Sara rubbed her eyes. "I know. I just hope I can be as strong as you."

Okay, this is it. You're going to march right into his office and say it. I'm pregnant.

Sara inhaled a shaky breath as the elevator climbed. She'd deliberately come in late, so he'd be there and she wouldn't have time to sit around at her desk and think of reasons not to tell him. She'd even bicycled here in a smart pantsuit so she'd be "dressed for the occasion." Unfortunately, there was now a black chain print smudge near the inside of the right ankle. She'd deal with that later.

The elevator doors opened, and her anxiety turned to chilling surprise.

Her desk, which had sat right in front of the elevator, was now moved to one side, sharing the space with a second identical desk. The piles of papers covering her workspace threatened to keel over onto the stark gray surface of the new desk pushed up next to it.

"Sara." Elan's large form dominated even the cavernous space of the foyer. His greeting caused her heart to pound louder.

I'm pregnant.

But she couldn't tell him now because there was another person in the room.

"This is Mrs. Dixon," Elan said. A satisfied smile roamed across his mouth. "She's a new member of our team. Her title is Executive Assistant."

Sara's blood froze. Was she being replaced?

"Mrs. Dixon will perform the secretarial duties that were your responsibility. Answering my phone, preparing my correspondence, filing my papers and such."

Sara struggled to keep her face expressionless. *And what will I do?*

"You will focus your time and energy on special projects I assign you. This arrangement is somewhat inconvenient," he indicated the two desks with a sweep of his hand. His gold watch glinted beneath a starched cuff. "But it's temporary. I'd like you to gain more experience in the field, to become familiar with the day-to-day operations at our job sites."

Sara blinked, the lights suddenly too bright for her eyes. She glanced at Mrs. Dixon. Steel-gray hair sprayed into a bouffant, mouth pursed into a prim line, the stiffly suited older woman regarded her with what looked like distaste.

I prefer my executive assistant to be a woman with decades of experience, and preferably gray hairs on her head.

Elan's words on that first day flew into her head.

She was being replaced. And banished. He meant to be rid of her, and since she wouldn't quit he planned to send her away to "gain experience." And he'd installed her replacement before she was even gone.

"Your salary will increase, of course." Elan's words jerked her attention back to him. He surveyed her through narrowed eyes. "Commensurate with your new responsibilities and the inconvenience of frequent travel."

Frequent travel. On a plane. Her gut clenched at the prospect. Is this how he meant to drive her away? To play on her one weakness?

"It is a promotion, though your title will remain the same." An overhead spotlight threw his arrogant features into harsh relief as a smile crossed his lips.

A promotion. Higher pay. A reward for excellence?

Or a smoke screen to cover his plan to force her resignation?

"Thank you. I look forward to the new challenges," she said stiffly.

"Good. I have a meeting to attend. Please familiarize Mrs. Dixon with the workings of our office. I'll be at home this afternoon as I have a new mare being delivered. You may handle my calls for me."

With a brusque nod, he strode toward the elevator leaving Sara alone with…

The Other Woman.

She wanted to laugh. Her rival was not the long-lashed, pouty-lipped casino bunny she might have imagined. No. She was a heavily powdered, sturdy-legged matron of at least fifty-five.

"Pleased to meet you," she said, holding out her hand to Mrs. Dixon.

"Likewise." Mrs. Dixon's hair remained firmly in place as she nodded a greeting and met Sara's sweating palm with her own cool, meaty hand. "Have you worked here long?"

"Nearly five months."

Oh, and I'm having his baby, by the way.

How would she ever tell him now? With this steel-haired battle-ax perched outside the office door, ear probably glued to the intercom?

As hers had once been.

"I have thirty-five years of experience assisting executives." Mrs. Dixon's thin lips pressed together for a moment as she glanced from Sara's travel-wrinkled suit to the teetering piles of folders and correspondence on her desk. "We'll soon get this office whipped into shape."

I have to tell him. Today.

She pumped down on the pedals, pushing her bike along the dusty road that cut through the sagebrush-strewn desert. She pedaled slowly, trying to conserve her energy, trying not to work up too much of a sweat as the summer sun glared down at her from the fierce blue sky. It was already eleven o'clock, the journey taking longer than she'd expected. When she'd looked up Elan's address she hadn't realized his ranch was so far from town. But she had to go there and tell him away from the prying eyes of their coworkers.

She'd tried, time and time again over the past two weeks, to get a moment alone with Elan behind the closed door of his office. But Mrs. Dixon hovered around him like a ministering angel, bearing cups of steaming coffee, bags of dry-cleaned shirts and freshly collated reports. She even took shorthand, which seemed to delight Elan, who now dictated most of his personal correspondence instead of typing it himself on his computer. There was no escaping the woman, whose old-school solicitude was a stark contrast to Sara's own ambitious careerism.

And Elan was using her ambition as a rope to hang her with. She was scheduled to leave next Thursday for three weeks on an offshore rig in the Gulf of Mexico. After that she was headed to Canada, for a long stint at three different sites there. The opportunity was exciting, she couldn't deny it, but it was sure to be a challenge in ways she probably couldn't even imagine. No question, he was pushing her, testing her, trying to find her limits.

He'd wanted her gone, and now she would be. Good. No more struggling to keep her eyes off the broad strength of his shoulders, the dexterous power of his hands, the dark magnetism of his gaze.

What a relief. So why the hollow ache inside her at the thought of leaving?

Probably that hollow space was there because she'd been up half the night drafting projections for a new client, with nothing more than a quick plate of fruit and cheese to keep her going.

She didn't think he'd fire her when he heard her news. She'd been at the company long enough to know that for all his brash demeanor Elan treated his employees with scrupulous fairness. There were several pregnant women in the office and he'd even raised the idea of an on-site daycare to encourage employee retention.

His objections would be *personal.*

If he was trying to force her out now, how would he react when he knew her secret? Even if he didn't fire her, he might push just hard enough to get her on that train home to Wisconsin.

Telling him was risky, but she wasn't the kind of person who could sit on a secret like this. It was his child, too, and he deserved to know of its existence.

She'd reached a flat expanse of land on which she couldn't see a man-made structure of any kind, let alone a house befitting a wealthy tycoon. Was she lost?

She hadn't phoned to tell him she was coming. She'd figured the surprise of her unexpected appearance would only herald the other, far more dramatic surprise that she had in store for him. But if she didn't find the place soon, the surprise would be finding her bleached bones out on the burning sands.

As she came to the top of a slight rise she spied movement off in the distance. Dark lines of pipe fencing crisscrossed the desert, marking boundaries on the open plain. She squinted against the high sun, trying to make out the shadowy shapes that darted to and fro in the distance.

A man and a horse.

A dark horse and a dark-skinned man silhouetted against the sun-bleached landscape. Gradually she saw the shape of the house emerge from its surroundings. Sand-colored, it blended almost totally into the environment. Other horses sheltered in the dark shade of earth-toned structures that became visible as she drew closer.

A trickle of sweat pricked at her spine, and her heart raced as much from fear as from physical exertion as she drew closer to her quarry.

He hadn't seen her.

Elan stood in the center of a round pen. The dark-red horse ran on the end of a long lead, as he chased it around in circles. When the horse slowed or tried to turn away from him, he cracked a whip to drive it forward.

His attention focused totally on the horse, he didn't look up even as she dismounted her bike. She leaned it against the sand-colored wall of the imposing bunkerlike structure that she assumed must be his house.

She approached slowly, her heart thundering against her ribs. The pen Elan worked in stood a good hundred yards away and she struggled to put one foot in front of the other and cover what suddenly seemed like an impossibly large distance.

She couldn't back out this time. Wouldn't leave until she'd told him.

"Yah!"

His shout startled her and she jumped. But he'd shouted at the horse. His expression frightened her, brows low over eyes narrowed against the bright sun, chin jutted in an expression of determination.

Her gaze dropped lower. He wore only a pair of dusty black jeans. His bare torso shone with sweat in the blazing midday heat. His hair was damp, black tendrils plastered to his forehead. He raised a muscled arm and buried his face in the crook of his elbow, streaking a mix of sweat and dirt across his face as he raised his focus again to his horse.

And then he saw her.

The rein to the horse went slack and the animal slowed to a halt. Elan raised his hand higher to shield his eyes from the sun and squinted at her as if doubting his vision.

"Sara?"

Her heart tripped over itself and her breathing quickened as she walked to him on unsteady legs. "Yes."

"What brings you to my home?" Still squinting against the sun, he started to stride toward her. The horse, however, had other ideas and tossed its head, almost jerking the rein from his hand.

Elan jerked back and let fly a string of words in a language she didn't know. "This mare, she has the stubbornness of an ox, the disdain of a camel!"

Sara looked at the mare. She had her head raised and one eye firmly fixed on Elan in an attitude of visibly insolent disregard. "I'm training her to see if she's suitable to breed to my stallions."

"But she has other ideas?" Sara raised an eyebrow. She was relieved by the minor distraction of talking about the horse. An icebreaker, if ice could even be imagined in the blazing heat of the desert.

"Yes. She'd like to train me to leave her alone with her food." Elan's lips curved into a smile. The mare seized the opportunity to turn her backside to him. Elan cracked the whip and goaded her into a swift canter around the pen, then brought her to a halt.

"There's no point in breeding a horse that cannot safely be ridden, no matter how lovely her conformation," he continued, as he gathered up the length of rein and led the horse across the pen to where Sara stood.

"She's beautiful."

"Yes, but beauty without loyalty can break hearts—and

bones." He smiled broadly and patted the horse's neck. "She'll bend to my will. It's only a matter of time. I feed her, I care for her, give her shelter from the sun. She will learn these things come with a price, and she'll learn to pay it."

Sara nodded and looked at the beautiful sorrel mare, who tossed her head constantly, obviously hating the confinement of her halter. Her heart swelled with pity for the creature that wanted to be free, but would have to learn that her days of illusory freedom were over.

She knew that feeling.

At that instant the child stirred inside her, a strange new fluttering sensation that tugged her attention back to her purpose. Her fingers drifted instinctively to the place where her baby was secreted in her belly. Elan's eyes narrowed as they followed the motion, and she yanked the traitorous hand behind her back.

"I need to talk to you." Her gut tightened and her breathing slowed, making her light-headed.

"Yes?"

"Can we…I know you're busy, but can we…go inside?" She couldn't stand there in the heat much longer without keeling over. Her fingers and toes stung with needle pricks of awful anticipation and her heart bumped almost painfully against her ribs.

"Of course." He paused for a moment, regarding her steadily. "I'll put Leila in her paddock." The expression on his face showed that he realized it was a serious matter. Elan was not a man to waste words teasing out the reason for her visit. They walked in silence together as he penned the horse and removed its halter.

The shade of the barn was a merciful relief from the unrelenting heat of the sun. He hung up the halter and lead in a tack room, then glanced down at his dusty, sweaty body.

"Please excuse me a moment." He picked up a hose and turned the spray directly on himself. A few stray drops splashed on Sara and the icy coldness of it startled her.

Rivulets of water streamed over his back and down the taut muscles of his torso as he held the hose above his skin. He bent his head forward and ran the water directly into his hair, ruffling it with his fingers and sighing as the cool liquid touched his scalp.

A rush of heat made Sara cringe as her body responded so predictably to the sight of his impressive physique as he cooled and cleaned his skin with the fresh water.

When he turned the hose off, his jeans were soaked down to midthigh and his upper body glistened with clear droplets. Sara struggled to keep her breathing inaudible as she watched the water drip sensuously over the curves of his thick muscles. Drops traced the deep hollow of his spine down to where his wet jeans hugged his rounded backside.

As he turned, her eyes automatically followed the trails of water that gathered between his pectorals and slid into the line of black hair tracing the distance from his belly button to the fly of his low-slung jeans.

She really was a hopeless case.

"Come this way," he said. Mercifully he didn't look at her long enough to notice the effect of his impromptu shower on her sanity.

He kicked off his boots outside a wide, arched doorway, then pushed open the door and ushered her inside. The thick earthen walls that blended so easily with the desert opened into a softly lit, cavernous space. A fountain trickled steadily in the center of the room, creating a cool and peaceful atmosphere. Subtle earth-toned patterns ornamented the bare walls.

"It's beautiful," breathed Sara, her eyes wide. "Should I take my shoes off?" The space felt like a sanctuary. It was, no doubt, Elan's refuge from the pressures of the business world.

"If you wish."

She slid off her sneakers and her tired feet reveled in the sensation of deliciously cool stone under their soles. Elan strode across the tiled floor toward another arched doorway.

"Come in here." He held a door open. She accidentally brushed against his arm as she moved past him. The drops of water that passed from his skin to hers sizzled as his touch stung her with a surge of electrical energy.

"Please sit and relax. I'll be right back."

Two vast leather sofas flanked a fireplace outlined in pale marble. A wall of windows was shaded from the sun by gauzy pale curtains that moved in the air-conditioned breeze.

She seated herself gingerly on one of the sofas, the leather cool against her skin. The painting above the fireplace looked like a Mark Rothko original, a cool square of blue hovering in a field of gray.

Elan returned wearing a clean pair of jeans and nothing else. Drops of water still glittered on his torso. His uncombed hair fell seductively to his eyes. What did she expect? She'd invaded his home without asking, interrupted his work, did she think he'd put on a suit for her?

He carried two frosted glasses of water. "Here, drink this."

She took it from him, icy drops stinging her fingertips. He sat on the opposite sofa and leaned back, broad bare shoulders sprawled on the dark leather. He took a sip of water and looked at her expectantly.

Silence hung in the air and a surge of panic shot through her as she realized the time had come for her confession. She cleared her throat and placed her glass on the floor with an awkward clunk.

"Er, Elan…" Blood rushed around her brain as she struggled to keep her thoughts coherent. She'd tried rehearsing what to say, but her attempts always dissolved into panicked babbling or tearful self-pity. This was no time for self-pity. She took a deep breath and straightened her spine. "I have something to tell you."

His brow furrowed. She waited for him to interject a polite response, along the lines of "Oh?" or "What is it?" but he didn't.

He merely took another sip of his water and regarded her steadily through hooded eyes.

"I...I don't know how to tell you this..." she paused again and wrapped her arms around herself as if assaulted by a cold gust of wind. Elan's eyes narrowed and he put his glass down. He adjusted the waist of his jeans against his hard, tanned belly and leaned forward a little. Expectant.

The baby shifted, flooding her with resolve.

"I'm pregnant."

He blinked. Other than that he didn't move a muscle. He stared at her, and his eyes searched her face. A furrow appeared above one eyebrow. Sara shrank inside. Did he not believe her?

"I...I...I'm four months along."

His brow creased into a deep frown and his lips parted. His eyes darted down to her belly, which she realized she was clutching, then back up to her face.

Sara struggled to find the words to make it seem real. "I'm going to have a baby."

The words hung in the air for a few seconds as he continued to gaze at her in astonishment. Then he sprang to his feet and strode across the room, bare feet on the stone floor.

He still hadn't uttered a word.

Sara shriveled inwardly and dropped her eyes to the floor as she heard his footfalls moving away from her. She'd tried and failed to imagine what his reaction might be. She'd never seen him fly into a rage at the office. His anger was always quiet and controlled, a fire burning deep within.

Was he angry?

She sneaked a glance across the room, and at that very moment he wheeled around and stared at her. His eyes were blazing, his face set in a stony expression that was unreadable, frightening.

"You've carried this secret for four months?" The words seemed to emerge from a closed mouth, hissed between tight lips.

"I've only known for two weeks," she whispered. Her heart clenched as she saw a shadow of confusion cross his features. He stared at her a few more seconds, then turned abruptly away again. He strode around the perimeter of the large room and approached her until he was standing over her, his shadow invading her space.

"May I see your belly?" His voice emerged low and quiet, yet clearly a demand. His request wasn't polite, but then it wasn't a gracious situation. Sara rose to her feet ungracefully. She knew her face was blazing as she lifted her T-shirt and pushed down the waistband of her bike shorts.

She avoided his eyes and looked down at her belly. It looked so vulnerable, pale and soft, a slight curve that announced the presence of a third person in the room.

Elan slowly lifted his right hand and reached out to her abdomen with his fingers extended. She heard his intake of breath as the tips came to rest on her skin. Gradually, gently, he lowered his hand until it covered her belly, cupping the roundness.

Her womb stirred under his touch. A sudden rush of sensation flooded her limbs. She struggled to keep her breathing under control. Didn't dare look at his face. Her nipples tightened involuntarily and she tore her eyes away, desperate that he not see the way her body responded to the gentle pressure of his hand.

For, even now, Elan's touch made her body hum with thrilling awareness. A dangerous awareness of his hard-sprung masculinity, his harsh beauty. Humbling awareness of the razor-sharp intellect that matched her own. But above all, awareness of the man who had loved her that night with a passion and tenderness that would haunt her as long as she walked the earth.

He pulled his hand back. "We must marry."

The words, spoken low and fast, blew away the fog of sensation that had engulfed her.

"What?" She barely recognized her own voice. It sounded

strangled, distant. With a tremendous effort of will she looked up at his face.

His eyes blazed with black fire. He looked directly at her, his features set in an expression of determination.

"You will be my wife."

She fumbled with her shorts and T-shirt, covering the exposed flesh of her belly. She felt altogether naked and exposed in the face of his authoritarian command.

But she shook her head.

Elan's eyes narrowed, but he didn't speak.

"I can't marry you." Her voice was clear, quiet but resolute.

"Why not?" The words flew from his mouth in a growl.

"Because…"

Because you don't love me.

She couldn't bring herself to say the words. Certainly in her mental anguish she'd imagined the possibility of a proposal. It was, after all, the honorable thing to do. And Elan was an honorable man.

She was "in trouble" and he was the man who'd gotten her that way. Even in the twenty-first century it was still common politeness that he should offer to give the child a name. It was the same reason her father had proposed to her mother, decades ago, when her oldest sister had come unexpectedly into existence.

Elan regarded her with total astonishment. His brow lowered farther he raised his hands to his hips. "You refuse me?"

Sara swallowed hard. Her hands flew to her belly and clutched each other, fingers trembling. "Yes," she whispered. "I can raise my child alone."

The confusion that darkened his face tore at her heart. For an instant she itched to step toward him, throw her arms around him and shout "Yes, I'll marry you, I'll be your wife and bear all your children and we'll live happily ever after!"

And the thought brought a fresh flush of color to her cheeks.

A twinge of embarrassment that she could harbor such childish fantasies. That she could dream even momentarily of a happy future with a man who'd made it crystal clear that ardent women were the bane of his existence.

No doubt her mother had nurtured those same foolish fantasies when she'd chosen marriage over single motherhood—a miserable marriage that had drained her strength and kept her constantly pregnant or tending to a baby, despite her increasingly poor health. That had kept her chained to a cruel man who cheated on her and to a succession of low-paying part-time jobs that would never give her the means to escape.

Sara didn't intend to make that same mistake.

Eight

Elan tore his eyes off her and strode across the room. His mind whirled with confused thoughts and he couldn't grab a single sensible one from the mix.

Sara is pregnant with my child.

He'd needed to place his hand on her belly to fully accept the truth of it. And nothing could prevent his heart from soaring with the knowledge.

He was assaulted with a vision of Sara living in his home, of the quiet desert ringing with the sounds of childish laughter. For an instant all the entanglements he'd dreaded seemed like the most blissful kind of bondage he could imagine. Sara in his bed each morning. A family to provide and care for the way a man is born to. A son or daughter—and the promise of more—to carry his legacy into the future.

Then she'd refused him.

His gut burned with unfamiliar emotion as he wheeled around

to face her. She looked so small and delicate standing there, clutching her belly with both hands as if he might try to rip the baby right from her womb.

"You wish to deny me the right to raise my child?"

She flinched as he said *my child*. Blinked and looked down at the floor. An ugly thought sneaked up on him, bringing with it a cold chill of fear.

She'd said she was pregnant, but she had not said the baby was his.

Was it possible that she carried another man's child and was merely informing him of her pregnancy as a professional courtesy? The image of Sara with another man assaulted him like a kick in the gut.

"Is it my child?" The words shot from his mouth like bullets from a gun. There was no dignified way to ask the question, but he had to know.

Sara nodded, her face flushing crimson. "Yes," she hissed between closed lips.

Recrimination seized him as he realized how he'd shamed her with his doubt. "I apologize. I didn't mean to imply…" He couldn't bring himself to spell it out. The idea of Sara with another man stole his breath.

Since that one night in the desert he'd been tormented by the longing to gather her in his arms again. He was haunted by memories of her gentle touch, her fiery passion. But the memories were tainted by the realization that he'd taken advantage of her.

She was a young girl, barely out of college. Even if she had desired him, too—at that moment—he should have known better than to let the situation get out of control. Than to let himself get out of control.

He was her boss. The abuse of his authority was inexcusable. When she'd accepted his apology without protest, she confirmed that night had been a terrible lapse of judgment. As he'd suggested, they had never mentioned it again.

Determined to rid himself forever of his craving to hold her, of the memories he couldn't seem to shake, he'd done his best to challenge her beyond her capacity and drive her away.

When that hadn't worked he'd planned to send her away. Push her out of sight, out of reach, out of his mind. To rid himself of the compulsion to take her in his arms, of the foolhardy urge to protect and care for her.

He didn't need her.

But now there was a child to consider. That changed everything.

She regarded him steadily with those cool, pale eyes that haunted his nights. A few strands of golden hair had escaped her bun and curled around her face. She reached up and gathered them in her hands, tucking them back into the knot behind her head.

The movement of raising her arms pulled her T-shirt tight against the new fullness of her belly and the heavier curve of her breasts and he looked away quickly as his breath hitched. Her pregnancy did not dampen his desire for her.

Anger sliced through him. Anger at the power she had over him, power only magnified by the fact that she carried his child.

Power he could harness only though marriage.

Why did she refuse him? It was hard to comprehend. Perhaps she felt guilty for breaking the pact that *she* had proposed on her first day of employment?

They had both broken it. That was moot and it was time to move forward.

"I hold myself fully accountable for this unfortunate situation. You bear no blame—"

"But I—" She began to protest and he held up his hand to silence her.

"Your pledge to me on the first day of employment was broken by my rash actions, not yours. Rest assured, we'll never mention it again. I will provide you and our child with every advantage and opportunity. As my wife, you'll want for nothing. You will bear my name and we'll share life as a family."

Already his heart swelled with the idea. How strange that the universe should provide such an opportunity! That fate should deliver a woman into his arms who was his match in every way.

Their marriage was an ideal outcome to this strange predicament.

"We'll make our announcement tomorrow. We'll be married before the month is out and our child will suffer no shame." He rubbed his hands together. "We shall plan the wedding immediately, perhaps by next week—"

"I can't marry you." She spoke quietly, but with no hesitation. Her renewed refusal struck him like a slap.

"But you must. Can't you see that?" He couldn't keep angry indignation out of his voice.

She looked away across the room for a moment, as if gathering her thoughts, then back at him, eyes wide. "I know that in some ways marriage does seem like the sensible thing, the obvious thing to do, but I also know that in the long run we'd both regret it. We'd feel trapped, like we were forced together."

"Arranged marriages are common in my country. Few matches arise out of love, but many achieve it."

The cruel irony stung him. He was making the argument his father had made to him when he came of age. A suitable bride, a lifetime of duty. He'd rejected it out of hand and claimed the right to choose his own bride, shape his own destiny, even if it meant abandoning his homeland for good. He'd given up enough already at the hands of his father.

"Did your parents have a happy marriage?"

Sara's question penetrated the dark fog of ugly memories that surrounded his last face-to-face encounter with the man who stole his childhood.

"No." He would not lie to her.

She turned to face him, fixed him with her wide-eyed stare. "So you know firsthand that a marriage of convenience doesn't always lead to—love." The last word caught in her throat slightly and Elan's heart constricted as she said it.

Love. It was not a commodity to be bought or sold, searched for, found or extracted with the aid of high-tech equipment. It was something strange, unknowable, elusive—that no amount of money could buy.

He doubted he would know it if he saw it. His life had been empty of love since his mother's death. Even his once-beloved brothers were now virtual strangers to him, all of them victims of his father's power games.

"What went wrong in your parents' marriage?" She asked the question cautiously. He bridled at the unpleasant prospect of airing his family's dirty linen with an outsider. Some things were better left unspoken. But her steady gaze called to him, demanded his honesty.

"My father liked to be in control and to have those around him know he was in control."

"And he tried to control your mother?" The pulse flickering at her throat contradicted her calm voice.

"Yes. She was much younger than he, bright and free-spirited, with her own way of doing things." Elan swallowed. Even after all these years he could still see her smiling face, feel the soft touch of her soothing hands. He'd clung to those memories as a balm to his loneliness. "My father did not brook any contradiction."

"So they argued?"

"Yes. About many things. Until my father declared that in his household he laid down the rules and everyone would obey. When my mother defied him he punished her in the harshest way he could think of. By taking her sons away and sending them abroad."

"Including you." Her eyes narrowed and he stiffened at what looked like pity in her expression.

"Yes. She died shortly afterward and his punishment was inflicted permanently on all of us. He died a lonely and bitter old man who had lost his sons, as well as his wife."

"That's terrible."

The soft expression in her eyes seemed to invite him to sink into the warm comfort of her arms, but her rigid posture held him at bay and those wide jade eyes begged him to keep his distance.

He straightened his shoulders, held his head erect. He didn't need her sympathy or anyone else's. A hard shell had formed around the tender core of his emotions and now he supposed there was nothing left inside it to give or receive love.

His deficiencies must be obvious to Sara. She was a lively young girl who hoped to spend her life with a whole man, not one whose spirit was hollowed by loneliness and toughened by exile.

"If you think it's best, I'll offer my resignation." Her words penetrated his grim thoughts.

"No!" Heat surged through him.

She took a quick step back as if he might hurl himself at her, then quickly steadied herself, one hand resting on her belly.

"You must not leave your job." The thought struck a chord of alarm. That she might get on a train, leave town and never come back… It was not something he could contemplate.

Conviction roared through him. Immediate marriage was the only possible course of action. It was the sensible thing to do. The right thing to do. His heart played no role in his decision. He would handle this situation as he would manage any business crisis, with decisive action.

"You will remain at the headquarters, of course. As for travel in your condition—"

"If I stay I shall continue my job exactly as planned. I do not wish for any special favors or considerations. I'll leave for Louisiana next week as we discussed."

He blew out a snort of laughter. "You can't stay on a drilling rig. It's dangerous and dirty."

"No more so than it was yesterday, when you briefed Mrs. Dixon and myself on my responsibilities there."

"Yesterday, you weren't pregnant." He shoved a hand through his hair. This situation was a challenge to his wits. "Of course, you *were* pregnant, but I didn't know that at the time. It is the nature of our business that it's dangerous and dirty, there's no avoiding those aspects of it, but you will certainly not risk exposure to pollutants while you're pregnant with our child."

"El Mansur Associates prides itself on the containment of potentially harmful substances at all phases of exploration and recovery," she said, her eyes flashing a challenge at him. "One of my tasks is to make sure those goals are being met."

He suppressed a chuckle. Yes, this woman was a match for him. "You will stay at the head office during your pregnancy. I have need of you here."

She lifted her chin. "I would prefer to be in the field," she said coolly.

"As I said, I have need of you here."

She stiffened and her eyes narrowed. "You are *the boss*."

A cool finger of sensation slid up his spine. He risked abusing his authority again in this situation. Still, the circumstances called for a strong guiding hand.

"I will exert my authority in matters of business. It's a question of liability, surely you understand that?"

She hesitated, drew in a breath. "I understand." She held her chin high, proud and beautiful, her face radiant and her body strong, yet soft and devastatingly female. Her eyes glittered, the flecks of gold catching light from the skylights overhead. Her cheeks were pink from the physical exertion of her long bike ride and the mental exertion of revealing her secret.

And what a secret!

A secret that would change his life forever. Until now he'd wanted nothing more than the quiet calm of solitude. He'd grown weary of eager females and the entanglements they tried to thrust on him.

But despite all his efforts to the contrary, this woman had crept into his mind and cast a spell on him. Now their blood was linked in a child they'd created and there was no way she could leave him now. He'd make sure of it.

Sara was growing light-headed under Elan's steady gaze. Her blood seemed to be draining away, and with growing terror she realized she might actually pass out. She'd been running on adrenaline all morning, and her blood sugar must be getting dangerously low.

"You look pale," his brow lowered in concern.

"I...I'm rather hungry. Would it be possible to—"

"Of course, you must eat. Come with me."

He held out his strong hand and reluctantly she took it. Heat coursed through her as his fingers closed around hers and his thickly muscled arm drew her gently to her feet. He gripped her hand, firm but gentle, as he led her across the cool stone.

As he guided her through the cavernous space of his house, emotions and sensations buzzed in her mind and body like a swarm of bees in a hive. There was massive relief that she'd finally let the proverbial cat out of the bag. She was grateful that he'd taken the news relatively calmly.

But not as calmly as she'd hoped. He wanted his child.

The situation paralleled that of her parents far too closely. She knew her mother had refused her father at first. She'd known he was a ladies' man who didn't love her. But he'd worn her down with his pleas that marriage to her child's father was the "sensible thing" to do.

And in some ways it *was* sensible, at least initially. But in the long run it made for a bitter, hate-filled marriage that cast a pall of misery over their home life and her childhood.

She was fiercely attracted to Elan, but that was just one more reason to guard against him. No doubt he was aware of the power he had over her. To him she was just another of those lecherous women who couldn't keep their eyes and hands off him.

He'd probably expected her to gleefully accept his proposal of marriage and rush into his arms, only to spend the rest of her life wrapped in a cocoon of regret as he grew to despise her more and more for each year he stayed in a marriage that sprang out of circumstance rather than love.

If Elan was anything like her father, he'd feel free to continue the lifestyle he'd pursued before marriage. He'd be out there under the desert moon, burning mesquite with another woman, while she stayed home taking care of the children.

Her heart squeezed at the thought of Elan with another woman. For all she knew, he did have a girlfriend, or a stable of them. She'd rather walk barefoot through the desert in the blazing midday heat than even catch a glimpse of him with someone else. Just one of the many reasons she'd prefer an oil rig on the open sea to a desk outside his office.

"The kitchen. Please, take a seat at the table. I'll find something for you to eat."

He released her hand and she breathed a sigh of relief as cool air replaced his warm grasp.

Commercial appliances gleamed amongst sheets of rare stone. The table she sat at was an extraordinary sliver of metal-flecked granite.

"Would you like some chicken salad?" Elan appeared relaxed and nonchalant as he moved about the large kitchen.

"That would be fine."

He was acting as if nothing had happened. But wasn't that what they did every day at the office? Elan went about the business at hand and she struggled to do her duties while her mind whirled with the torment of wanting to touch him.

And today was no different. The muscles of his powerful back flexed as he pulled open the heavy fridge door, causing an echoing ripple deep inside her. His jeans hugged and molded to the firm curves of his athletic backside and long, sturdy legs.

She drew in a silent breath and prayed to retain at least the appearance of dignity.

He stood in front of the fridge, examining the contents of the neatly stacked crocks inside. She couldn't help but notice his hair was freshly cut, cropped close in back to reveal the thick muscles of his neck.

She started as he turned to her.

"You must be hungry now you're eating for two."

"Er, yes." She was shocked that he could refer so casually to her pregnancy. She still struggled with the reality of it and had to remind herself constantly that she carried another being inside her. Apparently, Elan had no trouble accepting the idea.

He brought out two black ceramic containers and swung the heavy door closed with a denim-clad knee. His bare feet were silent on the stone tile as he moved toward her. Her heart skipped as his eyes met hers.

How could he take this so calmly? Did he really expect her to marry him?

She struggled to plaster a polite expression on her face while her body roiled with the usual mix of uncomfortable sensations that assailed her when Elan was in the room.

His broad hands moved with deft grace as he spooned two salads onto a large black stoneware platter. Even now she was haunted by the sensation of those hands on her, undressing her, roaming over her skin.

Get a grip. It was that kind of thinking that got her in this situation in the first place.

It wasn't fair. They'd used a condom. But she'd discovered to her chagrin that condoms were only about 95 percent effective at preventing pregnancy. She'd fallen into the other five percent.

"My cook is a health nut so you can be sure these salads are packed with nutrients. But I can tell you already take excellent care of yourself." His eyes dropped quickly to her body, then back up to meet hers. Their path left a smoking trail of heat that made her struggle to catch her breath.

She felt underdressed in her tight athletic clothes. She should accept the fact that she was a pregnant woman and start dressing differently. Clinging to her usual attire and habits was a form of denial she couldn't seem to shake.

"I do try to eat healthily. But I haven't gained as much weight as the doctor would like." The confession slipped out as she reached for her fork. She worried that her tendency to deny was somehow depriving her baby.

Concern flashed across his face as his brows lowered. "How much are you supposed to gain?"

"She'd like me to have gained eight to ten pounds by now," she mumbled as she dug her fork into Chinese chicken salad with a mouthwatering aroma of sesame oil. "Because I'm a little underweight."

"And how much have you gained?"

She hesitated. "Only four pounds. But the doctor says the baby's growing fine." She forked the salad into her mouth and chastised herself for telling him.

"You're underweight?" His eyes widened. "Forget these salads, they seemed refreshing for a hot day but you need something heartier."

He wheeled away from her and strode back to the fridge. "You must eat as I do—red meat and plenty of it."

Elan's expression was so serious that she couldn't help but laugh. "No, thanks, I've seen you eat and I don't think I'm up to the task."

He turned to face her and she flushed as she remembered the time they'd eaten together—*that night in the desert.*

They'd eaten food, and then they'd tasted each other.

His lips parted as if the memory assailed him, too. Sara felt her blush darken.

Why did you have to bring up that night?

Elan raked a hand through his hair. He took in an audible breath, "That night—"

"Was a terrible mistake," she burst. "It should never have happened." Tears welled up, gagging her throat.

A moment's indiscretion that had permanent repercussions.

His face darkened and he turned away.

Elan drew in a breath. He had been about to suggest that the night itself was unplanned but that its consequences might be…

Wonderful.

He had to make her see that, too.

"Sara, naturally the situation is unexpected. As I've said, I take full responsibility and I assure you that you will want for nothing."

"I don't want your money," she said quickly.

Elan felt a muscle twitch in his jaw. Money? He'd offered to share his life with her and she thought he meant to simply throw money at her? The insult stung him. "Money will be the very least of your needs," he growled.

"I'd like to continue at my job for as long as possible. And," she looked up at him, her soft eyes pleading, "I'd prefer if people didn't know the child was yours."

His gut muscles clenched at the blow.

"It's just that people at work won't respect me if they know that I…"

Slept with the boss.

His heart constricted unpleasantly. He could indeed imagine the snickering and gossiping around the water coolers if people knew she was pregnant—by him.

Of course, if she married him it would be a different story altogether.

He had to make her see reason.

He stood in front of the refrigerator, watching her as she quietly ate the chicken salad. They could be married this week—tomorrow perhaps? He was unsure of the laws involved—and she could announce her pregnancy and her marriage at the same time.

Mrs. Elan Al Mansur.

He had to admit the name didn't suit her well, with her soft pale hair and wide jade eyes. It sounded heavy, weighed down with the centuries of tradition that lay behind it.

But he knew they could make a marriage work. They were a crack team in business. And between the sheets… Well, there hadn't been any sheets, but his temperature spiked as he recalled the joy of being buried inside Sara.

That night, they'd had the world to themselves. The excitement had been explosive, the satisfaction—total. He had never experienced anything like it.

"Sara, I must press my point."

She looked up at him and he watched her bite her lip, anxious.

"*Why,* exactly, do you refuse my offer of marriage?"

If he knew her reasoning, he could make her see sense. He'd built a reputation as a tough negotiator in business. He was skilled at changing minds.

And to his mind marriage was the only reasonable course of action.

She looked up at him. "You don't love me."

She said the words so softly. She blinked, and again her skin flushed.

She was right, of course. He'd lost the capacity for love, but perhaps with her help he might regain it.

"Love grows within a marriage."

"Sometimes it does, sometimes it doesn't. As you know far too well." She straightened in her chair and her eyes glittered.

He regretted relating his family history, because she was right. His own parents' marriage had grown out of tradition and dissolved into disaster. He raked a hand through his hair as if the motion could dislodge sensible thoughts from his brain, but none were forthcoming.

"I like you, Sara. I respect you." His words seemed to come from miles away as they echoed off the stone surfaces in the room.

She looked down at the table and he watched a tear fall and splash on the granite surface as her eyes squeezed shut.

His breath caught in his throat and his hands clenched into fists at the sight.

"Sara, please…" Instinctively he strode toward her, no longer able to resist the powerful urge to take her in his arms. But as he watched, she stiffened. Her eyes sprang open to meet his, shining with tears, begging him to keep his distance.

"No one can predict the future, Elan." Her voice trembled, but she cleared her throat and her next words rang across the kitchen. "My parents married because my mother was pregnant. It proved to be an empty marriage that diminished both of them. I don't want that for myself or my child."

His chest tightened. Her harsh experience echoed his own. His arms still itched to hold her, to close around the slim shoulders she held so rigid.

But now wasn't the time.

Her fiery and stubborn nature demanded skillful handling, much like his new mare. He would take matters into his own hands for now.

Soon, she would be his.

"I'd like to go home now," she said softly.

"Of course."

As Elan sat behind the wheel of his car and watched Sara disappear through the doors of her apartment building, wheeling that infernal bike he'd just taken down from the roof rack, every atom of his being rebelled against letting her go, even for a few hours.

Tomorrow he was ordering her a car whether she liked it or not.

Their wedding would be simple and quiet, yet he would not stint on the luxuries a new bride deserved. Fine gems to bring out the sparkle in her eyes, a lavish gown to complement her lovely figure, gifts to make her laugh with delight.

I'd better get busy.

Nine

Sara stiffened as Elan rested his elbow on the desk, next to the dish of broccoli drenched in fragrant sesame oil, and dangled the keys from one broad finger.

He'd insisted that she join him behind the closed door of his office for a lavish lunch prepared and delivered by his personal chef.

Again he pressed her to accept the new Mercedes E500 he'd ordered without consulting her.

"No, I can't take it." She wiped her fingers on her napkin and sat back in her chair.

"It is a question of efficiency. Your time is better spent working than cycling."

Anger rushed through her. "I don't cycle on company time. I do it on my own time. Am I not always the first person here in the morning and the last to leave in the evening?"

He surveyed her in silence for a moment.

"Your doctor should counsel you not to ride that accursed thing while you're pregnant. Surely the exertion is too taxing on your body?"

"She says that as long as I don't feel overtired or breathless, I can continue all my normal activities. In fact, she told me exercise can make pregnancy and delivery easier."

"Bah. What do doctors know? Driving an air-conditioned sedan is far healthier—and the other drivers can see you coming." He raised an eyebrow as if defying her to deny it.

"I can't accept it." She crossed her arms.

She didn't want to feel beholden to him. She needed to make decisions based on what she truly felt was right, not because she owed anyone a debt of gratitude.

Elan leaned back in his chair and crossed his arms, mirroring her gesture. "There is no arguing with the fact that your cycling keeps you magnificently fit."

His eyes dropped momentarily to her significantly enlarged bust and a smile sneaked across his sensual mouth. She bristled as her nipples stung with awareness of his admiring gaze.

Damn him.

This was a new tactic. Since her announcement three days earlier, he'd taken to deliberately flirting with her. Actively trying to seduce her.

Instead of stiffly holding a door open as she passed through it, he settled his fingers delicately in the small of her back to guide her through. Rather than regard her with measured glances, he now allowed his eyes to linger on her, to drift across her face, hover over her neck and jawline, and occasionally plunge to the swell of her excruciatingly sensitive breasts.

Appreciation of what he saw darkened his eyes, and he did not hesitate to let her see it.

Always struggling with her attraction to Elan, Sara was becoming thoroughly unhinged by his behavior. She knew she should be rankling under the open sexuality of his gaze, bristling with thoughts of sexual harassment lawsuits.

But of course she wanted nothing more than to take him up on his unspoken offer to rip off her clothes and ravish her right there on the carpeted floor of his office.

This new strategy was very, very dangerous.

She pushed her plate of beef teriyaki aside and picked up the drilling proposal they were drafting for a new client.

"Item three, depth of well. It has been determined that the well depth must be no less than thirty-five hundred feet," she said crisply. "That's deep. It'll be expensive."

He paused, looked at her steadily. "Yes, but the rewards promise to be magnificent." He cocked his head and narrowed his eyes slightly. His voice dropped. "Once we establish *steady flow.*"

Perfectly ordinary terminology, said over a perfectly ordinary desk in a perfectly ordinary office. But nothing between her and Elan was ever ordinary, and his husky voice had its intended effect. All sorts of things began to flow inside her—heat, crazy thoughts and warm fluids.

She straightened in her chair. "Indeed," she said, narrowing her eyes. "Is this light, sweet, *crude* we're talking about?"

Elan raised an eyebrow, his full lips curving into a smile.

A treacherous smile threatened to rip across her own mouth.

At that moment the door flung open and Sara jumped in her seat.

Mrs. Dixon's stiff bouffant hair appeared in the gap. "Excuse the interruption, Mr. Al Mansur, I have an urgent phone call for you from Mr. Redding."

"Let me get these dishes out of here." Sara rose and gathered the plates, glad of an excuse to end a conversation that was heading into dangerous territory.

This morning, while his mouth had spoken of soil composition and rock density, his glances had assaulted her with a thousand unspoken words.

Part of her wanted to hear those words—craved them, even—but at the same time she was afraid.

Elan didn't love her. He wanted to marry her for all the wrong reasons.

He was a strong man in every way, his impressive physique only mirrored his fierce determination. She had to make sure she kept her perspective and her distance, and didn't allow herself to be swept away by the sheer force of his will—or by the thrall of desire that still held her captive.

"Let me take those from you, dear." Mrs. Dixon rose to her feet as Sara emerged with the dishes.

"That's okay. I'll just carry them down to the kitchen and put them in the dishwasher."

"Here, let me at least take the plates." She lifted the dirty plates from on top of the stack of serving dishes and pressed the button on the elevator. "Do me good to stretch my legs anyway. Can't have the varicose veins getting the upper hand, now, can we?"

She smiled and Sara smiled back. Despite her formidable exterior Mrs. Dixon was proving to be a nice woman. Helpful to a fault, in a way that made Sara feel selfish and self-important in her hunger for experience and advancement. She hadn't had time to water Elan's plants lately.

They stepped into the elevator.

"Mrs. Dixon, I know you've been doing this type of work for years, and I'm pretty new to it. How do you draw the line between the kinds of tasks you will and won't do?"

"Line? There's no line. I'm employed to keep my executive happy, and I'll do everything within my power to fulfill his needs."

"That sounds rather dangerous!" Sara laughed. "What's the most outrageous thing your boss has ever asked you to do?"

Lie naked beneath him on the desert floor? What on earth

would the prim Mrs. Dixon think if she knew? If she learned that Elan's baby was growing inside her, right now?

"Well." Mrs. Dixon pursed her lips for a moment. Color rose in her powdered cheeks. "I'm afraid that it sometimes falls to me to procure gifts and arrange favors for…how shall I put it?" She tilted her head. "For their mistresses."

"Goodness, do they all cheat on their wives?" The back of Sara's neck prickled.

"Not all of them." Mrs. Dixon pressed her lips together. "But we must remember that these powerful men handle problems and crises that would break an ordinary man. They must have some outlet for their stress." She blinked rapidly.

"I'd certainly draw the line there. There's no way I'd run errands for my boss's bit on the side." The prickling sensation had descended down Sara's arms, causing goose bumps to form.

"Perhaps that's why women of my generation are still in demand." An ice-blue gaze accompanied Mrs. Dixon's tight smile.

Sara blinked. The prickling crept to her fingertips.

"Men have their needs, dear. It's best to accept that." She leaned into Sara with a conspiratorial whisper. "In fact, just this morning Mr. Al Mansur had me arrange insurance and shipping for some gems for one of his ladies."

"What?" Sara spoke too loudly. She'd rattled the plates.

"Yes." They walked into the small galley kitchen and put the dishes on the countertop. "You should see them. Exquisite. Ordered from Mappin & Webb in London. He even showed me some images on the computer and asked for my opinion." She placed her hand on Sara's arm. "Sixty thousand dollars," she whispered. "Whoever gets those will be a very lucky girl."

Spots danced before Sara's eyes as she pulled her arm back and she slid a plate into the dishwasher. A girlfriend? She struggled to keep her breathing inaudible.

Or are they for me?

They hadn't spoken again about his demand that she be his wife. He appeared to have lost interest in the issue for now, which was both reassuring and unsettling at the same time. Did he plan to ply her with gems, as well as heated glances and eighty-thousand-dollar cars? To try and buy her as he'd purchase an expensive new mare?

"Yes, a very lucky girl. They're being delivered to an address on the Vegas strip."

The words hit her like a blow to the solar plexus. Vegas? That was hundreds of miles away.

What a joke that she'd thought they were for her. As if anyone would buy her sixty thousand dollars worth of jewels. The idea was laughable. She gritted her teeth. Would she never learn?

Mrs. Dixon chuckled. "I know you probably find it hard to picture our Mr. Al Mansur with a showgirl, but I've been around long enough to know that even the most serious and business-minded gentlemen enjoy the company of those gay young girls. And why shouldn't he have a beautiful girlfriend, or ten of them? He's not married, after all."

No. He's not married.

The thought of Elan with another woman chilled her. Did he truly plan to marry her, and keep another woman—or women— on the side?

Just like her father.

"Are you all right, dear? You look a bit peaky."

"I'm fine," she rasped. "A touch of indigestion."

"Well, we'd best be getting back to our desks. We don't want Mr. Al Mansur to come out of his office and find we've both gone on the lam, now, do we?"

"No." Sara stumbled behind Mrs. Dixon.

She was *very, very* glad she'd turned down that car. If Elan thought he could buy her for his stable of women, he was very much mistaken.

* * *

The intercom light flared on Sara's phone. What did he want now? She was just getting ready to go home. He'd been calling her into his office all day on one pretext or other and her nerves were in tatters. What she needed right now was to be as far away from him as possible.

"Yes?"

"Please come in."

"I'll be right there." She gathered herself together, tucking a stray strand of hair into her bun.

"Close the door." Elan lounged in his chair, hands behind his head, elbows in the air, broad chest flexed beneath his white shirt.

She closed the door behind her. The baby fluttered in her stomach.

"Congratulations." He smiled enigmatically for a moment. "You won us the Anderson account. They found your presentation and your proposal *very* impressive."

Yes! She narrowly resisted the urge to pump her fist in the air. "Excellent."

"*Excellent* is the only word to describe your performance of late. Though sadly, as a result, my plants are wilting from lack of your tender care and attention. Mrs. Dixon doesn't seem to share your green thumb." His mouth tilted into a smile.

Or your appetite for seduction. He didn't say it aloud, but his stare, heavy-lidded and lingering, conjured the words in the air.

Already her body had started to respond to the unspoken suggestion. She cleared her throat. "I have had my hands full with important projects, as you know."

"Exactly. And, under the circumstances, I intend to lighten your workload considerably." He leaned forward and planted his elbows on the desk. "You should be getting a good night's sleep, conserving your energy, eating carefully prepared, nutritious meals. I'll delegate the Farouk proposal to Andrew, Claire and

Patrick will work on the MacDormand project and I shall take over the Anderson project myself."

A seeping sensation of relief grew into alarm as he spoke. "But that leaves me with—"

"Time to relax and enjoy your pregnancy. You've looked tired lately, and, as you've admitted, your weight gain is not adequate. We must ensure that our baby has every advantage, don't you agree?"

"Well, yes, but…" He was taking away *all* her projects? And he'd already delegated her administrative duties to Mrs. Dixon. Did he intend her to sit in a chair filing her nails all day? Or to spend her time watering his plants?

Or tending to other needs.

Needs that might be better met by an experienced Vegas showgirl.

She clenched her fists. "I'd like to finish calculating the projections for the Farouk proposal myself. I've done a good deal of research and I feel that at this point I can offer the most detailed and comprehensive—" her voice was rising.

Elan silenced her by holding up his hand. "As you wish. Abdul Farouk told me himself how impressed he was by your insight into the complexities of the situation. But be sure to update Andrew on all aspects of the project." He leaned forward and subjected her to another blood-heating stare. "Because imminently I will have another, *very important* project for you."

He held her gaze and she struggled to keep still. To keep her face expressionless as her synapses crackled with a mix of anger and arousal. How did he do this to her?

"I'd better get going," she hissed. "I have a doctor's appointment first thing in the morning. It should be done by nine-thirty so I'll be here before the implementations meeting. I'll have the Farouk proposal on your desk by noon."

"I'm sure you will." A half smile lingered on his full lips. "I have *absolute* faith in you."

The dark rumble of his voice echoed in her ears as she hurried out of the office. Why did it sound as though he meant so much more than her ability to complete an assignment on time? What was he up to?

As she nudged up her kickstand in the parking lot, she looked wistfully at the gleaming silver sedan parked right next to Elan's identical black one. For a moment she allowed herself to feel sad that she couldn't accept it. That she couldn't accept Elan's offer to make her his wife. When her thoughts sneaked off in that direction, the idea of spending her life with him made her spirit soar for a brief, blissful moment.

Until she remembered her mother's stern warnings: "Don't marry a man who doesn't love you. You'll live to regret it. I know I did."

Those words always chilled the heat of her fevered imaginings and brought her back to earth. An earth where she was determined to be dependent on and beholden to no one but herself.

Elan checked his watch. Again. Where was Sara? Her doctor's appointment was supposed to be over by 9:30 a.m. He strode to the window and scanned the parking lot for signs of that accursed bicycle she was so attached to.

A broad smile spread across his face as he saw her turn into the parking lot. A chuckle rose in his throat. She was so graceful, wonderfully athletic, and she carried herself with the dignity of a queen. A queen in Spandex shorts and a sporty maternity top. At least he'd convinced her to start wearing a helmet.

A pleasant warm sensation eased his limbs as he watched her raise herself up to glide over the speed bumps. She made her last turn and headed toward the bike rack that never held more than one bike.

A gray sedan jerked out and sent her sprawling to the hard asphalt.

Yaha!

Terror gripped him and fired every neuron in his body. He grabbed the phone off his desk, shoved out of his office and hurled himself down the stairs, dialing 911 as he ran.

"What is your emergency?"

"Ambulance! She's been hit!"

"Sorry, sir, can you slow down please."

"Sara's been hit by a car.... On her bike." His breathing labored, he pushed out of the emergency exit into the blinding sun of the parking lot. "Five hundred Canyon Road. Please hurry!"

His blood froze as he saw Sara limp and lifeless on the asphalt, the driver of the car standing over her.

He sprinted across the lot and dropped to his knees beside her. He pressed his fingers gently to her neck. Her pulse thumped steadily.

"I didn't see her," said the driver plaintively. Elan ignored him. Sara lay in an awkward position, her eyes closed. But she was breathing.

He fought an overwhelming urge to gather her in his arms. He knew she needed to remain still in case there were internal injuries. He stroked the soft skin of her cheek and heard his own breathing emerge in ragged gasps. He wanted to shout at the ambulance to hurry up, but he didn't want to frighten her in case she could hear him.

Could she hear him?

"Sara?"

No answer, not a flicker of her pale lashes. A fist of fear clenched his heart and he cursed under his breath.

He'd forgotten the phone for a moment, but he pressed it to his ear. "Where is the ambulance?"

"It's on its way, sir. Is the victim conscious?"

"No." He gulped air as his body pounded with adrenaline. "She is not conscious. Hurry! She's pregnant."

"Is her airway clear?"

"Yes, she's breathing."

"Don't move her. The ambulance should be there within five minutes."

The minutes ticked by with agonizing slowness while he held her hand and watched her chest rise and fall silently. Her arms and legs sprawled haphazardly on the hot pavement. He'd never felt so helpless and he burned with the need to do something, anything, he could to help her.

"Sara, can you hear me?"

No answer.

A crowd had gathered around him and he shouted at them to divert the traffic and guide the ambulance in.

Her body looked so small and frail lying there on the ground, the hot desert sun pounding down on her. He wanted to shield her from the harsh rays, to cool the burning asphalt that supported her limp form.

"Sara," he whispered.

No answer.

At last the ambulance roared into the parking lot, siren screaming. The crowd parted as the EMTs unloaded the stretcher, took Sara's vital signs and loaded her onto it.

Elan made a nuisance of himself, begging them to be careful, his gut churning at the sight of her being poked, prodded and hauled into a truck by strangers.

"Stand back!" shouted the EMT, as they prepared to close the doors.

"Let me in!" cried Elan.

"Sorry, sir, no room."

"But she's my...I'm her...I'm the father of her child!" His shout tore through the voices buzzing in the air.

"I'm sorry, sir, we're taking her to General. You can follow the ambulance."

Rage and desperation roared through him as the ambulance doors closed and it ground slowly out of the parking lot. As the vehicle merged back into the highway traffic and its siren turned on, he cursed the skies—his car keys!

He pushed through the crowd of gawking onlookers and shoved back into the building. Ignoring the elevator, he pelted up the stairs, crashed into his office and snatched the keys off the desk. He was sweating and panting by the time he finally got behind the searing-hot wheel of his car and started the ignition.

"Do not let her die!" His angry shout gave no relief.

He blasted the horn hard as a group of pedestrians crossed the road, chatting and laughing. They scowled at him and he banged his hand helplessly on the dashboard. He blamed himself for her accident. How could he have been so negligent as to let her keep riding that ridiculous bicycle in her condition?

From now on he would make sure he took good care of her, whether she liked it or not. It was his duty and he wasn't going to fail again.

He screeched into the parking lot at General and parked directly in front of the emergency room entrance. He abandoned the car with the keys in the ignition and pushed his way through the glass doors into the stark white lobby.

"Sara Daly, where is she?" he demanded of the receptionist, interrupting her conversation with a woman in front of him.

"One moment, please, sir."

"She just came in—she's badly hurt!" He tore away from the desk and moved toward the double doors behind the desk.

"No, sir, you can't go back there!"

"But I need to—" Two orderlies sprang forward and grabbed his arms to restrain him as he attempted to shove his way past the desk. "You don't understand—I'm her…"

Her what? He wasn't her husband, he wasn't even her boy-friend. He was her boss.

"Sir, if you'll please come this way." He'd stopped fighting against the orderlies and allowed them to lead him to a different desk and deposit him unceremoniously in a chair.

"Sara Daly," he said to the silver-haired woman at the glowing computer screen. "I need to be with her," Elan added with force.

"I understand, sir. Let me check her records." She flashed him a kindly glance before turning her attention to her computer screen. "She's been taken into an examination room, the doctor is with her now."

Elan's chest tightened and his fists balled at the thought of Sara laid out on a hard table with a stranger's hands upon her.

"You'll have to wait out here until the doctor—"

"I can't!" He sprang to his feet and instantly the orderlies were at his side again, hands gripping him.

"I know it's a difficult time, sir, but you don't want to distract the doctors and nurses from doing their job."

"No, of course not." He glanced at the orderly to his right and the man shrugged and shot him an expression of sympathy. "I'll wait."

He paced back and forth in the waiting room. This predica-ment was entirely his fault. He'd broken all his own rules and gotten into a situation where he no longer had complete control. Sara *had* to live. She *must*. And when she did, he'd make sure that they could never be torn apart again.

Sara glanced around the small "room" where the nurse had left her sitting on a wheeled bed. Only a blue curtain separated her from the hallway and the other curtained cubicles. She could hear the patient opposite her speaking to someone in Spanish.

Her ankle throbbed painfully and she half wished she'd accepted the painkillers they'd offered, but the reassuring sight of the slight curve to her belly made her glad she hadn't.

She had no idea how long she'd been in the hospital, though she'd regained consciousness in the ambulance. It seemed an eternity of strangers shining lights in her eyes, attaching electrodes to her belly, kneading and binding her injured ankle. Fear had faded into exhaustion and she couldn't wait to get home.

The curtain twitched aside and Elan entered, eyes fixed on hers. He strode up to her and snatched her hand from her lap.

"Sara." His voice was rough.

"I'm okay, just a badly sprained ankle," she said with forced bravado. "And the baby's kicking like a karate expert."

Elan pressed his lips to her hand and she felt a shudder of warmth reverberate through her bruised and aching limbs. She had a sudden urge to throw her arms around him and hug him, but her battered body and her cautious mind prevented her.

"It's a miracle you weren't seriously injured. In an accident like that, *anything* could have happened." His low voice quivered through her sore muscles. The intensity of his expression threatened to unleash the tangle of emotions she'd been suppressing since she'd awakened—with light blasting in her eyes and strange voices buzzing in her ears—and threatened her calm demeanor.

"I ache all over," she admitted. And she wasn't really talking about her ankle. That hurt, sure, but all of her ached for the love and comfort of someone who cared about her.

Just as the temptation to reach out and hold him became overwhelming, his face hardened. "We must get you home."

"I think the nurse is bringing my discharge papers any minute. The doctor initially wanted to keep me overnight because I lost consciousness. But since the baby is moving well and my vital signs were all good, he agreed to let me go."

"Excellent." Elan clapped his hands together. "Where's that nurse?" He tugged the curtain back and scanned the hallway. "You're coming home with me, by the way. Don't even think of arguing."

"On the contrary, I'd be very grateful if you'd drive me home."

He turned back, a dark eyebrow raised. "When I said 'home with me' I meant home to my house."

"Oh, no. No, I couldn't."

"Did I ask you?" He ducked out of the curtained area in search of the nurse.

Sara tried to struggle to her feet but her right ankle screamed with agony as she put weight on it, and she was unable to suppress a gasp that emerged with a slight shriek.

Elan instantly appeared back in the room. "What happened?"

"I tried to stand," she said sheepishly.

Exasperation twisted his mouth. "Don't compound your injury. There's no need for standing. I'll carry you about in my arms if necessary." His deadly serious tone and demeanor made Sara want to chuckle. She was assailed by an image of him bearing her around belly outward, like an enormous china Buddha.

"I really, really want to go back to my place." She needed to collapse in her own bed and sleep.

"Impossible." He didn't even turn to face her. Sara bridled with indignation. He might be her boss but he couldn't order her around outside the office.

"You have no right!" Her voice sounded shrill.

"Possibly not, but I have two good legs and strong arms, which is more than you can say right now. Where is that damned nurse? I'll carry you out of here right now if I have to." He craned his neck outside the curtains. "Nurse!"

The nurse entered, carrying a clipboard. "I have your release here, if you'll just sign down at the bottom." She handed the clipboard to Sara.

"Sara sustained a blow to the head," said Elan, "there is still a risk of concussion, correct?"

"Yes, she was knocked unconscious. There's no swelling, but—"

"So it's important for her to be with a friend who can care for her and drive her here immediately if symptoms of concussion appear?"

"Absolutely."

Elan assured the nurse she'd be in excellent hands. He went so far as to hold out the hands for examination and the nurse smilingly agreed that she'd never seen a more capable pair.

His expression of smug satisfaction made Sara's hackles rise higher with each second. The tender affection she'd *almost* felt for him a few minutes ago evaporated entirely in the heat of her anger.

She was sure this insistence on taking her to his house tied in somehow with his campaign to get her to marry him—whether she wanted to or not.

As Elan pushed her down the hallway in a wheelchair that he and the nurse had insisted on, she could almost feel the blazing heat of his grin irritating the back of her head.

"Relax, Sara, tension will only slow the healing process." She could hear the smile in his voice and it made bile rise in her gut.

She gritted her teeth. She certainly didn't want anything to slow the process of getting her out of Elan's *capable hands,* and back into the peace and privacy of her own apartment.

If he thought this kind of behavior was going to convince her to marry him, he could not be more wrong.

Ten

"I have a confession to make, Sara."

She was comfortably propped up on pillows in his cozy den, snacks and juice within reach, a thick stack of good books and the TV remote by her hand. Elan enjoyed a surge of satisfaction at seeing her so well settled.

"What?" She lifted an eyebrow and fixed him with a steely stare.

"I may have inadvertently announced the paternity of your baby."

Her head kicked back slightly, but she didn't speak.

He raked his fingers through his hair. "There were a lot of people in the parking lot when the ambulance arrived." He held her gaze. "I may have said something along the lines of 'She's having my baby.'"

He settled his hands on his hips.

Sara's mouth dropped open, then snapped shut.

He shrugged. "They had to find out sooner or later."

She turned her face toward her knees and he watched her shoulders tense.

"They were taking you away, and they wouldn't let me in the ambulance. To be honest, I'm not quite sure what I said. I know I wanted to say 'She's my wife.'"

Her eyes flicked up at him for a split second, then darted back to her knees.

"But since you've not accepted my proposal—*yet*—I merely stated the truth."

His heart quietly thrilled at the knowledge that their secret was out. Such a powerful truth was not a force for good if it remained hidden. Secrets bred secrets, festering into lies, half truths, ugly shadows that warped reality.

"Did they let you in?" She didn't look at him, but the question was not asked unkindly.

"No, but it's no matter. I came anyway."

"I'm sorry they wouldn't let you in the ambulance." She studied her legs—one of them strapped in a black elastic bandage. The other leg looked so delicate beside it, long, slender, suntanned, her bare foot resting on a soft pillow.

She glanced across the room, avoiding him, her pretty brow lined with consternation. "I guess they had to find out eventually." She lifted a slim eyebrow, "I bet they're pretty surprised."

"Their thoughts are no concern of mine."

"I guess I'll just have to get used to it." Her face softened a little, and his own posture relaxed as an odd surge of joy warmed him.

"Does your ankle hurt?"

"A little."

"Can I get you anything?"

She pressed her finger to her lips for an instant, pondering. "Yeah, the moon on a string."

He raised his eyebrows. "Is that some kind of candy?"

"It's a joke." She looked at him, eyes narrowed, mouth utterly unsmiling. "I'm cosseted here with every convenience known to man. I don't think there is anything else I could possibly need. Except the liberty to return to my *own* home."

Her eyes snapped away from him and she tugged at the hem of the boxer shorts he'd lent her. They swam on her charmingly, as did the extra-large T-shirt he'd given her. It was odd how two people who fit together so perfectly could be such completely different sizes.

"I can hear you grinning," she murmured, between gritted teeth.

"The smile is officially wiped from my face." He dragged a hand dramatically over his mouth. The smile, however, was reluctant to depart. While he did not like keeping her prisoner, he certainly did like having her safely within reach.

He did not wish Sara to suffer pain, but he didn't want that ankle to heal any faster than it had to. Settled comfortably in his home, enjoying his tender care, she was sure to see that partnership with him was a welcome, even joyous outcome to the events taking place inside her lovely body.

So everyone knew she'd slept with the boss. Embarrassing, but there it was. The truth. So much for her carefully cultivated air of cool professionalism. That was blown high on the four winds like everything else in her life right now.

And she was going stark, staring, eyes-popping-out, ranting and raving crazy. Elan hovered around her like a giant genie tethered over his bottle, demanding to know her wishes. Didn't he have a company to run?

The sight of him in a crisply tailored suit was enough to send her to the land of gaga. The big, hunky, warm, masculine presence of him dressed in nothing more than a pair of faded jeans threatened to make her beg for mercy.

She knew he was doing it on purpose. He wanted to make sure she saw every tiny ripple that might occur amongst the hundreds of perfectly toned muscles that covered his towering and agonizingly fit physique.

It was cruel and inhumane torture.

It wasn't bad enough that she had a pounding ankle and a bruised butt. No, he had to make sure that her insides pulsed and quivered and simmered uncomfortably in all sorts of inconvenient places. That her nipples were constantly erect and straining against the soft cotton of her borrowed T-shirt. That she couldn't possibly focus on any of the magazines or books or videos he plied her with.

Because she couldn't get her mind off him.

What a jerk.

And he was being so nice. Tending to her needs day and night, arranging the room for her comfort, bringing her favorite foods and an endless stream of hot and cold drinks, fluffing her pillows. Wanting to make her his wife.

It was enough to make a woman lose her resolve. Enough to make her forget about the outside world and cozy up here for good on the Isle of the Lotus Eaters. Enough to make all her plans and dreams and goals evaporate in the face of a plate of handmade bonbons served by a broad hand.

Almost.

"Would you like a massage?" He'd materialized again, heavily muscled arms crossed genie-style, a cheerful smile playing infuriatingly across his bold features.

"No, I would not like a massage!" Her shouted words surprised them both. "Gosh, sorry. I guess being cooped up like this has me wound up."

A mischievous gleam shone in his eyes. "Would you take care of me if I lay injured?" He cocked his head to one side.

"No way. I'd have left you rotting by the roadside." She snapped open a magazine.

"I don't believe you."

"No?" She looked up, an eyebrow raised, daring him to argue

with her. "If I was Florence Nightingale, I'd have majored in nursing, not business management."

"Then perhaps it's lucky our children will have me to tend their wounds." His mouth curved into a crooked smile that made pinpricks of—annoyance, surely?—come alive all over her skin.

"Our children?" Her voice was strangled with fury. "I'm having *one* baby. I've seen an ultrasound. There's only one in there."

"For now." He smiled enigmatically. "I think a massage is definitely in order. You seem very tense." His voice was soft, low, and she could swear for a second that he licked his lips.

Before she had a chance to protest, he'd sprung up onto the chaise behind her and lifted her hair off her neck. He placed his large thumbs on either side of her spine and pushed them, gently but firmly, into the knotted muscle.

"Ohhh!" she cried out with a mix of pain and relief.

"You are in need of *deep tissue* massage," he growled softly, his breath hot on her ear. "*Very* deep."

She whimpered as his callused thumbs found a whorl of painful tension. His masculine scent wound around her, assaulting her senses with a dangerous blend of soap, horse and musky male. Maybe even a dash of crude oil in there to spice the mix. Why did he smell so damn good?

She groaned as his thumbs trailed down her spine, moving in circles that teased pain from deep within. His hot breath tickled the back of her neck as his lips hovered above her skin.

"I have another confession to make," he murmured, his words vibrating off her skin.

Sara gulped. Was he going to confess to his affairs?

I don't want to hear it.

"I must apologize for the way I challenged you with such a demanding workload." His thumbs pressed deep into the tight muscle above her waist. "It was inexcusable."

"On the contrary," she could hardly get the words out as his forceful touch relieved weeks of built-up tension. "I'm grateful for the opportunity to prove myself. Not many bosses would have offered such an opportunity."

Elan chuckled, a low, dangerous sound that echoed deep in her belly. "I don't think *any* would. I confess, my intentions were not entirely honorable."

She froze.

His thumbs stilled. "I meant to push you to your limits, to make you regret the day you met me."

I knew it. Anger sparked inside her, crackled through her muscles.

"Little did I know…" his hot breath tickled the hairs on the back of her neck, "that you would rise so brilliantly to every challenge. Instead, I managed to prove that—without a doubt—you are the only woman for me."

As his words shivered through her like a streak of lightning and sparked a flash of pride, his lips touched the base of her neck. She felt teeth, tongue and then a sensation of being devoured whole crept over her as his fingers roved around her waist and seized her from behind.

A low moan escaped her lips.

Alarm bells sounded in her head. "Wait—"

"You don't mean that." His teeth grazed her neck as his words sank into her consciousness.

He was right. She had no power to resist as his hands moved over her skin, teasing and chafing the surface as his breathing quickened in her ear.

"You are my destiny, Sara. The one woman chosen by the universe to be my bride. I was too stubborn to see that—too blind—until the hand of fate placed my child in your belly and made it clear that we *must* be man and wife."

Sara shuddered as his words struck to her core. Why did it sound so obvious—*so right?*

A swift movement of his powerful legs had him sitting on the chaise in front of her, his handsome face inches from her own. His lids lowered, he picked up the hem of her T-shirt and lifted it. "I want to feel your skin against mine."

His demand rippled through her as he pulled the cotton T-shirt over her head before she could conjure so much as a whimper of protest. Now she wore only shorts and a white sports bra. His big hands settled around her waist and pulled her to him, just as he'd done that night in the desert.

"My Sara." His possessive claim both alarmed and thrilled her, quickening her arousal as his thumb grazed her nipple. Her breathing came faster as his hard-edged cheekbones and aristocratic nose crowded her vision. For a single agonizing second his lips hovered a mere atom's length away from hers. She could feel the heat of his skin, inhale the spicy maleness of his scent. For that single second she thought she might just die if he didn't kiss her *right now.*

Then his lips closed over hers and swept her away in a windstorm of emotion.

She'd never met a man like this. Dangerous in his power, fierce with passion, yet tender in his deft touch. A man of strong emotions buried deep by a lifetime of trial and triumph.

The way he'd reached out to console her during her terror on the plane showed the kind and caring spirit hidden by his stern facade.

Now, as his groan filled her mouth, she knew his bullying insistence on keeping her his prisoner here was driven by his desire to protect her. To keep her safe.

With his powerful arms wrapped around her, her whole body claiming her, she wanted him to keep her safe—forever.

I love you.

She felt the words rising up from deep inside her. Elan kissed her lips repeatedly, licking and teasing them apart until the words felt ready to fall out.

But something still kept them bottled inside her.

She tunneled her fingers into his thick hair, pulled him to her as her body hummed and quivered with maddening arousal.

Why couldn't she tell him? Why couldn't she let him know her feelings for him went far beyond mere lust?

Why?

Because she didn't trust him.

Like a douse of cold water, the memory of sixty thousand dollars in jewels washed through her brain and sent goose bumps racing over her skin.

She pulled back, gasping, her lips stinging with the force of his kisses.

Elan's eyes slitted open, dark with passion. His full lips parted, moist, as he looked at her.

"I can't." Her words rang clear, decisive, in the deafening silence.

His heavy-lidded stare seared into her. A smile tugged at the corner of his mouth, then he wrapped his hand around her waist and pulled her to him.

"No!" she rasped, stiffening and pulling back. "I won't be the latest addition to your stable. I won't be your new mare."

The slight lift of his lip deepened into an arrogant grin that only intensified her fury. "Every stallion needs a fine mare." His dark words, accompanied by a humorous twinkle of his eyes, challenged her resistance.

"Every stallion has a *herd* of mares. I won't live like that. I already told you, that's how my father treated my mother. I'd rather starve."

By the time she'd finished speaking she'd sprung off the chaise, at the cost of pain shooting through her injured ankle. She stood on the floor, in her bra and borrowed shorts, glaring at him.

His brow furrowed. "What are you talking about? I have no intention of admitting other women to my life. You of all people should know I was fed up with women until you came along."

She lifted her chin and narrowed her eyes. "Mrs. Dixon told

me about the jewelry you ordered. To be delivered to an address in Las Vegas. I think we all know what goes on in Sin City."

Heat flooded her face. Spoken aloud, the gossip—secretarial chitchat about his personal business—cheapened her.

Elan burst out in a laugh. "Mrs. Dixon told you about that? Well, that does surprise me. She seemed the soul of discretion. I'd thought I could trust her with my secrets."

His casual dismissal of her concern made rage streak through her, white-hot.

"How can you laugh it off? How do you think I feel that you're promising me a lifetime commitment when just a few days ago you bought jewelry for another woman?"

Elan laughed again. His throaty chuckle shook his broad chest. "Oh, my, she's jealous as a she-cat! Any minute now I shall have scratch marks on my chest. Sara, you are truly the most wonderful woman alive."

"And you are a…a…" She struggled for words. "A swine!"

Elan laughed again—with delight!—and rubbed a hand over his face, then pushed his fingers back into his tousled hair. His face creased into a broad grin.

The nerve of him! Any minute now she was going to lose her cool and smack him one.

Elan seemed to notice the imminent loss of her last marble, and his expression became more serious. "I ordered those gems for *you.*"

Ice crystals formed in her blood as his words seeped into her consciousness.

He's lying.

"I don't believe you. I don't live in Las Vegas."

"No." He hesitated. "But the planner I hired to coordinate the details of our wedding does. She wished to see the gems so she could choose a dress to complement them. I see my subterfuge has undone me."

Sara's brain couldn't seem to process this information. "Our wedding?" She blinked rapidly.

Elan tilted his head and looked sheepish for a moment. "Sara, wait here."

He strode out of the room. Her ankle throbbed and she hopped over to the chaise and sat back down. He'd gone ahead and planned their wedding even though she'd said no?

She should be furious about that. His arrogance had no limit! So why did the idea of him scheming to buy her treasures and dresses and make her his wife cause her whole body to tingle with excitement in a very alarming way?

He returned with his hands behind his back and laughter in his eyes. "Sara, I would like to present you with a small gift that has obviously been the source of some confusion. It was couriered back to me from Las Vegas this morning along with some other items for our wedding."

He held out his hands. Splayed over his broad palms and long fingers, a tangle of gems glittered in the bright sunlight streaming through the skylight. He plucked at one and lifted it between finger and thumb. A string of diamonds linked by a filigree of metal strands. "May I place it around your neck?"

She swallowed. He'd obviously gone to a lot of trouble. "Um, okay."

He sat opposite her, and his musky warmth calmed her as he raised his powerful arms and placed the necklace around her neck. Her skin prickled with awareness as his forearms brushed her shoulders.

He leaned back to survey the result and a smile crept across his lips. "The beauty of this fine design is greatly enhanced by the loveliness of the woman wearing it. Let me get a mirror."

He returned a moment later with a black-rimmed shaving mirror and held it up to her.

"Oh, my goodness." Slim strands of a pale metal—platinum?—danced between brilliant-cut diamonds, weaving back and forth in an intricate pattern that seemed both modern and timeless. The sparkling gems brightened the tones of her skin and picked up the light in her eyes.

"Allow me to fasten the bracelet."

She held out her wrist and was impressed by how easily his large fingers managed the tiny clasp. "I didn't buy earrings as I've noticed you don't wear them. Your lovely ears need no ornamentation." He leaned in and sucked her earlobe in a bold hot swipe that made her catch her breath.

"I…I…don't know what to say." Her hand flew to the jewels at her neck.

Sixty thousand dollars worth of gems.

For her.

"They're a simple token of my affection. A brilliant and beautiful woman such as yourself deserves gifts far more impressive and meaningful than a few sparkly trinkets."

I do?

He took her hand, which trembled in his warm grasp. Her body responded instantly to his touch, heating and straining toward him, nipples tight, fingers and toes tingling.

He touched her chin and lifted it until her gaze met his. "You are my Sara."

"I think I am." She sounded as surprised as she felt. A rush of unexpected tears pricked at her throat and made her bite her lip harder.

He stepped forward, fingers cupped around her jaw. Their mouths came together with magnetic force as his lips closed over hers.

Her head tipped back as she wound her arms around his neck, hugged him to her. She welcomed his tongue, tunneled her fingers into his thick hair and dug them into the hard muscle of his shoulders.

Her breasts, heavy and stirring, craved his touch. He obeyed their call, lifting her bra swiftly over her head before cupping them in his broad palms. Her nipples hummed with pleasure as calloused fingers rubbed them delicately to the point of maddening arousal.

She moaned as his tongue grazed her teeth and danced over the tender skin behind her lips. He licked the outside of her lips, then kissed her chin, before diving to lay a trail of kisses along her belly.

They both let out a soft groan as he whisked off her shorts and his mouth penetrated the pale hair at the apex of her thighs. His tongue flicked over her and she jumped, neurons firing as he lit the fuse to what promised to be an awesome fireworks display.

Burying his face between her legs, he licked and sucked, milking her juices with his mouth. Sara's breasts and belly quivered as he drove her to new heights of sensation. Her fingers grasped at his hair and scratched him as she rocked under his fierce caress.

And then the fireworks went off, a whirling Catherine wheel whipped her into a frenzy, seizing her limbs as she braced against the intense sensation. An array of sparklers rained down as her skin sizzled with the heat of passion. Every inch of her felt alive with joy, with sweet wonder at the thrill of making love to Elan.

The weeks of longing, of holding herself back, blew away like distant memories as she gave herself over to the man she loved. With her whole soul she yearned to join with him, to share everything with him, every aspect of her life, herself, her love.

The final barrage of rockets shot through her and left her gasping, breathless, shaken and throbbing in ecstatic release. As she lay in Elan's arms, a sense of peace claimed her, along with the man who had laid siege to her heart and won it.

He trailed a hand over her belly as he raised himself up to bury his face in her neck. Sara wrapped her arms around him and rested her head on his chest. She couldn't imagine being anywhere other than right here, with this man.

He eased up onto the chaise with her and showered her hair and face with tender kisses as their bodies mingled intimately. Resting his head next to hers he snuggled against her and settled a hand on her waist.

His big hand seemed to claim her, and their child.

"We're good together, you and I." He looked at her steadily. His dark eyes shone with wonder she felt, too.

Tentatively, she placed her hand on top of his, then he slid his hand over hers and wrapped his fingers around it.

"We make a good partnership in business," his voice was rough yet soft, like velvet. "And in the bedroom."

"We're not in the bedroom."

Elan nuzzled her and chuckled deep into her ear. "Ah, Sara, you're a breath of life to me. And you're right. I don't think we've ever entered a bedroom together. But that can be rectified immediately."

He slid his powerful arms under her and swept her off the chaise. For once she had no desire to kick and wriggle from his grasp as he carried her down the cool, tiled hallway toward a pair of double oak doors.

"The bedchamber awaits, my lady."

"Thank you, my lord," she mugged.

Elan eased a door open with his elbow and Sara gasped at the sight of the most beautiful bedroom she had ever seen. Everything was white: the smooth travertine-tiled floor, chalky plastered walls, and a giant four-poster bed with gauzy curtains that billowed gently in a mysterious breeze.

A wall of windows spread the desert before them like a giant oil painting, rich in color from the ochre earth to the cloudless indigo sky.

He strode into the oasis of cool whiteness and laid her carefully on snowy satin sheets.

"It's so…white."

"We can change it to whatever you want. My surroundings matter little to me."

"I love it. I've just never seen anything quite like it."

"It's practical in the heat of summer. In my country we know white stays coolest in the hot sun."

"Do you ever wish you could go back to Oman?"

"Yes." His eyes twinkled. "I'd like to show it to you. You'll like it. From the heat and fierce windstorms of the desert, to the soft beaches and calm seas of the coast, it's a study in contrasts that reminds me of someone." A smile tugged at his lips. "It's beautiful, but this is my home."

And you are my wife. He didn't say the words but his eyes claimed her, sweeping over her, taking in her upturned face, her neck encircled by his lavish gift, her full breasts and soft belly, the unfolded length of her legs, before fixing her again with his purposeful stare. Sara suppressed a shudder at the strange feeling of being taken by force—with a mere glance.

Her reaction to Elan overwhelmed her. The connection between them was so powerful, beyond her control, a little frightening. But the maddening undercurrent of constant desire that had threatened their professional partnership now revealed itself as a fire that could fuel the most intense kind of partnership possible.

"Sara," Elan raised her fingers almost to his lips, which parted, poised for a kiss. His eyes lifted to hers, and the intensity of his dark gaze stole her breath. "Will you be my wife?"

Eleven

"Yes."

The only possible answer slipped from her mouth. Every cell in her body breathed it as a massive exhale of relief.

Elan reached into the pocket of his jeans, and retrieved one last piece from the matching set of jewelry.

The ring.

A single diamond in an exquisite setting of smooth pale metal.

She struggled to hold her hand steady as he slid the ring onto her finger. A rush of emotion swept through her as his mouth closed over hers, inhaling her as they seized each other. She gave herself over to him totally, all doubt and fear evaporating in the heat of their kiss. Their baby stirred in her belly, shifting and settling between them as they fell back on the bed to spend the morning in each other's arms.

* * *

Sara shifted restlessly on the leather chaise in the den, flipping idly through a book as the white spotlight of high-noon sun rose to fill the skylight above her.

Elan blew into the room like a desert sirocco, but instead of the work-worn jeans she'd grown used to, he looked devastatingly elegant in a dark suit, white shirt and red-striped tie. His "boss" uniform.

"Are you going into the office?" Sara sat up and put her book aside. "I'll come with you. I'm ready to get back into the swing of things." Three days in the lap of air-conditioned, no-comforts-denied luxury had her a little stir-crazy.

"No need." He smiled. "I've conducted all today's meetings via videoconference from my study."

"Oh."

His smile widened, and excitement shone in his eyes. "And I've made our announcement."

An unexpected rush of fear assaulted her. "You told people at the office we're getting married?"

"And that we're having a child together." He pinned her with a midnight stare that defied her to protest.

"Gosh, it seems so…sudden." The baby shifted, kneeing her in the ribs, and she laid a hand on her belly to calm it.

He lifted his chin. "Don't you wish to share our joy with the world?"

"Yes, but…" But what? "Maybe it would have been nice for us to tell people together."

Elan pursed his lips slightly and nodded. "You're right. From now on we'll be doing many things together. But you need rest. You're recovering from an injury. The less you do right now, the better."

"My leg hardly hurts at all anymore."

"Excellent. And your beautiful posterior?"

She smiled. "I think all those kisses had magical healing powers."

He grinned. "Perhaps tonight we'll apply more 'medicine,' but now I have an appointment to keep. I've applied for the licenses and contacted a justice to perform the ceremony."

"What?" Her stomach clenched as another wave of apprehension rose inside her.

"We must marry right away. You're already my wife in many ways, but I wish you to be my wife in the eyes of the world."

He reached out and took her hand. "It'll be a simple ceremony, just you, me, the justice, and Olga my cook to bear witness. The wedding planner has secured a talented photographer who'll record the event, and take pictures of the bride."

"But I…" Sara was speechless that he'd gone ahead and arranged everything without asking her. She gently pulled her hand out of his grasp and used it to steady herself on the chaise that was starting to feel like a jail bunk.

"What, my sweet?"

"I…I always wanted a big wedding." Tears threatened, stinging her eyes and tugging at the back of her throat. "With all my family there. My brothers and sisters. I always wanted my oldest brother to give me away." She looked up at him. "His name's Derek." She blinked her tears back. "You don't even know the names of my siblings. I want them to meet you."

"There'll be time for that later. I look forward to meeting your family. We'll fly them all here to visit. Perhaps we'll have a big celebration party with them after our baby is born."

She realized she hadn't even phoned her family to tell them she was getting married. Elan had her so thoroughly cosseted in a cocoon of comfort that the outside world—including her own beloved brothers and sisters—seemed a universe away, almost forgotten.

"A skilled seamstress will visit the house tomorrow afternoon to fit you for your dress."

"My dress? The one the planner chose to match the jewels?"

"Exactly."

He laid both hands on her belly, one on either side. The gesture sent a warm shudder of sensation rippling through her. Elan lowered his lips and kissed her belly so tenderly that her heart squeezed with irrational joy.

His cheek rested just above her belly button, his ear pressed to her skin, as if he listened to their child. "I long to give our baby a name. My name."

He lifted his head and looked at her, dark eyes glittering. "And I long for you to bear my name, to be mine forever."

Her heart clenched again, but this time anxiety mingled with her joy. Everything was moving so fast, and she wasn't in control at all. "I left several things unfinished at the office. I really need to go in and sort through some files so I can work effectively from here."

"Sara," Elan chuckled as he rose to his feet. "You'll be my wife, there's no need for you to labor to make a living. You'll want for nothing."

"But I like working, and I have debts to pay off, huge debts." She looked at him cautiously, wondering what his reaction would be.

He waved a dismissive hand in the air. "Your debts are erased."

"What? You paid them?"

He nodded.

"How did you know…?"

"I have my ways." He tapped the side of his nose mysteriously. "As I said, you won't need to think about money from now on. Rest my sweet, so you'll walk with ease at our wedding next week."

He leaned forward and settled a kiss on her cheek. Her blood heated at the mere touch of his lips. As he drew back, her hand flew to the spot where the skin still burned. Her breasts stirred and her nipples lifted, as she yearned—as always—for his caress.

She struggled to regain control of her senses. To regain control of her life. "I want to do my job. I want to have a career, I'm ambitious and I've worked hard...."

Elan leaned into her and licked her mouth as she spoke, swiping his tongue across her lips in a way that erased her words and scattered her thoughts like dust in a breeze.

His left hand cupped her breast and his thumb strummed her nipple as his right hand seized her by the back of her neck. He plunged his tongue into her mouth and she gasped as a throb of agonizing pleasure shook her.

His fingers drifted down the curve of her waist to her hip, then jerked hard on her silk shorts and panties, tugging them down as he leaned into her, pushing her back on the chaise.

Her body melted like wax as his fingers penetrated the treacherously moist flesh of her sex. As his tongue probed her mouth, his broad, stiff finger entered her and she gasped with pleasure, her cry lost against his kiss.

She shuddered hard as he took control of her, working her with his fingers and mouth, driving her beyond the bounds of reason into a different realm where she wanted nothing more than to give herself to him totally, holding nothing back.

As she lay quivering and powerless from the force of her release, Elan eased up her shorts, kissed her once more on the lips, and said, "I have legal business in town, my Sara. I'll be back soon."

His smile was one of confident mastery as he gave her one last, lingering look before he turned on his heel and swept out of the room.

My Sara.

The words reverberated in her ears as she lay there, her limbs heavy with sated desire.

Elan was a hurricane that lifted her off her feet and swept her away on a gust of passion. Drained of strength, will, everything but the waves of pure pleasure she floated on, she drifted into a fitful daytime sleep.

* * *

She jolted awake with a gasp, shaking her head to try and dislodge the ugly images of her nightmare. She'd been covered with gold paint, gleaming, sweating in the hot, desert sun.

"How lovely you look," people had murmured as they passed her.

"I can't breathe!" she'd tried to shout. But no words came out. She recognized the image from an article she'd read about the making of the movie *Goldfinger*. When the actress was painted gold for her role, they had to be careful to leave a large area of skin on her stomach unpainted, or else she would suffocate.

"I'm suffocating!" she burst out.

She didn't know how long she'd been asleep. She wasn't even entirely sure what day it was. She thought she'd been here three days, but maybe it was more?

Elan had seized her life and painted it gold. She sprang off the chaise and winced as her injured ankle reminded her of its existence.

But it was almost healed. There was no reason for her to lie around like a pig being fattened for slaughter.

A movie preview of her life flashed through her mind. A pampered existence where all her needs were taken care of, where she wanted for nothing, wanted nothing…except Elan.

The power he had over her frightened her. That he could silence her protests with his mouth, invade her body with pleasure that stole all rational thought. That he could snatch her life from under her, keep her cosseted in a gilded existence, even pay off what she owed—to leave her permanently in his debt.

She couldn't live like that.

Was he back? She stole across the cool tiled floor in her bare feet and opened the door out into the hallway.

"Elan?"

She had to tell him, right now, that her life was her own, that she needed to make her own decisions, pursue her career goals, pave her own path. She couldn't be a whole person, or a good mother to her child, any other way.

"Elan?" He must still be out.

She limped slightly as she hurried along the long hallway. Shafts of light beaming through the skylights told her it must be late afternoon. She hadn't been outside in three whole days.

She opened the back door and stepped outside to drink in the warm desert air. And she saw something that made her breath catch in her throat.

Her bike. Or what was left of it.

She hobbled over to the disconnected, mangled pile of metal: the wheels stripped of their tires, the chain limp, the handlebars upside down so the fork of the bike stuck in the air. Goose bumps crawled over her arms as she noticed the padded covering had been ripped right off the seat. The bike might have been damaged in the accident, but not to this extent. Amid the clutter lay a wrench and a greasy rag.

Her bike had been deliberately pulled apart.

How on earth had her bike made it to his house? Elan was a man who made things happen. Whatever he wanted.

She knew he hated her bike, and now he'd destroyed it. Nuts and bolts littered the sandy ground and the tires wilted in the sun like molted snake skins. The last symbol of her freedom and independence lay in ruins.

"No!"

The protest emerged as a howl of anguish that reverberated in the desert air, rang across the flat plain, bounced off the buildings, and carried toward the distant mountains. But there was no one to hear it.

Where was her family? Her friends? She had only Elan.

He's never said he loves me. He wanted her to be his wife, yes, but as she knew from harsh personal experience that was *not* the same thing.

When he grew tired of her she'd have nothing and no one. She'd be just like her mother, trapped by guilt, obligation, tradition, and without the means to leave.

I've got to get out of here.

Her throat so tight that she gasped for breath, Sara scanned the horizon. Her bike was far beyond repair. She ran back into the house and hunted for a phone.

She asked information for the name of a taxi service, called, and gave them directions to Elan's ranch. She found her backpack, which mercifully still contained her wallet and the now-wrinkled work attire she'd been carrying when she'd had her accident.

The taxi was coming from miles away. Would it get there before Elan returned? She prayed it would. Elan would never willingly let her go and she knew she didn't have the power to stop him. One look from him, not even a single word, and she'd be falling into his arms, all other considerations forgotten.

"She'll bend to my will. It's only a matter of time." His words came back to her, mocking her with her own vulnerability. She was like the horse he sought to subdue on her first visit to his ranch. *I feed her, care for her, give her shelter from the sun. She will learn these things come with a price. And she'll learn to pay it.*

The price is too high.

A tear rolled down her cheek as she removed her ring, and she shivered at the naked sensation she felt without it. She placed it with its glittering companions on the kitchen table and wrote Elan a letter in which she tried to be as honest as possible. He deserved at least that much. She wrote that she hoped some time—in the future—they would establish a means to give him some access to his child. But not yet. First she needed time to get over him.

A lot of time.

The distant hum of a car engine made her dart to the window, clutching her letter.

Thank God, the cab was here. She'd worried about not being able to make the once-a-day train to Chicago if it didn't come fast enough.

She left the letter on the kitchen table despite a stab of regret. She snatched up her backpack, and hurried outside as fast as her sore ankle would let her.

"The train station, please." The train station was only a few hundred yards from her apartment but she didn't dare go there. Elan might find her. Her neighbor Sylvia would be willing to box up her few possessions and forward them to Wisconsin for a couple of hundred dollars. Money well spent if it would buy her freedom back. And she'd pay Elan back every penny he'd put toward her debts, no matter how long it took.

She didn't look behind her as the cab roared away along the straight road. If she did she might weaken at the sight of the lovely house that might have been her home.

Don't think about it. Just go. Run while you can, there'll be time for crying later.

At the station she paced back and forth waiting for the train, ankle throbbing. Her baby was madly active, kicking and rolling, jumping and bumping against her. It must be her nerves, jangled and sizzling with adrenaline that had her and her child in such turmoil.

She wished the train would come before she might weaken.

Don't think about him.

She didn't even want to think his name. But a fragmentary memory would slip unbidden into her mind—the black hairs that dusted the backs of his powerful hands, the small, delicate ears that sat atop his thickly muscled neck, the way he ran his fingers through his thick hair while he was thinking…

No!

At last the train pulled in and she found herself a seat in the final car, her eyes tearless, fists clenched in resolve. She'd make it. She always had.

* * *

"My Sara!" Elan flung open the front door and tossed his jacket on a chair. Preparing all those papers, adding Sara's name to his bank and brokerage accounts, had taken far longer than he expected. He couldn't wait to lose himself in her arms.

He strode along the corridor and gently pushed open the door to the den. He didn't want to awaken her if she was sleeping. The den was empty.

"Sara!" he called along the corridor and his voice echoed back to him off the hard stone.

Where on earth is she?

He hurried to the kitchen. Perhaps she was hungry. But the room was empty, as was the dining room, the living room, his bedroom…. She wasn't anywhere to be found in the entire house.

Could she have been abducted? He had never been vulnerable to kidnappers before, since he'd never had any dependents. But since he'd been blabbing all over town about his upcoming marriage to Sara, perhaps he'd placed her life in jeopardy?

He grabbed the phone off the hook in the kitchen and was about to dial 911 when he saw a folded note lying on the stone table.

Amidst the diamonds he given her.

He dropped the phone and seized the folded paper.

Dear Elan,
I'm afraid I cannot marry you…

The rest of the words were a blur as he scanned them, looking for where she had gone.

I am leaving for Wisconsin today. Please don't follow me.
I'll contact you when I'm ready.

The train. It had to be. The local route ended in Chicago—a short distance from her home state. He knew she couldn't drive with her injured ankle, and a plane was unlikely with her fear of flying.

He grabbed his keys and spun out the door, slammed into his car and roared off across the desert. He realized with a jolt that he had no clear idea where she was headed. He knew her debts were with a bank in Milwaukee, the P.I. who'd uncovered them had told him that much, but he didn't know if she was originally from that city. He didn't even know the names of her relatives.

And he had a sickening premonition that once she was gone he would never get her back.

The train left the station only once a day at 4:30 p.m. The clock on the dash read 4:22. He pushed the accelerator to the floor and dust clouds whirled around the car as he ate up the sandy desert road.

He blew into town going way over the speed limit and hammered his hands on the wheel as he sat for precious seconds at a stop light.

4:29.

4:30.

The light changed and he revved away, tires squealing. He turned onto the road leading to the station only to see the train just beginning to move.

Its progress was excruciatingly slow—slow motion—but it was leaving the station without him.

He followed the paved road past its end onto the sandy dirt that followed the track out into the desert. He sped past the train, driving several hundred yards out into the desert, then skidded to a halt on the sand and leaped out.

And he ran. Pelting alongside the track, he glanced back at the train coming up behind him. He would have one chance. He kept a steady pace, looking back to find the handhold he'd aim for—the long metal handles on either side of the doors.

The rattling sound of metal wheels on the track clamored in his ears as the first car caught up with him. He quickened his pace and as the handle sped past him he grabbed it and swung himself up onto the steps. He tugged the heavy door open with tremendous effort and hurled himself headlong into the moving car.

The force of the motion flung him to his knees on the floor inside and he paused there a moment on all fours, catching his breath as a wave of stinging relief seared him.

Heads craned to look at him as he scrambled to his feet.

Sara? He scanned the seats, looking for her soft, pale hair amongst the few passengers and not seeing it. He wrenched open the connecting door to the car behind, and stepped through.

Striding along the car, he searched faces, and each one that wasn't her pricked him with a sharp needle of anxiety. He shoved into the next car, heart pounding and sweat trickling along his spine as he prowled down the aisle.

Where was she?

The sight of blond hair falling over a down turned face made his heart seize, but a stranger looked up at him—eyes wide with alarm—as he stopped to lean over her.

The third car had one occupant, an elderly male whose eyes tracked Elan as he plowed onward down the aisle. Only one more car. If he'd miscalculated and she wasn't on the train…

But she was.

As he tugged aside the heavy door between the cars he recognized her instantly. She stood at the end of the aisle, her back to him as she gazed out the rear window of the train at the track streaming out behind.

"Sara!"

She wheeled around, startled by his strangled cry of joy. Relief roared through him. He closed the distance between them at a run, and seized her wrist as he reached her.

"Why did you leave me?" The question flew from his mouth.

Her eyes glittered with tears that streamed down her cheeks. The sight of them tore at his heart.

"Don't cry, my Sara. There are no problems we can't solve together." He pressed his lips to her hand as fierce emotion flared in his chest. The prospect of losing Sara had almost deprived him of his senses. "Thank the stars I've found you. We can get off at the next station and take a cab home."

She looked at him, and her forehead wrinkled in perplexity as her eyes blinked back tears.

"I can't."

Her words emerged as a choking sob. Ten seconds earlier she'd clawed at the window, muttering his name under her breath. She wanted to stay, no matter what the cost. She loved him, she needed him more than her independence, more than her pride.

But now, as he gripped her hand, his black eyes bored into her and his mouth issued another command, her only impulse was to resist.

"You can't leave me." Elan's face was contorted with emotion.

"I can," she whispered, her eyes dropping to avoid the raw pain she saw in his. "I must."

"But why?"

"You read my letter?" She struggled to keep her voice audible.

"It said you couldn't marry me, and that you were leaving today…there wasn't time to read the rest." He dropped her wrist and shoved his hands into his pockets, as if hunting for the paper. "I don't have it with me."

A choking sound, half sob, half laugh, escaped Sara's throat. "You didn't even read it!" She shook her head. "You didn't even care what I had to say. You just knew you had to come after me, regardless of what I wanted."

"I… I…" He held out his hands, his gesture pleading with her. "I couldn't let you go."

"That's just it," her voice emerged high-pitched with desperation. "You couldn't *let* me. You know best, in your mind you always know best. You knew you had to marry me, and you didn't quit trying until I said yes.

"Once you had my assent you whipped my life out from under me and replaced it with a new one, without even asking what I wanted. I'm my own person, Elan, whether you like it or not, and I'm not going to become anyone's pampered possession, locked in a golden cage while you fly free."

She paused for breath.

His lips twitched, no doubt with the urge to protest and silence her, but he didn't speak. He held her gaze, silent. The emotion she read in his dark eyes threatened to rock her resolve.

At last he spoke. "I love you, Sara." His words didn't emerge as a demand, or an order. They were soft, an apology, an offering. "I simply love you."

Her heart quivered at his declaration.

He loved her.

Part of her wanted to jump in his arms, but caution held her steady. "I love you too, Elan," she whispered, the words torn from her by the raw agony she read in his stiff posture. "But sometimes even love isn't enough."

She squeezed her eyelids against fresh tears.

"You're my wife, you know you are, we don't need a piece of paper or a fancy gown. Our marriage is written in the stars."

As he said it she could see his hands jerk as he fought to keep from reaching out to her. She ached with the need to touch him, to hold him, to take him in her arms and soothe him—to comfort them both.

He lifted his chin slightly. "If you don't wish to marry me, so be it." His eyes glittered with pain and defiance, then softened. "But live with me, be my companion, share my life. I won't seek to control you, only to love you—and our child."

A fearful trembling shook Sara as every atom vibrated with longing so intense it was literally painful.

I love you.

Her whole being issued the words and she softened as the force of their love filled the rattling, pounding space of the jolting train car.

Could love be enough? And did she dare take the risk to find out?

"You've entered my empty home—my empty heart—and filled them with love." He stood before her, hands spread, palms up, opening himself to her. "Our love is precious, and we've made a child together. Come home with me."

The appeal of his words loosened her limbs and she longed to fall into his arms and literally let him carry her home. But at the same time her brain crackled with warnings that flashed across her consciousness like electronic billboards.

"What happened to my bike? Did you rip it apart?"

"Yes," he admitted.

The alarms in her brain grew louder. "You deliberately destroyed my only means of transportation?"

"It was broken in the accident. And you know I bought you a new car." He shoved a hand through his hair. "To be honest, the accident scared the hell out of me. It made me so afraid to lose you." He paused, breathing, dark eyes fixed on hers. "I took my emotions out on your bike. I shouldn't have done it and I apologize. I'll buy you a new bike."

The contrition in his eyes and the strong emotion on his face tugged at her heart. Was he truly sorry? She steadied herself against the metal wall as the train rattled onward. Drew in a deep breath. "*I'll* buy me a new bike."

"Yes." His eyes brightened. "Or even better, we can buy it together. I won't prevent you from living the life you want. I'll be right with you, by your side."

Could he see her resolve weakening? "What about at the office? I want to work." She held her chin high.

"Absolutely. We'll share the boardroom—" the gleam in his

eyes turned into a sparkle, "as well as the bedroom. We'll raise our child together and build our company together. A true marriage of equals."

Was it possible? Her heart swelled with the answer *yes* and her arms ached to grab him and hug him.

But doubts—fears—still sneaked around the edges of her mind.

"Elan, neither you nor I knows what a happy marriage is. Our parents were miserable—they destroyed each other—how can we escape that legacy?"

Elan stood, feet apart, braced against the rattling of the train. "We'll forge a new legacy, one not based on worn-out patterns that limit us both. Already you've proved you're strong enough to stand beside me, to stand up to me, to shape our lives with a force equal to mine. Let us break the mold."

He held out a broad hand, palm up, the lines where a palmist could read his future raised to her like an offering. Sara studied the dark creases bisecting his palm, the roadmap that held his fate—and hers.

She rocked a little, shifted to keep her footing on the moving train and suddenly her hand was on Elan's as she grabbed him for balance.

His fingers closed around hers, and she shivered at the reassuring sensation of his big hand steadying her, offering her the support she needed. She could almost feel the lines of their hands fuse together—lifeline, head line, heart line—their destinies becoming inseparable.

Something flowed between them—from his eyes to hers, from her hands to his, a flow of love and positive energy that could power them both for a lifetime.

"Come home with *me*," she whispered, filled with sudden resolve. "Come to Wisconsin with me and meet my family. Come on this journey with me and learn who I am."

Surprise widened Elan's eyes and he blinked. His lips parted as emotion washed across his face, softening his hard features. His eyes shone as his hand tightened around hers. "Yes," he said forcefully. "Yes. We'll go on this journey together." A smile quivered across his mouth. "I'll travel with you wherever you wish to go, my Sara."

He squeezed her hand and she felt a big grin spread across her face. They flew together, arms and legs tangling in the rush to close any distance between them. Her lips stung with the force of his kiss as his mouth closed over hers.

Her body melted into his as his tongue filled her mouth. She buried her hands in his shirt, tugging at it as she strained to touch the hot, vivid skin beneath. Her head thrown back, she writhed as Elan sucked at the pulse point on her neck.

Then she gasped as she realized the train was pulling into the next station.

Elan's eyes opened as she pulled away from him. His pupils were dilated and his face glazed with a sheen of lust and perspiration.

"What?"

"The station."

They collapsed in laughter as they fell toward the closest seats.

"I have no ticket," said Elan, his mouth fighting a grin. "I don't even have my wallet."

"Don't worry, I'll take care of you." She looked at him as she reached into her backpack, wondering how he'd take this first assertion of her right to pay her own way—and his.

He'd settled back into his seat with a satisfied smile, hands behind his head, elbows in the air.

"Take care of me, my Sara, and I'll take care of you."

"It will be my pleasure."

Epilogue

Nine months later, Lions Club Hall, Seminee, Wisconsin

"Oh, he looks so sweet in his tiny tux!" Erin chucked the baby's chubby chin. "I can't believe you managed to find one that small."

"Find it? Are you kidding? Elan had it made by his tailor in London. We had to measure little Ben's inside leg. You should have seen him kicking." Sara giggled. "I'm just glad he's outside of me so I can fit into a real wedding dress, not a white satin tent."

"You look lovely." Her sister bit her lip.

"Oh, don't start bawling again!"

"I'm just so happy for you, and for Elan. I can't believe we've only known him a few months. I feel like he's always been part of our family."

"He does, too. And being around us has triggered his dormant family instincts. You've seen him with his brothers over the past

week. It's like…he's not afraid to care about people anymore."
Uh-oh. She was getting choked up now. There was such affection between the three handsome men that it was hard to believe—and so sad—they'd missed so much time together. Things would be different from now on, she'd make sure of it.

"Speaking of his brothers…" Erin fanned herself, sending blond hair and chiffon dress ruffles fluttering. "Hot!"

Sara smiled. "Stay away from Quasar, he's a notorious playboy," she whispered, glancing at the blue-eyed charmer surrounded—as usual—by a circle of blushing girls.

"Will do. I have bad luck with that type," Erin winked. "But what about Salim? He looks so…dignified. Like he needs someone to loosen him up."

"A tall order, I suspect. He inherited the family business and all the responsibilities that come with it at a young age. And Elan says he never got over his college girlfriend."

"Bummer. Maybe I could help him get over her?" Erin raised her eyebrows. "Then again, I'm not sure I want to move all the way to Oman."

"You'd better not! We're counting on you coming down to Nevada. Elan has a grand vision of our entire family gathered around the table for dinner every evening."

"Does he really? He's so sweet. Then I guess he's not going to quit trying to get us all to move down there, is he?"

Sara shook her head. "Nope. Elan doesn't quit until he gets what he wants. I have firsthand experience of that."

"Well, maybe I'd like the desert air. And the job offer is pretty tempting. Do you really think I have what it takes to be an event planner?"

"Definitely." She squeezed her sister's arm. "If I can be VP of Business Development, you can be an event planner. You run your family single-handed—there's no challenge greater than that. And our kids will have a great time together in the new on-site daycare."

Erin narrowed her eyes as she raised them to look behind Sara. "You're as bad as he is."

"She's worse." Elan's voice tickled Sara's ear as he slid his arms around her waist, surprising her from behind. A warm shiver of pleasure rippled though her. "But think how your children will thrive in the healthy climate where they can play outdoors all year long."

"I've heard the sales pitch," Erin winked at him and hoisted Ben up onto her shoulder.

"I hope Ben doesn't spit up on your lovely dress." Sara turned to Elan. "Where's Derek? Does he have the rings?" She was anxious to get started on the ceremony.

"Salim has the rings, my Sara. He's the best man. Your brother will be walking down the aisle with you, remember."

She sucked in a long breath and smiled. "I do have it all straight in my head, really, I'm just so…so…"

"Happy?" Elan had moved in front of her and he lifted an eyebrow as his lips curved into a smile.

"Yes. So happy." She bit her lip. "I just can't wait to be your wife."

"Nor I to be your husband."

He laid a gentle kiss on her cheek and heat bloomed under his lips in a way that never failed to surprise her, though they spent every day together.

He looked at her for a moment, eyes shining, then turned to lift his son from Erin's arms. He smoothed the baby's thick, dark hair off his tiny forehead and settled him against his broad, tuxedo-clad shoulder. "There's no rush. We have the rest of our lives together, and I mean to savor every glorious minute."

He leaned forward until his mouth brushed her ear and

sparked a sizzling response. "Though I confess, I'm anxious to enjoy the pleasures of our wedding night."

Sara felt her body flush inside her virginal white dress as her nipples strained against the delicate satin. "Just keep your hands off me until after the ceremony. You know I'm not that kind of girl."

They all exploded into helpless giggles as little Ben surprised them with the wonderful throaty chuckle of his first laugh.

* * * * *

SOMETHING ABOUT
THE BOSS...

BY
YVONNE LINDSAY

New Zealand born, to Dutch immigrant parents, **Yvonne Lindsay** became an avid romance reader at the age of thirteen. Now, married to her "blind date" and with two fabulous children, she remains a firm believer in the power of romance. Yvonne feels privileged to be able to bring to her readers the stories of her heart. In her spare time, when not writing, she can be found with her nose firmly in a book, reliving the power of love in all walks of life. She can be contacted via her website, www. yvonnelindsay.com.

This one is for the amazing team at Harlequin who,
I'm sure, often miss out on thanks for all you do in the
foreground, the background and the playground. :-)

One

Sophie flew into the office five minutes later than usual. It drove her crazy to be late, for any reason. She'd woken way past her usual time and had had to forgo her morning coffee and bagel in an attempt to make up for it. With a vague wave at their receptionist and the skeleton staff already working at their stations in the open-plan office behind reception, Sophie went through to the executive office suite, smoothing her short blond bob with one hand.

She flung a glance at Zach's office door—it was open. Darn. He was already here. Despite her best efforts, Zach Lassiter had beaten her into the office, again. Not good. Not when she was doing her best to keep everything running on an even keel, and certainly not when she needed to do some snooping in his office. He was hiding something, she just knew it.

She dropped her shoulder bag on the corner of her

desk. The bag didn't quite make it, though, and it slid off the surface to fall silently onto the thick carpeting, its contents spilling at her feet.

"Damn!" The curse slipped from her lips and even now, though she hadn't lived under her mother's roof in more than four years, she felt the quiet reproof of her mother's gaze for dropping her standards so. They might have been poor, but her mother had always expected her to act like a lady.

She scrabbled to put everything back where it belonged—a place for everything and everything in its place; it had been her mantra for longer than she could remember. Her hand hovered over the photo she carried with her everywhere and she straightened with it still in her hand. They'd been so young, so innocent. Victims of circumstance.

Silently she renewed her vow to find her half-sister; Sophie owed it to them both. And she was getting closer. The latest report from the private investigator she'd hired to find her sister had listed a new possibility to explore. Thinking about it had kept her awake half the night, hence her sleeping past her alarm this morning.

A noise from behind her, from the kitchenette that she kept well stocked, sent a prickle of awareness tiptoeing between her shoulder blades.

"Cute kids."

Zach gave one of his lazy, killer smiles that always managed to send a bolt of longing straight to her gut, as he handed her a coffee. Sophie fought to quell the tremor that threatened to make her hand shake as she accepted the mug. She'd tried to shore up her defenses against her crazy attraction to him, but even after eighteen months she still failed miserably. Working in the same office space with him had been taxing enough, but now working directly for him—well, that was a whole new kettle of fish altogether.

"I'm supposed to be the one bringing you coffee," she said quietly. "Sorry I'm late."

"No problem. I was getting myself one. Is that you?" he asked gesturing to the photo in her hand.

It was the kind of snapshot that most kids had taken at some stage in their lives. Siblings, oldest behind, youngest in front. Gap-toothed smiles fixed on their freckled faces, hair pulled back into identical pigtails, bangs straight across their eyebrows. Oldest staring dead ahead, youngest—still baby-faced at age four—with eyes unfocused, distracted by whatever it was that day. Sophie certainly couldn't recall although she remembered well the sensation of her sister's bony shoulder beneath her hand, the steady warmth of Susannah's body standing close to hers, almost leaning into her in that way she did when she wasn't entirely comfortable with a situation.

"Yes, me and my younger sister."

"Are you guys close?"

"Not anymore," she hedged.

Suzie's father, Sophie's much-adored stepdad, had died suddenly shortly after that photo had been taken. With their mother struggling to make ends meet, Suzie had gone to live with her father's sister. Financially independent and also recently widowed, Suzie's aunt had an open heart and open arms for her brother's only child. Contact between the two families had been severed almost immediately—deemed to be in the best interests of the girls at the time. It had been more than twenty years since they'd seen each other and Sophie still felt the emptiness inside, even though she'd long since learned how to mask it.

She thumbed the well-worn edge of the photo before tucking the picture back in her bag. She was doing what she could to reestablish contact with her sister. She had to be satisfied with that. She gave herself a mental shake and locked her handbag away in the bottom drawer of her desk. Even though this was downtown Royal, Texas, Sophie didn't take chances. It wasn't her way.

Clearly taking the hint that the subject of her sister was closed, Zach turned his attention to work.

"What's on your agenda today?"

Sophie briefly outlined what she had planned in her other boss's absence before asking, "Is there something else you need me to work on instead? None of this is urgent right now, especially with Alex still out of the office."

Out of the office. She gave an inward sigh. Some euphemism for missing. It had been over a month since her boss had simply disappeared off the face of the earth. Each morning she still hoped that she'd come in and find him in his office, his energetic personality filling the room, but each morning she was disappointed. The police were now involved in the hunt for Alex Santiago and his disappearance looked more sinister by the day.

"Any news from Sheriff Battle?" Zach asked.

She shook her head. Sophie had racked her brain trying to think of anything that could have been a clue to why Alex had gone, and where. But nothing had been out of the usual. The guy had disappeared the same way as he'd arrived in Royal, although with a great deal less fanfare. He was the kind of man who *made* things happen—things didn't happen *to* him. Which made his disappearance all the more puzzling. Surely someone had to know something. Someone, somewhere was keeping secrets, and Sophie had a worried feeling it might be Zach.

The muscles around his mouth tightened slightly, his only tell that something was bothering him. If anyone knew anything about Alex, it should have been Zach, as the two men had become firm friends in the time they'd worked together and shared office space. She watched him carefully. Zach Lassiter had a reputation for keeping his cards close to his chest and only letting you know what he thought you should know, when he thought you needed to know it.

The man was locked tighter than the vault at Fort Knox. Goodness only knew he'd remained impervious to the subtle and not-so-subtle questioning from local men and women alike. All anyone knew about him was that just under two years ago he'd arrived here in Royal with his own investment company and a knack for turning high-risk investment opportunities into sure fortunes. When Alex Santiago had arrived a couple of months later and set up his venture capital business, they'd created the perfect successful partnership.

It hadn't taken a whole lot of research to find out that Zach Lassiter had been married, not when his ex still called him almost every day, although Sophie had been unable to find any photos online that included Anna Lassiter. It also hadn't taken a lot of poking to discover that Zach's knack for turning high-risk investment opportunities into gold had started several years ago with an investment firm in Midland.

But the man himself? What made him tick, what drove him? There was nothing. Dark good looks and urbane charm aside, he could be hiding anything beneath that smooth, sophisticated exterior. It was whether that "anything" involved Alex's disappearance that Sophie wanted to find out.

"What? Have I got something on my face?" Zach asked, reminding Sophie she was staring.

Color flooded her cheeks and she ducked her head. "No, sorry, I was just distracted for a minute."

The phone on Sophie's desk chimed discreetly. Zach's line. He usually took his own calls, but since he was here with her, Sophie reached for the handset.

"Zach Lassiter's office, this is Sophie speaking."

"I can't reach Zach on his phone. Is he there? Put me through to him," the woman's querulous voice demanded, belatedly adding, "Please."

"One moment please, I'll see if he's free to take your call." Recognizing the voice, and putting the woman on hold, Sophie said, "It's your ex-wife. You're not answering your cell phone. Do you want to take it?"

"Of course." He patted the breast pocket of his jacket. "I must have left my cell in the car again." He fished his keys out of his pocket and handed them to Sophie. "When you have a free moment, could you get it for me?"

"Sure," she said, taking the keys and trying desperately to ignore the buzz of attraction that warmed her skin as his fingertips brushed her palm.

She watched as he walked back to his office and heard the deep murmur of his voice through his closed door as he picked up the call. Not for the first time she wondered about the relationship Zach had with Anna Lassiter. She could count on one finger the number of people she knew who were still on speaking terms with their exes, let alone *daily* speaking terms. As far as she could ascertain, he and Anna had been divorced for nearly two years. She shook her head. He had to still be in love with the woman. Why else would he devote so much time to her?

Sophie fought to quell the pang of envy that struck deep in her chest. What would it be like to be the object of Zach's devotion? His closed demeanor aside, the man was sex on legs. Or maybe it was that very aloofness that made him so appealing to her. She took a sip of her rapidly cooling coffee. No, it was more visceral than that. To use a more colloquial expression, the man was prime beef. It was no hardship to imagine the lean, hard-muscled lines of his body beneath the tailored suits he wore.

A tiny thrill coursed down the length of her spine, setting a tingle up in her lower back. Lord, she had it bad. Just thinking about him was enough to send her pulse up a few notches and a flush of awareness to heat all those secret parts of her body that were hidden by her office clothes.

Combine a killer physique with a handsomely chiseled face, expensively cropped jet-black hair, green eyes that looked straight through you and a mind as sharp as a tack, and he became a very appealing package. From the first day he'd walked through the front door of the professional suite and taken up the spare office next to Alex's, Sophie had been mesmerized by him. He carried himself with an air of confidence that made it clear that he was there to succeed at whatever he turned his hand to. And succeed he did. His investment advice had made his client list an exceptionally large and equally wealthy one. Some even said he had a Midas touch and, if his address on the outskirts of town was any indicator, he certainly knew how to put his money to good use.

She also knew that you didn't get anywhere without hard work and dedication and if she didn't apply some of that to the list of things she had to do today, she'd have to answer to Alex when he came back. If he came back, whispered a small voice in the back of her head.

Zach hung up from the call and just for a moment allowed himself the indulgence of resting his head in his hands. He was worried about Anna. She'd always been high-strung, but right now she was acting as if she was stretched to the breaking point. He had to do something, and do it soon. Her parents still insisted there was nothing wrong with her, keeping their heads in the sand regarding any potential mental imbalance.

Their refusal to admit to her instability wasn't doing her any favors. She needed help—professional help—and it was up to him to find it for her. Drawing in a deep breath, Zach straightened and booted up his laptop, opening a search window. Before long he had a list of people and places to contact. He'd do more research tonight.

Zach pressed his fingertips against his closed eyelids. He felt so damned responsible. He should never have married Anna, never bowed down to her father's—his boss's—unstintingly direct pressure to court his only child.

Sure, Zach had been attracted to her. She was blonde and beautiful and had an air of delicacy about her that had appealed to the caveman inside him in a way he'd never experienced before. But he'd been all wrong for her. She'd needed someone less driven, more devoted. Certainly someone less earthy. It hadn't taken long for the fragility to wear thin, for him to feel trapped. Then, just when they'd begun separation proceedings, she'd discovered she was pregnant and it had become far too late to walk away. He'd tried to do his best by her—

after all, he'd vowed to her before man and God that he'd stand by her through all that life could throw at them.

But life had thrown them a complete curveball with the death of their baby son. And while Zach had learned to hide his pain beneath a shell of self-preservation, Anna's guilt over the car wreck that had taken ten-month-old Blake's life had seen her spiral deeper and deeper into depression.

"Zach? Is everything all right?"

He hadn't even heard Sophie come into his office. He snapped to attention. "Sure, everything's fine. Just a bit tired is all."

"I found your phone. You'd left it connected to your hands-free kit."

She slid it across the desk toward him, the screen letting him know exactly how many calls he'd missed from Anna. He sighed. Tonight he would definitely make some decisions. It was past time.

"Thanks, I appreciate it."

He lifted his gaze and met Sophie's. She was a sight for sore eyes, with her cute blond bob and those warm, whiskey-brown eyes of hers. Today had been the first time he'd seen her approach anything outside of her usual unflappable mien, when she'd arrived a few minutes late. He kind of liked seeing her a little off-kilter. It made her seem more human, more approachable.

She always looked immaculate—her clothes well cut but not flashy—and he'd long envied Alex her calm, capable efficiency. As Alex's executive assistant, she kept the place running like clockwork, keeping an overview of not only all the pies Alex had his thumb in but every aspect of every pie. You had to admire a mind that could compartmentalize and draw information out on command the way hers did. In Alex's absence, the cracks would surely have started to show by now without her talents.

Zach hadn't wasted a second on availing himself of her skills over the past month, when it had become clear that Alex's disappearance was more than the temporary foray they'd all thought he might have indulged in. With the police now handling the disappearance of his good friend, Zach had doubled his workload, juggling both his own clients' portfolios and Alex's venture capital concerns. Without Sophie he'd have dropped the ball by now.

He really ought to show her some appreciation. He spoke out loud before thinking on the subject long enough to talk himself out of it.

"Sophie, you've been a godsend these past weeks. I couldn't have managed it all without your help. I know you've been putting in some long hours and I'd like to make it up to you. How about dinner at Claire's at the end of the week? Sound good?"

"You don't need to do that, Zach. I'm only doing my job—one I'm very well compensated for."

"I know, but I am grateful and I'd like to show it. I'll make the reservation today, and Sophie? I won't take no for an answer."

She gave a little laugh, the sound a gurgle of amusement that removed the last of the dark cloud in the back of his mind and pulled an answering smile across his lips.

"Well, when you put it like that, what can I say? Thank you, I'll look forward to it."

He watched her turn and leave his office, noted the way the fabric of her straight skirt skimmed her hips and pulled across her buttocks with each no-nonsense step. An unwanted pull of desire tugged deep inside him and he forced himself to avert his gaze. Acknowledging that Sophie Beldon was an attractive woman was one thing, but actually doing something about it was off-limits. They worked together, and he didn't want to jeopardize that. Too much hinged on them continuing to work in synchronicity until Alex's return. Besides, look at the disaster of his last work-related relationship. It wasn't something he was in a hurry to repeat.

He'd asked her out to dinner to express his gratitude, that was all. There couldn't be any more to it than that—no matter what his clamoring libido insisted to the contrary.

Two

"Thank you, I shall look forward to it?" What on earth had she been thinking? The words played over and over in her head, so stilted, so... Argh! Why couldn't she have come back with something witty or sophisticated? Something that might have attracted his interest just that little bit more.

This was further proof that a man like Zach Lassiter was out of her league, Sophie castigated herself as she settled at her desk and tried to force her mind back to analyzing the projection figures that had come in on Alex's latest venture. They made for interesting reading and her fingers itched to compile her report. But even as she started entering the data into her computer, her mind kept flicking back to Zach's dinner invitation.

Her pulse skipped an excited beat. Claire's was not your run-of-the-mill restaurant and the prices there reflected that. She'd only ever made reservations there for Alex and his various business contacts—she'd never had the good fortune to dine there herself. Sophie quelled an inner squeal of delight and reminded herself she was a sage twenty-eight years old, not a giddy teenager. Besides, this wasn't anything like a date. It was a work-related bonus, that's all. And the sooner she started believing it, the better.

When her phone rang, she was glad for the interruption to her thoughts, even more so when she heard who was on the end of the line.

"Lila," she greeted one of her dearest friends, "how are you?"

Lila Hacket had been making a strong name for herself in set production design in Los Angeles. Sophie was so very proud of her for carving out such success in that competitive world. A world as far from hers as it was probably possible to get, when you thought about it. When Lila had been in Royal to work on a movie being filmed there, the two women had had scant opportunity to catch up beyond the barbecue Lila's father had hosted last month. Even then it had been so packed they'd had little chance to really talk. Except about Zach Lassiter, that was. Strange how he kept coming up in her thoughts and conversations, Sophie mused before pushing him to the back of her mind.

"I'm feeling just fine, thank you," Lila said. "Under the circumstances."

Sophie could hear the grin that was undoubtedly painted on her friend's face. She could always tell when Lila had news she was itching to share.

"Circumstances? C'mon, spill," she demanded. "I know you too well for you to keep a secret from me for long."

"I have news." Lila chuckled.

Sophie's lips twitched into a broad smile. "You and Sam? I knew it! There always were too many sparks between the two of you."

"More than sparks, we're getting married."

Sophie let go a shriek of delight, then, remembering where she was, rapidly tried to calm herself. "Congratulations! When?"

"Last Saturday of the month. We're having it on the Double H. We just want to keep it simple and low-key."

"And your father agreed to that? Low-key really isn't his style, is it?"

Lila laughed. "No, you're right, but I'm standing firm on this. Close friends and family only. Besides, any more than that will probably wear me out, seeing as how I'm pregnant and all."

Sophie's breath caught in her throat as the news sank in. Excitement and sheer joy swelled up within her.

"Pregnant? Oh my, that was quick. Congratulations again, that's wonderful news."

"Not so quick, actually, I'm just over four months along."

"You've been holding out on me," Sophie accused her in a teasing tone. "We'll need to talk this out face-to-face, I think."

"Definitely. Oh—" Lila hesitated for a moment and Sophie heard her draw in a deep breath "—and it's twins."

"Twins! How long have you known?"

"About the twins? Not all that long, although I have known for a while about being pregnant. I just needed some time to come to terms with it. To sort out in my own mind what I was doing next. It's part of why I came home last month."

Sophie could easily imagine what it was like to face

raising a child on her own. Although Lila's position, both financial and social, was vastly different from what Sophie's mother's had been. Lila would never have been short of support, emotional or monetary, which was a luxury Sophie's mom had never had. She pushed those sad thoughts aside, wanting instead to give her full focus to her friend's exciting announcement.

"I'm so very happy for you, Lila. A wedding and twin babies to look forward to? It's wonderful, *wonderful* news. You have to let me host your baby shower, please! My mind is already brimming with ideas."

"Are you sure it won't be too much work for you? You've got so much on your plate already, especially with your boss still gone."

Sophie made a shushing sound to her friend. "Don't be ridiculous. It would be an honor to host your shower. You just leave it all to me."

"Thank you, Sophie."

"You're very welcome. It's the least I can do for you. So does this mean you'll be staying in Royal?"

"Sam's offered to relocate to L.A. with me, to set up a branch of Gordon Construction there, but we're holding off making a decision until after the babies are born." She gave another breathy laugh. "I still can't believe it. Babies!"

"It's going to be amazing," Sophie reassured her. "But are you sure we're talking about the same Sam Gordon?"

Sam had vocalized his thoughts about a woman's place being in the home on more than one occasion. In fact he'd been one of the most vociferous in opposition to the new child-care center at the Texas Cattleman's Club when it was initially proposed.

"Just goes to show even a leopard can change his

spots with the right motivation," Lila answered, and Sophie could hear the happiness ringing through her voice. "So, tell me. You haven't done anything silly about what we talked about last month, have you? I'm worried about you."

Sophie huffed out a small breath and lowered her voice. "To even have an opportunity would be a fine thing. No, don't worry, I still haven't been able to do any snooping around Zach Lassiter. I'm quite safe."

Their conversation turned to more general matters and after Sophie replaced her handset on the cradle, she took a moment to hug Lila's exciting news to herself. Her friend had been fiercely independent for so long, had carved a strong career for herself against some pretty tough odds, and now here she was—on the precipice of a whole new adventure in her life. Marriage to a man she clearly loved with all her generous heart, and expecting his babies.

Truth be told, Sophie felt a little envious of Lila. What would it be like, she wondered, to carry the baby of the man you loved? Without realizing it her eyes strayed to Zach's closed office door. She shook her head. She wasn't in love with Zach Lassiter. Of course she wasn't.

Sure, she was attracted to him. Majorly attracted to him, even though she had some niggling suspicions that he knew more about Alex's disappearance than he was letting on. But she didn't know him. Not really. Certainly not enough to begin contemplating what it would be like to have his child, and certainly not enough to fully trust him. Even so, she couldn't help wondering what it would be like to be the sole focus of his attention. To feel not only his gaze upon her, but his lips, his hands, his body, as well. Zach stood a good six inches taller than her own five and a half feet and he had a strong build. How he found the time to stay in shape with the hours he spent in the office or out on business calls she didn't know, but it was easy to see in the way he walked and in the fit of his clothing that he took care of himself.

She could only begin to imagine what it would be like to trace the outlines of his muscles from shoulder to chest...and lower. Tendrils of heat spread from the pit of her belly and made her insides clench on a surge of need so intense it almost made her gasp out loud.

Sophie pushed away from her desk and went through to the kitchenette to grab a glass of water. She took a long drink of the chilled liquid, but it did little to quell the turmoil in her body. She was being ridiculous. A woman like her was not Zach Lassiter's type. She lacked the refinement he'd surely expect in his women. Not that anyone ever saw him out with a woman on his arm. He was as closed and careful about his relationships, if he had them, as he was about everything else in his life.

It made her wonder again just how much he knew about Alex Santiago's disappearance. Unlike everyone else, he hadn't openly speculated on where Alex could be. Did that mean that he knew something and was keeping it secret, even from the police? Sophie shook her head slightly. She didn't want to contemplate it. Surely Zach wouldn't withhold vital information from what was now a police investigation.

Zach appeared in the doorway, a sheaf of papers in his hand and a worried frown on his forehead.

"Did you w-want me for something?" she asked, her voice a little wobbly.

An inner groan tore through her. Want her? Like she wanted him? She'd have to work harder to guard her tongue. She turned away to reach for a mug from the cupboard so he wouldn't see the twin spots of color she just knew would be glowing in her cheeks the way they always did when she was uncomfortable.

"Yeah, can you come into my office when you're finished in here? I've been going over the pitch we're sending out for potential investors in the Manson project. I need you to help me fine-tune some things."

"Sure, I'll be there right away. Coffee?"

"Thanks," he replied, already walking away.

Sophie quelled the sigh that built in her chest. Yes, he wanted her all right. For work, not for play.

Her nerves were stretched raw by the end of the week. She and Zach had worked late most nights, he even later than she, and he'd beaten her into the office each morning, as well. Even getting half the chance to check around his office was impossible. Lila certainly would have no worries on that score.

Sophie knew it was important that they get their pitch perfect for the Manson project. It was something that Alex had started before he had disappeared. It had become a matter of pride for both her and Zach to deliver no less than Alex would have when it came to sourcing investors for Ally Manson's start-up. The seventeen-year-old prodigy was an IT genius and Alex had been hugely excited by the opportunity to launch her idea of a nationwide computer-assisted home disability network. Astute investors at the outset would be integral to her success and, by association, theirs, as well.

For all the hard work and long hours they'd been putting in, Sophie was still surprised that Zach was spending so much extra time at the office, and most of it with his door closed. A couple of times she'd entered his office, only to hear him abruptly put his caller on hold or close his laptop so she wouldn't see what was on his screen. There was something going on that wasn't quite right, but she couldn't put her finger on it.

But it wasn't his hours that had unsettled her the most this week. It was just him. For some stupid reason, Lila's news had triggered something in her that had begun to blow out of proportion. She'd been able to control her attraction to him without any issues over the past eighteen months, even though they'd started working together more closely since Alex had disappeared. Now, though, the proximity was driving her crazy and affecting her concentration when it was more important than ever that she be on the ball.

It was as if her hormones had gone into overdrive, as if her friend's pregnancy had triggered a persistent reminder that Sophie was twenty-eight, painfully single and childless—and that time wouldn't forever be on her side. Her body remained in a heightened state of awareness even when she wasn't around Zach—but when she was, it was a hundred times worse.

He only had to brush past her for every cell in her body to spring to aching, and embarrassingly eager, attention. And her dreams…she didn't even want to think about them, or about waking—hot, sweaty and wanting in the worst way.

Several times this week she'd battled with canceling tonight's dinner but some masochistic inner demon stopped her whenever she found the words to tell him their date was off. But it wasn't a date, was it? It was a reward, a bonus. He'd made it clear in his invitation he wanted to say thank-you for her work. Technically, she'd earned it. Still, the prospect of an evening in his company was winding her as tight as a spring and her constant battle with herself had worn her defenses ragged.

Sophie shut down her computer at five-thirty and slid her backup drive into the side pocket of her bag. She planned to have a long, hot, invigorating shower and take her time over getting ready for this evening. She was going to enjoy herself, dammit. He was an attractive, well-educated and erudite male. Tonight was a reward for her hard work. She had earned every second of it and would savor every bite of what would no doubt be a delicious meal.

"Everything still okay for this evening? I thought I'd pick you up at your place around seven-thirty."

Zach's voice cut through her resolve like a hot knife through butter. She couldn't do it. She couldn't sit opposite him over an intimate meal and not be driven totally crazy with wanting him. She'd be hopelessly uncomfortable and make some stupid mistake, like letting him know how she felt, and no doubt he'd end up embarrassed for her. It would be a kindness to both of them to avoid being in that situation altogether.

"About tonight," she started.

"I've made our reservation for eight," he continued before stopping to give her a sharp, assessing look. "You're not pulling out on me, are you? Thinking about dinner at Claire's tonight has been the only thing that's kept me going through the TV dinners and takeout all week."

"Yes, I… Oh, um, no," she vacillated. "There's no need to pick me up. I can meet you there."

"What kind of a gentleman would I be if I didn't collect you? My mama would be ashamed." He gave her a cheeky smile, then rattled off her address. "That's right, isn't it?"

She gave a brief nod.

"Good, I'll see you at seven-thirty."

He was gone and out the door before she could say another word. The faint chime of the elevator in the outer reception area galvanized her into action. If she didn't hurry, she wouldn't have time to gather her wits together for tonight, let alone present herself respectably.

Forty-five minutes later, she surveyed the underwear she'd chosen to wear for tonight. *Respectable* was the last word on her mind. She'd bought the tiny scraps of fabric during a girls' day out with her friend Mia Hughes, who worked as Alex's housekeeper. The pale-green silk had looked stunning against her ivory skin and the texture had felt deliciously sinful. The half-cup bra made it the perfect piece to wear beneath the deep-V-necked teal dress she'd bought for a "sometime" special occasion but hadn't yet had the opportunity to wear. Like the underwear, she'd bought it on impulse—something she rarely did after a childhood of poverty—and tonight seemed perfect to wear it for the first time. Armored with the expensive threads, she would feel like a million dollars—and right now she needed all the strength she could get.

Sophie luxuriated as long as she could under the stinging-hot spray of her shower, lathering her body twice with the expensive scented shower gel Lila had sent to her on her last birthday and which she saved only for special occasions. As she dragged her washcloth over her breasts, she felt her nipples pebble in anticipation of the evening ahead.

As conflicted as she felt about tonight's dinner, she knew one thing very clearly in her mind. She wanted Zach Lassiter with an ache that went straight to her core, and if all she could have of him was this meal together, then she was going to make the most of it.

By the time she'd toweled off, styled her hair and applied her makeup, she felt almost bulletproof. It felt decadently wicked sliding into the tiny panties and hooking the bra before stepping into her dress and shimmying it up her body. She cast an eye at the clock beside her bed. Darn, she was cutting it close. Sophie reached for the zipper and started to tug it upward while slipping her feet into the killer heels she'd bought with her dress, but the zipper halted in its tracks.

She squirmed, trying alternately to tug it down or ease it up. Blasted thing was stuck fast and no matter how much she wriggled, it just wouldn't budge. She tried to ease the gown off her shoulders but quickly gave that up as a bad idea. The dress was designed to be a skintight fit. There was no way she was going to get out of this one easily. What to do, what to do? She gave the tab on the zipper another jiggle, but still no luck.

This kind of thing did not happen to her. She was the consummate swan, gliding effortlessly across the lake of her life—outwardly, anyway. Control was the foundation of her life. Being at the mercy of something as inane as a stuck zipper was not something she was used to, not from this end, anyway.

But then again, the past week had been an exercise in levels of frustration she'd never experienced before. She huffed a sigh of exasperation. Zach would be here any minute now and, of course, right on cue, the doorbell rang.

Three

Zach pressed the doorbell again. He had said seven-thirty, hadn't he? He checked the TAG Heuer on his wrist. Yep, he was on time. He stepped back from the door and checked the side window. Lights were on inside and, yes, right there he saw a flash of movement through the crack in the drapes.

The door slowly opened.

"I'm sorry to keep you waiting," Sophie said, her light-brown eyes looking bigger and sexier than ever with the smoky makeup she wore.

"No problem, we have half an hour until our reservation." He hesitated, waiting a second for her to invite him in, but when no invitation was forthcoming he continued, "So, shall we head out?"

She gave him an awkward smile. "Yes, well, maybe in a minute or two. I've got a bit of a problem with my dress."

"Anything I can help with?"

Her dress? Maybe that explained why she wasn't opening the door fully and was talking to him with just her head popped around its edge.

Sophie sighed. "I think you might have to."

Huh. Well, there was no need for her to sound so eager, he thought. He waited again for her to open the door wider and to invite him inside. Still, she didn't move.

"Is this something we can fix here on the doorstep?" he inquired.

"Oh, no. No, of course not. You'd better come in."

She looked flustered, something he wasn't used to seeing in her. He raised his eyebrows slightly and, taking the hint, she finally eased the door wide enough for him to pass through. She closed it behind her, keeping her back to the door.

She was as skittish as a newborn colt. He wondered what had gotten her so riled up.

"It's my dress," she started, then stopped just as suddenly and worried her lower lip with her teeth.

His eyes were caught and mesmerized by the action. Sophie's lips were slick with gloss, several shades richer than what she normally wore to the office, he noted, and the color made him think of candy apples and all their sugary sweetness. Would she taste like that, too, if he nibbled on her lip the way she was doing right now?

Zach dragged his gaze from her mouth and from the forbidden thoughts she incited in him. She was strictly off-limits. What had she been talking about again? Yeah, that was right. Her dress.

"What's wrong with it? You look great to me," he said, letting his eyes skim over her.

Oh, yeah, she was the full package tonight. Her hair sat smooth and sleek in its unassuming bob. Fine, pale-blond hair that made his hand itch to reach out and feel if it was as silky soft as it looked. Desire hit hard and hot, driving a surge of lust straight to his groin. He fought to control it. This wasn't what tonight was supposed to be about. He firmed his jaw and wrestled his libido back under control, right up until she turned around, exposing the long ivory column of her back.

"My zipper. It's stuck. I think I've caught it on the lining. Do you think you can work it loose for me?"

Think? The woman expected him to think? Without realizing it, his hands moved to her back. One knuckle grazed against her warm skin. He felt her flinch beneath his touch.

"Sorry," he muttered and forced himself to concentrate on closing his fingers on the delicate tab of the zipper.

"Do you think you'll be able to work it loose?" she asked over her shoulder. "I'd hate to have to rip the dress."

He quelled a groan at the image of doing just that. Of ripping the dress from her slender form and exposing more than the hint of sheer green confection that was masquerading as underwear beneath her gown. If that was the back of her bra, he could only begin to imagine how alluring the front would be. On second thought, better not to imagine it, or his current discomfort would be nothing compared to what his body would do next.

"Sure," he ground out through gritted teeth. "Just give me a minute."

His knuckle brushed against her skin again. This time she didn't flinch, but he could see the reaction to his touch as tiny goose bumps rose in a scatter across her skin.

"I'm going to have to pull your dress down a bit,"

he said, warning her of his intention to hold the fabric firmly against her as he pulled the tab gently up.

There, he could feel the teeth letting go their grip on the smooth silk lining of the dress. He was almost sorry when the tab pulled free and he slid it up, closing that enticing view of her back and the band of her sheer bra.

"You're all set," he said, dropping his hands to his sides and stepping back from her. "And you look amazing."

"Oh, thank you," Sophie said, turning around to face him.

"Shall we go?" he suggested, eager now to put them in a position where they were surrounded by other people and where he wouldn't have to continually fight this urge to reach out to pull her to him and find out just how good those candy-apple lips tasted after all.

"Let me get my bag."

He looked around the apartment as she went into what he assumed was her bedroom. He liked what she'd created here. Despite its compact size the apartment had a light, airy feel to it—the furnishings combining a few good pieces with what were obviously refurbished yard-sale finds. It felt like a home. More so than his expertly furnished mansion on the outskirts of town. He loved living there, but it lacked the small touches that made a place more than just somewhere to eat and sleep. Mind you, for the amount of time he'd spent there lately, what did it matter? Besides, it was a prime investment. One he wouldn't hesitate to flick off when he was ready to move on or when the market was right. He didn't like to attach sentiment to assets the way his parents did. You never got ahead that way.

"I'm ready. Sorry for the delay, Zach."

She'd replenished her lip gloss while she'd been in

her room and looked so incredibly perfect from head to toe it was difficult to equate the woman in front of him with the slightly nervy creature who'd greeted him when he'd arrived. Women. He'd never understand them fully, nor did he really want to. Who had the time? But he certainly was in the right frame of mind to appreciate this one.

He guided her outside and waited on the path while she locked the front door, then escorted her to his gleaming black Cadillac CTS-V Coupe.

"New car?" Sophie inquired as he held open the passenger door for her.

"Not so new, but it's my fun car. For weekends and special occasions only," he said before closing the door on the inviting view of her slender legs.

He settled himself in the driver's seat and started up the engine, allowing the growl of the 6.2-liter V8 engine to course through him for just a moment.

"You like it?" he said with boyish enthusiasm.

"It certainly looks and sounds sleek and fast, but somehow I would never have pictured you driving something like this," she commented as she fastened her seat belt.

"No, why so?"

"With your reputation, I'd have picked you for European flash."

"My reputation?" He raised an eyebrow.

"For being a risk taker. I would have thought your idea of a fun car would be some imported speed machine."

He smiled. "No, proudly American all the way, that's me."

She was easy company on the drive to Claire's, not being one of those women who felt the need to fill empty space with constant idle chatter. By the time they entered the restaurant, he felt it safe enough to lay his hand at the small of her back without worrying that it would trigger a wave of heat and desire. He couldn't have been more wrong.

The instant his hand rested against the fabric of her dress, he could sense the warmth of her skin through its fine weave. The effect was more of a tsunami, threatening to swamp him. This was ridiculous, he thought as they were promptly shown to their table. He worked with Sophie every day. She was attractive, he'd always found her so, but he'd never had this kind of trouble keeping his attraction under control before.

He'd also never been quite this close to her before, never touched her, never smelled the light fragrance that trailed her now—a scent that reminded him of summer and roses and long hot aching nights. Maybe this was the real reason he'd envied his friend his capable assistant. Maybe it had nothing to do with her efficiency and all too much to do with the fact he hadn't been laid in far, far too long. He'd have to remedy that. For now, though, he had to exert his self-control—and remind himself that Sophie was off-limits.

They sat at the table, Sophie refusing an aperitif when the waiter offered.

"Did you want to have a glass of wine with dinner?" Zach asked as he perused the menu once the waiter had left.

"Sure, just one."

"Not much of a drinker, then?"

"No, I don't like losing control."

For a second there she looked surprised that she'd admitted as much. Zach gave her a nod.

"I know what you mean. It can bring out the best and the worst in people."

She smiled back at him, relief evident in her eyes.

"I'm glad you understand. Most people just think I'm some kind of control freak."

"I've seen you at work. I *know* you're a control freak," he teased gently.

A light flush colored her cheeks and she ducked her head, her short blond hair swinging forward to obstruct his view of her face as she put her attention to studying her menu.

"Anything in particular take your fancy?" he asked. "I know the steak is always good here."

"I've never been here before, but it all looks good to me."

"Did you want an appetizer?"

"No, I'll save myself for dessert."

"Ah," he said, "a sweet tooth, huh? I didn't know that about you."

"I would think there's a lot you don't know about me."

Her tone was slightly quelling, but Zach was nothing if not challenged by her statement. He noticed the exact second she realized the light of that challenge had reflected in his eyes.

"Not that I expect you to know anything about me, that is," she said, her voice flustered.

"I'd like to know more about you," he answered, closing his menu and laying it on the crisp white linen of the tablecloth. "We work together. There's no reason why we can't be friends also."

Sophie swallowed. There was a determined set to his jaw that she knew from watching him at work meant he wasn't going to let this go. Why, oh why had she been so careless with her tongue? From the second she'd agreed to this dinner she'd been off balance. Could she be friends with someone like Zach? She very much doubted it; especially considering how *unfriendlike* she'd felt when he'd ever so slightly touched her while rescuing her dress from the voracious teeth of the zipper.

She'd all but melted at the unintentional caress, and had had to draw on every last ounce of self-control to stifle the gasp that had threatened to expose her reaction to his touch. No, *friendly* was the last word she'd ever employ to describe how he made her feel.

Could she be friends with him, though? Honestly?

It would be tantamount to torture. But worse, how on earth could she explain *that* to him? She took a deep breath and let it go slowly before speaking. "I'm pretty boring, really."

"You think so?" he answered, cocking his head and locking those startlingly green eyes of his onto her like twin lasers.

She squirmed a little in her seat, and immediately regretted the action as she became even more aware of the silky softness of her underthings against her skin and of the way the silk lining of her dress whispered against her body.

"Well, by comparison to you, for example," she deflected, quite neatly she thought, right up until he let loose with a rich belt of laughter.

"Oh, Sophie, you couldn't be more wrong. I've been told I live to work. There's not much more boring than that."

Even though he joked at his own expense, she could see the light of an old hurt lingering in the back of his gaze. Compassion flooded her. A man in his early thirties, in his prime both mentally and physically, living to work? It was sad. Something must have shown on her face, because he sobered and reached across the table to grasp her hand.

"Don't worry about me," he said, his voice dropping intimately.

Oh, she wasn't worried about him, not exactly. Of more immediate concern was the crazy flip-flop her stomach did as his thumb lightly stroked the inside of her palm. She gently pulled her hand away from his, relief and regret fighting for supremacy as he made no move to stop her.

"What makes you think I'm worried?" she asked, a note of defense in her voice.

"You have the most expressive face," he answered, his eyes not shifting an inch. "It's easy to see when something's troubling you."

As long as that was all he could see, she thought worriedly. What if he could see the longing she felt every time she looked at him? A man like Zach Lassiter was so far out of her league it wasn't even funny. But a girl could dream, couldn't she?

"There's not much that troubles me," Sophie said, closing her menu and placing it in front of her. She could barely concentrate on the culinary delights the pages offered. It wouldn't matter what she ordered, it was bound to be delicious.

"But you're worried about Alex, aren't you? I can see it on your face every morning when you arrive in the office and he's not there."

"Aren't you?" she countered. "He's your friend as well as your colleague. Aren't you worried about where he is, what might have happened to him?"

"Sure I am," Zach replied. "I feel frustrated I can't do more. The only thing I know I *can* do is keep all those plates he had spinning from falling down so that when he comes back everything will still be as it should."

"Is that why you're in the office so early each morning and don't leave until after I do?" Sophie asked without thinking.

He looked startled at her question and his eyes became slightly shuttered before he replied. "Yeah, there's a lot going on right now."

"Can I take more of your load off you?" she offered.

"No, of course not. You already are the glue that holds the office together. No one could expect more of you than you already give. In fact, let's make that the end of the subject of work. We're here tonight because I wanted to thank you for everything you've done, not discuss how you can do more."

He smiled at that last sentence but Sophie could tell it was a deflection. She'd been wondering what it was that was keeping him in the office for such long hours. He was right, she did keep the office running, and she knew exactly what stage each of Alex's projects had been at before he'd disappeared. Unless Zach had suddenly become wildly incompetent, he should have been able to handle everything—his own portfolios included—within normal business hours, which made her wonder: What was he really up to?

Four

She reached for her water glass and took a tiny sip, letting the cool water slide down her throat while her mind worked overtime. The mere fact that he hadn't sent more work her way for all the extra hours he was putting in was a glaring red flag to her. Why hadn't she seen that earlier?

Her work had always increased incrementally depending on Alex's output. Zach was doing something he didn't want her to know about, he had to be. She was almost certain of it. But it was anyone's guess what, exactly, that was. Could he somehow be involved in Alex's disappearance? Was he actively hiding his tracks? The questions were never far from the back of her mind, even though she didn't want to believe Zach was entangled in whatever had led to Alex virtually vanishing off the face of the earth.

There had to be some way she could find out.

"I do appreciate your hard work, Sophie," he said,

dragging her attention back. "And I know you put in some very long hours. Doesn't your boyfriend object?"

"I don't have a boyfriend," she answered, feeling warm color flood her cheeks again.

Silently she cursed her fair complexion. There was only one man she was interested in and he was sitting right opposite her. What would he say, she wondered, if she told him exactly that? She fought back a smile. He'd probably make some excuse to draw the evening to a close early.

"I'm surprised. You're a very attractive woman," Zach said seriously, ensnaring her in his gaze like a predatory cat with its prey.

"Thank you," she said, dipping her head.

"So, no boyfriend, huh? What do you like to do in your spare time if you don't have a significant other filling it with you?"

"I read a lot, romances mostly and the occasional crime thriller." She shrugged. "And I keep house, see friends. The usual things."

"Did you grow up around here?"

She nodded, "Sure did, and I couldn't imagine living anywhere else. Big cities aren't my thing and I love the lifestyle that Royal has to offer."

"It's a different pace here, that's for sure."

"What about you?" she asked, happy to turn the tables on him for a change. Even though she was fairly certain of the answer, she couldn't help probing. "Girlfriend?"

His face closed again, all warmth replaced by a sorrow that flashed briefly across his face. "No girlfriend," he said emphatically. "Too many other things going on in my life."

And what would they be? Sophie wondered as the

waiter interrupted them to take their orders. After ordering a lamb shank braised in red wine, she wasn't at all surprised to hear Zach order the eye fillet steak. He looked like a man who liked his red meat.

"Lamb?" he said to her after the waiter had taken their orders and moved away from the table. "You come to what is essentially the best steak house in Texas and you order lamb?"

Sophie shrugged. "It's what appealed to me at the time. At least I ordered a domestic wine, not some fancy imported beer. And here I thought you were proudly American all the way?"

"Fair point." Zach nodded slowly, then smiled as said fancy imported beer was put in front of him and her Californian white zinfandel placed before her.

She watched as he took a long pull of the chilled lager, her eyes mesmerized by the muscles working in his throat and then by the smile of satisfaction on his beautiful features as he put the glass back down in front of him. Oh, how she wished that she could be the reason behind a smile like that from him one day. The second the thought formed, she beat it to the back of her mind again. That way could only lead to trouble.

"Now that makes a hard day at the office worthwhile," he said with a soul-deep gratification that brought another smile to her face.

"Simple pleasures, huh?"

He looked at her as if to check if she was still teasing him after the imported beer comment, then gave another nod of acknowledgment. "Yeah, when it comes down to it, it's the simple things that matter the most. Don't you agree?"

"Totally. For me it's home and family. One day I hope to have both."

"You've made a lovely home out of your apartment."

"Thank you, but it's still not mine, y'know? Soon I hope to be able to put a deposit on a place of my own. Something small, with a bit of a garden. Somewhere that I can truly call mine."

And that was another reason why she was so darned worried about Alex Santiago. What if he didn't come back? Would Zach continue to keep the business running or would he fold things up and go back to where he'd come from? Where would she be then? She earned good money now and her options within Royal to earn the same weren't bountiful. If she lost her job, that could be the end of her dream of owning her own home—she'd never earn enough to make mortgage payments and to afford extras like the private investigator she'd hired to find her sister.

"And that's important to you because?" Zach coaxed.

She took a moment to think before answering. "Stability, not being at someone else's whim or mercy."

"Sounds like there's some history there."

She shrugged. "Isn't there always?"

"Can you tell me?"

Sophie sighed. It wasn't something she tended to bandy about, but there was something about Zach's gentle questioning that made her actually want to tell him.

"Nothing spectacular. My dad died when I was a baby and my mom remarried. They had my sister and life was great for a while, but then a few years later my new dad died in an accident at work and our lives turned upside down. We had to move out of our home and my sister went to live with her aunt, because Mom couldn't cope with us both with the hours she had to work to make the rent. It was hard for her," Sophie added just in case Zach felt inclined to be judgmental. "We had to keep moving around, which I hated, but even then I used to keep house to help Mom out. She'd usually juggle two jobs, or pull double shifts when she only had one source of income. Things settled down a bit after I finished college. She met someone new, they married and I moved out and got my own place."

"They kicked you out?"

Zach sounded defensive and Sophie rushed to disabuse him of that. "No, not at all. But I was ready to stand on my own two feet. Mom and Jim marrying didn't make any difference to that. No, that's not entirely true. I felt better about moving to a place of my own, knowing she'd be taken care of."

Zach looked at Sophie across the table. She'd talked more personally to him tonight than she ever had in the time they'd worked together, but there was a huge amount she wasn't saying. Listening to her, he could begin to understand why she was so good at what she did. She was used to keeping things together, keeping things calm. It was a sure bet that she'd done her best to help her mother out at home from an early age—that capable manner of hers was second nature now, but there had probably been a time when it was all about security.

His own upbringing had been completely the opposite. At least up until his dad had been laid off from his job. Even then, forced to take on a menial position at a much lower wage, his father had insisted on paying Zach's way through college. It was one of the reasons Zach worked so hard now. He didn't ever want to be in the position his parents had been when his father's job had been downsized. And he'd made it up to them for all the sacrifices they'd made to ensure he'd had the best opportunities available to him. It didn't sound like Sophie had been so lucky.

"And your sister? She's the one in that photo you had with you on Monday, right?"

Sophie inclined her head, her cap of hair swinging gently forward to caress her cheek. His fingers itched to do the same and he reached for the dewy glass in front of him instead.

"You said you don't stay in touch. How come?"

"Her aunt formally adopted her several months after she took Suzie to live with them. She told Mom they didn't think it was good for Suzie to continue to have contact with us. Said it was too disruptive."

There was a world full of hurt and loss in her simply chosen words.

"And your mother agreed to that?" he said incredulously.

Sophie's eyes flamed. "You have no idea of what it was like for my mother. Don't you dare judge her."

Zach put up both hands in surrender. "Whoa, I'm sorry. I didn't mean to touch a nerve there."

After Anna's car wreck, he'd fought tooth and nail to keep his son—arguing with doctors and specialists until he was blue in the face. But after Blake had been on life support for six weeks and the doctors had repeatedly told him his son had no brain activity, Zach and Anna had had to let him go. For the life of him he couldn't understand how a parent could give up a child the way Sophie's mother had, not when she had every reason to fight to keep her.

"Mom couldn't work and take care of us both at the same time. I was in school. Mom couldn't afford day care and Suzie, well, she was a bit of a handful. She had been a demanding baby and that didn't change as she got older. She was always just that bit more vulnerable than I was, needed that much more attention. Giving Suzie up wasn't Mom's first choice, not by any means, but she had to do what was best—for all of us. And Suzie's aunt, well, family money aside, her late husband had been a very wealthy man. She didn't have to work and she was childless. Mom knew that Suzie would be the center of her world, that she'd be loved and cared for as she deserved to be—in ways we couldn't."

Her choice of words—saying "we" rather than "she"—explained so much about the person she was today. He didn't doubt that Sophie harbored some guilt that she hadn't been able to look after her sister enough or to help her mother more so that their small family wouldn't have to be broken up. He tried to imagine what it would be like growing up feeling like that, and couldn't.

"Sophie," he said reaching across the small table to take her trembling hand in his, "I'm sorry. I didn't mean to sound judgmental. It must have been tough."

She hesitated a moment and he could feel her inner battle rage as she fought to drag her emotions back under control. Eventually she pulled her hand out from beneath his.

"It was, but it's in the past now."

But it wasn't in the past. He could see that just by looking at her. The hurts, the loss—they were all still there. Their shadows lingered beneath the calm surface she presented to the rest of the world.

Zach fought the nearly overwhelming urge he had to tell her it would be all right, that he would do what he could to assuage the pain of her past, that he'd fight her dragons for her and lay them at her feet. Grappling to get his own emotions under control, he reminded himself that he'd already taken that road once before, with Anna, and look where that had led them. No, the last thing he needed was to complicate his life with another wounded bird.

He all but welcomed the waiter out loud when the man arrived with their plates of steaming-hot food, and Zach turned the conversation to more general things, including the latest developments at the Texas Cattleman's Club. He entertained Sophie with a passable impersonation of Beau Hacket's blustering about the new child-care center. By the time they'd finished their meal and enjoyed dessert and coffee, he thought he'd managed to chase those shadows from her eyes. Even if only for an evening.

He wished he had a reason to make their night last longer. She was good company and, when the conversation stayed well and truly off the personal, a great talker. Even more, she was a perceptive listener—he supposed that was part of why she was so darn good at her job. She was always subconsciously taking note of what was happening around her, always ready to put her hand on what was needed almost before the need arose.

Sophie Beldon appealed to him on an intellectual level, and her subtle beauty was a siren call—from the way her eyes began to sparkle before she would laugh right down to the enticing shadow of her breasts at the V of her neckline. And her mouth. God, her mouth. A jolt of longing shook him to his core. What would it be like to taste her, to feel the softness of those lips against his, to command their surrender?

Zach placed his coffee cup back on its saucer none too gently, a tremor in his hand betraying the need that fought for dominance over his heretofore steely control. Control won in the end as he signaled to the waiter for their check. He slid his card in the wallet and when the waiter returned with the receipt, he signed off with a generous tip.

He had to get Sophie home before he did or said something stupid. Before he went over the invisible line he'd drawn in respect of his working relationship, and *only* his working relationship, with her.

They made small talk on the short journey to her apartment building, extolling the virtues of the chef at Claire's and how much they'd enjoyed the food. When they pulled up outside her ground-floor unit, it was second nature to Zach to get out of the car first and open her door for her. He walked her up the short path and waited while she extracted her key from her bag.

"Well, thank you for a lovely meal. I really enjoyed it," she said simply once the key was in her hand.

Before he could reply, she stepped in closer and leaned up to place a kiss on his cheek. That was all it took for his instincts to kick in, for him to turn his face so that her lips met his instead. His arm curled around her waist to draw her more closely against his body and he angled his head ever so slightly so he could deepen their kiss.

Heat sizzled along his veins. Her lips were every bit as soft and delicious as he'd imagined and the tiny sound she made in the back of her throat sent his pulse racing. This was way more than he'd imagined—this scorching desire combined with the raging need he'd managed to keep firmly under control for so very long. Emotion rocked him, sharp and intense, and he knew their working relationship could never be the same again. He wanted Sophie Beldon from the gleaming top of her blond head to the tips of her dainty feet and everything, yes, definitely everything in between.

His hips flexed lightly against the softness of her belly. Her answering press back against him reminded him of what it felt like to be a man—to want with a gut-aching need so strong that it almost hurt to desire another human being this much.

And then, just like that, it was over. Cool night air swirled in the space between them. She was pulling away, her eyes glittering like whiskey-colored topaz, her lips still moist from their kiss and slightly swollen with the evidence of their all-too-brief passion. She dipped her head in that way she had, closing her eyes briefly.

"Don't," he said sharply.

"Don't?"

"Don't hide from me. From us."

"There is no us, is there?" she asked, her voice slightly shaky.

Every cell in his body urged him to say, "Yes, there is an us." To take her back into his arms again and to repeat the intimacy of what they'd just shared. But reason intruded with harsh reality. They worked together. More than that, they had to hold things together in the office until Alex's absence could be explained and he, hopefully, returned. And then there was Anna. The reminder was as sobering as an icy-cold shower.

"No, you're right. I'll see you Monday?" he said, stepping back from her—away from temptation.

"Yes, Monday."

He waited by his car until she let herself inside her apartment, and watched as her outside light went out, followed by the living room lights being turned on. Even then he had to force himself to get in his car and to start it up, put it in gear and drive away. He was a fool. He should never have let things get away like that. Never. It went against his code of ethics in so many ways, and yet there was still this invisible thread that pulled between them. A thread that grew tighter with the more distance he put between them.

Five

"You kissed him!"

"Mia, please, shh!" Sophie hissed across the table of the booth she shared with her friend Mia Hughes. "Besides, it was only supposed to be a short peck, a good-night and thank-you, not…not what it turned into, that's for sure."

Her nerve endings still buzzed with excitement even now, fourteen hours since Zach had seen her to her door. Fourteen hours since she'd been introduced to the most searing, blistering ardor she'd ever experienced in her entire twenty-eight years.

Mia moved in closer. "So, tell me. Did he make your toes curl?"

"Oh, Lord, yes. And everything in between."

"I knew it!" Mia laughed, leaning back against the back of the banquette. "Beneath that *GQ* look, he definitely has that smoldering-hot thing going on. Plus, he's so dark and mysterious."

Sophie squirmed in her seat and almost immediately wished she hadn't. Her body still hummed from the aftereffects of their kiss and the action just seemed to increase her discomfort.

"I still don't know what possessed me to do it," she confided in her friend.

"I know," Mia said confidently. "You've been attracted to him for the longest time. It was the next natural step."

"Well, natural or not, it isn't happening again. I kind of put him off."

"You what?"

Mia's voice rose again, attracting the attention of the other patrons of the Royal Diner. Sophie felt her cheeks flame.

"Do you think you could maybe keep it down a bit?" she pleaded with her friend.

Mia looked like she was all control—her long dark-brown hair wound into a tight knot at the back of her head, her complexion flawless, the makeup around her bright-blue eyes subtle yet still managing to emphasize her natural beauty. She was usually quiet and no-nonsense, so her outburst surprised them both.

"I'm sorry," Mia said, contrite. "It's just you surprised me. You've been hungering for this guy for the longest time and you're telling me *you* were the one to back off?"

"It was too much."

"What, exactly, was too much?"

"Don't you put your counselor face on with me," Sophie laughed.

"Hey, I haven't finished my degree yet," Mia reminded her. "And don't try to distract me."

Sophie sighed. "Everything. Being with him for a

meal out, kissing him good night." She rubbed her eyes with the fingers of her right hand. "Even when he arrived and I had to get him to help me do up my dress."

Mia's face said everything her mouth didn't.

"Yeah, I got my zipper stuck just before he arrived. I couldn't get it loose and I had to ask Zach for help. He... he touched me. It was totally accidental and it was only with the backs of his fingers, but all evening I couldn't help but wonder—if I felt like that at a slight touch, what would it be like to have him really touch me?"

"You got it bad, girl," her friend teased.

"I know. If I'm not careful I'll ruin everything. We have to work together, for goodness' sake."

Mia smiled. "No reason why you can't have work and a bit of play."

"I dunno." Sophie shook her head. "I keep feeling like there's something going on with him. Something that he's trying to keep quiet. What if it's to do with Alex's disappearance?"

Mia was employed as Alex's housekeeper at his mansion in Pine Valley—it was a personal arrangement that Alex handled himself and fell outside of Sophie's responsibilities in the office. The hours were perfect for her while she finished up her counseling degree, and Sophie knew for herself what a generous boss Alex was. The work had never been terribly demanding, but with Alex missing Mia had become more of a well-paid house sitter than housekeeper. Sophie's words brought a frown to Mia's brow.

"You really think he might be involved?"

Sophie shrugged. "I don't want to think he is, but he's working strange hours lately and he's kind of secretive, y'know? Like putting people on hold if I come into his office while he's on the phone, or closing his laptop so I can't see the screen. It's not like him. I mean, sure, he's not exactly an open book on any day of the week, but he's even more closed than usual. And even last night he kept turning the conversation to me every time I tried to learn a bit more about him. He said he wanted us to be friends."

"Friends?"

"Yeah, and in my book, friendship is a two-way street."

"Hmm," Mia answered, looking thoughtful.

"What are you thinking about?"

"Well, of anyone, you're probably in the best position to figure out what he's up to, wouldn't you say?"

"Except I don't know what he's up to, that's the problem. It's not as if I haven't tried, but he's always a step ahead of me."

"Maybe you need to investigate a bit more. Check his computer? Check his phone log? Alex has to be somewhere. No one just disappears into thin air. He could even have planned this all along and Zach could have helped him. We can't automatically assume that Zach could be a bad guy in this."

"You're right," Sophie agreed slowly. "He might be helping Alex. I sure hope if he is involved, it's for that reason and not for anything sinister."

"I don't think he's involved in anything bad. If anyone is, it'd be that rat-bag David Firestone. Before Alex went missing, he asked me to make sure he had some champagne on ice. When I asked him what he was celebrating, he told me he'd beaten Firestone on an investment property deal. Apparently Firestone wasn't very happy when Alex beat him to the punch."

"Do you think Firestone could have done something to Alex? Was he really that angry?" Sophie asked.

"From what I understand, he was pretty steamed up. And I dunno, but he looks to me like the kind of guy who'd exact revenge if he thought it was due." Mia lifted her coffee cup and took a sip, then shuddered. "Cold, yuck!"

"I wonder where Alex is," Sophie mused.

"Yeah. I still can't help thinking that something bad has happened to him. He took nothing from the house. Not a change of clothes, nothing."

Sophie pushed away her plate, half her lunch still uneaten. "What can we do?"

"Information. We can gather information. It's the only thing we can do. You need to find out whatever you can from Zach if he knows more than he's letting on and I'll do what I can from Alex's side of things, especially about what he might have known about David Firestone. There has to be something at the house that can point us in the right direction." Mia leaned forward and reached for Sophie's hand. "By the way, speaking of information. How is it going with the investigator you hired to find your sister? Any luck?"

Sophie shook her head. "No. We thought he had a lead earlier in the week but it turned out to be another dead end." She met her friend's compassionate gaze. "What if it's all a waste of time, Mia? What if she's dead?"

"Wouldn't you rather know?" her friend said softly, giving her hand a reassuring squeeze.

"I guess so, and something tells me she's still out there."

"Then trust that feeling to bring her home." Mia cast a glance at her watch. "Speaking of home, I'd better head back to Pine Valley."

"How are things there? Are the media still camping out at the gates?"

Mia pulled a face. "They are. It's getting so bad I almost pulled out of coming today. I'm worried sick someone will break into the property and start poking around."

"But the police already went through the house, didn't they? If they couldn't find anything to explain where Alex might have gone, then I doubt any journalists could, either."

"Try telling them that," Mia answered with a wry grin. "Anyway, I'd better get going, I still have some studying to do. My turn to treat for lunch, okay?"

"That makes it my turn to tip," Sophie answered, leaving a few bills on the table.

The two women took turns to pay for lunch, even though Sophie would have been more than happy to have treated Mia more often. She knew her friend had tuition due soon, and while Alex was a generous boss, Sophie doubted that Mia could afford to splurge too frequently.

But at the cash register, both women were surprised when Mia's card was declined.

"Don't worry, I'll cover it." Sophie rapidly stepped up and unfolded the necessary bills.

"I don't understand it," Mia said, her face a little paler than usual and a worried frown creasing her brow.

"It'll just be some glitch at the bank. Give them a call and I'm sure you'll have it sorted out in no time. Look, can I loan you some money to tide you over the weekend? At least until you can sort things out with the bank?"

"No, no. I'll be fine. I'm sure."

Mia unlocked her car and threw her friend a quick

smile, but Sophie could tell she wasn't mollified. She didn't want to push. Mia was nothing if not proud and guarded her independence carefully.

"Well, don't hesitate to ask if I can do anything for you, okay? I mean it, Mia."

It was all she could do under the circumstances.

"Sure," Mia answered although Sophie knew her friend would rather walk through a field filled with ornery rodeo bulls than ask for help.

"Oh, and be careful about that guy, Firestone."

"I will, don't you worry," Mia said with a smile and a cheeky wink. "And don't do anything with your Mr. Lassiter that I wouldn't do."

Sophie couldn't help it. She blushed red hot again. She opened her car and settled inside, accompanied by the ring of Mia's laughter at her reaction. As she drove back home, she wondered just how far she'd be prepared to go to elicit information from Zach.

"Don't be ridiculous," she growled at her reflection in the rearview mirror. "You're no Mata Hari."

No, she definitely wasn't, but it didn't stop a ripple of anticipation from undulating from her core to her extremities. Could she do it? Could she try to seduce the information out of him? It went against everything she had inside of her and even if he did prove willing, there was nothing to say that he was the kind of guy who'd divulge his secrets during a bit of pillow talk.

Her inner muscles clenched tight at the thought of what it would take to actually lead to said pillow talk. She weighed it in her head during the journey home and all through her afternoon tidying around her home and getting her laundry done—her work outfits all pressed and ready for the week ahead. By the time she donned her nightgown and tucked herself into fresh, clean sheets, together with the latest novel she'd picked up, she was still a bundle of nervous energy and sick to death of the inner battle she'd waged with herself.

"Toss a coin," she said out loud when she couldn't settle into reading her book.

Sophie pushed back her covers and rose from the bed to cross the room and take her coin purse from her handbag. She grabbed a nickel and studied it carefully for a full minute before placing it on her thumbnail, ready to flick it into the air.

"Heads, I do it. Tails, I don't," she muttered grimly.

She flicked. The coin executed a graceful arc before she grabbed it with one hand, laying it flat on the back of the other with her fingers still covering what decision it had made. Slowly, she lifted her fingers.

Heads.

Six

"Best of three," she said on a whoosh of air.

Heads.

Heads.

Somewhere out there, someone had to be laughing at her, Sophie decided before returning the coin to her purse and climbing back between the sheets.

So the fates had decided she was to seduce whatever information she could out of Zach regarding his knowledge, or otherwise, of Alex's disappearance. Sounded simple, really. She flopped back against her perfectly aligned feather pillows and huffed out a sigh. She'd never succeed. She'd been the one to stop things going any further when he'd kissed her good night.

Then, surely, she had the right to change her mind…

Sophie reached out to flick off her bedside light and lay in the darkness staring blindly toward her ceiling. This was big. More than big, it was monumental. It went against everything she'd ever been brought up to be. But she owed it to Alex, didn't she? Her boss deserved someone in his corner. Oh, sure, she knew the police were investigating, but so far they'd been unable to turn up any solid leads. What if Zach had been actively pushing them in the wrong direction?

She rolled onto her side and closed her eyes. What if he hadn't? What if her conjecture was nothing but smoke and mirrors? At worst she'd potentially embarrass herself horribly, and she cringed at the thought. But at best, well, at best she could possibly find out vital information about Alex while in all likelihood having the very best sex of her life. And if this crazy scheme of hers turned out to be completely off the mark, well, it wasn't as if she wasn't powerfully attracted to Zach or that interest wasn't reciprocated. Who knew where things could lead?

A groan ripped from her throat and she threw herself onto her other side in disgust. It all sounded so mercenary. She was nothing like the kind of person who could carry this off. She wasn't designed for intrigue and seduction. She liked order, security. But that very security was threatened if she lost her job. While Alex and Zach were business partners, Zach could just as easily conduct his business anywhere but Royal. There was nothing and no one to hold him here.

She tried to think it all through logically, to weigh the pros against the cons, but as sleep claimed her she was no closer to a resolution. The next morning, after a surprisingly restful sleep, Sophie woke with the answer clear in her mind. Zach had already shown he was attracted to her, but he'd respected her when she'd stepped back. She'd leave it to him to make her decision for her. But nothing said she couldn't try to sway that decision in her favor.

She crossed the room to her wardrobe and considered the five outfits she'd hung in order for her Monday to Friday office wear. No, these wouldn't do at all. Not in their current incarnations, anyway. Sophie unhooked the suit and camisole that she'd decided on for Monday and tossed the camisole onto her bed. Was the neckline of the suit too bold or, with the right bra, would it be perfect for Operation: Seduction?

She giggled to herself as she put the suit back on the rail and considered Tuesday's ensemble. Yes, this could work, too. Instead of buttoning the form-fitting blouse to her throat, she could easily flick a few extra buttons open, and maybe wear a pendant—she had exactly the right one in her jewelry box—that would draw the eye, specifically Zach's eye, down.

Was he a boob man or a leg man, she wondered. No harm in covering all bases, she decided, eschewing Wednesday's getup as way too staid for the new Sophie Beldon. Instead, she reached for a short, straight skirt she saved for nights out with her girlfriends. Even her legs, which she'd always considered too short to be beautiful, looked good in this. Stacked with a set of heels she'd be invincible.

Sophie laughed out loud. She was starting to enjoy this.

"Roll on Monday," she said to herself as she closed her wardrobe and went to get herself some breakfast. "I can't wait."

Zach felt every one of his thirty-four years come Monday morning. Over the weekend he'd spent time on a video conference with a panel of doctors at the private mental health clinic he wanted to admit Anna to. Problem was, she'd dropped off the radar. Her parents said they hadn't heard from her over the weekend, something that wasn't unusual in their experience but, for Zach, combined with Anna's ultrafragile state of mind, it was red flag of titanic proportions.

When he hadn't been able to reach Anna on her mobile phone all day Saturday, he'd driven the fifty miles to Midland on Sunday morning. But the house they'd previously shared had been empty, without even a sign of recent occupation. It had all but slaughtered him to go upstairs to check the bedrooms and to discover that even now, almost two years since Blake's death, his nursery was still in the same state of casual disarray as it had been on the day Anna had taken him in the car and driven away after yet another argument with Zach.

None of her friends seemed to know where she was and it frustrated the hell out of him that he seemed to be the only person truly concerned about her whereabouts. If she'd ended up hurting herself, or worse, he didn't know if he would ever be able to forgive himself for not acting sooner to keep her safe.

Compounding his concern for his ex-wife was the complication of how he felt about Sophie Beldon. Taking her out on Friday night had seemed like a good idea at the time, but after a chillingly cold shower when he'd arrived home, he'd begun to examine his sanity in pursuing her as he had, even if it was as subtle as turning a chaste good night peck on the cheek to something so much more. He could have sworn the air around them had crackled with the energy that sprang to life between them. But she'd pulled back, and he'd been gentlemanly enough not to attempt to override her decision, no matter how much his libido had screamed at him to do otherwise.

Zach pushed open the door to the executive suite and started toward his office, only to be halted by Sophie coming out of the kitchenette.

"Ah, there you are. Good morning. Would you like coffee?"

He stopped in his tracks, his eyes locked on her as if seeing her for the first time, his mouth suddenly dry. Words failed him. He'd seen her wear this suit before, several times in fact. But he'd never seen her wear it quite like this. The rich amber fabric was a perfect foil for her eyes and the shining cap of her blond hair, but it wasn't the color that had arrested him. No, it was the fact that she most definitely wasn't wearing her usual demure something underneath it. And her breasts, they were soft gentle mounds peaking up against the lapels of her jacket.

"Zach? Coffee?" she prompted with a sweet smile.

"Uh, yeah. Coffee. Thanks. That'd be great."

He forced himself to turn toward his office and get himself under control. He felt as if he'd been ambushed and shook his head slightly. No. He had to be imagining things. And he continued to console himself with that thought right up until she came into his office with a steaming mug of coffee and bent down to place it on his desk.

Oh, yes, definitely ambushed. A hint of white musk and vanilla and something else that made him want to reach for her and repeat their embrace of Friday night— and more. Worse, though, was the glimpse he got of soft, warm flesh encased in some frothy cream-colored lingerie.

"Thanks," he said through gritted teeth. "Any news from the sheriff this morning?"

Sophie straightened and made a little moue with her lips. Darn it all. What was it with him and her lips?

"Nothing yet," she said. "Is there anything in particular you need me for today?"

He could think of several things right off the top of his head. None of them had anything to do with the work at hand, however.

"I'm fine," he said, reaching for the coffee and taking a long sip of the brew, burning his tongue and the roof of his mouth in the process.

He welcomed the pain; it was the perfect distraction from the torture his body was going through.

"Okay, then. Well, if you need me, you know where to find me."

She exited his office and he couldn't tear his eyes off her. It wasn't just his imagination. She was different from last week. Way different, and yet no less appealing.

And so it went each day. Her new fragrance, while subtle, managed to stay with him every hour in the office, driving him crazy. He was on edge constantly, and in a state of semiarousal from the instant he set foot in the executive suite until he drove himself back to his empty mansion containing his all-too-empty bed each night.

But it was her subtle brushes against his body when he least expected it that were his undoing. They were working late on Thursday night and she'd brought him the reports he'd been waiting on so he could send them out to investors with his recommendation. She brushed lightly past him as he stood staring at the mounting piles of paper on his desk, the outside edge of her breast touching ever so slightly against his shoulder.

The heat of her body seared through the blue silk blouse she wore and transferred past the high-quality cotton of his tailor-made shirt with the conductivity of electricity.

"Sorry," he said, pulling away from her even though it was her contact.

"No problem. Will that be all tonight?" she asked, barely moving a scant inch from his side.

"Yeah, you can go. Thanks for staying with me."

"No problem. What about you? Are you heading home now?"

"No, I still want to give these a final pass-through and compose the individual letters."

She turned slightly so her cutely shaped backside was resting against the edge of his desk.

"You're working too hard, Zach. Don't you think you should lighten up, loosen that tie of yours a little and cut yourself some slack?"

Slack? There was nothing slack in his body right now, in fact, every working part of him was exactly the opposite—taut and aching and frustratingly unsatisfied. Words failed him as she leaned a little closer.

"Or maybe I should just loosen it for you?"

Her fingers undid the work of his perfect Windsor knot in a matter of seconds, then gently flicked the top button of his shirt undone.

"There, isn't that more comfortable?" she said with a curve of her lips.

Before he knew it his hands were at her wrists, tugging her toward him until they were face-to-face.

"Comfortable? I'll show you comfortable."

He leaned forward and captured her mouth with his.

The relief was instant but short-lived as the perfection of kissing her incited a whole raft of new sensations within him. He pulled away.

"Tell me to stop now and I will," he growled, barely able to hold on to his instincts a moment longer.

In answer, Sophie captured his face between her hands and pulled him back toward her, her tongue slipping between his lips to caress and entice and thoroughly chase away any last rational thought of control. He gave over to the moment, to the rush of desire that consumed his body. For the first time this week, everything felt right. He sank into her warmth, her welcome.

She tasted of coffee and a sweetness that was pure Sophie and he couldn't get enough of her. His hands skimmed up her rib cage to touch the sides of her breasts. She groaned and pressed herself against him, her hands now on the buttons of her blouse, pulling them open and exposing the silver-gray lace cups of her bra. Behind the sheer fabric he could see her nipples, taut and prominent nubs of palest pink.

Zach bent his head to the warm swells of her flesh, pressing his lips to the crevice created by the push-up effect of her bra. Sophie shuddered in his arms as he reached behind her and unsnapped the hooks on her bra, releasing her breasts.

"You're beautiful, so beautiful," he said reverently, palming the full globes, his thumbs brushing over her nipples, drawing them to attention even more.

"You make me feel beautiful," she whispered in return, her hands now busy yanking his tie from his collar and loosening the rest of his buttons.

"I want you, Sophie."

"I want you, too. So much. For so long."

Her words slowly sank in. He'd been holding back,

determined not to engage in a relationship with her and she'd been willing all along? He was a crazy fool. Here she was, as hungry for him as he was for her, and he'd been nobly refusing to follow what his body had been begging for all this time.

Her small hands pushed his shirt aside before spreading across his chest. He gasped at the sensation of her fingers on his skin. It had been so long since he'd allowed himself to give and receive physical affection, to have pleasure from meeting a need that went soul deep.

He kissed her again, and again and again, his mind a haze of need and want and sensation. Somewhere along the line she shed her skirt, revealing tiny panties to match her bra and thigh-high stockings with lacy tops. His fingers skimmed the lace, stroked the softness of her skin, felt her tremble at his touch. His hand worked slowly past the edge of her underwear to the neatly trimmed thatch of hair at the apex of her thighs, his fingers stroking her heated core, feeling her wetness, her desire for him.

He reached behind her to push aside the papers he'd been so fixated on only moments ago and gently coaxed her backward onto the surface of his desk. Her legs splayed over the edge and he felt his breath catch in his throat. He'd never seen anything more wanton, nor more exquisitely feminine in his life. Zach slid his fingers into the sides of her panties, drawing them down her legs, exposing her lush femininity to him. She was spread before him like a feast to be devoured, and he a man who hadn't dined in so long he'd almost forgotten what pleasure was anymore.

Zach stood between her legs and bent over Sophie's prone figure and kissed her again, her hands thrusting in his hair, then down the back of his neck and to his shoulders, her nails digging into him as he trailed one hand up and down her body, taking his time discovering the shape of her, the feel of her skin against his palms.

"You feel so good," he murmured against her lips.

Beneath his mouth he felt her lips pull into an answering smile. "You should feel it from my side," she said teasingly, her voice ending on a gasp, her body going rigid as his hands trailed lower to tease the tops of her thighs.

"How about I feel *in*side," he responded, his voice thick with longing.

He gently parted her moist flesh and felt her tense in anticipation as he stroked the heated entrance to her body.

"You're enjoying this, aren't you?" she said, her voice strangled.

"Oh, yes."

Zach eased one finger inside her, her heat enveloping him and making another part of his body all the more eager to follow in kind. He stroked her inner walls and gently pressed his palm against her clitoris. The instant he did so, it was as if it catalyzed her body into paroxysms of pleasure. Her inner muscles clenched rhythmically around his finger, her hips strained upward and her cry of satisfaction filled the office. He slowed his movements, taking his time, easing his hand free even as she reached for him, dragging his belt undone and unzipping his trousers.

He almost lost it as her hands closed around his straining erection through his boxer briefs, but somehow he managed to regain control.

"I don't have any protection," he said through clenched teeth as she freed him from his underwear and stroked him from base to tip.

"I'm protected," she said in invitation. "Seriously, I'm clean, I have regular checks, I haven't had a partner in at least a year and I'm on the injection."

"Same, except more than two years and while my shots are up-to-date, we're probably not talking about the same thing."

He smiled, caught by the random humor of the situation even as his body trembled and his brain, and other parts of him, demanded he simply take her and be done with it. Take both of them on a ride to deliver a maelstrom of feeling. Sophie stroked his length once more, making him hiss a sharp breath in between his teeth.

"Then what on earth are you waiting for?"

"Are you certain you want this?" he asked, desperately trying to maintain his equilibrium even though he felt as if the top of his head would blow off any second now from the pressure building inside him. "I'm—I… I haven't been with anyone in a long time."

She met his gaze full-on. "I'm certain. I trust you, Zach, and you can trust me, too. I'm not the kind of girl who—"

It was all he needed to hear. "Shh, I know. I trust you."

And with those words of acceptance, he slid inexorably inside her body. Zach dragged in a deep breath and slowly withdrew again. This was pleasure and pain and everything in between. The gratifying impression of her slick body clasped around him, the piercing agony of holding back, of gripping the last vestiges of control. It was too much, especially when Sophie drew her feet up behind him. He heard her shoes drop to the floor seconds before her heels dug into his buttocks.

"Take me, Zach. I'm all yours."

The dam of constraint burst and he surged forward,

again and again until the sensations that drove him spiraled out of control. Vaguely he was aware of Sophie cresting another climax before his own flashed through his body—a kaleidoscope of color and sensuality, of connection and completion, of give and take.

He groaned as he collapsed, none too gently, upon her. Sophie's arms closed tight around his body, holding him as if she'd never let him go. His heartbeat pounded at a mega rate as aftershocks of fulfillment shuddered through him. Finally he pushed himself up, mindful of his weight on Sophie's much smaller frame.

Zach reluctantly withdrew from her body, his own instantly mourning the unforgettably sweet intimacy of their skin-to-skin contact.

"Are you okay?" he asked, extending a hand to her and helping her to her feet.

"Never better," she answered and went up on tiptoes to kiss him.

Despite having enjoyed mind-numbing sex with her only seconds ago, desire slammed into him anew and he wrapped his arms around her slender form and drew her firmly against his body, deepening their embrace. The buzz of his mobile phone caught his attention.

Sophie pulled out of his arms.

"I'll go and tidy myself up while you take that," she said, with another quick buss against his cheek.

He watched as she collected her things, her movements graceful as she walked naked out his office door and toward the private bathrooms that were part of the executive suite. He ached to follow her but his phone continued to buzz insistently.

He swept it up and answered it without checking the caller ID.

"Zach? Is that you?"

Anna.

Guilt slammed into him with the weight of a runaway freight train.

Seven

Guilt laced with a hefty dose of relief. They hadn't been a couple in any sense of the word for years—their marriage broken long before the ink was dry on their divorce papers—but she still needed him and relief won out as he silently thanked God she was okay.

"Yeah, it's me. Where have you been?"

"Oh, just away. I—I needed some space, some time to think about things. The neighbors said you were around, looking for me. Was it something special you needed me for?"

She sounded distant, as if her mind was on something else. Zach's concern inched up a few notches.

"No, nothing special. I just couldn't get hold of you and I was worried about you. Is everything okay?"

"I'm fine, Zach. No need to worry. Everything's just fine."

"Have you been taking your meds?"

"Of course I have. Despite what you may think, I can look after myself."

That was something he very much doubted. And the way she was talking worried him even more. She'd gone from calling him every day, crying through the phone, racked with grief for their dead son, to this. He'd call her parents and see if they could persuade her to stay with them for a few days. At least then he'd be able to relax in the knowledge someone was keeping an eye on her until he could convince her to see the doctors at the clinic.

"Okay," he said, forcing himself to sound calm. "I believe you, Anna. I depend on you to take care of yourself."

"Not to disappoint you, you mean."

He flinched. He didn't deserve that. "You don't disappoint me."

"But I did, didn't I?"

He sighed and closed his eyes. "We've moved past that now."

"Have we?"

"Anna, please. Don't do this to yourself."

"I'm sorry, Zach. Have I told you how sorry I am?"

Her earlier calm gone, her words were threaded with the grief he knew was on the verge of consuming her whole.

"You have, Anna, and it's okay. You have to believe me. It's time to move forward."

"I'm trying, but it's so hard."

"I know," he consoled. And he did know. There wasn't a day that went by that he didn't think about what Blake would have been doing had he lived. "But you're stronger than you think, Anna. You will get through this. Look, why don't you pack a bag? I'll call your parents and get them to take you back to their place for the weekend so you have some company, okay?"

"Okay. Yeah, I'd like that."

Zach quietly sighed and felt his body relax. She would be safe for now, at least. Getting her assurance she would pack her bag right that minute, he ended the call and then dialed his former in-laws, who were only too happy to agree to his suggestion that they take her into their home for a few nights. This disappearance of hers had given them a wake-up call and he could only hope that they'd be on board when he talked to them about Anna entering a professional care facility to guide her out of the black hole her grief had become before it consumed her whole.

Zach disconnected the call with his ex-father-in-law, closed his eyes and hoped with all his heart that Anna would be safe with them. Her parents had brushed off two earlier suicide attempts as accidental overdoses. Of course she hadn't meant to do it, her parents had argued when he'd struggled to make them see she needed more than just their help to get through. Their favored excuse was that she just had trouble sleeping since the accident, the other that she had trouble controlling the pain in her neck that continued to be a reminder of the whiplash she'd sustained in the crash.

He didn't deny that Anna had trouble with both those things, but her problems went far deeper, and since her parents were stubbornly oblivious to them, it was up to him to make sure she found a path out of her darkness. She needed someone in her corner to fight for her—to fight for her life, in fact.

The tension in his shoulders tightened when Zach opened his eyes and saw the chaos that was his desk. The reminder of what had just transpired in his office.

He reached to the floor to pick up his shirt and dragged it over his body. What an evening of contrasts. To peak on such a glorious high, and then descend to an all-too-sobering low.

Zach finished getting dressed and made a vague attempt to straighten his desk before giving up the idea as hopeless. He'd sort it out in the morning when everything was clearer. He slotted his laptop in its case and, stuffing his tie in his pocket, grabbed his jacket in the other hand and walked out into the reception area of the executive suite.

Sophie stood at her desk. She started to walk toward him, but then hesitated. Uncertainty was clear on her face.

"Are you okay?" she asked, her voice tentative, as if she wasn't sure if she should say anything to him.

Need filled him at the sight and sound of her. Not sexual, just the pure and physical need of one person desperately craving solace from another. He put his things on her desk and opened his arms to her, closing them around her slender form and feeling a deep sense of relief as hers closed around him in return. They stood like that for several minutes, not saying anything, just being—together. It gave him the strength he needed, for now.

Confusion chased through Sophie's mind. When she'd left Zach's office he'd been happy, satisfied. So who had been on the phone and what had they said or done to reduce him to this somber creature in her arms? She held on to him tightly, as if somehow she could infuse her spirit into him—give him the comfort he silently requested and so obviously sought from her.

That he'd come to her and that she could give it to

him made her heart swell with emotion. That he needed it, however, made that knowledge a bittersweet one.

She stroked her hands up and down the long muscles that bordered his spine, relishing the heat and strength of him through the fine cotton of his shirt, and felt him relax in increments. Sophie breathed his scent, like a spray of sea air, crisp and fresh. She'd never be able to visit a beach again, smell the tang of the ocean, without thinking of Zach Lassiter and this moment.

Beneath her cheek on his chest she felt him inhale deeply and then slowly let it go.

"Thank you," he said, loosening his embrace. "I needed that."

"Tough call?" she asked, burning with curiosity yet not knowing exactly how to inquire as to whom he'd spoken to.

His eyes dulled a little and his lips firmed into a straight line before he gave a small nod. "Yeah, but it's okay for now. I'm sorry it had to inter—"

Sophie laid a finger on his lips. "No, don't. Life intrudes. I accept that."

It intruded all too often and too harshly in her experience, which was why she was going to grab this time with him with both hands and hold on with all her might. Her discussions with Mia about seducing information out of Zach paled into insignificance in view of what they'd done here today. The chemistry they shared was all too rare and she knew she wanted more. More of him.

She looked him square in the eyes. "I never thought I'd ever say this to a guy, but here goes. Your place or mine?"

Zach didn't hesitate. "Mine," he said firmly and linked his fingers through hers. "We can stop by your place in the morning for a change of clothes, but up until about then I don't think you're going to need anything else."

Sophie smiled back at him, squeezing his fingers tight. She didn't trust herself to speak, her body racked by a surge of desire so sharp and so extreme it literally made her feel weak in the knees. They moved swiftly through the outer office. She was relieved that the hour was late and the space was empty of their receptionist and handful of admin and accounting staff because she was sure she glowed brightly with what they'd just shared—and what they were about to.

The drive to his home took about thirty minutes and it felt like the longest drive of her life. Every nerve in her body, every cell quivered on high alert. She tried to keep a grip on her thoughts and feelings but everything seemed determined to run through her entire being at Mach speed.

She'd never done anything like she'd done this night—ever. She'd never been the one to take control. Her relationships had always been so organized, for want of a better word. Courtships had followed a set procedure and sex, if it had progressed that far, had been satisfactory. Certainly not the mind-shattering culmination of pleasure she'd experienced tonight beneath Zach's ministrations.

A quiver ran through her at the thought of spending a whole night with him. It had taken every ounce of courage for her to say what she had and she'd fully expected him to bow out, to be polite but firm and excuse himself on one pretext or another. But he hadn't. A tiny inner voice squeed in delight at the prospect of enjoying more of what they'd already shared, of learning more about what pleased him as well as how he could please her.

Her stomach tied in a knot of anticipation as Zach slowed down the SUV he obviously used as his "non-fun" car and pressed a remote, causing the tall iron gates in front of them to swing slowly open. He accelerated up the long driveway and into a large circle, coming to a halt in front of an imposing two-story mansion sprawled at the end of the driveway. Subtle exterior lighting shone on the perfectly manicured lawns and hedges and trees that had been trimmed and topiaried within an inch of their lives.

Everything about the exterior screamed money and for a moment Sophie wondered if she was doing the right thing. Zach belonged to an entirely different world than her own. He had money. Real money, and lots of it.

"Are you coming?" Zach asked as he flung open his door and started to get out.

Sophie nodded and undid her seat belt. By the time she'd picked her bag up from the car floor, Zach was at her door and holding it open for her. His manners never failed to charm her and she unhesitatingly put her hand in his outstretched one. The instant she did so she was assailed by desire for Zach—raw, potent, demanding.

She was all but oblivious to moving past the pillared entryway and over the acres of cream and gold Italian tile. She automatically placed one foot after the other up the sweeping carpeted staircase—one hand resting lightly on the ornately turned black iron railing, the other still clasped firmly in Zach's heated grip. They traversed a gallery and stopped momentarily at a set of double wooden doors.

Zach twisted the handle and thrust the doors open, pulling Sophie along behind him as he entered the room.

Then all haste ended as he turned to close the doors behind him again. Elegant twin alabaster lamps cast a warm glow over the room from either side of the bed, but Sophie wasn't interested in the rich furnishings or the mile-wide bed on its slightly raised pedestal. She only had eyes for the man standing before her with longing on his face and a promise of more exquisite pleasure in his eyes.

And she wasn't disappointed. While their first coupling had been all haste and achieving satisfaction as quickly as humanly possible, this time they took their time. Learning one another's bodies, discovering the secret places that could reduce them to a quivering mass of need or laughing out loud. And this time when they came together it was slow, languorous and so very, very good.

As Sophie drifted off to sleep in Zach's arms, she knew she'd done the right thing, for both of them. The simmering tension between them had to let go somewhere. How much better was it to have simply given in to the attraction between them? There were no words to describe the drowsy contentment that suffused her—all she knew was that this was way, way more than a crush. She had feelings for Zach Lassiter that went beyond the magnetism that had drawn them together tonight.

Feelings that made her want to chase the shadows from his eyes, to see only joy and laughter reflected there. Feelings that made her wish tonight could be the first of many such nights—for the rest of her life, and his.

Eight

Zach knew the exact moment Sophie drifted off to sleep by the way her body relaxed and grew heavy against him. He pressed his lips to the top of her head, silently wishing her sweet dreams.

Although he was physically shattered, his mind was racing. What had he done? His life was complicated enough already without dragging Sophie into the mix. He should have exhibited some of the restraint Alex had always teased him about—sealed himself behind his so-called ice-man exterior and kept Sophie at bay.

Until last weekend's dinner, he'd had no real clue about how she felt about him. She'd always been warm and friendly, efficient and accommodating. But their kiss that night and her behavior since had steadily chipped through his resolve.

He inhaled the scent of her hair mixed with the fragrance she'd worn recently. Together, they were a heady blend and he could feel his body stir in response. Feel the tendrils of heat curl through him, inch by inch.

No one had ever made him feel like this. He'd never *wanted* anyone with quite this unadulterated desperation. He wanted more, he wanted to explore whether they could actually enjoy a relationship together. Learn all there was to know about one another. They already had the physical harmony down pat. There had been none of the awkwardness of discovering what worked or didn't. Every stroke had been sure, every touch adept. And the way he felt when he entered her body—it was the most sublime experience he'd ever enjoyed. If they could achieve the same synchronicity and understanding mentally, theirs would be a relationship without comparison.

A stab of guilt hit him fair and square in the chest. With Anna in such a vulnerable position, could he allow himself the indulgence of thinking like this, of feeling this way about another woman? What would it do to her? He didn't want to begin to think of how she might react. She depended on him emotionally, so much. It was a burden he'd taken without question. He owed it to her. After all, he should never have bowed to her father's pressure to marry her. He'd been ambitious and stupid, losing sight of his long-term goals and believing that he could shortcut the steps he himself had laid out for his future. Anna had been innocent in all of that.

He was doing his best for her now. Short of actually staying with her and physically taking care of her, which she'd made perfectly clear to him on several occasions that she did not want, he'd done the next best thing in sending her home to her mom and dad.

How would she cope, he wondered, if she heard he was in a new relationship? Zach tightened his hold on

Sophie's sleeping form and relished the warmth and feel of her against his naked body. He had barely dated since he and Anna had divorced. He certainly hadn't entered into any intimacy with anyone else—until now. Since she'd fielded the occasional call at the office, Sophie had some idea of Anna's dependency on him. How would she feel, he wondered, about his ex-wife's strong presence in his life? While he was concerned that finding out he had a new woman in his life could be the proverbial straw that broke the camel's back in Anna's case, would Anna be that for Sophie in return?

He clenched his eyes shut. Life could be so complicated. He'd thought he'd had it all under control when he was younger. What a stupid, arrogant fool he'd been to think he could merely follow a plan. People couldn't be categorized so easily, lives couldn't be forced to conform to his expectations. If he'd learned anything from his marriage to Anna, it had been how to adapt to change.

So what about the current change in his life now? Could he embark on what was a potentially precarious office romance, at a time when the office was already in a state of flux? Had the instability of having his business partner missing driven the two of them together and artificially accelerated their feelings for one another? Zach turned the thoughts over and over in his head.

He buried his face in the curve of Sophie's neck, inhaled the scent of her skin and her hair and felt the tension that had been coiling tight inside of him begin to unwind. Even while she was asleep, she did that for him. Soothed him. Eased his worries. And didn't he deserve that? Didn't he deserve some happiness? Some respite from his responsibilities? Sophie brought him that, and more. A decision settled over him before he even realized it. He was going to take what was his to take and let their affair lead where it may. He owed it to himself and he owed it to Sophie.

His body began to relax and he finally allowed sleep to claim him, secure in the knowledge that he could cope with this—one step at a time.

They were running late when they finally hit the office the next morning. A couple of times during the night they'd stirred, reaching for one another in the plush darkness of Zach's master suite to rediscover the highs they could share together. By the time dawn broke, Sophie felt both well used and completely sated. After breakfast in his gourmet kitchen, which had had her itching to inspect the contents of the refrigerator and try out the appliances with some of her favorite recipes, they'd made it to her house in time for her to shower and change into fresh work clothes, applying her makeup even as they drove to work.

Aside from a few raised eyebrows as they entered the building together—Sophie's cheeks flushed and eyes bright from the kiss Zach had planted on her in the elevator—no one had said anything. In fact, it seemed as if today was business as usual, with the exception that her body still hummed with contentment even though she had the odd twinge here and there to remind her of muscles she hadn't used in a while.

She hugged her arms around herself tightly for just a moment and let loose with a grin that spread from ear to ear.

"You look happy," Zach said from behind her. His hand pushed away a swath of her hair, exposing her neck, where he placed a hot, wet kiss just behind her ear. "I have a bone to pick with you."

"Really?" she said, fighting to control the shiver of longing that swept her body at his touch.

"I'm finding it incredibly difficult to focus on the work on my desk today."

Sophie swallowed. She could quite imagine. She got tingles every time she had looked toward his office door this morning.

Zach continued. "Do you have plans for tomorrow night?"

"Me? No, why?"

"The welcome party at the TCC is tomorrow evening, now that my application for membership has been approved. Would you like to come?"

He cast the invitation her way very casually, but she knew what a big deal this was. It was Royal's mark of acceptance from the very elite—the people to whom he looked for business, the people he asked to trust him with their financial stability. No small ask in these turbulent times.

"I'd be honored to attend with you. These events are usually quite formal, aren't they?"

"Yeah, I think so."

"Then I'll make sure I do you proud." She hesitated a moment, seeing a small frown crease his forehead, seeing his eyes look just that little bit distant. "You're thinking about Alex, aren't you?"

"Yeah. It'll be strange accepting the membership offer without my sponsor there. It won't be the same without Alex."

Sophie studied his face carefully, confused by her conflicting thoughts. If Zach truly did have something to do with Alex's disappearance, would he look so genuinely sorry that his friend couldn't be there with him to share the occasion of his entrée into Royal society? Or was he simply a very good actor?

If that was the case, what did that make her? All kidding aside, when she'd decided to investigate whether Zach had anything to do with Alex going missing—at any cost—had she really considered the emotional cost of entering into a physical relationship with him? She'd been stupidly naive not to realize that her heart was already intrinsically wound up in this man. Knowing she was falling for him, could she honestly believe that he was involved?

"Hey," Zach said, tipping her chin up with his knuckle. "I didn't mean to bring you down."

"It's okay. I can only imagine how tough it'll be for you tomorrow."

"I'm glad you'll be there with me," he said simply and the words hit her like blows to her gut.

The laughter she and Mia had shared over Operation: Seduction was a far cry from this reality. From the obvious pain Zach was feeling. There were probably a million reasons why he'd been more reserved than usual recently, why he was spending so much time on the telephone behind a closed office door. Lost for words, she could only give Zach a smile in return.

Work was busy and Zach was out most of the rest of the day with client meetings. It was later in the afternoon and Sophie had just received the call logs for the office and was about to go through them when she picked up an incoming call on Zach's line. Usually he diverted his calls to his cell phone when he was out, because the nature of his work meant he needed to be accessible to his clients, so Sophie was surprised to see his line light up.

"Zach Lassiter's office, this is Sophie speaking," she answered crisply.

"Mr. Lassiter, please," a male voice responded.

"I'm sorry, he's unable to take your call. I could get him to phone when he's available. Who's calling, please?"

"No, I won't leave a message, thanks."

And just like that, the call ended. Sophie couldn't quite put her finger on it, but something about the call, about the man making the call, set off her suspicions. She made a note on a message pad and tried to put it out of her mind for now, but curiosity kept pecking at her like a demented hen. There'd been noise in the caller's background, busy noise, and a voice over a PA system if she wasn't mistaken, paging someone. She closed her eyes and replayed the call in the back of her mind, but for the life of her she couldn't filter through the sounds to identify anything conclusive.

"Dreaming of me?"

Zach's voice startled her and her eyes flew open.

"Oh, always," she answered dryly. "You just missed a call, by the way. He wouldn't leave a message."

Zach flicked a glance at his watch. "Darn, I'd hoped to be here in time for that. Never mind, I'll give them a call back."

So he'd been expecting the call? Sophie tried to ignore the frisson of unease that raised the hairs on the back of her neck as he turned his back on her and went to his office and firmly closed the door behind him. Whatever it was he expected to discuss, it wasn't something he wanted her to overhear—again.

She forced her attention to the call logs, coding them as she went so the accounts department could apportion them accordingly. Alex had been a stickler for detail and while this was the kind of work normally assigned to someone on a far lower pay scale than Sophie's, he'd insisted it be part of her duties. So many of the numbers were familiar to her already, being those of people she knew who lived in and around Royal, but there was a new number cropping up in there over and over again. Sophie flicked back through the pages. There was no sign of that number being called while Alex had still been at the office, in fact, it appeared to be something that had only begun to occur recently and only from Zach's line.

Curious, Sophie picked up her phone and dialed the number.

"Good afternoon, you've reached the Philmore Clinic, how may I help you?"

"I'm sorry, I've dialed the wrong number."

Sophie put the phone down and turned to her computer, searching for the clinic. Her breath caught in her throat as the results lined up on her screen. She clicked on the main one, the website of the Philmore Clinic itself. Her eyes flicked across the screen as she read the home page, then more on the "about us" section of the site. It seemed the center was one for rehabilitation but also housed a secure-care facility for patients deemed mentally unstable and a danger to themselves or others.

Her thoughts boggled on the information even as she closed the window on her computer. Was that where Alex was? Had Zach somehow had him committed? Surely not. He wouldn't have been able to do something like that without medical intervention in some form, and surely if Alex had been unstable she or others would have noticed something, seen some warning signs. Maybe Zach just had a client who worked from there. Yes, that's what it had to be, she tried to convince herself. But even so, a little niggle of concern continued to hover at the back of her mind.

Maybe she should just ask Zach outright, she thought, her pen still hovering over the numbers. He came out of his office—his face drawn and his short hair rumpled, as if he'd been running his fingers through it—and his laptop case in his hand.

"Something's come up," he said heading for the main office door. "I'm going to a meeting, and I probably won't be back to the office tonight."

"Before you go, can you check this off for me? It's a number I can't code on the call log."

He strode over to her desk and swiveled the paper around to face him. "Just code it to me, personally," he said, his face grim.

"Personally," she repeated.

"Yeah, anything else?"

"Um, no," she replied, stung a little by his abruptness. Last night and this morning, Zach had been a different man altogether. It was clear something was bothering him. "Except, is there anything I can help you out with?"

"I wish you could, but no."

"Well, when do you expect to be back?" she asked, pressing gently for some kind of response that might give her an insight as to where he was going. "I thought maybe I could cook for you tonight, at my place."

"I'm sorry, I can't. I have no idea of when I'll be free tonight, so better not make plans. I'll pick you up tomorrow evening for the TCC event, okay? Look, I'm sorry I have to race out now. I'd hoped…"

"Don't worry. I understand."

Sophie interrupted before he delivered some platitude she couldn't bear to hear and while she mouthed

the words of understanding, she did so without sentiment. She didn't understand. Not one bit. Where had
the man she'd spent the night with gone? She'd thought
they were maybe at the start of something new together.
Something they both wanted. But here she was—left
staring at the door as he went out to the main office and
then, presumably, off to his unexpected meeting, leaving her with far more questions than answers.

Nine

Zach watched with mixed emotions as the other members of the TCC circulated around the room. Pride swirled foremost among them. That a boy from a middle-class upbringing could count membership in the Texas Cattleman's Club among his achievements was something else. His dad would be puffed up with pride when he heard.

He made a mental note to call his parents on Sunday at their retirement villa in Florida. A villa he'd bought for them, pushing past his father's stubborn pride, which wouldn't allow him to accept Zach's offer of relocating them to their dream destination. But Zach had been firm. He wanted them to be able to enjoy their retirement years—they'd both worked so hard all their lives to create a stable and happy home for him. Even when his dad had been made redundant from his work at an electronics design and manufacturing firm, they'd scraped by to make ends meet, refusing to touch the money they'd set aside for Zach's college education even though doing so would have lightened their load considerably. It was the least he could do to see them into comfortable and carefree years now.

Yeah, his dad would be proud of him, all right. But the man he'd most wanted to have by his side tonight wasn't here, and that troubled him deeply. Judging by the slightly more somber tone to the evening, he wasn't the only one who felt that way. Alex's disappearance remained the hot topic of conversation.

"Zach, now that the formalities are over, let me personally welcome you to the club." Gil Addison, the club president, extended his hand.

Zach shook it warmly. "Thank you. I'm honored to be a member."

"I see you're here with Sophie Beldon. She's Alex Santiago's assistant, isn't she?"

"And mine until he gets back," Zach said, his eyes finding Sophie across the room.

She was dressed in a simple black dress in a wraparound style that had him eager to unwrap her the minute he had her to himself. Before picking her up this evening, he'd called and left a message to suggest she bring an overnight bag and stay at his place. He hadn't realized just how much he'd been hoping she'd agree until he'd arrived at her apartment and seen the bag just inside the front door.

"You still think he's coming back?"

"I sure hope so."

"I take it you haven't heard any more?"

Zach shook his head. "Nothing."

Gil nodded. "It's a puzzle all right. I understand Nate Battle has been coordinating with a state investigator out of Dallas. I imagine she'll be in touch with you at some stage, too. Since you two worked together."

"Glad to hear the sheriff is making the most of all resources."

"Yeah. The investigator, Bailey Collins, seems to believe that Alex Santiago may not even be his real name. Kinda makes you wonder who he really is."

"And where," Zach added, shocked to hear that his friend might not be who he said he was.

Given the nature of their business and the massive volumes of money they handled on behalf of their clients, the news set alarm bells ringing in Zach's head. He knew the police had frozen Alex's personal accounts and the business accounts were running as normal at the moment, but he made a mental note to change the passwords again just to be certain. While they changed their passwords regularly, they were done in a system that Alex was familiar with. If he turned out to be some kind of criminal, they ran the risk of losing everything, especially with the Manson project about to go live in another week with a massive cash injection from investors.

"Let me know if you hear anything else," Gil asked before excusing himself as someone gestured to him from the other side of the room.

Sophie cut through the crowd to his side and Zach pushed aside his concerns about Alex to mull over later on.

"Enjoying yourself? It's quite a turnout for the new member welcome ceremony, isn't it?"

The night almost read like a who's who of Royal. Longtime TCC member Beau Hacket sat at a table with a bunch of his cronies—many of whom, he'd heard, had objected vociferously to Abigail Price's run for the club presidency a couple of years ago. Beau's wife, Barbara, mingled with a group of older women who'd circled around her daughter, Lila, and another TCC member, Sam Gordon. And those were just a few of the faces he knew or recognized.

"Sure is," Zach agreed. "Do you want to stay for the dancing?"

"Is that what you want to do?" she asked, looking up at him with those sinfully sexy whiskey-colored eyes.

Her eye makeup was a burnished gold, emphasizing the width and beauty of her gaze and Zach met the unspoken question in her eyes with an answering twist deep in his groin.

"Not by any stretch of the imagination, unless—" he bent to speak privately in the shell of her ear "—you and I are dancing naked."

He felt her shiver in response. "Then, in the interests of not scandalizing the company we're in, I'd say we should make our apologies and go, wouldn't you?"

Zach couldn't have agreed more. He reached for her hand and they began to make their way out of the room, stopping here and there to shake a hand or exchange a brief farewell. He'd brought the Cadillac coupe tonight and after the valet pulled the car to the entrance of the club for him, he ushered Sophie into her seat, getting an eyeful of her décolletage at the same time. She wasn't wearing a bra.

His mouth went dry, his fingers spasmed into a tight grip on the edge of the car door. In an instant he'd gone from semiaroused to rock hard, his pulse throbbing with all the pent-up longing of a flamenco guitar. He couldn't wait to find out what other surprises she had for him under that dress. He forced himself to let go of the door and close it before walking around the car and easing himself into the driver's seat.

Sophie, oblivious to his discomfort, flung him a smile in the darkened interior as he crawled past the cars lining the driveway and out onto the road. He completed the journey back to his place in record time— prepared to risk a speeding violation to get her home before the top of his head exploded, not to mention other parts of his body.

Not bothering to garage the coupe, he climbed from the car and grabbed Sophie's overnight bag from the trunk. She was waiting on the front step as he slammed it closed. He pressed his finger on the biometric scanner to allow him access to the house and to disable the alarm and forced himself to draw in a deep breath. They had all night and all day tomorrow. He could take his time, he could savor every second with Sophie rather than rush at her like the randy teenager who suddenly seemed to have control of his mind. And his body.

"It's a beautiful night, isn't it?" Sophie said, inhaling the night air redolent with the scent of the standard roses that lined the turning bay of the driveway.

He stopped a second and looked at her. Really looked. She all but glowed, the exterior lighting making her blond hair a shining cap of palest spun gold.

"You know what's beautiful," he responded, coming up the steps to stand beside her, "you."

He bent his head and kissed her, long and deep and wet, until he felt her tremble beneath him. It took all of his control not to drop her bag and sweep her off her feet and carry her to the nearest soft horizontal surface, but somehow he managed it.

"Come on inside. Would you like a drink before we go to bed?"

Surprise flitted across her face ever so briefly and he contained an inner smile. It was good to know she was as eager as he was to make it up to the master suite, but a little more anticipation never hurt anybody, even though certain parts of his body were making their objections to that statement well known right now.

"Sure, that'd be nice."

"Let's go outside," he suggested. "There's a wet bar in the loggia by the pool."

He placed her bag near the bottom of the staircase and took her by the hand again, leading her through the house and out to the pool terrace.

"Oh, my goodness!" Sophie exclaimed. "I never realized you had all this here behind the house."

He smiled. "The last time you were here we didn't exactly make time for the full tour, did we?"

A flush spread over her cheeks in response. "No, we didn't. Seriously, though, Zach. All this for one person?"

"It's an investment," he said as they crossed the terrace to the loggia and he gestured for her to sit down in one of the deep, cushioned wicker chairs facing the massive stone fireplace he'd commissioned for when the weather began to cool.

"Some investment," she muttered. "What's that way?"

Zach followed where her finger pointed down a colonnaded walkway. "My fitness center and spa, and beyond that there's a private putting green for when I'm entertaining clients. What would you like to drink? Champagne or something stronger?"

"Oh, champagne, please. You've entertained clients here?"

"I've had a few visitors stay in the guest house."

He popped the cork of the bottle he'd withdrawn from the wine fridge under the bar and poured two glasses. Sophie had risen from her seat and drifted over closer to the pool and even now was bending down to trail her fingers in the clear water.

"It feels like silk," she said, straightening and accepting the glass from him as he drew closer.

"Did you feel like a swim?"

"I didn't bring a suit."

"There are plenty in the changing rooms, but, with no neighbors for at least a couple of acres and no staff on duty except you and me," he said, clinking his glass to hers and taking a sip of the foaming golden liquid, "suits are entirely optional."

Sophie looked at him for a moment and allowed the sip of champagne she'd taken to trickle past the restriction of her throat. The idea of swimming naked with Zach all but made her throat close up in anticipation. The night air was still warm, the water of the pool just right. Beneath her dress she felt her nipples harden, her insides clench on a rolling pull that started deep inside her body and radiated out to her extremities.

She'd never done anything so risqué or erotic before in her life, never wanted to. But she couldn't think of anything she'd rather do right here, right now with the gorgeous man standing in this unbelievable setting with her.

"Well," she said, stepping out of his hold and placing her champagne flute carefully on a nearby patio table, "since suits are optional…"

She saw his fingers clench on the slender stem of his glass as her hands went to the knot at the side of her dress. Very slowly, she worked the fabric loose and unwrapped the gown from her body. She'd prevaricated over what to wear beneath it all day, but the lady in the shop had suggested she go braless—something she couldn't remember doing in polite company since she was about twelve years old.

At home she'd realized she really didn't have any other choice. The undergarment would have spoiled the visual line of the front of the dress and the way it was bound around her it provided sufficient support for her breasts. Her skin tingled on exposure to the night air that gently moved around them, laden with herbaceous scents from the manicured gardens that surrounded them.

Sophie's eyes flew to Zach's face. He was staring straight at her, his jaw clenched, his eyes shimmering. She let go of the ties and wriggled her shoulders, feeling the silk of her dress slide down her back to fall behind her, leaving her exposed in only her black lace panties, sheer black thigh-high stockings and her patent high-heeled pumps.

One by one, she stepped out of her shoes then, resting first one foot and then the other on a nearby lounger, she slowly rolled down her stockings. She flicked a glance at Zach. He hadn't moved so much as an inch and she could see the cords of his neck standing out prominently as he clearly battled to keep himself under control. A bulge behind the fabric of his trousers left her no doubt just how strained that control was right now.

With a private smile she hooked her thumbs in the waistband of her panties and slowly slid them off her hips. A strangled sound escaped his throat as she turned away from him and leaned over the table to pick up her wine, taking another sip before replacing the glass once more. As she stood, Sophie ran her tongue around her lips.

"Mmm, I really like that," she said and sauntered toward the edge of the pool before flinging another glance his way once she was poised at the edge. "So, are you joining me?"

Without waiting for a response, she executed a perfect dive into the silky water, relishing the sensation of it over her naked body. She'd barely made it to the end of the pool before a splash alerted her she had company. A rumpled pile of clothing lay where Zach had previously stood, and a dark shadow now approached her beneath the water.

Sophie put her feet down, relieved to discover she could touch the base of the pool, and waited for him to break the surface. She didn't have to wait long. Zach's arms caught around her middle and dragged her to him, his mouth closing on hers in a hungry caress that left her in no doubt that her little striptease had driven him to the edge.

She lifted her feet and clasped her legs around his hips, his erection trapped between their bodies.

"Do you feel what you do to me?" he growled against her mouth.

He lifted her slightly so her breasts were free of the water and buried his face against them. She shuddered at the feel of his lips, his tongue delving into the valley created when she'd clasped her arms around his shoulders. She tilted her head back a little, thrusting her chest out, her breasts aching for more.

Zach's hands loosened their grasp at her waist and slid up the ridges of her rib cage, slowly rising up her body to cup her tender globes. The ache inside her intensified as his mouth, so hot compared to the lukewarm water of the pool, closed around one tightly beaded nipple. His tongue swirled the sensitive tip, his lips suckling, his teeth gently rasping until she squirmed against him.

She felt the heavy ridge of his desire against her entrance and tilted her hips to stroke his length with her body. She craved him with a force she had never felt before, her entire being attuned to him, his breath on her skin, his heat against her body, his hardness against that part of her that was soft and willing and compliant—begging for his possession.

He completed his worship of her breasts, his hands dropping down now to cup her buttocks, to lift her ever so slightly higher so his erection sprang free, no longer trapped between them. Sophie clung to Zach's shoulders as he positioned her over him, as he slowly began to lower her down. She felt the blunt tip of him probing her body and she gasped her pleasure as he slowly filled her. He waited, allowing her body to adjust around him or simply to rein in some control; she could feel his muscles straining as if he was holding back.

"Let go, Zach," she whispered against his ear, and she flicked her tongue out to caress his earlobe before catching the neat nub of flesh between her teeth and biting gently. "Let go."

His fingers tightened on her buttocks and she felt the muscles in his thighs bunch beneath her before he withdrew slightly then surged back again. Sophie loosened her grip on his shoulders and caught his face in her hands, sealing his lips with hers and putting all her desire, all her hopes, all her dreams into her kiss. Her tongue caught and dueled with his and she suckled against it, drawing it gently into her mouth before letting him go and doing it all again. Zach moved again, this time settling deeper than before. She felt as if he knocked at the door to her soul as the first ripples of pleasure began to radiate out from her core, as her thighs clenched tight about him as she broke off their kiss to drop her head back.

A sharp cry ripped from her throat as those ripples sharpened, deepened into something even more concentrated, more powerful than anything she'd experienced before—as her body began to shake and all but implode on the bliss that ripped her from reality and flung her into a sea of sensual gratification far richer than her dreams.

Zach's mouth fastened on her where her neck flared to meet her shoulder, his teeth sinking ever so gently into her skin. All her nerves concentrated on that one spot, heightening her consciousness as he ground his lower body against her, as he drove her toward yet another peak. This time her climax was more gentle, more indulgent—and as she welcomed the rolling sense of completion that spread through her body once more, she felt Zach stiffen and tremble in her arms, his head now resting in the crook of her neck, his breath coming in sharp gasps against her skin.

It was several minutes before she could move, before she even wanted to move, but eventually Sophie untangled her legs from their grip around his hips. Zach lifted her off his body before gathering her tightly to him.

"I can't get enough of you," he admitted softly in the night air.

"I feel the same way," she answered, spreading her hands across his chest, feeling his heart hammering in his chest at a rate similar to her own.

Sophie's feet found the floor of the pool and she was grateful for the buoyancy of the water and Zach's steadying embrace, because she doubted she'd have been capable of standing on her own otherwise.

"Good, let's go and rinse off and head inside."

Zach guided her to the steps at the corner of the pool and together they ascended onto the patio. Sophie was surprised when she saw the outdoor shower, with multiple heads, set off to one side of the loggia and changing rooms. Although she wondered why she was surprised, since Zach had surrounded himself with the very best of everything.

Suddenly, despite her boldness these past few days, a small kernel of doubt invaded her mind. She knew she'd virtually thrown herself at him the other night in the office, but he'd chosen to take her out with him tonight. If a man like Zach only indulged in the best, what was he doing with her?

Ten

Zach felt Sophie's withdrawal as if it was a physical thing. Up until now they'd been so in tune with one another, yet he could feel her pulling away—mentally, if not physically.

Determined to get to the bottom of it, he turned off the shower faucets and walked a short distance to the changing room to grab towels and robes. Sophie followed him and grabbed a towel off the stack and began to dry herself.

"Here," he said, taking the towel from her, "let me."

"It's okay, I can—"

"I want to, Sophie."

She submitted to his request and once he'd finished drying her and helped her into a fluffy white robe, he swiftly dried himself off. Then, collecting their champagne and glasses, he showed her back inside.

"You hungry?" he asked.

"A little bit," she admitted with one of those sweet smiles of hers. "That was quite a workout."

He loved the way color stung her cheeks when she was embarrassed.

He led the way into the kitchen and pulled out a bar stool for her. As she sat down, he topped off their wineglasses and lifted his in a toast.

"To us," he said, "and a great weekend."

She lifted her glass also but remained silent.

"What is it, Sophie? What's the matter?" he asked.

He hadn't been imagining it out by the pool. Something was definitely playing on her mind. Something he'd rather she shove out in the open now so they could deal with it and move on.

"Nothing's the matter," she denied, taking a sip of her wine and firing a smile at him that could have fooled a man who hadn't made an art form over the past couple weeks out of watching her and finding out what made her tick.

He'd felt a pull of something toward Sophie when he'd started working with Alex but, as raw as he was after his son's death and the finality of his divorce he hadn't been ready to take a step in that direction. Now, though, was an entirely different matter. With the distance of time acting as a buffer, Sophie Beldon had brought so many aspects of him back to aching life.

"There's something. You've been fine up until just a while ago. Is it something someone said tonight? Something I said, or did?"

"No! It's not you. Seriously, it's not you. You're... well, you're perfect," she ended softly, her eyes downcast.

He snorted inelegantly. "I'm hardly perfect."

"But you are. You're successful, you have this amazing home. You can have just about anything money can buy and probably just about anything it can't."

He was puzzled. "And that's a problem?"

"Why me, Zach? Out of all the women you could have taken out with you tonight, of all the women you could sleep with, why me?"

He stilled, forcing himself to take his time answering her. He moved across the kitchen, grabbing a half loaf of French bread and slicing it into medallions and then taking some sliced cold cuts, relish and fresh cheese from the refrigerator. He laid the food on a platter and put it on the granite island where she was sitting before taking the seat beside her.

"Why you?" he repeated, lifting a hand to smooth an errant strand of hair from her beautiful, worried face. "Because deep down I know you're as lovely on the inside as you are on the outside. You forget, I've had over a year to get to know you, over a year feeling my way through my growing attraction to you. I'll be honest. As short a time as only a few weeks ago, I thought it would mess things up in the office if I acted on my feelings—not to mention complicate things in my already complicated world. But when you made it clear to me the other night that you felt the same way, that you wanted me, I knew I couldn't keep you at arm's length any longer."

He spread some ripe Brie onto a slice of bread and added a small dollop of relish before handing it to her. She remained silent, as if digesting what he'd said.

Zach continued. "And you talk about this place, my *amazing home*. It's not a home. It's where I live, sure, but it's not a home. I know what it takes to make a home and that is usually a family. I was lucky, I had that growing up. I had the security of having two parents who loved me and who I knew would move heaven and earth to give me every opportunity in the world to excel. And I have. I have excelled because I'm determined to always be the best I can be. Sure, I've taken risks. Some have paid off. Some haven't. I've learned to judge better what's right and what's wrong, and Sophie?" He reached out to cup her cheek, tracing the outline of her sensually full and wide lower lip with the edge of his thumb. "I mixed business with pleasure once before and it put me off ever wanting to do that again, but you, you're a risk I'm definitely ready to take. I want to know you better."

He leaned forward and kissed her, keeping it gentle, trying to imbue into his action what he suspected his words hadn't quite gotten through to her yet. When he broke off their kiss, her eyes glistened in the overhead lighting.

"Thank you," she said. "For being so honest."

"No problem," he answered with a quirk of his lip. "More to eat?"

"Yes, please. I'm suddenly starving."

The quirk spread into a smile. If she had an appetite, it was a good thing he knew exactly how to appease it. After they'd eaten and finished the champagne, they went upstairs to his room.

Zach turned down the bed while Sophie freshened up in the en suite bathroom. He reached for her as she walked back into the bedroom, tugging at the sash of her robe.

"In a hurry, Mr. Lassiter?" she asked teasingly, stepping just out of his reach.

"For you? Always."

And it was shockingly true. Since that first time they'd made love in his office, he'd been in a state of heightened awareness. A state of readiness that demanded to be assuaged. Not even last night's hurried trip to meet with Dr. Philmore to discuss a potential treatment plan for Anna had taken the edge off his craving for Sophie.

She stepped into the circle of his arms, her hands going to the lapels of his robe and pushing them aside and stroking across his chest. Her hands were silky soft as they traced the definition of his pecs before tracking a line down the center of his chest and lower, to his waist. Her fingers made quick work of the knot on his robe and she let the garment hang loose as her hands continued their voyage of discovery down his body.

He hissed in a breath when she reached his erection and closed a fist around him.

"Ready for more, I see," she observed.

"Always willing to please," Zach replied, trying to keep his voice light but failing miserably as his awareness of her touch, of the gentle pressure of her fingers, increased by increments.

"This time I want to please you."

"You always please me, Sophie."

"I don't think you fully understand me," she sighed with a wicked twinkle in her eyes, "but you will."

Before he could do anything to stop her, she'd sunk to her knees. Strands of her fine blond hair caught on the smattering of hair of his upper thighs, making him all too aware of what she'd planned. His muscles tautened, bracing themselves for what was to come. It didn't stop the groan of sheer delight from escaping his throat when her warm lips closed around the swollen head of his penis. Or when her tongue stroked the underside of the tip, where his skin was most sensitive. Sophie began to move her head, to take him deeper into the warm, wet cavern of her mouth, her lips and tongue continuing to cause flame after flame of heat to lick through him.

She made a sound deep in the back of her throat, a sound that sent a vibration rippling through him. It was his undoing. He'd planned to hold on, to maintain control, to take, but only so much—but with that one action she dominated him fully and his climax hit hard, unexpectedly, rocking him to the very center of his being.

As pulse after pulse pounded through him, she slowed her actions, the slick softness of her tongue now almost unbearable against his hypersensitized flesh. Almost, but not quite, he admitted as another jolt of completion made his hips jerk involuntarily. She let him go, stroking him once with her hand before rising to her feet.

Zach's heart was still pounding in his chest but he reached for her, closing her in the circle of his arms and holding her, his chin resting on the top of her golden head. She felt so perfect in his arms. How could he have continued to deny himself this?

Eventually he loosened his hold and sat on the bed, pulling Sophie down with him. They lay down together, facing one another.

"What did I do to deserve you?" he asked.

She smiled in return. "I've been asking myself that question all night."

Zach traced the edge of the lapel of her robe, delighting in the fine trail of goose bumps that followed the path of his fingertip. He moved in closer, flicking out his tongue to follow that same path down the V of her robe and then back up the other side.

"I think this should go, don't you?" he murmured, undoing her sash and tugging it loose.

Slowly he traced the outside edge of her robe with his tongue once more, then blew cool air from his mouth over her moistened skin. She gave a small shiver, one that had little to do with temperature, judging by the blush that now spread across her chest. Her breasts lifted on each breath she took and he followed their shape with his tongue, again blowing that cool air over her skin. Sophie's nipples grew tight and extended, their pink tips thrusting out. He kept up his gentle assault, touching her lightly each time, then blowing once again until she squirmed against the sheets.

"More, Zach. I need more," she implored him.

"In a hurry? You'll have to be patient. Now, where was I?"

It tormented him no less that he went back to the very beginning, commencing anew his tantalizing touches—each one awakening his body even as he knew it stoked hers to scorching life. Eventually, though, he could resist no longer. He had to feel her beneath his hands and he eased the robe off her shoulders, spreading the fabric wide on either side of her, exposing her nakedness for his eyes to feast on.

She moaned and pressed into his hands as he cupped her breasts, kneading them gently, his mouth alternating from one distended tip to the other. Beneath him he felt her legs move restlessly and he settled between them, one knee drawing up to her core. She was hot and wet against him, and it took every ounce of his considerable control not to simply take her there and then.

Zach began a journey down her body, forcing himself to take his time, to make sure that every caress, every touch brought her new waves of enjoyment. By the time he reached the delicate hollow at the top of her thighs, that enticing arrowed apex, he could smell her sweet, musky scent. It made everything in his body clench tight.

"You're torturing me, Zach," she said breathlessly. Her hands reaching for him, her fingers knotting in his hair.

"That's the plan," he said with a smile and lowered his lips to her heat.

She all but lifted off the bed as he closed his mouth around her, as his tongue unerringly found the pearl of nerve endings that he knew would drive her crazy, mad, over the edge. He wasn't wrong. His touch was like a match set to paper; she was a skyrocket waiting to be set free. Her body bowed, her hips lifting off the bed, her legs clamped tight around his shoulders as he swirled his tongue around that tiny bud of flesh, as his lips tugged and pulled, until with a scream of abandon she hurtled over the edge and into orgasm.

She was still a supple mass of limbs and torso when he pushed himself up over her, when he guided his length within her swollen, still-contracting center. Zach laced his fingers through hers, lifted her hands up, holding them beside her head. It was as if a line drew all the way down his spine to where they connected. Down his spine and then back up hers again, as if they were always meant to be this perfect together. Sophie's eyes flew wide open.

"Oh, my Lord. Again?"

Her climax chased the surprise from her eyes and she shuddered against him, her fingers now so tight around his own he'd begun to lose feeling in them. Her powerful, rhythmic contractions were enough to tip him completely over the edge, his climax drawing from the soles of his feet and reverberating through his body until he collapsed on top of her, breathless, stunned, pleasured beyond his imagination.

Sophie woke several hours later. It was still dark outside. She reached for Zach but she was alone, his side of the bed warm but very definitely empty. There was no light from the bathroom, either. She started a little as the bedroom door opened. Zach slid, naked, into the bed.

"Are you okay?" she whispered.

"Better than I've ever been," he said, feeling for her hand and lifting it to his lips to kiss it.

"Me, too," she sighed in satisfaction. "But how come you're awake? Can't sleep?"

Zach settled onto his back and she snuggled up against his chest.

"No, I can't stop thinking about Alex. Wondering where the hell he is and what might have happened to him."

"I know. It's never far from anyone's thoughts these days. So many people were discussing it at the club tonight. I hope he's going to be okay."

"Gil told me that the sheriff has brought in a state investigator from Dallas. She believes that Alex Santiago isn't even his real name."

Sophie stiffened. "Seriously?" Her mind raced. "You don't think he could be a fraud, do you? I'd find it hard to believe. It just doesn't jell with the guy we know and have worked with."

"I know. He's my friend and I'm worried now that maybe I didn't know him after all. But what worries me most is that, for one reason or another, someone's hurt him, badly. Otherwise I know he'd have done everything in his power to come back to us here in Royal. He has too much here to simply walk away from it.

"For a while there this evening I got angry, and started to consider it might be true, that he is a fraud. But I've been playing it over in my mind and it just doesn't fit."

Sophie lay quietly, listening to the confusion and frustration in Zach's voice and wishing she could do more to alleviate his concern. He certainly didn't sound like the kind of guy who could be involved in his friend's disappearance. If he was, he was a very good actor. She eschewed that idea the instant it came to her mind—the one that made her so anal about dotting every *i* and crossing every *t*—just wouldn't let it go.

That devil demanded one hundred percent certainty and it made Sophie nothing if not persistent, a trait her mother had frequently complained of while Sophie had been growing up. But it had gotten her where she was in life today; it had helped her growing up more times than she could remember, especially after Susannah had gone. And now as an adult, it had stood her in good stead as she fought to find her sister.

"What if you're wrong, Zach? What if he is a fraud, a very good one? People fool other people all the time."

As he could be fooling her right now.

"Yeah, I can't discount that. To be on the safe side I've just been online to change the password sequence for the bank accounts. With the Manson project going live soon, there is going to be a lot of money transferring through those accounts starting Monday. I can't risk anything happening to our investors' funds."

"Oh, Lord. I didn't even think about that."

Zach held her close. "Don't worry, I'm sure it would never come to anything."

They lay together, quiet in the darkness. After a while, Sophie realized that Zach had drifted off to sleep. She wasn't as lucky, as their short conversation kept playing around in her head, keeping her awake. So Alex might not have been who he said he was, but who was Zach Lassiter, exactly? He hadn't grown up here in Royal. No one really knew his background, a background that he kept very close to his chest.

It was still within the realm of possibility that he might have had something to do with Alex's disappearance, for all that he'd sounded genuinely concerned only moments ago. Maybe he'd even locked up Alex at that clinic he'd been in contact with so often. And now he'd changed the banking passwords. Sure, it made sense if he was genuinely concerned about Alex accessing funds illegally, but who was to say that it wasn't Zach who planned to do the exact same thing?

Sophie's stomach churned and she eased herself away from his sleeping form. All joking aside, had she just begun to sleep with the enemy?

Eleven

Logic warred with instinct. Instinct told her, over and over, that Zach couldn't be involved—that he was genuinely concerned for his friend. Logic told to her to make sure.

But how? All she'd managed to find out so far was he had been calling a private clinic frequently and very recently. He could have an investment client there for all she knew. She discarded the thought as soon as it popped into her head. Zach had a standard procedure for new clients, one that had always involved her creating a personal file for the client in their computer system. If his calls had been work related, she would have known. Besides, hadn't he told her only yesterday to mark those calls to his personal expense when she queried them on the call log?

He was up to something. Everything inside her said so. But what was it? His laptop! He carried it with him everywhere. If she could access his computer, she was sure she could find out just what was going on.

Sophie slipped from the bed and grabbed one of the robes off the bedroom floor. She stilled in her actions as Zach muttered something in his sleep and rolled over. In seconds he was breathing deeply again. She walked carefully across the thickly carpeted floor and let herself out of the room.

Where would be the most logical place to look for his computer, she wondered. She hadn't seen it in the kitchen when they'd been in there, but just off the kitchen was a high-tech den that had looked well used. Since every other area of the house appeared to be in show-home condition, she kept her fingers crossed that when Zach was home he used his den as more of a family room or office.

A trickle of unease ran through her as she made her way down the curved staircase to the ground floor and walked across the tiles toward the back of the house. She was going out on a very shaky limb doing this. Chances were she'd find nothing incriminating at all. At least she fervently hoped not.

Thankful that the outdoor lighting cast enough light through the floor-to-ceiling downstairs windows that she didn't need to turn on any lights, Sophie made her way through to the den. Long plush sofas faced one another across a large marble coffee table and two deep armchairs were positioned at one end, facing the large-screen television mounted on the wall above the fireplace. It was a cozy room, even in the semidark but, she reminded herself, she wasn't there to admire the decor.

Her eyes, now well adjusted to the half light, scanned the room. Yes! Right there, on the table, sat his computer. He'd left it open, obviously in a hurry to get back to bed after he'd secured the new passwords on the bank accounts. Had he simply let it go into sleep mode, or had he shut it down completely, she wondered, picking her way through the furniture. She really wanted to get this over with as quickly as possible. She had no idea how long it would be before he realized she was missing from the bed.

Sophie lowered herself onto the sofa and placed her finger on the mouse pad, a sigh of relief sawing through her as the screen brightened and came to life. She keyed in Zach's password, one he'd given her several months ago when he'd needed her to retrieve data for him on a rare occasion that he'd left the computer behind in the office.

She caught her lower lip between her teeth, worrying at the tender flesh as she decided where the best place to start looking for information might be. Email or general files? Email, she decided, and opened the program, then quickly typed *Philmore Center* into the search window.

As she did so, a worrying thought occurred to her. She'd been so quick to suspect Zach of some wrongdoing, but what if he was in contact with the Philmore Center because of something wrong with *his* health? A sharp stab of concern struck her square in her chest. He was always such a loner, mixing but never really socializing, always working long hours.

Alex had probably been his closest friend, and Alex was missing. Had Alex discovered something about Zach and his past, his mental health even, that Zach wasn't happy about? Sophie tried to quell her overactive mind and focus instead on the results that had come up from her search. There were several emails both to and from the Philmore Center. She scrolled down to the earliest one, dated only days after Alex was last seen.

She opened the email and began to read. The more she read, the angrier she became. Okay, so her investigating hadn't led her to any answers about Alex Santiago's whereabouts, but it had certainly led her into some new insights into Zach's character. From the looks of things, despite no support from the rest of her family, he was about to commit his ex-wife into a mental institution. She'd heard of some crazy things in her time but what kind of man did that to his ex?

He didn't know what had woken him, but Zach was surprised to discover he was alone in his bed. He waited a few minutes, but Sophie didn't return from wherever she'd gone. Dawn was still some time away, so he doubted she'd woken hungry and gone looking for food. He rose from the bed and grabbed a pair of sweatpants from his drawer, hoisting them to his hips before heading out of the room. No lights on anywhere, he noticed, his concern rising. Had she gotten up and headed downstairs, only to fall somewhere?

He checked each of the formal rooms off the main entrance. No, no sign of her there. The kitchen, maybe? As he entered the kitchen, he heard a click from the den. What the…?

He stopped in the doorway, watching Sophie as, with her face lit from the computer screen, she clicked and scrolled her way through something. A cold, burning fury lit deep inside of him. He should have known she was too good to be true. What was her angle, he wondered. And what the hell was she finding so damn interesting on his laptop? He stepped forward. Sophie was so engrossed in what was on the screen she didn't hear or see him. He stepped closer, looking at the computer screen as he did so. She was reading his private email.

Zach moved swiftly, leaning over her, his hand reaching for the laptop and closing it with a snap. Sophie jumped backward against the sofa before rising swiftly to her feet.

"What do you think you're doing?" Zach asked, working double time to keep his voice low and even.

It was no small feat, given the wild anger and sense of betrayal that warred for supremacy inside him. To his absolute surprise, though, instead of making some excuse or even some apology, Sophie blasted straight back at him with both barrels.

"More to the point, what on earth do you think *you're* doing? I knew there was something up with you, I just knew it. I thought it had something to do with Alex, but it's worse than that."

"Worse?" Zach gripped the back of the sofa with both hands to stop himself from reaching for her and giving her a darn good shake. "What could be worse than a friend, a well-respected businessman, going missing for no apparent reason?"

"Locking your wife into an institution and throwing away the key, for one!"

Zach straightened and shoved a hand through his hair. "This is ridiculous. You don't even know what you're talking about."

"I've read enough to see that you want her out of your hair. You forget, I've fielded her phone calls to you. I've seen how distant you are afterward. For whatever reason, she's still very dependent on you. You even mention it in your emails to Dr. Philmore. I used to think it was strange that you two still had so much contact together since your divorce, and clearly you do, too. I guess you've had enough, haven't you? Why else would you be planning to lock her away? Don't you think that's just a bit too draconian?"

"Draconian?" He shook his head slowly, his cynicism clear in the smile he gave her. "You really have no idea."

"You think?" Sophie replied with a snap, her arms crossed tight in front of her. "Well, let me tell you, it looks like you want her out of your hair. You want her institutionalized. How on earth can you even consider such an act against her?"

"Maybe to save her life?" Zach shot back. "I told you, you have no idea what you're talking about. Anna is a danger to herself. She's already made a couple of unsuccessful attempts on her life since our son died two years ago."

"Your son?" Sophie looked shocked. "You have a son?"

"Had," he corrected. "He died six weeks after he and his mother were in a car wreck. He was only ten months old. Anna lost control of her car on a wet road and slid sideways into a bridge abutment."

The words he spoke were simple, yet every one tore at his heart again as if the loss had been only yesterday.

"A-and Anna?" Sophie asked, sinking onto the chair again.

"She walked away with nothing but whiplash and more guilt than any parent should ever have to bear."

"Oh, my Lord. That's awful."

"She'd been trying to teach me a lesson that night. Showing me that she wouldn't be there waiting for me when I came home late. That she wasn't at my beck and call. Things had been strained between us before Blake was conceived, in fact we'd already begun separation proceedings when she discovered she was pregnant." Zach dropped onto one of the sofas and leaned his elbows on his thighs, his head dropping between his shoulders, the weight of all that had gone wrong in his marriage like a millstone around his neck. "We'd argued on the phone when she told me she was going out. I'd warned her the roads were tricky, to just wait until I got home—that we'd talk then. But she wouldn't listen."

The memory burned, painful and fresh in his mind. His mad dash home to discover her car gone from the garage, the house empty—worse, Blake's crib empty when he should have been tucked up asleep with his favorite teddy.

"I didn't know where to begin to look for her, but I didn't have to wait long. The police came to my door within minutes of me getting home. She was hysterical, they said, but that was nothing compared to the quiet after she was released from the hospital. Her parents just put it down to grief, both for Blake and for our marriage when she insisted we continue with the divorce we'd begun almost two years prior, but it was much more than that. She'd always been fragile, but losing Blake, being responsible for his death, that broke something inside her."

Zach dragged in a deep breath and let it out again before continuing. "It's nearly two years exactly since Blake died and Anna went missing this week. I was fearing the worst. Thankfully she's turned up again, but I'm not prepared to take that risk again that next time she won't turn up and that it'll be a policeman instead, on her parents' doorstep or mine, telling us that this time she's succeeded in taking her own life. She desperately needs help before it's too late. I'm determined she will receive it."

"Zach, I'm sorry. I really don't know what to say."

Sophie's voice sounded small. She looked small, as if she'd retreated in on herself. All her anger against him had dissipated in the face of what he'd told her.

But his anger had not. It welled anew and filled his heart, where he'd begun to care, begun to think that perhaps with Sophie he could think about a new start, a new relationship.

"There's nothing you can say, now, is there? You know, if you had any questions, all you had to do was ask me. You didn't need to go snooping behind my back."

"I thought you were hiding something to do with Alex. I never had any idea that you were trying to help your wife."

"My *ex*-wife," he corrected, but then her words slowly sank in. "You actually thought I had something to do with Alex's disappearance? You slept with me, thinking that I might be responsible—perhaps even for Alex's death? Oh, yeah, that's right. You were prepared to come at me, guns blazing, over putting Anna in a secure unit. Of course you'd suspect me of doing something terrible to Alex." He stood up and shook his head in disbelief seasoned with a fair dose of disgust. "What kind of woman are you? I thought we had the start of something special but you were just using me, weren't you?"

"Zach, I'm sorry, I didn't know," she protested, also rising to her feet, throwing her hands out as if imploring him to believe her.

"But you believed I might be capable of it. What were you planning to do? *Seduce* the information out of me?"

He watched as her face flamed with color—as her eyes dropped, unable to meet his accusing gaze a second longer.

"You were so secretive. I know I should have known better, should have trusted you, but every time I'd come into your office you'd obscure your computer screen or cover the mouthpiece on your phone if you were on a call. I don't know." She shook her head. "In light of everything that had happened, I just started to get suspicious. And while it started that way, with wanting to seduce information out of you, it's not like that now."

"You seriously expect me to believe that when I've just walked in on you on my laptop reading my private email? Excuse me if I find your protestations just a little hard to believe. Besides, don't you think the police questioned me thoroughly enough? You thought you possibly knew more than them or at least enough to believe I was guilty of doing something so stupid?"

"I'm so sorry, Zach. Please forgive me. Like I said, I should have known better. What you're trying to do for Anna is noble and kind and good. Just like you are. I can see that. I could see it all along, but I wouldn't let myself believe it. I'm the fool here. The crazy, stupid fool."

"And what if you were right, Sophie? What if I was the kind of guy who was capable of dispatching another man to wherever, whatever Alex has gone to? Don't you think that if you had concerns you should have taken them to the police and not embarked on some ill-advised personal investigation? Didn't you think that you might be putting yourself at risk, too?"

"Please, Zach, please give me, us, another chance."

Tears shone in her eyes. Tears of genuine regret, he had no doubt. But he couldn't find it in himself to forgive her. Not for believing something as nefarious as him possibly being responsible for another man vanishing from the face of the earth—a man who was not only his friend and business partner, but her boss, as well.

"That first time we made love, you said I could trust you. I believed you, and now you've proven me wrong. Go get dressed, I'll call you a cab," he said flatly.

Sophie took a step toward him, her hand out as if to touch him, but he stepped back, avoiding her.

"Don't," he warned. "I can't be in the same room as you right now. Just…go."

Twelve

Sophie let herself into her apartment just as the sun was beginning to peek its pale-golden face over the horizon. A new day, yet to her it felt like the end of the world. She'd betrayed Zach's trust in the worst way possible.

Her apartment looked just the same as it always did, yet Sophie knew without doubt that everything inside her had changed. She'd ruined everything. She—who was always so careful, always so considered—had destroyed her chance at happiness with a wonderful and worthy man. It was one thing to plot, however far-fetched it was, with Mia over lunch, and another thing entirely to act upon it.

She walked into her bedroom and turned back the bed before methodically unpacking her weekend bag and putting things away, with the exception of her dress, which she put in the hamper for dry cleaning. For once she couldn't take any comfort in mundane activities. Not when it felt as if her heart was breaking in two.

Sophie dragged on a pair of cotton pajamas and crawled into her bed, pulling the covers up over her and blocking out the cheerful light of day. Right now she didn't want to face the world, or anything or anyone within it. She'd made what was probably the worst mistake in her entire life and against every caution she'd given herself, too.

It was midafternoon when she awoke with a bitter taste in her mouth and a heaviness in her chest that made her want to cry out loud. She scrubbed her teeth in the bathroom, then went to the kitchen and poured herself a glass of water before curling up on her couch and staring emptily at the blank television screen.

No matter which way she turned things around in her mind, she'd been in the wrong. Zach had been decent and good and professional every step of the way. *She* had been the one to promulgate the kiss between them after that dinner at Claire's, not him. *She* had been the one to actively entice him and flirt with him in the office in the days afterward, even after pushing him away after their first kiss. *She* had been the one to make that first move, to make love to him, to experience the most incredibly uplifting and fulfilling lovemaking she'd ever had the pleasure to encounter. And she knew why it had been so very special because, somewhere along the line, she'd fallen completely and utterly in love with Zach Lassiter. And she'd been the one to destroy that love with her senseless suspicions and irresponsible behavior.

She lifted a hand to her face and pressed her fingertips tightly to her mouth to hold in the wail of grief that rose from deep inside her.

All her life she'd been the one who fixed things, who made things right by taking the load of others, by organizing the sphere in which she lived. But now she'd done the exact opposite. She'd hurt Zach; she'd pulled apart his trust when he'd so carefully, so cautiously, given it to her.

How could she fix this? Was it something she was even capable of? She doubted it. A man like Zach didn't commit easily, not when he already had so much happening in his life. The fact that he continued to work so hard to save his ex-wife from hurting herself and her family—no matter how blind they remained to her vulnerability—spoke volumes about his character.

Deep down Sophie had always known he was that kind of man. So why had she been so imprudent as to believe he had something sinister to hide? What business had it been of hers?

She owed him a massive apology and she needed to know exactly where they stood. Okay, so she knew he probably wasn't in the frame of mind to accept anything from her right now, but at the very least they still had to work together until this business with Alex was resolved. If she could prove to him that she fully accepted she'd been in the wrong, that she could make it up to him somehow, that she'd be even better at her job than she had been before, then maybe, just maybe, he might consider giving her, them, another chance.

Before she could change her mind, Sophie picked up her phone and dialed Zach's cell. He picked up on the fifth ring and she couldn't help wondering if he'd been prevaricating between answering and letting her go to voicemail. Before he could answer, she began to speak.

"Zach, please, hear me out. I know you probably don't want to talk to me right now—"

"And you'd be right. What is it, Sophie?" he replied, weariness weighting his every word.

"I…I…" The words that had been clear in her mind faded on a swell of insecurity. Silence echoed through the earpiece of her phone, forcing her to fill it. "Zach, do I still have a job?"

"That's a good question," he answered slowly. "You betrayed my trust. In the same position, would you continue to work with someone like that?"

Sophie wrinkled her brow. She could discern nothing from the tone of his voice. Nothing of the boss she'd worked with these past weeks. Nothing of the lover who'd filled her heart and driven her body to heights of pleasure she'd only ever dreamed of. A small sound of pain rose from deep inside her. She'd ruined everything.

"No, I guess I wouldn't. Not without a very good reason, anyway. But Zach, we have good reason to keep working together. Without me there you'll only be able to work at one-third capacity. Even with a temp to help you, between Alex's responsibilities and yours, you'd still be struggling."

She heard him sigh through the phone as her words rang true. Pressing her advantage, she continued.

"I know I deceived you, Zach. I went against everything I know in my heart to do so and I'm more sorry than you'll probably ever understand, but I can't leave you in the lurch at work. Not now. Please, at least let me have another chance there."

"All right, but step one toe out of line and—"

"You won't regret it, Zach, I promise you."

He made a sound, somewhere between a snort and a laugh, before answering. His words, when they came, chilled her to the bone.

"I already do. Every second," he said before severing their connection.

Sophie sank slowly to the floor, the phone still

clutched in her hand. She'd wanted to know where she stood and now she knew.

Sophie had to haul herself into work the next morning. Getting up early wasn't the problem; she'd barely slept a wink all night anyway. No, it was the prospect of seeing the recrimination in Zach's eyes that was the hardest thing to deal with. She knew she couldn't put it off. She, of all people, knew how important it was to face up to things, to keep putting one foot in front of the other, day after day, week after week. Eventually a new normal asserted itself. One you could live with. After all, wasn't that how she and her mother had coped after Susannah had gone to live with her aunt?

Somewhere in the dark hours of the night, Sophie had formed a plan to carry her through today, and if that was successful, it would hopefully see her through the next day, and the next.

"New normal, here I come," she said under her breath as she let herself out of her apartment and walked to her car parked on the side of the building.

By the time she reached the office she'd all but convinced herself she could do this. Right up until the moment she saw Zach's SUV in the office's basement parking lot. Her palms grew sweaty on her steering wheel and she had to concentrate to breathe properly. It would have been so much easier had she been the first to arrive today.

"New normal, remember?" she chided herself in the rearview mirror before alighting from the car and making her way to the elevator.

The main office was still unstaffed and despite the fact they had no idea of what she'd been up to over the weekend, she was grateful she didn't have to run the gauntlet. She knew she looked terrible. Two nights of broken sleep did that to a person. Two very different nights, she thought briefly before assembling her features into an expression she hoped would appear calm and capable and letting herself into the executive suite.

Zach's office door was closed and she could hear voices coming from inside. As she was putting her bag away, she heard his door open and Zach and an older couple came out. Past them she could see another woman sitting by Zach's desk. Zach closed the office door behind him and shook the man's hand, then leaned forward to kiss the woman on the cheek, only to be enveloped in a huge hug before, on a strangled sob, she reached for her husband and they walked straight out without so much as acknowledging her.

Zach's face looked strained. It didn't look as if he'd had any more sleep than Sophie had, she realized as he turned and went back into his office, closing the door once again.

There had been something vaguely familiar about the woman who'd left. She wondered if she should offer Zach and the person she'd seen still sitting in his office a hot drink. She supposed if she was going to break the ice between her and Zach, it would certainly be easier to do it with another person there to act as a buffer.

She put her coffee mug on her desk and walked the short distance to Zach's door, knocking sharply before twisting the knob and opening the door.

"Good morning," she said as smoothly as she could. "I wondered if you and your guest would like coffee or tea? Or perhaps some water?"

"Coffee, thanks," Zach bit out crisply. "Anna?"

Sophie felt a frozen chunk of lead settle in the pit of her stomach. This was Zach's ex-wife? Oh, Lord, she didn't know if she was ready for this. Coming face-to-face with the woman he'd chosen to marry, the woman who'd borne his son. The woman who so needed him now that he'd moved heaven and earth to do what he could to help her.

"Just water, thanks," the other woman said, her voice wobbly as if she was crying.

Sophie turned to her with a smile. "Sure thing, I'll be back in a mom—"

Her heart shuddered to a halt in her chest. The walls of Zach's spacious office began to close in on her. Too afraid to speak, to even draw a breath, Sophie straightened and walked out of the office, shutting the door behind her and leaning against its solid surface as if that was the only thing keeping her upright at this point in time.

No wonder the woman who'd just left looked vaguely familiar. The last time Sophie had seen her was twenty-two years ago. The day her sister had left the small rented apartment she'd shared with Sophie and their mother. The day Sophie, in her six-year-old innocence, had believed her four-year-old sister was going for a vacation with her daddy's sister. A vacation? It had been a lifetime. She could still see her baby sister waving excitedly as she was led away by her aunt. Sophie hadn't been able to understand why her mother was sobbing quietly in her bedroom when Suzie was going to come back soon, wasn't she?

It had been several weeks before her mother could even tell Sophie the truth. By then, her mother had become a brittle shell, even worse than she'd been after burying her second husband. It was as if, with Suzie gone, all the light had gone from her world, leaving Sophie to pick up the pieces of the life they'd had before. A simple life, certainly not one with any extravagances in it, but they'd had love. Six-year-old Sophie had made it her mission to show her mother every day that it would be all right, that they still had one another, that they could cope with the gaping hole in their lives where Suzie had been.

Suzie. *Anna Lassiter was Suzie.*

Sure, she'd grown up, she'd changed, and obviously her name had been changed, but Sophie would have recognized her little sister anywhere. The knowledge slowly seeped into her mind, spreading through her body with something akin to hope. But that hope was brought to an uncompromising end when she remembered exactly who Suzie was now.

Zach's ex-wife. An ex-wife she knew he still spoke to almost daily. An ex-wife he still felt duty bound to care for, and Anna desperately needed care if what Zach had told her over the weekend was true.

Sophie pushed off the door and went quickly to the kitchenette, automatically going through the motions of pouring Zach's coffee and a glass of ice water for Anna, complete with a slice of lemon. She put the drinks on a small tray and closed her eyes a moment, drawing in a stabilizing breath before she went back to his office and knocked on the door and let herself in.

She fought the urge to say something to her sister, to beg her to look her in the eyes and recognize what they had lost when they had been split apart all those long years ago. Her hand shook slightly as she put the water glass on a coaster on the edge of Zach's desk, beside where Anna was sitting. She took the opportunity for an assessing glance at the woman little Suzie had become.

It broke Sophie's heart to see the person sitting slightly hunched over in the chair, her blond hair long and stringy—desperately in need of a decent wash and style—her blue eyes, a legacy from her father, dull and filled with misery. She was far too thin, her clothes hanging off her shoulders. Sophie ached to put her arms around her, to try to assure her sister that everything would now be okay, but she didn't have that right.

Suzie was gone. *Anna* sat in the chair here in Zach's office. Anna who'd grown up with another life, another world, a husband, a child—the loss of that child. Sophie felt that loss now, as immediate and as sharp as if she'd experienced it herself.

"Sophie?"

Zach's voice reminded her of her task, of where she was.

"Oh, um, I'm sorry. Here's your coffee. Will there be anything else?"

She met his eyes for the first time since he'd sent her packing from his home, from his bed. She expected to see something there, some flicker or spark, but his gaze remained inscrutable, devoid of any feeling—for her, at least.

"No, thank you. Anna and I will be leaving shortly. I don't expect to be back in the office today and I'd like you to take care of my calls for me."

"Certainly," she said, taking refuge in her old persona. The superefficient executive assistant who never put a foot wrong. The one who hadn't been disloyal to her boss by suspecting him of being party to a heinous crime. The one who hadn't fallen irrevocably in love with him. "It was nice to meet you, Mrs. Lassiter."

The other woman didn't even acknowledge her and continued to sit, staring down at her hands, a slow, steady trail of tears rolling down her cheeks.

Sophie collected the empty tray and left the office,

her legs working automatically, her heart beating so hard in her chest she was surprised Zach and Anna hadn't heard it. In the kitchenette she bent to stow the tray in its cupboard then stood, unmoving, as if not knowing what to do next.

And she didn't know. Not in all honesty. She'd waited all this time to be with her sister again, yet now, having discovered who and where she was, there was no way she could land her discovery on the poor creature in Zach's office.

At least Suzie—no, Anna, she scolded herself—had Zach on her side, Sophie consoled herself as she felt the burning-hot sting of tears in her own eyes. The fact he had her right here, that he'd spent so much time in the past month or so trying to find help and that he'd apparently now convinced her parents—her adoptive parents—to support him in his quest to get treatment for Anna, spoke volumes as to how much he must still love his ex-wife.

Acknowledging the truth of that love was both a blessing and heartrendingly painful. A blessing because now, hopefully, her sister would have the chance to get well again, to be whole. To learn to accept her grief without allowing it to consume her very reason for continuing to live. The pain came in accepting that no matter how much Sophie loved Zach, no matter what chance she'd ever stood of maybe earning his forgiveness for letting him down the way she had, he wasn't hers to love. Never had been, never could be—not when he still loved Anna and when Anna needed him so much.

There was no light at the end of her tunnel. No hope. Even if, by some unexpected and unbelievable twist of fate, Sophie did receive Zach's forgiveness, she could never do that to her little sister.

Anna needed help, pure and simple. It started with Zach and the doctor he'd been consulting with at the Philmore Clinic, and maybe one day it could end with Sophie. She'd been incapable of helping her sister before today but there had to be something Sophie could do for Anna—even if it meant giving up the man she loved with all her heart.

Thirteen

Around visits to the Philmore Clinic, Zach poured himself into his work. It should have been a panacea, but what relief was it when each day he came face-to-face with the woman who invaded his every sleeping moment and most of his waking ones, too?

He hadn't known how Sophie would react at the office the first Monday they were back, but she'd behaved with her old consummate professionalism—her clothing tasteful and not in any way revealing, although with how thoroughly and intimately he knew her now, it didn't take any stretch of the imagination before his body was aching and seething with frustration. If only it could be as simple as just keeping it physical, but what had begun to grow between them had been more than that. At least he'd begun to think so. Foolishly, it seemed—and that was why the discovery of what she'd believed him capable of was even more agonizing. And although Sophie kept her physical distance during the times they had to occupy space together in the office, as intangible as it was, he still *felt* her with him.

The only good thing about the past week and a half was that Anna had finally agreed, with her parents' blessing, to be admitted to the Philmore Clinic and was actively participating in her rehabilitation. Even so, Zach experienced a clutch of fear in his gut each time his cell phone rang. What if she decided to leave, decided that she didn't need Dr. Philmore's treatment any longer? Or worse, that she felt well enough to leave long before she'd been medically cleared? It was a secure facility, but the choice to remain there was hers alone.

He could only hope as each day passed that she could see the good the clinic could do for her and find the strength from somewhere to battle back to the woman she used to be.

At work, though, there was a new tension in the air. Understandable, given the circumstances, but no less comfortable to live and work with. Sophie had been professionalism incarnate, keeping their interactions brief and to the point. Even so, he still felt uncomfortable around her, his mind plagued with memories of the intimacies they'd shared and of the shock of finding out she'd duped him all along. Added to that, the police had recently confirmed there were no new leads as to what the hell had happened to Alex. Some of their clients had grown antsy and Zach had spent a good portion of the week soothing the more volatile among them and talking them down from wanting to take their investment capital elsewhere. He hadn't been a hundred percent successful and that failure rankled him.

He was mentally exhausted by the time he drove home toward the end of the week, wanting nothing more than a scotch on the rocks and a good movie, but tonight he was expected at his first official TCC members' meeting. He could only hope that nothing contentious sprang up to make the meeting take longer than absolutely necessary. After all, per the agenda he'd been emailed earlier in the week, they were to discuss hiring a child-care-center manager. How contentious could that get?

It didn't take long to figure that one out, Zach discovered a couple of hours later.

"I still say it's outrageous that we're even contemplating the need for this here appointment of a center manager," Beau Hacket said, his color rising in his face in step with the volume of his voice. "Waste of club funds, in my opinion. What's wrong with a roster of parent helpers?"

"Beau," past president Brad Price said wearily from his position as chairman of the meeting, "stop hashing over something that's a done deal. The child-care center is happening, voted and agreed upon, whether you like it or not, and it will be a professionally run and certified entity in its own right. The appointment of a suitable and qualified manager is an integral part of that process."

"I don't like it and I don't mind telling anybody that," the older man blustered.

"So we've heard," came a wry voice from the back of the room.

Zach couldn't be sure who had said it, but the round of suppressed laughter through the meeting room that followed suggested there were several there who were totally over Hacket's old-school views.

One of the other older members stood up. "I still don't see why this is even an agenda issue."

"That's right," interjected Beau. "What difference does it make who runs the dang thing? It'll be nothing but a hyped-up babysitter service for women who ought to be looking after their babies at home anyway."

Zach could see Brad's wife, Abigail, starting to get hot under the collar. She'd held her peace up until now, but the old man had just pushed one too many buttons.

"Now just one minute—" she started angrily as her husband banged his gavel on the table.

Zach got to his feet and put up his hand. He could hear the others in the room shift in their seats as he did so—some curious as to why he'd stood to speak, others clearly just wishing the meeting would get over and done with.

"I think we need to look at this item calmly and carefully. What has been proposed is clearly far more than a babysitting service, don't you all agree?" He looked around the room, meeting the eyes of those who were clearly on his side as well as a few who weren't.

He continued. "We're talking about child care. Your *children's* care. Your *grandchildren's* care. This isn't just some short-term setup so your wives can enjoy a game of tennis or two on those new courts while your kids are cared for by some glorified nanny. There are enough of you who already have one of those, right?" A smattering of laughter, this time more of camaraderie than ridicule, filled the room. "This is to be a place where your children and grandchildren can learn to be worthwhile people, where they can learn to socialize and interact with other kids and their caretakers in a safe, happy and healthy environment. Where they can learn and grow and allow their parents the time they too need to be worthy citizens of Royal, doing the works they do to make our town great. It would be narrow-minded and shortsighted not to realize that the appointment of a suitable manager is paramount."

He turned and faced Beau Hacket outright. As the old man was the powerful and respected ringleader of the members who'd been most vocal in their disapproval, Zach knew he had to get Hacket onboard if they were to avoid further trouble down the line.

"Mr. Hacket, your daughter has brought new business and capital to our town with her work, work that will hopefully stand Royal in good stead for future movie locations. After all, look at what *Lord of the Rings* did for New Zealand. Why wouldn't we want a piece of that?" Zach could feel the mood in the room beginning to lighten, the tide beginning to turn. "Now she's expecting a family—twins, I'm told. Should Lila put all her hard work—work I'm also told you're incredibly proud of—on a back burner, perhaps never to be touched again, simply because there is nowhere suitable for your grandchildren to be cared for? Don't your grandchildren deserve the very best?"

Beau Hacket spoke gruffly. "Of course they do. But that's why they should be cared for by their mother, at home."

"But what if caring for her babies isn't the best thing for Lila? What if her work is so important to her, so vital to her happiness, that a few hours a week in a center such as we're creating gives your daughter the best of both worlds? Can't you see now how important it is that we consider carefully each and every application so that when an appointment is made we can all be secure in the knowledge that we've found the very best person for the job? For our children, and our grandchildren?"

"He makes a good point, Beau. You don't want any old biddy in charge of our kids," commented the gentleman who'd supported Beau Hacket earlier. "I know I don't want my grandbabies in the hands of some random stranger."

Zach could feel the mood in the room shift, becoming less combative, less old-school versus new.

"Why are you so all-fired keen on this idea, Lassiter? You're not even married," someone yelled from the back of the room.

"No, I'm not. But one day I'd like to think I'll marry again, and have a family of my own—" *again,* he added silently "—and I'd like to think that my wife and I would have a choice about where our children will receive their early learning. I'd like it to be somewhere like here, within the TCC. In a child-care center that embraces the same values that we've all sworn to uphold."

Zach sat down again, satisfied he'd said his piece and satisfied that he'd been heard. As the discussion continued around him, and he fielded the occasional pat on his shoulder or sidelong comment of "Well said" and "Bravo," he began to feel the acceptance of his peers within the TCC. While no one had been overtly unfriendly to him as his membership was under consideration, it seemed that any barriers left between him and the other members had fallen on the heels of what he'd had to say. As the meeting drew to a close, Sam Gordon, Lila Hacket's fiancé, approached.

"Well said, Lassiter. You've given me something to think about, thank you. Can I buy you a drink at the bar?"

And there it was, that sense of acceptance. That sense that no matter his background, no matter what he might have done before, here, at the TCC, Zach was a valued and accepted member.

"Thanks, I'd like that, and call me Zach," he accepted with a shake of the other man's hand. "Everything sorted out for your wedding this weekend?"

Sam put both hands up in the air in a gesture of surrender. "It's all out of my hands and that's the way I'm keeping it. I'm just glad I finally got her to agree to marry me."

By the time Zach returned home that night, Sam Gordon hadn't been the only one offering to buy him a drink. In fact, if he'd taken them all up, he'd have been blind drunk in a cab by now, he thought ruefully as he rolled his Cadillac into its space in his multicar garage. Not ready for bed yet, Zach went through to his den, where he threw himself on the sofa and loosened his tie. All in all, today had been a good day.

He picked up the TV remote and started to surf through the channels, but nothing caught his eye. Instead he muted the TV and just sat for a moment, absorbing the quiet that surrounded him.

Normally he didn't mind being on his own. In fact, by the time his day staff had left the house, he relished it at the end of a hard day. He thought back to the meeting, to how the members had listened to him, allowed him to take charge of the issue, and he realized that the feeling it had left him with was one of happiness.

Zach wasn't usually the kind of guy to dwell on his feelings, but tonight he couldn't stop thinking about two things—people, in particular. He knew Alex would have been proud of him tonight. Even though he and his friend had never discussed the child-care center in depth—after all, they were both leading bachelor lifestyles—he had gotten the feeling that Alex was a deeply family-oriented guy. That providing the best for children was as intrinsic to him as turning the best deal or finding the best investors to make that deal happen.

He missed his friend with a physical ache. Missed their late-afternoon debriefings over a beer in the office after everyone else had gone home for the night.

"Where are you, buddy?" he asked out loud, wishing with all his might that somehow, some way, he'd get the answer he wanted.

The only person in the world who could possibly understand how much he missed his friend was Sophie. Just thinking about her gave him a pang in his chest and he realized, despite seeing her each day in the office, that he missed her and what they'd begun to share together just as much as he missed Alex.

Two people absent from his life. Two things that if set to rights could make him feel wholeheartedly happy again.

Could he set to rights the emptiness that now existed between him and Sophie? Did he even want to try? He weighed the pros and cons in his mind, first examining in depth the hurt he'd felt when he'd found her here, in his den, snooping in his private email. Even now he still tasted the anger that had flooded his entire body when she'd admitted why she'd been poking around. The sense of having been taken for a fool, *used,* by her as she continued with her duplicity.

He'd thought she had genuine feelings for him, had known he was developing them for her. God only knew how long he'd kept her at arm's length, kept his own desires under lock and key. After Anna, he'd been wary of commencing a new relationship. Then, when the feelings between him and Sophie had swelled to the boiling point, it was no wonder they'd spilled over and combusted the way they had.

The way she'd behaved still had the power to rile him up but, he asked himself for the very first time, if the tables had been turned, if he'd suspected she had information about this business with Alex, what would he have done?

Whatever he could.

The answer echoed in his mind. In reality, Sophie had done no more or less than he would have done in the same situation. The only problem had been that she'd discovered things about his personal life that he'd have preferred, out of respect for Anna and her parents, to keep private.

So why had he been so worried about that? Sophie had proven herself to be nothing but the soul of discretion the whole time she'd worked alongside him. Even now, in the face of what had happened between them—with both the highs and lows of what they'd gone through together—she had kept her counsel. She behaved as if nothing had ever transpired between them, as if the status quo had never been ruffled. As if they had never had the wildest sex he'd enjoyed in a long time on the surface of his desk.

Need punched deep and low in his gut. He missed her, all right. Missed what they'd begun to share, missed what they could have continued to share if only he hadn't caught her on his laptop that night. If only he had remained rational in the face of her accusations. If only he hadn't all but banished her from his private life.

It had been the intensity of his protectiveness toward that privacy that he'd reacted to. He could see that now. By keeping Anna and her problems, *his* problems, secured within a box, he hadn't had to face his own feelings about what she was going through—or, more importantly, his own grief.

Zach stood and reached into his back trouser pocket for his wallet and opened it. There, behind a plastic shield, was a photo of Blake, taken shortly before the accident that had claimed his son's life. An accident he, in all honesty, blamed himself for as much as he blamed Anna. If he'd been any kind of husband to her, any decent kind of father, he would have been home that night instead of working late in an attempt to earn a partnership in her father's investment firm.

What had it all been for, he wondered. After the accident, what was left of their marriage had disintegrated—exposed for the empty, guilt-ridden sham it had been from the start. Zach had resigned his position with Anna's father's firm and struck out on his own, quickly getting a reputation for taking risks that paid off, risks that drew Alex Santiago's attention and his offer of a partnership that had quickly led to a strong friendship based on mutual respect.

He dragged his mind away from his missing friend and back to the woman who linked them. The woman who'd been as concerned as Zach about where Alex was. The woman who'd been prepared to do whatever it took to find out. Could he forgive her for not trusting him, for not trusting herself to even approach him about her concerns?

Of course he could. Sophie was good from the tip of her shining golden head to the soles of her delectable feet. Good in a way he had rarely seen outside of his own parents and good in a way he'd almost forgotten existed within the world he'd chosen to inhabit.

Could he forgive Sophie for what she'd done? Of course he could. In fact, how could he not when he'd already admitted to himself that he would have done exactly the same thing to find information if the tables had been turned?

She was hurting inside just as much as he was, he knew it. He'd caught her gaze upon him several times this past week before she'd rapidly averted it and continued with whatever she'd been doing. But within those beautiful, soft brown eyes he'd seen the longing mixed with pain and regret. He wanted to erase that hurt. Ease that longing.

He wanted Sophie Beldon.

Fourteen

The only good thing about getting to the end of this interminable week, Sophie thought, was being able to look forward to Lila and Sam's wedding over the weekend. How Lila and her mother had managed to pull something as important as this together in three weeks defied even Sophie's normally logical and practical mind. They were keeping things small, which made it a great deal more manageable to host at the Double H.

They couldn't want for a more beautiful setting than the Double H. No matter what anyone said about Beau Hacket, or how stuck in the Dark Ages he appeared to be with regard to a woman's place in the world, he had worked hard to build a very special home for his family.

She turned her attention away from the wedding and back to the report she was finalizing for Zach. She'd barely seen him today, but a tiny knot of tension in her stomach reminded her he was due any moment.

He'd been visiting the Philmore Clinic again. She was burning to ask him how Anna was doing, but given how strained the atmosphere was between the two of them, she had no idea where to start. A call to the clinic hadn't elicited any information, either, and had earned a terse remark regarding patient confidentiality. She'd even toyed with phoning Anna's aunt, except she still had no idea what name the woman went by now and had taken that particular frustration out on the private investigator she'd engaged, and now fired. How difficult should it have been for them, with all their resources, to discover that Anna's aunt had married—that Anna's surname had changed and her first name had also been shortened?

Her goal, though, had been reached. She had found her sister, for all the good that it did her.

Sophie's mother had been over the moon with joy when she had phoned her with the news that she'd found Suzie, but she'd been understandably upset and concerned when Sophie told her how ill her sister was. Sophie had briefly toyed with not telling her mom about Anna's mental collapse, worried it might raise old demons of guilt that stemmed from letting her daughter go in the first place, but her mother had been stronger than she'd expected and had coped remarkably well with the news. Even now she and Jim were driving their RV back to Royal from the Reagan Library in California, putting their vacation plans on hold indefinitely. Sophie would be glad of their support but until they got here she was on her own.

Sophie looked up as Zach entered the executive suite.

"Any messages?" he asked.

"Nothing today. I guess everyone's busy getting ready for the wedding tomorrow."

"About that, do you have a plus one on your invitation?"

"Y-yes, I do," she answered hesitantly.

Why on earth would he want to know that? She knew he had received his own invitation, one that had arrived by special delivery this morning.

"And? Are you taking anyone with you?"

"No, I'm going on my own," she said, her spine stiffening in reaction.

"Seems silly for us to take two cars. Why don't I pick you up about three, we can go together?"

She stood there stunned into silence.

"What?" he asked. "You don't think that's a good idea?"

"I'm just confused, is all. Especially after..."

"I'll pick you up at three," he reiterated. "Now, if there's nothing else that's urgent today, we may as well finish up for the week."

Sophie didn't need to be told twice. She'd booked an appointment at Saint Tropez, the upscale spa and hair salon in town, for early tomorrow morning. *Me and half of the invited wedding guests,* she'd thought when she'd been forced to accept an early-morning appointment. Now she was glad she'd gone ahead with it. If she was to spend any time in Zach's company at the wedding, she'd need the armor of perfect hair, face and nails. All the better to claw him with? She almost laughed out loud at the thought. As if she'd ever get that close to him again.

Tears stung Sophie's eyes as she watched Lila and Sam walk together down the aisle toward the celebrant. They'd decided to forgo attendants and the usual traditions, saying they came to this marriage together and that's exactly how they wanted it. Their vows were simple and poignant, each one a very personal testament to the love they shared and the promises they now made to each other. Their shared joy shone through their voices and their eyes, eyes they could barely take off one another throughout the short ceremony.

A gentle breeze blew softly against the bride's diaphanous strapless gown, exposing the soft roundness of her early pregnancy as if with a loving caress. And when the bride and groom kissed, there was an uproar from the crowd as congratulations, whistles and applause filled the air. Finally united as man and wife, they turned to face the gathering, their happiness beaming over everyone present.

While Sophie wished her friend all of the very best, she couldn't help but feel a chasm opening between their lives. Lila was married now, with a family on the way and with a bright successful career. Before, Sophie had barely felt the difference between herself and her married friends, but today in particular created a wistful ache deep in her chest. She was no closer now to long-term happiness than she'd been five years ago, than she'd maybe even be in another five years. It was an incredibly painful truth, and hard to bear—even more so watching Lila's wedding while the man Sophie loved with all her heart, but whom she could never have, stood at her side.

Sophie felt a gentle nudge against her arm.

"Here," Zach said softly.

She looked down, surprised to see a crisply ironed white handkerchief in his hand. She touched a hand to her cheek, surprised to find the tears she'd thought she'd contained liberally running down her face—no doubt ruining the makeup applied so carefully at Saint Tropez that morning.

"Thanks," she said, her voice husky, and dabbed carefully at her eyes and cheeks.

"It was a beautiful ceremony," he said simply.

"Yes, it was. Perfect." Her voice closed on a hitch. "Ex-excuse me, please."

She couldn't bear it a second longer; she needed a moment or two to herself. Without waiting for Zach's response, Sophie turned and pushed her way through the well-wishers crowded around the happy couple and made for one of the guest bathrooms inside the main house. Once inside, she locked the door firmly behind her. She leaned against the solid wood, dropping her head back and closing her eyes, now acutely aware of the hot, inexorable slide of tears down her cheeks.

Pull it together, she told herself sharply. *You're happy for Sam and Lila. Thrilled that they've pulled the threads of their attraction together into a tightly woven future.* And she was truly happy for them—just insanely miserable for herself.

She pushed off the door, opened her eyes and stepped up to the cream marble vanity unit, turning on the cold tap with a vicious twist before thrusting her hands under the cool, gushing water. As it poured over her wrists, she began to calm down, get control of the crazy emotions that ran rampant through her body.

So she'd failed with Zach. She'd abused his trust and she'd failed, coming up with a big fat zero. She could overcome this. There was nothing keeping her in Royal, not now with her mom happily remarried and enjoying her retirement traveling around the country in a luxury RV. She could relocate, find another job somewhere else. Maybe even in Midland. No one said she had to stay in Maverick County. Maybe she could travel farther afield to Dallas or Houston, or even out of state. Her savings and her skills could travel with her and she'd proven over and over again while she was growing up that she could pretty much make a home anywhere.

But what about Anna? a little voice deep inside her asked. *Now you've found her, do you really want to go away?*

Sophie met her gaze in her reflection in the gilt-edged mirror. Could she honestly do it? Could she walk away from the sister she'd been searching for? The sister she'd missed from her life for the past twenty-two years?

No. She couldn't walk away now. Even if she couldn't tell Anna who she was right now, eventually she'd be well enough and Sophie wanted to be there when that happened—for both their sakes. She was just going to have to suck it up, plaster over her broken heart and keep on going. Besides, she couldn't let Alex down now, wherever he was.

Matter-of-factly, Sophie opened her clutch and took out her lipstick and powder. There wasn't much she could do to repair her eye makeup, but thankfully the reception was outdoors and she could probably get away with wearing her sunglasses. She did the best she could to repair the ravages of her tears and then straightened in front of the mirror, pulling her shoulders back and meeting herself square in the eye.

"You can do this," she said firmly. "You're strong, you're intelligent, you're in control. You will survive."

She spied Zach's handkerchief on the vanity and shoved it in her clutch. No doubt he'd prefer it returned without the streaks of mascara and foundation that currently marred its pristine whiteness. She'd launder it for him and return it on Monday.

With one last check in the mirror, Sophie opened the door and walked straight into the last man on earth she expected to see waiting for her.

"I was getting ready to knock the door down. Are you okay?"

"Have you been waiting here all this time?" she asked, incredulous and a little embarrassed.

What if he'd heard her little pep talk to herself in there? She stifled an inner groan of dismay.

"When you didn't immediately come back, I got worried. Then when you didn't come out of the bathroom I began to get even more worried."

"Well, thank you, but you didn't need to bother. I'm fine," she breathed with an insouciance she was far from feeling.

"They're asking everyone to take their seats at the tables. We're together," he said, offering her his arm.

Of course they were seated together, she thought with a tiny sigh. Could today get any worse? She put her hand in the crook of his elbow and tried to ignore the instant flare of heat that burned from her fingertips to the very center of her being. Of course it could, but she'd get through it. She had to.

Fifteen

Sophie's face ached with the effort of keeping a smile plastered on it, but that was nothing compared to the pain in her heart. Every time she'd attempted to create a bit of physical distance between her and Zach, he'd closed it right back up again. It was as if he was doing it on purpose, or as if he didn't trust her to let her out of his sight.

She sighed. It was probably the latter. Although she didn't quite know what he thought she could get up to here. No, she decided. She was just being foolish. The past two weeks had been emotionally taxing and she wasn't her usual self. These stupid, fanciful imaginings were a perfect case in point.

"Dance?" Zach's voice interrupted her thoughts.

"Wh-what?" she asked, momentarily confused.

"I was asking you to dance," he replied with a small quirk of his lips. "It's a common enough custom at weddings, I understand."

"O-of course it is," she stammered.

"So, will you join me on the dance floor?"

He rose and held out a hand to her and with the eyes of several of their clients, who were seated at other tables, upon them, she couldn't very well refuse. She put her hand in his, steeling herself for the reaction she knew was to come, but that was nothing compared to when they joined the swirl of couples on the dance floor. It seemed everyone had decided to join them, which forced them into far closer proximity than was reasonable or comfortable.

Worse, the music had slowed to a dreamy number, one where couples took advantage of the crowded floor to move together hip to hip, their eyes locked on one another, their hands entwined. As beautiful as it was, it was also well-nigh unbearable, Sophie decided as she fought to keep a scant few inches between herself and Zach—a distance that was suddenly closed as another couple bumped into them.

"I'm sorry," Sophie said, pulling slightly away.

The heat of his body had seared through the gown she wore and her hips had brushed all too intimately close to his.

"No problem, but I think you're fighting a losing battle. Why don't you just give in and enjoy it?" he murmured, even as he increased the pressure of his hand against the small of her back, drawing her against him.

Their closeness was both an exquisite pleasure and an excruciating agony at the same time. Her body recognized his instantly, her blood heating and her pulse increasing as they moved together in time to the music. Hip to hip, belly to belly, it was an intoxicating temptation and a cruel torment. Sophie was aware of every flex of muscle, every breath he took.

His light cologne, boosted on the scent of his skin, teased her nostrils and the warm clasp of his hand holding hers made her all too aware of the memory of what that hand had felt like on other parts of her body. Parts that were now taut and aching for more. She stood it for about two minutes, but even that was two minutes more than enough.

"I can't do this," she said abruptly, pulling out of his grasp. Turning away, she made her way through the throng and back to their table.

Zach was instantly by her side. Typical, she thought bitterly. Why give her a few minutes to pull herself together when he could just prolong the torture?

"Come on," he said. "I'll take you home."

"No, I'm fine. Besides, it'd be rude to leave before Lila and Sam do."

He looked at her, a small frown of concern marring his broad forehead.

"Are you sure?"

She painted on a smile. "Of course I'm sure. Oh, look, I've just seen someone I need to catch up with. Will you excuse me?"

Sophie slipped away and began walking toward the opposite side of the festivities. She felt Zach's burning gaze on a spot between her shoulder blades for about the first twenty steps then, mercifully, it was gone. Her shoulders slumped in relief. Having to work with Zach all week was one thing, but having to spend time with him socially, as well—well, that was about more than any woman should be asked to bear.

Circulating among Lila's friends wouldn't normally have been a problem, but Sophie was beginning to feel as if she was playing a sophisticated game of tag by the time Lila was getting ready to toss her bouquet. She'd moved from one group to another, each time shadowed only a few minutes later by Zach. It was exhausting trying to stay ahead of him. Thankfully she could leave soon.

Amid much cajoling and friendly rivalry, she joined the single ladies in a group, waiting for Lila to throw her flowers. She hung well to the back, not at all eager to win the prize. She already knew that she couldn't be with the man she wanted, and no bouquet would magically change that fact—more was the pity.

"Are you all ready?" Lila called out to the group with a beaming smile.

A chorus of voices assured her it was time to hurry up and get on with it. With another smile Lila turned her back and her arm swung in a graceful arc upward, releasing the flowers to fly through the air. Sophie didn't want to catch it, she really didn't. She didn't even so much as have her hands up, but fate had a seriously sick sense of humor right now because sure enough, the flowers sailed directly toward her and would have struck her full in the chest if she hadn't put up her hands to catch them.

For the briefest moment she clutched them to her chest, inhaling the sweet, rich scent of the pale-pink roses interspersed through lush white chrysanthemums, before thrusting them back out and away from her.

"Here," she said to Piper Kindred, who'd been a year ahead of her at school. "You have them."

Before Piper could respond, Sophie thrust the flowers in her hands and turned to walk swiftly away.

"But you won them, fair and square," the curly redhead called out to her retreating form.

"They're all yours," Sophie threw over her shoulder before making her way to her table and collecting her clutch.

She couldn't wait to get out of here and she counted the minutes until Lila and Sam made their goodbyes to everyone. As the departing couple reached her, Sophie put her arms out to her friend and gave her an enormous hug.

"Be happy," she whispered in Lila's ear.

"Oh, I am," her friend answered with a squeeze. "Your turn next. Don't think it won't happen just because you off-loaded the bouquet to someone else."

Sophie forced a smile to her face as she pulled away from Lila's embrace, allowing her to move on to the next person. Then, in a flurry of rose petals, the newlyweds were driven away—a "Just Married" sign in the back window and tin cans clanking the full length of the Double H driveway and lending a slightly incongruous note to the gleaming black stretch limousine Beau had arranged for his daughter and her new husband.

Zach moved beside her.

"Okay?" he asked, his eyes searching hers as if looking for something.

"Yes, I'm fine, although I am rather tired. I'd like to go now but please, do stay if you want to. I'll get a ride with someone else heading back to town."

She gestured in the direction of a small group of people heading toward their cars.

"You came with me," Zach said firmly, "so I'll see you safely home."

The drive back to her house was a long and silent one and when they pulled up outside her apartment, Sophie all but shot out of the car.

"Thank you," she said through the open door. "I'll see you at work on Monday."

She pushed the door closed with a solid thunk and started up the path as fast as her high heels could carry her.

"Sophie, wait!" Zach called out.

She turned and swallowed hard as she saw him striding determinedly toward her.

"Could I come in for a minute?"

Refusal hovered on the tip of her tongue but good manners prevailed. "Sure," she said slightly ungraciously.

Good manners were one thing but she didn't have to sound happy about it. Her hand shook slightly as she tried to insert her key in the door and she startled as Zach's hand closed around hers, guiding the metal key into the keyhole.

"Thank you," she muttered grimly as the door swung open.

He followed her inside, altogether too closely for her equilibrium. She gestured for him to take a seat while she went through to her bedroom and tossed her clutch onto the bed, taking a moment to drag in a steadying breath. Composed again, she went back to the living room.

"Can I offer you something to drink? Tea, coffee, something stronger?" she said as brightly as she could manage.

"Whiskey and water, thanks."

Zach watched as Sophie went to her compact kitchen and he could hear her opening and closing cupboards, then the sound of liquid pouring. She came back through with one glass on a tray together with a small matching jug, its cut crystal cloudy with ice water.

"You're not joining me in a drink?"

"No," she answered matter-of-factly before perching on the edge of the seat farthest from him.

He added water to his whiskey and took an appreciative sip. "Thank you. This is good."

"You're welcome. Are you sure you will be safe to drive home after that?"

"Why? Worried you might be forced to allow me to stay?" he teased.

From the rigid set of her posture, his comment didn't go down at all well. He sighed softly and put his glass down on a coaster.

"Don't worry, Sophie. I'll be fine. I stuck to club soda at the wedding."

"Good," she said abruptly, then frowned. "Although I would have called you a cab."

Zach let loose with a full-bellied laugh, earning a look of censure from his hostess.

"I'm sorry, Sophie. I shouldn't have teased you. Not about that. Seriously, though, I wanted to talk to you tonight."

She stiffened and braced her shoulders, as if expecting bad news. "Really? Nothing that could wait until Monday?"

"No, I didn't want to discuss this at work. I've been thinking a great deal about our last night together." A great deal? Who was he kidding? He hadn't been able to get it out of his mind. He couldn't walk past the windows by the pool without remembering what it had been like to make love to her in the blue water. He'd even considered moving into another bedroom, except he knew he'd never be able to rid himself of the memories they'd created together there, no matter where he did or didn't sleep.

"Oh?" Sophie answered. "I would have thought you'd have managed to move on from that by now."

"I would have, too. But it seems I can't. I can't sleep without dreaming about you, I can't be awake without thinking about you." He shook his head. "Look, I'm going about this all wrong. In fact, I went about everything all wrong that night when I saw you on my computer."

"I was in the wrong. I shouldn't have—"

"No, wait, let me speak. I overreacted, Sophie, and I'm sorry. I was stressed out about Anna and about Alex, and it made me unreasonably defensive."

"But I had no right to go snooping in your private affairs," she said more strongly.

"Actually, you had every right. You suspected, wrongly, thank God, that I was involved in Alex's disappearance. And yes, I had been cagey at work about what I was doing. It's no wonder you put two and two together and managed to get five or more. Seriously, if I had suspected you of being involved in Alex going missing, I would have done exactly the same thing— probably even less subtly." He shoved a hand through his hair, then reached for his drink and took another sip. "Look, I'm really sorry, Sophie. It's been a hellish time and you bore the brunt of it. What with Anna going missing a few days beforehand and then finally getting her parents to agree she needed help, I just lashed out at the most convenient person."

"Me?"

"Yeah, they say you tend to do that with the ones closest to you." He paused, letting his words sink in a little before he continued. "And I do want to be close to you, Sophie. This past week has taught me that. I'm really sorry I hurt you and that I was so cruel. I hope you can forgive me and, more importantly, that you'll give me, us, another chance. I care for you, I really do, and I think we could make a strong future together. Obviously, Anna will always be a part of our lives—"

"No! Stop!" Sophie held up one hand, shaking her head frantically, her eyes wide open, stark against the paleness of her skin. "Don't, I can't. *We* can't. It's impossible."

Her words cut like razors across his nerves. *Can't? Impossible?* When he spoke he tried to infuse his words with as much persuasion as he possibly could.

"Sophie, please. I have very strong feelings for you, and I'm pretty sure you do for me, too. Can't we at least try to make it work? Don't you think we deserve one more chance?"

Sophie's head dropped and she stared at her hands clenched on her knees. He clearly heard the shuddering breath she drew in before she spoke.

"Zach, please, don't get me wrong. I'm honored that you think you have feelings for me—"

"I don't *think* I do, Sophie. I *know*," he said with quiet conviction.

He'd expected resistance—it was only natural after the way he'd treated her—but he would wear that resistance down, however much it took to do so.

She lifted her head and looked directly at him, her beautiful eyes swimming with unshed tears. "I can't accept them, Zach. Please respect that."

"Respect what? You're not telling me anything. At least tell me why."

She shook her head just as a tear began to track a silvered trail down one cheek. A tear that just about rent his heart in two.

"Please, Zach, please go. This is painful for me. I need you to leave, now."

There was nothing else for it. She'd asked him to go and while every cell in his body protested, commanding that he stay—comfort her, argue with her, figure out what the hell it was that was keeping her from him—he rose from his chair and saw himself to the door.

Sixteen

Zach sat in his car, still parked at the curb outside Sophie's place. One hand on the wheel, the other poised to turn on the ignition. But he didn't move. All he could do was think about the woman he'd walked away from. It was crazy. He hadn't gotten where he was today by giving up, by simply walking away because someone had asked him to. His entire reputation had been built on taking risks and winning. And he wasn't about to stop doing that now.

Decision made, he flung open his car door and slammed it behind him, keying the remote locking button as he strode back up Sophie's path. He reached the door and, only just resisting the urge to pound on its painted surface and holler at her to let him back in, politely pressed the doorbell.

"Who is it?"

"It's me."

"Zach, I asked you to go. I'm all done talking about this."

He could hear the weary unhappiness in her voice and it made his gut twist.

"And I'm not," he insisted. "I'm also not leaving until you tell me exactly why you're not prepared to give us another chance. The way I see it, we can do this one of two ways. Either I stand here shouting through your door, or you can let me in and we can do this face-to-face."

Silence.

"Sophie—" he pressed the doorbell again "—just how much sleep do you think you're going to get with me doing this every five seconds?"

Slowly the door opened in front of him.

"About as much as I've had all week. Fine, come in then, before you disturb my neighbors."

"Thank you."

He couldn't quite keep the smug satisfaction out of his voice. She'd caved far sooner than he'd have guessed.

"I don't know why you're doing this," she said wearily, wrapping her arms around herself. "I'm entitled to not want to be with you, you know."

"Sure you are, but you really *do* want to be with me, you just won't let yourself. That's different. Here," he said, taking her by her shoulders and gently guiding her down onto one end of the sofa before settling beside her. "Now tell me why you're prepared to let go of what is probably the best thing ever to happen to either of us."

Sophie looked at him and from the expression on her face, it was almost as if doing so caused her immeasurable pain. "I...I don't know where to begin," she said shakily.

"Try the beginning," he coaxed, his hands reaching to hold hers as if to infuse her with the courage she needed to get started.

"You know that my sister was separated from us when we were little. Mom and I started over. Just the two of us for over twenty years. Mom met a really great guy four years ago and she finally remarried. It took her all that time to be willing to take a risk on loving another man again, and she finally had the courage to take what he offered her with both hands. They've been away, fulfilling their dreams of visiting every presidential library around America, and she's finally happy."

Sophie fell silent for a moment, then rose abruptly from her seat to begin pacing the floor.

"Over the years I'd asked Mom about finding Suzie, but it would always make her cry, so I learned to shut up about it—to just tuck it away inside. But then a couple of months ago, Mom asked if I still wanted to find her. We talked about it and decided now was a good time for us to try. To see if we could establish a bond again, if she was willing.

"It hasn't been easy. All the information we had on my stepdad's sister lead to dead ends." Her mouth curved into a rueful twist. "And as you know, my investigative skills aren't up to much. Recently, I hired a private investigator, but that proved to be an exercise in futility. He was either lazy or useless or both," she said bitterly. "And then Suzie just turned up in front of me one day. Just like that."

"Seriously? But that's wonderful news, isn't it?" Zach was even more confused.

While he still didn't see what this had to do with him and Sophie, surely it had to be exactly what she'd hoped for, especially after all this time.

"Yes, and no," Sophie prevaricated.

He could see she was battling with what she had to say. Choosing her words and turning them over in her mind carefully before speaking.

"Explain," he demanded, impatient now to get to the root of what Sophie saw as the problem keeping them apart.

"Suzie's full name was Susannah, and it seems that her aunt changed her name when she adopted her. And it would also seem that she remarried soon after, with Suzie taking her aunt's new surname, as well. Of course, since then, Suzie herself has married and had a child."

Zach started to get a cold prickling feeling down his spine. Suddenly he didn't like where this was heading.

"Zach, Anna Lassiter, your ex-wife, is my sister."

Seventeen

Sophie watched as her words slowly sank in for Zach. Before he could say anything, though, she plowed on with what she knew had to come next.

"It's impossible for us to have another chance. As much as I'm attracted to you—" she closed her eyes briefly, summoning all the courage she could muster "—as much as I love you, I cannot take my sister's chance of happiness and recovery away from her."

Zach got up and put his hands on her shoulders, forcing him to face her.

"Anna and I are good friends, Sophie. Nothing more than that now, and we haven't been anything more for a very long time."

"How can you say that?" she demanded. "You forget I've seen you taking calls from her almost daily for the past eighteen months. I've seen how much you care about her. Can you categorically say that there's no way that when she's better you two won't make a go of your marriage again?"

"Yes, I do care for her, deeply, but not in the way you're thinking. Not as a lover, not as a husband. We're divorced," he said calmly, "and we're staying that way. We found out very early on in our marriage that we were wrong for each other, and we remedied that."

"But she can't live without you, Zach. She needs you like she needs no one else."

He fell silent. Even he couldn't argue with that, she thought painfully. His hands dropped from her shoulders and he turned away from her, one hand reaching up to rub at his face. Sophie went to step forward, to offer him comfort, but she stopped herself just in time. They were at an impasse. An awful and horrible stalemate where another person's very well-being hung in the balance.

"Zach, I'm not going to do anything to upset her world. Not now I've finally found her. I'd like to get to know her again, to be a part of her life, to be her sister. Can you deny me that?"

Zach threw himself back down on the sofa. "This is all such a mess," he said, shaking his head. "You know, when I met her I thought she was cute. Pretty, but not in a stuck-up kind of way, despite her upbringing. Her parents were older and she was a much-cherished daughter. I never knew she wasn't their biological child and she never said anything herself. Do you think she knows?"

Sophie shrugged. Even though it hurt she had to say it. "How much do you remember of your life when you were only four? It's possible that with time she's forgotten all about Mom and me."

"Whether she remembers you guys or not, it may explain why she has always been more emotionally delicate than most people. As if she was afraid that people would abandon her, you know? I never really thought about it much. In fact, that whole vulnerability about her really drew me in. I wanted to be the big strong man for her. I guess I'm still doing that now.

"I worked for her father and I have to admit that when I first met Anna, I did see an opportunity to get a leg up within the company. Initially, at least. When we married, though, I really thought I loved her. At least I'd convinced myself I did. It didn't take long before we both realized we'd made a mistake. We were taking steps to formalize our separation when Anna discovered she was pregnant with Blake."

He sighed again, deeply. "She struggled after the birth. She felt trapped in a marriage neither of us wanted anymore and motherhood didn't come instinctively for her. It didn't help that I was pulling extralong hours at the office because, with Blake's birth, I was offered the promotion I'd wanted. The night of the accident she'd called me at the office, begging me to come home. Threatened to take Blake away from me if I didn't come home right there and then. She was unreasonable and I couldn't calm her over the phone, no matter what I said. It scared me. I headed home as fast as I could but I was already too late.

"Anna has never been able to get over her guilt over what happened. It's eaten her up inside, bringing her to where you saw her the other day."

"Thank you," Sophie said. "Thank you for telling me, for being honest."

"Too many people tried to hide Anna's condition for far too long already, including her parents. They thought—hoped—that all she needed was time, but she needs more than that. The only way she'll ever stand a chance of getting better is if she and the people around her are up front about all of it."

"Her parents finally came around?"

Even though it stuck in Sophie's craw to call them Anna's parents, they had brought her up to the very best of their ability, and she'd seen for herself when they'd left the office last Monday morning just how distraught they were for Anna.

"Reluctantly, but as with everything they do, now that they're on board they're behind her recovery all the way. They've even started organizing a fundraiser back in Midland for the Philmore Clinic." He shook his head with a rueful smile. "You have to hand it to them. They may be late to the party, but they sure know how to arrive."

Sophie couldn't be as magnanimous. "But if they'd stood behind you sooner, Anna wouldn't be in this position."

"Possibly, but we'll never know that. Which, I guess, brings us back to us. Anna and I are not a couple. If anything I'm her best friend, Sophie, that's all. How she'd handle you and me being a couple, well, I guess I'd have to discuss that with her doctor."

Sophie shook her head sadly. "I really want my sister back, and I'm not prepared to do a single thing that might jeopardize that."

"Not even if it means our future happiness? Sophie, I love you. Please, let's work this out."

"I can't," she sobbed, unable to hold back her emotions a second longer. "I just can't."

Zach rose to his feet and reached for her, but she put up both hands and shook her head.

"No, please don't. Don't touch me. Just...please, don't!"

"Okay," he said, his expression somber. "But I'm not giving up."

She couldn't even summon a reply and when the front door closed behind him, she sank to her knees on the carpet and let it all out. All the fear, all the longing she'd had to find her baby sister. All the yearning she'd had for her love for Zach to be returned, only to finally receive it and have it snatched out of her hands by fate.

By Monday morning Sophie was still a mess. She'd barely slept all weekend and getting out of her bed for work had taken the last of her energy. She went through the motions, checking the mail, scanning email, readjusting her schedule accordingly. By midmorning she was beginning to feel almost human again, except for the constant tenterhooks she was on waiting for Zach to show up at the office.

He finally came through the door about midday, looking little better than she did herself. He walked straight up to her desk and stopped in front of her.

"Are you okay?" he asked.

"I'll live," she replied, not bothering to dress up her fractured emotions into anything pretty.

He cracked a small smile. "I'm pleased to hear that. Do you have anything vitally pressing for the rest of the day?"

She shook her head.

"Good," he continued. "Then you'll be able to come with me."

"Come with you? Where?"

"To see Dr. Philmore."

"What? Why?"

"We've been talking. He'd like to meet you."

"But why? Does he think I need help, too?"

Zach let out a short bark of laughter. "No, you goose, of course he doesn't. But he does want to talk to you about Anna. Can you come with me?"

"Of course. When do you want to leave?"

"How about now?"

"Just give me a minute to back up and I'll be ready."

Sophie's shaking hands flew over her keyboard. She was going to meet the doctor who was treating Anna. Did that mean he might even let her see her sister? Lord, she could only hope so.

She felt sick with excitement and trepidation as they drove to the Philmore Clinic. Zach seemed equally tense and reluctant to speak. The clinic was some ways out of Royal, set on sprawling grounds with massive oak trees providing shade across the well-kept lawns.

"It looks more like a country club than a clinic," Sophie remarked as Zach pulled up his SUV in the gravel parking lot.

"Yeah, it has that feel about it, but don't let that fool you. The place is one of the best of its kind. I wouldn't have suggested Anna come here if it wasn't."

"Of course," Sophie agreed, wondering anew just how deeply Zach's feelings ran for his ex-wife.

While his protestations on Saturday night had been very much to the contrary, he seemed prepared to go a great deal further than someone who was simply a good friend. What was she worried about anyway, she asked herself. It wasn't as if she was going to take him up on his offer to pick up where they'd left off. Not now with her sister so obviously dependent on him. It just wouldn't be right.

They ascended the wide, shallow stairs to the front door of the clinic together and Zach held the door for Sophie before following her inside.

A woman greeted them. "Ah, Mr. Lassiter, Dr. Philmore is expecting you in his office. You know the way?"

"Yes, thank you, Betty."

"They seem friendly enough here," Sophie commented nervously.

"They are, and they're devoted to their patients, too."

Sophie tried to ignore the burning sensation in her stomach as Zach guided her along the carpeted hallway before stopping outside a paneled door. He rapped on the surface, then opened the door upon the command of the man inside. She didn't know what she'd been expecting of the doctor, but it wasn't the trim and attractive man who rose to greet them as they entered. He couldn't have been much older than Zach, she thought, maybe mid- to late thirties at most.

His handshake was firm and dry and the warm light in his blue eyes instantly put her at ease as he gestured for them to take a seat in the easy chairs grouped near a bay window overlooking the grounds.

"Thank you for coming, Ms. Beldon," he said, settling himself into one of the chairs. "Can I offer you two anything? Tea? Coffee or a cool drink?"

"No, thank you, I'm fine," Sophie managed through dry lips.

"Same here," answered Zach.

"All right then, I suppose you want to know why I requested that Zach bring you here, so let's cut to the chase. I understand you haven't seen Anna, your sister, for a little over twenty years?" the doctor said smoothly.

"That's right. Twenty-two years, to be exact."

He nodded. "That's some time to be apart. I can see why you'd be anxious to find her. Zach tells me that you recently began searching for her."

Sophie nodded in response.

"Can I ask you why you didn't try earlier?"

She stiffened in her seat. "I beg your pardon?"

Was he implying she should have tried harder? Earlier?

"Please, don't take offense. I'm merely getting the full picture."

"Up until recently my mother was still too unhappy and too fragile herself to instigate a search for my sister. I think finding her earlier would have only reopened old wounds that were already too painful to bear. My mother is remarried now, she's happy. We recently decided, together, to instigate a search for her. We thought if we could find Suzie—Anna—then that might just bring everything full circle, for all of us. Besides which, we needed to know for ourselves that she was okay, that she was happy without us."

Dr. Philmore nodded. "Anna's is a complex case but I think, in part, the complexity comes from her vulnerability in being alienated from you and your mother when she was so young. She obviously had a very strong bond with you both and while she's suppressed many of her early memories, she has begun to talk about you."

"She has? She remembers me?" Sophie sat forward on the edge of her seat.

"She does. More importantly she remembers how safe she felt with you. I think it would be good for you to visit with her, reestablish your contact with one another, get to know one another again."

She couldn't believe it. She'd been worried that with Anna's illness she might have to put off meeting her again, maybe even forever. It had been one of the many things that had plagued her through Saturday night and most of Sunday.

"When can we start?" she asked, eagerly.

"How about now?" the doctor answered with a warm smile.

"Is she in her room?" Zach asked. "Perhaps I should introduce them."

"Yes, and yes, I think that's a great idea. Well," he said, standing up and offering his hand to them both, "it's been lovely meeting you, Ms. Beldon. Always a pleasure, Zach."

As they rode the elevator to the floor where Anna's room was, there were butterflies in Sophie's belly, great big butterflies doing loop-de-loops.

"You'll stay with us, won't you?" she asked Zach as they began to walk down a long, wide corridor.

"As long as you need me to," he promised and took her hand to give it a reassuring squeeze.

Instantly Sophie felt at ease. He did that for her. Thinking about it, he did that for everyone. While he might have built his reputation on being a risk taker, he also had the unerring ability to make people feel secure about his decisions. No wonder Anna depended upon him so much.

"We're here," he said, interrupting her thoughts.

The butterflies zoomed back big-time as Zach knocked on the door and slowly opened it.

Eighteen

"Zach!"

Obvious delight at seeing Zach filled Anna's voice, reminding Sophie of the bond between these two. A bond she could never break, nor did she want to. Sophie hung back slightly behind Zach. This was going to be more difficult than she had anticipated.

The woman who rose to meet them was a far cry from the broken creature Sophie had last seen in Zach's office. Her hair was clean and gleaming, caught back off her beautiful face with a couple of clips. She wore a little makeup, too, which emphasized her blue eyes and the sculpted cheekbones both girls had inherited from their mother.

"I've brought you a visitor today," he said, turning slightly to draw Sophie forward.

Sophie met her sister's gaze, wondering if this time Anna might recognize her. Either way, she decided, it wouldn't matter. They'd make new memories now. Better ones, ones that would take them through the rest of their lives, because Sophie knew to the depths of her soul that she'd never lose hold of her sister ever again.

Anna's brow creased as she looked at her, her eyes suddenly unsure before a new light dawned within their depths.

"Sophie? Is it really you?" Anna said, taking another step forward.

Before Sophie realized it, the two women had closed the gap between them and were in one another's arms.

"Yes," she whispered, her throat thick and her eyes burning with tears of relief and joy. "It's me, at last."

The sound of Zach clearing his throat made them draw apart, but still Anna clutched Sophie's hand as she had so very many years ago.

"I'll leave you two to get reacquainted, okay? Call me when you need me to come and get you, Sophie."

"Thank you," she said softly.

He lifted his chin in acknowledgment. "It was the very least I could do, for you both."

There was something in the tone of his voice that made Sophie take a harder look at him. To look beyond the weariness that painted his features into tight lines, and to the pain that lay behind his eyes. He stared at her, as if willing her to change her mind about them, but she knew she couldn't. Not now. Not when it could hurt her sister, whose psyche was already frail and brittle.

When Zach was gone, Sophie suggested they make the most of the early-fall afternoon and take a walk outside around the grounds. Once outside she linked arms with Anna and began to stroll.

"I never thought I'd see you again," Anna said softly

when they got outside, her voice choking. "Or our mom. Is she…?"

"She's fine. She's due back home any day. She's missed you so much, we both have."

Anna nodded slowly, as if assimilating the words in her mind. "I remember her perfume, her hugs, her smile. I missed them. I used to think that if I was very good I'd be allowed to go home and I tried so very hard, but it never happened."

Sophie's throat tightened again as she battled to hold back tears. Her sister spoke with an air of detachment, as if she was talking about someone else, not the confused four-year-old she had been. She threaded her fingers through Anna's and gave them a gentle squeeze. She had no words. There was nothing she could say that could ever fill the years they had lost. Any bitterness, any ill will she'd ever felt toward Anna's adoptive family had to be put aside and she reminded herself to give thanks for the fact that, despite the past, they had a chance for a new start now.

"She still wears the same fragrance," Sophie eventually managed with a watery smile. "Some things don't change."

"I've changed," Anna answered flatly. "I'm not Suzie anymore."

"I know," Sophie acknowledged with another gentle squeeze. "But you're still my sister and I love you. That will never change."

"You don't know what I did."

Agitation filled Anna's voice. She stopped walking and pulled her hand free from Sophie's clasp. Fine tremors racked her frail form.

"I know." Sophie worked hard to keep her voice level,

reassuring. "I also know you can't keep blaming your-self."

Looking at her sister, Sophie couldn't help but be aware of the massive gulf that lay between them. A gulf created by time and upbringing. By choices they themselves had no say over.

"I'm a monster."

"Anna, you're not a monster. Not by any stretch of the imagination," she hastened to reassure her sister.

"I didn't want him at first," Anna said, assuming that air of detachment she'd had earlier.

Was that how she coped, Sophie wondered, distancing herself from what had happened, from her feelings, until it all became too much and it overwhelmed her again?

"I wanted a termination but Zach wouldn't hear of it. We were already separating, I wanted out of that marriage as much as he did. He changed his mind. He said we could make it work, for the baby's sake. For a while I believed him."

The tremors increased. Alarmed, Sophie guided Anna to sit on a bench beneath one of the spreading oak trees that dotted the expansive lawns. If Anna continued to become upset, she'd need to call for help. Maybe coming outside together hadn't been such a great idea.

"We don't have to talk about this right now," she soothed.

"No," Anna said, her voice suddenly firmer than it had been before. "I need to. I need you to hear it, from me."

"Okay, I'm listening."

"I loved him when he was born, but he terrified me. This tiny baby so dependent on me, and our marriage dependent on him. It was all wrong. So wrong." Anna rubbed her arms, up and down, up and down. "I couldn't cope and I couldn't ask for help. Zach did what he could, but I became such a bitch to live with."

Anna got up suddenly and began to pace, still rubbing her arms, her movements jerky, haphazard. Sophie watched her with concern twisting her gut. Everything in her wanted Anna to stop telling her story, to stop torturing herself like this, but her sister had made it clear she needed to tell it. Sophie could only honor that wish and give her the attention she deserved.

"I drove the car when I shouldn't have, drove too fast on wet roads, and I was angry. Angry at Zach for not being there for me every second of the day, angry at myself for needing him so damn much—angry at Blake for being born. He didn't deserve to bear the brunt of my chaotic emotions, neither of them did.

"Zach and I married for all the wrong reasons. We were destined to fail. I saw Zach as a way out. I knew he wanted to get ahead at my father's firm, so I used him. I convinced myself I loved him and that I would make the best wife in the world. After all, hadn't I been the best daughter for most of my life?"

Anna stopped pacing, stopped rubbing and instead wrapped her arms around herself. Sophie smiled a little, recognizing the very same action she did when she was unsure or unsettled about something.

"Oh, Anna." Sophie got up and put her arms around her sister, trying to absorb the misery and cynicism projecting from her every word.

"No, don't." Anna pushed Sophie away. "Don't make it all right. I have to take responsibility for my part in all this. It's the only way I'll ever get better."

Sophie took a step back. It was a harsh reality, but her sister wasn't the little four-year-old who'd relied upon her for everything anymore. She was a grown woman. A woman who'd completed her education, married, had a child and then seen the death of that child and her marriage. Sophie had concentrated for so long on the young Suzie that she'd completely forgotten to rationalize that she had grown up, become a mature adult. They were contemporaries now, neither needing the care of the other but there for support, for friendship, for love.

"I'm sorry. I can't help wanting to make it all better for you. It's the way I'm wired, I suppose," she said with a small uncomfortable laugh.

Anna stared back at her. "Even after everything I've just said?"

"Especially after everything you have just said," Sophie affirmed. "I'm here for you and our mom will be, too. For as long as you need or want us. I promise."

"Zach said the same thing. He's a good friend. I don't deserve it. Not from him. Not from you. Not any of it." Tears began to track down Anna's face. At first slowly, then faster and faster until she shook with sobs. She didn't object when Sophie put her arms around her again.

"You do," Sophie said firmly. "You deserve our support and our love."

"I just feel so guilty. Not just for what I did, but for what I'm doing now. I'm holding him back. He's so damn noble I know he's putting me ahead of other things in his life, other people. I want him to move on, but I'm too frightened to do this on my own."

"You're not on your own. We'll all be here for you, with you. Trust me, Zach wants you well again, we all do."

She held her sister until the sobs calmed down, until she just gave a tiny hiccup every now and then. Sophie rubbed her sister's back, trying to infuse her love and comfort into Anna's gaunt frame.

"I want to go back inside now," Anna said plaintively.

Sophie tucked her arm around her sister's slender waist and walked her slowly to the main building. She accompanied Anna to her room, settling her in the easy chair near the window that looked out over the gardens.

"Can I get you anything? Call anyone?" she asked, reluctant to leave her.

"No. I just want to think."

"Okay, I'll be going, then."

Sophie got as far as the door before Anna's voice halted her in her tracks. "Will you come back?"

"Sure, every day if you'll have me. And you can call me, too, if you like. Here." Sophie reached into her bag for her notebook and a pen and scratched her details down. "Anytime, okay? If you need me, or just want to talk—call."

"I'd like that."

"Me, too," Sophie said softly, then let herself out of the room.

Downstairs, she phoned Zach and waited outside for him to arrive, replaying her time with Anna over in her head. One thing kept sticking in her mind: Anna's guilt over holding Zach back, together with her adamant statement that she and Zach were just friends. Her feelings about their marriage exactly mirrored what Zach had told her himself. Sophie's head spun. Could she do it? Could she have it all? Could she have a new relationship with her long-lost sister and have the man she loved, as well? In time, could Anna accept that Zach and her big sister were a couple?

She could only hope and pray it was so.

Nineteen

Zach drove carefully back from the clinic, his eyes flicking to Sophie sitting next to him then back to the road ahead. She hadn't said much about her visit with Anna, only that it had been good to see her sister again and that she was looking forward to spending more time with her. He hoped against hope that maybe now she'd begin to see that there was no grand passion between him and his ex-wife—only a friendship based on all they'd been through together.

They pulled up outside Sophie's apartment and he walked her to the door.

"Will you come in?" she asked.

"Sure."

"I'll get us something to drink. What would you like?"

"Just iced water or a soda, thanks."

He watched her as she walked to her kitchen, unable

to tear his eyes off her and biting his tongue hard to prevent himself from bombarding her with questions about her meeting with Anna. She returned with two glasses filled with ice and soda.

"Thank you for taking me to see Anna today," she said as she perched on the seat opposite him.

"You needed to see each other. To reconnect. It's been far too long."

"Yeah, it has. So much has changed."

She sounded wistful. Was that regret in her voice? Had he done the wrong thing?

"You're not sorry you went, are you?"

"No, not at all. I'm just sad for all we've missed out on. We've grown up into such different people."

"You were bound to be different, whether you grew up together or not," he pointed out carefully.

"I know." Sophie shrugged. "But for so long in my mind she's been my baby sister, you know? Someone I had to look out for."

"And now she's all grown up?"

"Yeah, she doesn't need me like she used to."

"She still needs you, Sophie. But as an equal, I think."

She nodded and smiled. "I pretty much came to that conclusion, too. It's a strange thing to have to admit that you're not needed anymore when you've spent your whole life feeling guilty for not being there for someone, for not being able to do more."

"I need you," he said simply. "I love you, Sophie, and I need you in my life like I've never needed anyone before."

"Even after everything I've put you through?"

"After trying to seduce my secrets from me?" he asked. "More than ever. After being my right hand since

Alex went missing? Like you could never know. After working your way into my heart and my mind until all I think about every day, all I want is you? Definitely."

"I don't deserve you."

"Then we don't deserve each other, but who says we have to? Can't we just reach for what we want and love each other, for the rest of our lives? Do you believe me now when I say that Anna and are not in love with one another? Sophie, are you prepared to try again—to put the past behind us and to move on and build a future together?"

His heart hammered in his chest as he waited for her reply. This was the hardest thing he'd ever had to do, this waiting. He'd known after what she'd told him on Saturday night that he'd have to prove to her that he and Anna were not a couple in a romantic sense any longer. That was why he'd spoken with Dr. Philmore and arranged for Sophie to meet with him. Yes, he and Anna would always be friends—you didn't go through what they'd been through without forging some sort of lifelong connection—but that's where they began and ended. The kind of lifelong connection he wanted with Sophie was another bond entirely. It was the kind of bond his parents had, the kind of bond he'd never dreamed he would be lucky enough to have with another person, especially after the disaster of his first marriage.

Now everything lay in Sophie's hands. His heart, his hopes, his future.

"I—I would like to," she said hesitantly, then her voice strengthened and she spoke with more conviction. "But I need to know something first."

"Anything, just ask," he said, hardly daring to hope.

"I can understand your grief over the failure of your marriage with Anna, over what it has cost both of you, especially with losing your son. And I could understand if you never wanted to take that step again, to have a family. I just need you to know that if you're ever ready to be a father again, I want with all my heart to be the one to give you that gift."

Zach moved from his chair to kneel in front of Sophie. He clasped her hands in his and drew them to his lips.

"Sophie, I couldn't imagine a better mother for our children. Will you be my partner in life, in everything that matters to me? Will you marry me?"

She gave him a tremulous smile. "Yes, I love you, Zach. I would be honored to marry you."

"Thank God," he said, pulling her into his arms and closing his lips over hers.

He held her tight to his body, loving the way she fit against him. Two halves of the same whole. She kissed him back with every bit as much fervor as he kissed her, their lips igniting a slow-burning fire between them. A fire he knew, after all they'd been through, nothing could extinguish. Zach pushed his hands through the silken strands of her hair to cup the back of her head as he deepened the kiss, as their tongues stroked and probed, retreated and returned again in a dance that made his blood sing in his veins.

This was right in every way. *She* was right for *him* in every way.

Their clothes seemed to melt from their bodies with the heat of their passion for one another and with each touch, each caress, they rediscovered each other's bodies. Zach rolled onto his back right there on her living room floor and pulled Sophie on top of him. She straddled his hips, her hands tracing circles over his chest, his abdomen and lower.

"I love you, Sophie," he said again as she lifted her hips and positioned her body over his aching arousal.

"I love you, Zach, always," she answered as she slowly accepted him into her body and, he hoped, forever into her heart.

She rocked gently against him and his hands gripped her hips, holding her in place as her hands braced on his chest. She increased her tempo, making his pulse rocket upward in increments. He reached up to palm her breasts, to roll her nipples between his fingertips and squeeze them gently. He could feel the tension building in her body, building in his, and then she tumbled over the edge with a cry, her body reaching its peak and dragging his answering response from deep inside of him.

Their lovemaking had never been more perfect, more in sync. When she collapsed against him, he closed his arms around her and made a silent vow that she would forever be safe in his embrace, that she and any children they were lucky enough to have would always come first in his life, no matter what. He would never make the same mistakes again. This marriage would be based on love, pure and simple—not on duty, not on doing the right thing, unless doing the right thing was loving someone with your heart and soul for the rest of your days.

Much later, after they'd made it to her bed and made love again, they lay in the encroaching darkness just holding one another and Zach admitted he'd never before felt such contentment in his life. Anna would get well again. He and Sophie would build a new life together. There was only one fly left in the ointment. Alex. Where on earth was he?

As if sensing where his thoughts had traveled, Sophie

lifted her head from his chest and met his gaze, tracing the outline of his brow with one finger.

"Problem?"

"Just thinking," he said.

She continued to trace the angles of his face and began to outline his lips with the barest touch. He opened his mouth and caught her finger gently between his teeth, laving it with his tongue. He felt her response as every muscle in her body tightened.

"About Alex?" she asked, gently extricating her finger and leaning up on one elbow.

"How did you know?"

"Because not knowing where he is, that's the only thing that stops the future being perfect right now."

He knew what she meant. It had felt strange accepting the TCC membership without his friend and sponsor by his side, and now he was embarking on marriage with the woman he loved without even knowing where his friend was.

"Zach?"

"Hmm."

"With Anna's recovery still underway and Alex still missing, let's not plan our wedding just yet. We need to be sure that Anna is going to be okay and I know how important your friendship with Alex is. Let's wait until we have some idea if—*when,*" she corrected herself firmly, "he's coming back."

"Are you sure?"

"Absolutely. He's your best friend and he means a lot to me, too, both as a boss and a friend. Somehow it doesn't feel right to plan a date until we know more."

Zach pulled Sophie down against him, folding his arms around her. "How did I ever get so lucky as to find you?"

"I'm the lucky one," she argued back, reaching up to kiss him. "I plan to keep reminding you of that for the rest of our lives."

"And I plan to hold you to that." He smiled in return, confident that the future would be a whole lot brighter with her in it.

* * * * *

BEGUILING THE BOSS

BY
JOAN HOHL

Joan Hohl is a bestselling author of more than sixty books. She has received numerous awards for her work, including a Romance Writers of America Golden Medallion award. In addition to contemporary romance, this prolific author also writes historical and time-travel romances. Joan lives in eastern Pennsylvania with her husband, Marv, and their family consisting of: two daughters, Lori and Amy, two grandchildren, Erica and Cammeron, and three great-grandsons, Jaden, Kieran and Sorin.

To my own "Gang". . .six writers from
various parts of the country, all of us different in
interests and politics, yet close no matter the distance
in miles. . .because we love one another and we
are all a little wacky! We stay connected by email
and refer to each other as the gang.
They are as follows:

Kasey Michaels. Leslie Lafoy. Mary McBride.
Karen Katz and myself.

Yes, I know, that is only five.

Marcia Evanick was number six.
Marcie, as we called her, was warm and kind and
compassionate. At our occasional meetings, when she
smiled or laughed, we had to smile and laugh with her.

Last July, after a valiant, courageous fight,
our beloved Marcie lost the battle of her life to ALS.
May she rest in peace.

I will miss you forever, Marce.

Joan

One

Jennifer Dunning had always been indulged and she knew it. How could she not? From the day of her birth she had been pampered and cooed over, not only by her parents but by anyone and everyone who saw her. And yet, as far as she could recall, she had never acted out or thrown temper tantrums when she didn't get her way. She accepted a "no" as final and quietly moved on.

But now she sat on her bed in her room, where she had been hiding for the better part of the past two weeks, searching desperately on her electric-blue laptop for her new life. It was time to leave her parents' home in the exclusive gated community on the outskirts of Dallas. It was time to leave her parents, period.

Jennifer was stunningly beautiful—she had been as a baby, and was even more so at the age of twenty-eight. Tall and willowy with curves in all the right places, she was blessed with long honey-blond hair, dark brown eyes and classic features.

Jennifer was also restless, frustrated and edgy. She had quit her high-paying job as a personal assistant to the CEO of a large company two weeks ago. She was simply sick and tired of listening to the endless daily pep rallies given by her boss—the son of the company owner—who Jennifer considered unfit for the position he held. She was also tired of him eyeing her up and down every time they happened to be in the same room. He was a creep. So, deciding she had had enough, she had resigned.

Jennifer didn't actually need to work. Her parents were wealthy and she was their only child. She also had a large trust fund from her departed fraternal grandmother, and a smaller one from her maternal grandfather, who was still alive. But she liked working. She was intelligent, had a bachelor's degree in science and an MBA, and she enjoyed keeping busy, doing something useful. As a personal assistant, she'd been on her way up the career ladder.

Besides, working was much more interesting than the Dallas social scene. She found the scene boring, as well as pointless. As a youngster she had enjoyed the dancing lessons her mother insisted upon, and she also loved riding, after getting over the initial fear of her horse, which was huge compared to her six-year-old frame. No small ponies for her daughter, her mother had declared. Jennifer would attain her seat while on the back of a full-size Thoroughbred. And she had. Her seat was as elegant by the time she was eleven as that of any expert equestrian.

It was later, as she grew into her late teens, that Jennifer had become tired of the social scene. Lunch with the girls every Wednesday, listening to gossip she couldn't care less about—it had all started to feel so frivolous, and Jennifer had big plans for herself. She'd been preparing to go east, to the University of Pennsylvania and the Wharton School of Business. Her friends all had plans to attend the same college right there in Texas. In short, they were parting ways. But Jennifer decided she'd bear the lunches and the silly talk, as she thought of it, until the end of summer. Then she'd be on her own.

In contrast, her parents had been immersed in the social whirl all her life, unfortunately. It wasn't that they were uncaring—Jennifer knew her parents loved her. It was simply that they weren't there all that much. As a kid, she spent most of her free time with the housekeeper, Ida, who taught her how to clean, or with the cook, Tony, who practically made her a professional chef. As it turned out, Jennifer loved doing hard, honest work with her hands. It filled her with a purpose she hadn't known she'd needed.

After Jennifer finished school, she came back to Dallas and lived in her own apartment with a private entrance in her parents' house. She could have invited anyone she wanted to her place, but she had never had a man stay over. Not that her parents would have minded or objected. She was an adult, after all. It was just that none of the men she knew affected her *that* way.

Maybe because of what had happened during her junior year of high school.

She had never told her parents—or anyone else—about being caught alone on campus by a boy. She'd been leaving school later than most of the students following a meeting with her math teacher. It was January and almost dark, and she was distracted by thoughts of her conversation with the teacher. She wasn't fully alert while weaving through the rows of vehicles in the parking lot as she headed for her car.

The boy was a senior—a clean-cut, all-American star football player. Most of Jennifer's friends had crushes on him. Jennifer didn't, thinking him too cocky and into himself. Perhaps that was the reason he had accosted her that afternoon.

Trapping her between two parked cars, he fumbled with his pants zipper, exposing himself to her. At first, she was too shocked to think. But she came to her senses when he shoved his other hand up her skirt, attempting to yank her panties off.

Frantic, Jennifer had let out an earsplitting scream. Although the parking lot had appeared deserted, a male voice responded with a shouted, "Hey, what the hell?"

Mr. All-American let loose a savage curse, snarling, "You better keep your mouth shut about this, bitch." He sprinted away in the opposite direction.

Without thinking, Jennifer ran to her car, even as she could hear the man who had shouted running toward her. Her parents weren't home when she arrived there, shaken and teary-eyed. Hearing the boy's snarled threat echo in her mind, she had never told anyone of the incident.

Though Jennifer had been physically uninjured, the experience had left her wary of the opposite sex. Over time her anxiety had faded as she realized all males were not like Mr. All-American. She had even indulged her curiosity one time while in college. Although she liked the young man, the act was disappointing, leaving her feeling empty. And so, she had never invited a man to spend the night.

Not that her parents would have noticed even if their

daughter was having a mad, passionate affair. They were busy socializing in Dallas and in the exclusive gated community where they resided, changing partners with their closest friends.

Yes, changing partners.

Jennifer had only recently found out about her parents' game. She hadn't a clue how many friends there had been or how many years they had been experimenting. In truth, she didn't want to know. She could barely look at her parents' faces or be in their company for more than a few minutes. Even though she knew her parents' lifestyle was their business, she felt betrayed, as if they had been lying to her for years about who they really were underneath the façade of "social appropriateness" and their picture-perfect marriage. It made her want to do something to shock them right back.

So she had resigned from her job the day after coming home from work and catching a glimpse of her father and his best friend's wife, Annette Terrell, in a compromising position in one room, and her mother and the woman's husband, William, in a similar position in another.

Now, two weeks later, Jennifer knew she had to leave home, to take a break until the hurt subsided. She could barely look at her parents without feeling ill, and wanting to cry. She loved them, but what she had witnessed had deeply shocked her. Perhaps someday, she would be able to be in the company of her parents without that awful image tormenting her. But that day had not yet arrived.

Alone in her bedroom, Jennifer sat cross-legged on her bed, her laptop balanced on her knees. She was searching for escape, and employment, to keep her mind occupied. In effect, she was intent on running away from home…and her memories. It was time to stop living in a house of lies.

One week later, Jen left her parents a note. It read: *I'm off to see the Wizard—Marsh Grainger, that is, the famously elusive business wizard of Dallas. It's about a new job. I'll be in touch.*

She also emailed her best friends, whom she had met her first year in college. They had remained close ever since, staying in touch mostly by email, phone and texts. Although they all lived within driving distance, they led busy lives—three of the women were married with children, and the other two were busy chasing careers. Even so, "the gang" managed to get together every couple of months.

Hi, all, she wrote them. *I'm taking off for a while, will be in touch soon.*

Jennifer knew the next time she checked her email, there would be long messages from her friends, demanding to know exactly where she was and what she was up to, but she just wasn't ready to talk about what had happened. And she wasn't ready to tell them that she was interviewing with Marshall Grainger, whom they knew had a reputation as a womanizer.

Her mother probably knew, too. She fully expected her mother to start calling her cell phone as soon as she discovered that Jennifer was gone. That was okay— her parents could call all they wanted. It didn't mean she had to answer. After all, even she couldn't entirely explain why Marsh Grainger's ad for an office assistant had appealed to her. But she needed space and distance—and she was pretty sure the wizard, who was rumored to prefer his hill country ranch to the craziness of high society in Dallas, could help her with that.

* * *

Marshall Grainger needed help. He needed an office assistant as well as a cook who would also clean the sprawling Texas hill country home that doubled as his workplace.

A cousin in the wealthy Grainger family of Wyoming, South Dakota and Montana, Marsh was, in a word, loaded. He owned a huge cattle ranch in Colorado, run by an excellent manager and former Marine buddy, Matt Hayes. The ranch had been in Marsh's family for generations. Growing up, he had spent most of his summers there and he knew the ranching business inside and out.

But Marsh was not a cattleman at heart. He was a businessman, considered a force to be reckoned with in more ways than one. He was six foot four inches tall, slim and rangy with rugged features defined by high cheekbones and a strong, square, rock-hard jaw. A thick mane of gleaming hair the exact shade of rich dark chocolate matched the slightly arched brows above slate-gray eyes.

While Marsh owned the building that housed his company, nestled among many other tall buildings in Dallas, he rarely traveled into the city. He avoided the scene in Dallas like the plague, preferring to work at home in the large house set dead center on more than fifty acres.

At present, Marsh was desperately trying not to allow himself to be hopeful. After weeks of using all avenues of advertisements available to him, there was a chance he'd soon be able to hand the ranch books, the household bills and several duties of his main business over to a new assistant.

Someone who was actually qualified had applied for the job. So what if she was a *she?*

Finished paying his current household and ranch bills, he picked up his coffee mug and glanced at his watch as he walked out of the assistant's office, hoping he wouldn't have to spend any time there again in the near future.

It was 1:36 p.m. The appointment with the applicant was at 2. Rinsing his mug, he proceeded to make a fresh pot of coffee. Then again, he mused, after her long drive, the woman might appreciate a cold drink. He checked the fridge; there was cola as well as bottled water. The beer was his. Now all he had to do was wait, which was not Marsh's strong suit. He got busy scouring the sink and wiping down the long countertop.

His former assistant had up and quit on him three months ago, and he hadn't been able to sleep since then—until last night. Just the thought of interviewing someone who was actually qualified and could lighten his load had allowed him to enjoy his first full night's sleep in a long time. Hopefully she would take to the place. At that thought, he grimaced as he sent a quick look around. While tidy, the kitchen needed a thorough cleaning. The same went for the rest of the house. He had done his best to keep up with everything, but the majority of his time was consumed by the myriad details of his businesses. At the end of the day he was only one man.

Marsh had never dreamed finding help would be so hard. After his assistant left, he had received many responses to his ads, but only a few were qualified, and even fewer of those were willing to relocate to "the sticks," as one respondent called it.

The sticks? Marsh had thought with amazement.

Didn't these city dwellers know how popular the hill country was with tourists? Apparently not. They hadn't a clue what they were missing.

But now, hopefully, things would return to normal.

If he could just replace his assistant—and the house-keeper that the man had taken with him to Vegas, to marry—life would be good again.

Marsh thought about what his assistant and the housekeeper had said to him when they'd quit. They had said they were in love.

Love. Yeah. Right.

And if that hadn't been bad enough, the teenage daughter of his nearest neighbor, who had been coming to the house once a week to help the housekeeper, had been ordered to quit. Her parents thought her being alone with him was a bad idea.

Marsh knew precisely what they meant by "bad idea." So he had a reputation with women. So what? He was a healthy male, and the key word was *women*. He was not interested in teenagers. He'd have laughed at the thought if he hadn't been so ticked off.

At the ripe old age of thirty-four, Marsh was bitter and he knew it. He hugged the truth to him like a heating pad, keeping the bitterness alive so he'd never forget.

He had been betrayed—twice. The first time was when he was six years old, by his mother, who had left his father to seek fun in the bright lights, taking a hefty chunk of his father's money with her. Marsh had doubled down on the pain of betrayal at age twenty-four by marrying in a haze of lust only to be told by his young wife that she wasn't about to waste her youth and beauty stuck in the hill country of Texas, popping out babies and ruining her figure. In hindsight, Marsh knew he should have discussed his desire for children before they were married. It would have saved him a lot of trouble and money—especially since he had known deep down inside that he wasn't in love with her. In his estimation, love was an illusion dreamed up by poets and romance writers. But he still would have had children with her, because he truly felt as if he was meant to be a father. He wanted an heir, someone to lavish love on—the only love he truly believed in—who would take over when he was gone.

In some ways, he got lucky. Though his ex took an even larger chunk of his money than his mother had taken of his father's, Marsh gladly wrote the check, happy to get the selfish woman who had clearly married him just for his wealth out of his life and his home.

Then, to top it all off, a couple years later his father had retired, retreating to the ranch where he completed his slow decline toward death, thus also deserting Marsh.

It had been a tough time.

The coffeemaker drew Marsh from his unpleasant reverie with one last gurgle as it finished brewing. Marsh filled his mug and took a careful test sip. The brew was scalding hot but good just the same, even though the carafe, too, needed a thorough washing.

Marsh sighed. As much as he cringed at the very thought of having another female in the house, he hoped this young woman took the job. Jennifer Dunning was her name, and on paper she seemed like a mature, intelligent adult. Her credentials were excellent, almost unbelievably so. Every reference she had listed had come up aces and the investigator's report gave her a clean slate. She was from a wealthy family but apparently enjoyed working. He had even met her prominent parents on one or two occasions but he had never met her. One report he had received said she was not a part of the Dallas social scene, which seemed strange, given her family circumstances.

Basically, he had no idea what to expect.

He had requested an interview at his home. As she was located in Dallas, he was certain she would refuse to travel the considerable distance to his house merely for an interview and that would be the end of it. But she had agreed. Against his better judgment, Marsh set a date and time. Well, today was the day, and it was almost the time...if she showed up.

As a rule, Marsh usually worked in his office until late into the evening hours after dinner. For the past three months, he'd had no choice but to do the work of his assistant and housekeeper as well, which included keeping current on the cattle breeding information and managing the finances for the ranch and the payroll for the men. He barely had time to clean, although he did manage to keep his own bedroom spotless. And forget about cooking—his cooking skills were limited to slapping a sandwich together and heating a can of soup. He did brew a damn good cup of coffee, though.

He shot another look at his watch. Three minutes until two. Carrying his cup, he strolled along the wide slate-covered walkway to the front of the smooth white adobe house. Narrowing his eyes he stared at the black-topped road that turned off the highway to wind its way to the main house. After a long, dry summer, the driveway was coated by a layer of dust.

The beginnings of a frown nudged his eyebrows together as he looked again at his watch. Never late himself, he expected punctuality from others—especially someone applying for employment.

A low beep sounded from a small device attached to his belt. Security was alerting him that someone had driven onto the property. At that moment, he noticed a plume of dust rising from the back of a vehicle moving at a speed that would have made Richard Petty grin. No way was it Jennifer Dunning—he'd never met a woman who drove like that in all his life. It was Matt, or a special delivery, which was probably for the best anyway.

Marsh slashed another glance at his watch. It was exactly two when the old white Cadillac came to a screeching stop directly in front of the flagstone entranceway. The driver's-side door was thrown open and a woman stepped out, slamming the door behind her.

Oh, hell.

She was absolutely gorgeous. A bit above average height, maybe five-eight or so, she had a long mass of honey-blond hair, dark brown eyes, a lovely face with well-defined features, a lush mouth and a curvaceous body. She was basically a man's fantasy come to life.

Dammit, Marsh thought as every muscle in his body grew taut. Jennifer Dunning was the last thing he needed within a hundred miles, let alone inside his home. It had been over two weeks since he had forced himself to leave the ranch and go to his office in Dallas…and as long since he'd been with a woman. How was he going to manage this?

"Mr. Grainger?" Her voice was both cool and seductive. She extended a slim-fingered hand and smiled, revealing perfect white teeth. What else? "I'm Jennifer Dunning."

I was afraid you'd say that. Marsh kept the thought to himself and offered a faint smile in return. He took her hand, surprised by her strong grip.

Something too close to awareness caused an itch in

his palm. He released her hand and gestured for her to precede him along the walkway.

"This will lead to the kitchen," he said, trying to ignore the enticing movement of her rounded hips as she walked ahead of him. "I thought you might like something to drink after your long drive. We can talk there."

"That's fine with me. I'd love a cup of coffee." She turned to offer him another one of those heart-stopping smiles that set off every alarm bell in Marsh's head.

The interview didn't last long. Her intelligent answers exceeded his expectations. Marsh hired her before she had finished her coffee. He was immediately sorry he'd done so, but dammit, he needed the help. He was a grown man—he could keep things under control.

Couldn't he?

Jennifer Dunning was walking, talking temptation. And Marsh certainly wasn't immune to women. Every man needed R & R now and then. But he was confident he could handle the situation—and her. Hell, they'd be in two separate offices located in two separate rooms.

He sighed. He'd be fine…if she turned out to be a nice, quiet assistant who did her job and stayed out of his way.

A woman who drives like that? Not a chance. "So, when can you start?" he asked, holding out hope she would say as soon as next week.

As if she hadn't heard, Jennifer glanced around the room. "Have you found someone for the housekeeping position?"

Marsh frowned. "No, why do you ask? Does the place look that messy?"

She smiled. "Not at all. The ad online mentioned living quarters for the housekeeper attached to the house."

He nodded, curious. What was she getting at? "Yes… why?"

She didn't hesitate. "I can start tomorrow, if I can move into those quarters until you hire a housekeeper. I have my stuff in my car."

Dead silence, for a moment. "You brought all your things with you on the basis of an interview?" Marsh asked. "What if I hadn't hired you?"

Jennifer shrugged. "I'd have found something else, somewhere else. I'm not in a hurry. But no, I didn't bring *all* my things." She flashed a brilliant smile at him, and this one Marsh felt from his hairline to his… never mind. "I would have needed an 18-wheeler for that."

Uh-huh, he thought, aching in all the wrong places and wondering if he had just made the biggest mistake of his life. "Miss Dunning, are you certain you want this job?"

"Jen," she said.

"What?"

"I prefer Jen," she answered. "And yes, I am certain. I wouldn't have bothered interviewing if I didn't want it." She gave him a strange look. "Why, have you changed your mind?"

"No." Marsh gave a quick shake of his head, ignoring the voice inside himself that was telling him to take the out she'd just offered. "I haven't changed my mind…Jen."

"Okay, then can I use the housekeeper's living quarters temporarily?"

"Yeah, sure, why not," he said. "Considering the kind of responses I've had, it might be a while."

She frowned. "Exactly what kind of responses have you received?"

He shrugged. "Oh, things like, 'it's too isolated,' 'too far from Dallas or any other decent-size city,' and on and on."

"Too isolated?" Jen repeated in a tone of disbelief. "There are a lot of towns in this area. From what I gather, the entire hill country is overrun with tourists." She paused, and seemed to size him up for a moment, as if suddenly questioning the wisdom of what she'd just done. "That was one of the reasons I asked if I could have the housekeeper's quarters. I wasn't certain I could find accommodations anywhere close by."

Marsh ignored the way she was looking at him. "Well, glad to be of help," he said, as neutrally as possible.

She relaxed and flashed that smile. "I think the location is perfect."

Marsh felt as if a cool finger had just trailed his spine. Ignoring it, he said the first thing that jumped into his rattled mind.

"Would you like to look at the apartment now?"

"Yes, please." Finishing off her coffee, she stood and started for the door. "I'll go get my stuff."

"I'll help you," Marsh said. "Drive your car around to the garages at the side. There's a private entrance to the apartment there."

To Marsh's surprise, Jen didn't have all that much. He had expected to find her car packed solid with all the "necessities" most of the women he knew needed for a week away. But Jen had two suitcases, a canvas carry-on bag, a computer case and a midsize carton, which drew a mild grunt from him when he hoisted it from the trunk.

"Books," she said, smiling at him.

"No kidding," Marsh said, sliding the heavy carton

under one arm. "And I was just about to tell you how light you were traveling."

"A girl's got to have her books," Jen said as she headed off in the direction he indicated, giving him a luscious view that made him sure he was going to regret the day Jennifer Dunning came into his life.

As they walked through the garage to the apartment, Jen took note of the four very expensive cars parked in each bay and the workhorse truck in the fifth one. The cars—and the garage itself—were cleaner than the interior of the house. Jen smiled to herself as Marsh crossed the spotless cement floor to a side door.

"Will you get the door, please? It's unlocked."

"Of course," she said, skirting around him to open it and stepping back for him to precede her. Nodding in thanks, he started up a flight of stairs. To her surprise, the stairway led into a long hallway inside the house, not above the garage, as she had assumed. So, the quarters weren't attached to the house, they were *inside* the house.

Mmm, she mused, *maybe this wasn't such a good idea after all.* That thought was immediately followed by, *Oh, grow up, Jennifer, surely Mr. Grainger wouldn't try anything with his assistant, would he?* At the thought, Jen felt a strange twinge in the pit of her stomach that wasn't altogether unpleasant.

She ignored the sensation and decided she was being ridiculous. The door would have a lock…or so she hoped.

Dropping the suitcase, Marsh dug a ring of keys from his pocket and removed one, unlocking and opening the door. "After you," he said, standing back to let her pass.

"Thank you." Jen entered, pleasantly surprised by the cozy living room. She heard him sigh behind her.

"I'm sorry," he said, following her into the room. "The place needs a good cleaning. If I'd have known…"

"It's fine," she said, cutting him off. "I'll take care of it."

"Possibly I could get the young woman who used to help out once a week before the housekeeper…"

"It's all right. Really." She smiled. "I learned how to clean from the best." Jen was on the move as she spoke, checking out the bedroom, the bathroom, the small dining area and lastly the kitchen. He trailed behind her.

Making a quick turn, she almost crashed into him.

"Sorry." They spoke in unison.

Jen laughed.

Marsh smiled. "So, what do you think?"

"I like it," she said. "This kitchen is fabulous."

"You can cook?"

She swung a wicked grin at him. "I'm a damn good cook. I practically grew up with the chef in my mother's kitchen."

"Uh-huh." He hesitated before saying, "I'm a disaster in the kitchen. The last decent meal I had was in a restaurant two weeks ago."

"Too bad," she commiserated with him. "I love to cook."

"Wanna get paid for it?"

Jen frowned. "What do you mean?"

"I'll up your salary by half if you'll take over the cooking in the main kitchen downstairs."

Jen extended her hand to him. "You've got yourself a cook." Her palm tingled at the touch of his rough, callused skin against hers. It wasn't the first time—she had felt the same sensation when they had shaken hands before, only then she had put it down to nervousness over the interview. Then there was that funny twist in her midsection a short time ago.

She didn't know what it all was exactly, but she didn't like it.

Fortunately, the contact lasted only a moment. He released her hand and moved to the door, pausing again to glance back at her.

"You don't have to start your administrative duties tomorrow, as you offered. Take the next three days to get set up in here. I'll be in my office. If you need anything—" he nodded at the slim phone on the countertop "—just hit number one. Any questions?"

"Yes," Jen said. "Since I assume there is no food here, where is the nearest grocery store?"

He frowned.

Jen had the distinct impression he frowned a lot.

"I thought you were going to cook in the kitchen downstairs."

Men. Squashing an urge to roll her eyes, Jen made do with a silent sigh. "I will need a few things in here, as well. You know, coffee, milk, other staples." Straight-faced, she admitted, "I'm a night snacker."

A shade of a smile crossed his lips. Jen had another distinct impression: that he didn't smile all that often. Shame. It was quite an attractive smile.

"Look, leave the grocery shopping until tomorrow. There is stuff in the downstairs kitchen—in the pantry, fridge and freezer. If you'll come along now, you can take things for tonight and make a shopping list for tomorrow."

"Okay." Jen followed him from the room. Getting to the kitchen was simple. They walked to the end of the hallway to a large landing, where a broad open staircase curved down to an equally broad foyer at the front of the house.

At the bottom of the stairs, Marsh turned left and strode along another hallway that led to the kitchen at the back of the house. By Jen's calculations, her new living quarters were directly above the kitchen and formal dining room. From the dining room's sliding glass doors, she caught a glimpse of a large patio and a swimming pool.

Gorgeous property, nicer than the too-formal look of her parents' home, she was thinking. *What will it feel like to live in a place like this as the hired help?*

"Okay, the kitchen's all yours," Marsh said. "I've got work to do."

"Wait," Jen said.

He frowned again but this time, impatience flashed across his features, making them look severe. Slowly, he raised one eyebrow.

If he meant to intimidate, he succeeded.

But Jen was not about to let him know it. "Jot down a few of your food preferences," she said, fully aware that her request sounded like an order. "Meanwhile, I'll start a list of the things we'll need." She raised an eyebrow right back at him. "Okay?"

He sighed, gave her a terse nod and left the room.

When he was gone, Jen exhaled. Working for Marshall Grainger was going to be a challenge, in a number of ways, not the least of which was remaining professional and not losing her temper right along with him.

Finding a notebook and pencils in a drawer, she began opening cabinets. None of them contained foodstuffs; a few were completely empty. Then she discovered the double pantry next to the fridge. Now she was getting somewhere. There were plenty of dried foods:

flour, sugar, cereals and canned goods, except for soup. There were only two cans in an otherwise empty area.

She stared at the shelf for a moment, wondering whether her new employer didn't like soup, or loved it so much it was a regular for him.

Recalling his words, she shook her head. He had admitted to being a lousy cook. Conclusion? The man had been practically living on soup. After checking out the fridge, she added sandwiches to the list of things he'd been living on. Other than two slices of cheese wrapped in plastic, a nearly empty carton of eggs, a small package of bacon, a half-empty carton of milk and a couple of slices of bread, along with some beer and soda, the fridge was empty.

Jen opened the freezer door on the side-by-side. Now, this looked better. The freezer was packed and everything was dated. Maybe there was hope for Marsh Grainger after all, she thought with a smile.

Her shopping list completed, she sent a slow look around the room. The countertop looked spotless, as if very recently cleaned. Hmm, she mused. Had her boss given it a quick cleaning before she arrived?

Had he done that for her benefit?

Giving herself a mental get-with-it shake, she glanced at the clock.

It was eight minutes after three. Jen figured she had time enough to clean the kitchen. But first, dinner. She rummaged around in the freezer and grabbed a package of ground turkey and a bag of mixed veggies with an herb sauce. Within minutes she had a turkey stew cooking in the slow cooker on the counter.

Turkey stew would have to do. Smiling at her silly rhyme, she pulled out some cleaning supplies, slipped on a pair of plastic gloves and got down to the business at hand.

A couple hours later, her skin moist with perspiration from her efforts, Jen stood in the kitchen doorway admiring the results. The room was spotless. A sense of satisfaction brought a small smile to her lips—Ida would be proud.

After touching the floor tiles to see if they were dry, Jen walked to the phone and hit the 1 button.

"What is it, Ms. Dunning?"

Jen didn't miss the exasperated note in Marshall's voice. Keeping her own voice carefree and chipper, she said, "Dinner is ready whenever you are." She paused, then deliberately added, "sir."

"Thank you. But don't call me that."

His tone had lightened a bit. Jen smirked. "You're welcome."

"I'll be there in a little while."

"Take your time, it will keep. I'm going up to my place now."

"What about you?"

She couldn't quite read his meaning. Was he worried she wanted to dine with him? Or did he want her to? "I've eaten, thank you. What time would you like breakfast?"

"Is six-thirty okay with you?"

Good grief, was he actually asking her instead of telling her? "Yes," she briskly answered, "six-thirty will be fine." She waited a heartbeat before saying, "Good night, *sir*."

Without giving him a chance to respond, Jen hit the off button, leaving the room with a jaunty step.

Two

Jen sat in a comfortable chair, sipping hot coffee while gazing around the living room in her new quarters. Though not very large, the room was cozy and would be even better with a bit of decorating.

She'd get at the cleaning tomorrow. Since she had the next three days off, she could take her time, she thought. But as she tried to make a mental list of everything she wanted to do, her mind kept drifting…to her new employer.

What was his deal, anyway? She mused, hearing an echo of his hard voice, seeing again the sharpness of his steel-gray eyes.

Tough man, Marshall Grainger. Though she had never seen him in person before, Jen had seen him in the paper and had heard about him. And there was plenty to hear—good and bad, but never indifferent.

He had married young, and divorced soon after—

a sticky affair from what Jen had heard. She gathered that the young woman, a genuine beauty, had expected Marsh to introduce her into the highest social circles in Texas. But apparently Mr. Marshall Grainger wasn't into the social scene, and never had been. So, goodbye wife—and goodbye to a large slice from his money pie.

But, rumor had it, his mother had done the same deal to his father, and Marsh was one bitter man. He disdained women, while not above using them for his own convenience.

Luckily for her she was only here to work. She had no interest in Marsh Grainger, and she intended to keep it that way. So what if he was as handsome as the day was long? Jen had never had a problem keeping her cool around good-looking men—she wasn't about to start now.

She rose from the comfy chair and walked to the kitchen to rinse her cup. It was time to put clean sheets on the bed, have a shower and hit the sack. *Breakfast for my steely-eyed boss at six-thirty,* she reminded herself.

Jen had a full breakfast of bacon, eggs, hash browns, toast and fresh coffee ready when Marsh strode into the kitchen at precisely six-thirty the next morning. Unlike most CEOs going to work, he was dressed in faded jeans, a chambray shirt and well-worn running shoes.

He looked terrific.

"Good morning," she greeted him cheerily, dishing up the meal onto two plates.

"Urmph," he responded as he seated himself at the solid-oak table.

Jen stifled a smile and placed his breakfast in front of him, then put her plate on a tray and started to head upstairs.

"Where are you going?" he asked, his forkful of eggs in midair between his plate and his mouth.

Gritting her teeth at his imperious tone, while reminding herself that this grouchy man was her employer, Jen managed to dredge up a pleasant reply. "I'm going upstairs."

He motioned at the chair opposite. "Have a seat. There are a few things I want to go over with you."

Offloading her food from the tray to the table, Jen sat and patiently watched him enjoying her culinary efforts.

"Eat," he said, snapping off a bite of crisp bacon with his strong white teeth. "We can talk over coffee."

They ate the meal in dead silence. Jen was tempted to speak, but she squashed the urge, determined to make him start the conversation.

As soon as he sat back and laid his napkin beside his plate, Jen was on her feet, clearing. Deliberately making him wait, she stashed the dishes in the dishwasher before pouring the coffee and then sitting down again. Wrapping her hands around the mug, she looked directly into his eyes, and was startled to find herself fascinated by the odd silvery color. She again felt that funny tingling sensation inside, deep inside, and again she didn't like it. The feeling was too...too out of her control. She quickly looked away.

"I'll be leaving later this morning," he said. "I have a few business appointments. You'll have the place to yourself for the entire weekend as I won't be back until Monday."

A strange relief washed through her at the thought that she wouldn't have to see Marsh for a few days. It was mixed with a sense of disappointment that she chose to ignore. "Great," she said. "It'll give me plenty of time to get settled in."

"You have no reason to be concerned about being alone here. I have—"

Jen frowned, interrupting. "Actually, I like being alone."

Marsh leveled a cool look at her; apparently he didn't appreciate being interrupted. "Any woman should be afraid of being alone on a property this size," he growled. "I'm a wealthy man. That, plus the size of the place, makes it a target. In addition to a man who takes care of the horses, I have security all over the grounds."

"I didn't notice any security when I drove up," she said, taking a sip of the coffee.

He gave her a wry look. "That's the idea—you're not supposed to notice them. But trust me, they were there, and I was notified of your arrival."

"You have horses?" she asked, ignoring his tone.

"Yes, I have horses."

When he didn't add anything further, she asked, "What about the office work?"

"That can wait until Monday. I brought everything up to date before you arrived." He lifted a hand to a breast pocket and withdrew a white bank envelope and a small black leather case. "That should be enough cash to purchase whatever you need," he said. "The case is an alarm. If you hear or see anything that doesn't seem right to you, press the button. There will be security here in minutes. It will also open the garage. I'm going to pull the truck out so you can park your car."

Sighing, she reluctantly took the case.

He frowned at her. "Keep it with you at all times. And that's an order."

"Yes, sir."

His eyes narrowed. "Oh, and I also listed a few of

my favorite meals…as you asked," he added in a dry-as-dust tone.

"Thank you." Jen pushed back her chair and stood. "If you'll excuse me now, I'm going up to clean the apartment…unless you have other instructions for me?" She raised her brows.

He nodded his head, also standing. "There is one more thing." He sent a slow glance around the room. "You did a good job on the kitchen. It's spotless."

A tiny smile played at the corners of her mouth. "Not quite," she said. "The curtains need laundering."

For a moment Marsh simply stared at her, then, with a shake of his head, he started for the hallway. "I'll see you sometime Monday." With that he strode from the room.

Jen watched him go, wondering just what kind of power struggle she had gotten herself into with Marsh Grainger.

She spent the rest of the day giving the apartment a thorough cleaning. By the time she looked up, it was time for supper. Yet as busy as she was, there were moments—too many, to Jen's way of thinking—when thoughts of Marsh pushed past her guard to tease her imagination.

Jen didn't appreciate his intrusion. He was her employer. Period. Nothing more. Who was he, really, other than a tough and bitter man? In all truth, he had a right to his bitterness, but it was none of her concern.

Still, the thoughts persisted. Why? In a word, Marshall Grainger was all male. A ruggedly handsome, sexy-as-hell male at that.

Startled by her last thought, Jen gave herself a mental shake. *Get it together, woman,* she told herself. *Marsh may be all those things, but he uses women, and you don't want any part of that.*

Forget him and get back to work.

When she had finished cleaning, Jen took a long, soothing shower, slipped into a nightshirt, then sat down with her laptop to contact her friends. Naturally there were emails from every one of them, demanding more information. She sent them a group email back, saying she had gotten a new job and would get back to them later, after she had settled into the position and had more complete information to offer.

The fact of the matter was, Jen was not quite ready to tell her friends what had happened to send her running from her home. Nor was she ready to tell them that she was living under Marsh Grainger's roof. Tired, muscles aching from the unusual flurry of physical activity, Jen was then content to drop into bed early. With any luck, she'd fall asleep quickly before she had time for more thoughts of Marshall Grainger.

Saturday morning Jen woke refreshed if still a bit achy, proof of the fact that she had been idle too long. She had stayed in shape playing tennis and horseback riding whenever she could, but while musing on her future options during the past several weeks she had barely left her apartment. The cleaning exercise had done her good.

She dressed in designer jeans, a pin-tucked white shirt and flat-heeled boots. Deciding to grab breakfast in town, she left the house for her shopping spree.

She looked inside the envelope Marsh had given her. Along with the short list of his favorite meals and directions to the nearest mall, Marsh had left her a ridiculous amount of money. Jen rolled her eyes but couldn't stop the smile that spread across her face.

Either Marsh Grainger had no idea what things actually cost, or he was an extremely generous man underneath that gruff exterior.

It was a lovely, warm autumn day, perfect for shopping. As she headed down the driveway, Jen kept an eye out for signs of the security he had told her about. She didn't see hide nor hair until she neared the stone pillars flanking the entranceway. A short distance off the road, barely visible, an all-terrain vehicle was parked next to a low hanging tree. As she drove through the entranceway, she thrust her arm out the window and waved as she hit the horn. She laughed as she received a wave and toot in return.

Well, at least the security is friendly, Jen thought, applying a little pressure to the gas pedal. She drove first to the mall Marsh had mentioned, and went into the first shop she came to displaying home decorations.

Not into knick-knacks, Jen chose three pictures in three different sizes. The smaller pictures she chose were pastoral scenes, one of a field covered with Texas bluebonnets, the other of a basket of wildflowers set on one end of a long library table. But the largest one, for the living room, was a rendering in black-and-white of a ship, alone on a wide sea. For some reason, it reminded her of Marsh, alone in that big, remote house.

The thought sent a little shiver through her. *Now, that's simply ridiculous,* she chided herself, trying and failing to ignore the feeling. *There's no reason to be thinking of Marsh as a lonely man—in fact, that's just plain dangerous.* Pushing away her thoughts, Jen left the mall and headed for the supermarket.

The sun was beginning to set as Jen drove back onto

the property. Her glance automatically shifted to the tree. There was a vehicle there, but a different one. Again she hit the horn and waved, and again she was greeted in kind.

In high spirits, satisfied with her selection of decorations for the apartment, Jen unloaded the car and set to work stashing the food in cabinets, fridge and freezer. As she worked, a curiosity set in about the rest of the house—and, if she was honest with herself, Marsh. It wouldn't exactly be snooping, she decided. Just… investigating. After all, she'd be working here—she might as well familiarize herself with the place. She quietly slipped into the main part of the house and found herself peeking into six bedrooms and five bathrooms, all of which were long past due for a good dusting and vacuuming. Stepping into the last room at the end of the hallway, Jen felt her breath catch when she opened the door to the huge room that obviously belonged to Marsh.

The room was the complete opposite of opulent—it was Spartan, and it was spotless, not a speck of dust anywhere. A tiny smile feathered her lips. It seemed Mr. Marshall Grainger liked a clean room just as much as she did.

The furniture was plain, straight lines, solid oak. The bed—his bed—was enormous. His color scheme consisted primarily of black, white and red, stark but effective, somehow perfect for him.

Feeling more like a snoop by the minute but unable to resist, Jen moved into the room, going to the row of sliding mirrored closet doors along one wall. One entire section was full of tailored suits, one of them a tuxedo. Another section held nothing but dress shirts in every color imaginable, including white with black stripes. She liked that one, imagining how sexy he'd look in it.

Sexy? she thought. *What am I doing in here?*

But Jen kept going—she couldn't seem to make herself stop. There was something too enticing about being this close to Marsh. The next section held jeans, some faded, some brand-new. They were the longest jeans she'd ever seen in her life, perfect for a tall drink of water like Marsh. The last section held casual shirts of every style and hue. On the floor beneath each area were shoes—dress shoes, work boots, riding boots, running shoes. Jen laughed. And she thought she was a shoe maniac!

Closing the sliding doors, she opened another door in the bedroom to find a good-size dressing room and a spacious bathroom. The bathtub was huge, with water jets set into the sides. A compact shower stall sat next to the tub. The black-and-white marble vanity top looked much like the surface of his dresser—sparse and neat. A toothbrush was set in a marble brush holder, and a woven metal basket contained a hairbrush, and several unopened bars of soap. Spartan indeed, she thought, slowly stepping back into the hallway.

She ignored the little twinge of guilt she felt about her "investigation," thinking that in the short time she was in his room, she had learned much about him.

Marshall Grainger was wealthy beyond belief—that was a given. He was also a man who lived life stripped to the bone, despite all the clothing. His bathroom vanity held nothing but the bare essentials, including what Jen knew was a very expensive bottle of cologne. She hadn't smelled it on him so far. She wondered if he'd been wearing it when he'd left for Houston. Perhaps he didn't have any meetings or appointments to attend—maybe there was a woman there, waiting for him.

The very idea caused a strange twist in Jen's chest, a twist that felt like jealousy. *What would the woman be like? Beautiful? Of course. Sophisticated? Naturally.* The strange jealousy she felt grew stronger. *Was this woman his lover?*

Bringing herself up abruptly, Jen quickly turned and went roaming through the rest of the house. It was absolutely gorgeous. Open rooms, one flowing into another. She stepped into one and somehow knew she had entered her office. It was roomy yet utilitarian, containing everything she would need. It even had two club chairs, one in front of the large desk, the other to one side. She liked it at once.

Exiting that room, Jen went to the next one: Marsh's office. It was locked.

Walking back toward her apartment, Jen contemplated the situation. The beautiful house needed some care. She hadn't been hired to clean, but damn, such a house should shine.

She sighed. She had all day tomorrow to herself with nothing pressing to do. A smile touched her lips as she made a decision. Tomorrow, she would clean the big house, just to see if the boss noticed anything different.

Of course, Jen assured herself as she mounted the stairs to her apartment, her decision had nothing to do with pleasing him. Why should it? She had nothing to prove except her ability as his assistant. It didn't matter what Marshall Grainger thought of her.

Did it?

She suddenly imagined herself back in Marsh's bedroom, tidying it up, making it perfect for his return. When she remembered that his room was already spotless and that there was no need for her to go back in there, she blushed, hot and fierce, and promised to push all thoughts of Marsh from her mind for the rest of the night.

Marsh sat across the table from the beautiful woman his business acquaintance had introduced him to mere hours ago. Admittedly, Marsh was on the prowl, itchier than usual for a woman. Without a twinge of conscience, he had invited the woman—Chandra was her name—to have dinner with him that evening. But now, after several hours, her appeal had faded, through no real fault of her own. She couldn't help it if she wasn't Miss Jennifer Dunning.

When Chandra looked at him expectantly, he realized she was waiting for some kind of response. He hadn't a clue what she was talking about; he hadn't exactly been paying attention. He took a chance and nodded, and that appeared to satisfy her.

Being inattentive, his conscience kicked into action. *What in hell am I doing here?*

Marsh knew the answer—he simply didn't want to look at it too closely. He had been hoping for a bed partner later in the evening, and Chandra had seemed a good choice. Now all he wanted was a bed to himself.

That wasn't quite true, either.

In truth, he ached for one woman: Jennifer Dunning.

He had been in her company…how long? Not much more than an hour or so, total? It was ridiculous. Plus, she was now an employee, and he never fooled around with employees. Of course, other than the previous housekeeper, who was pushing fifty, he had never had an employee living in his home, either. What was it about her that got to him so strongly?

"…and I told him he could just go to hell."

Marsh blinked himself back into the moment. "You did?" he asked, because Chandra had paused again and he knew he had to say something.

"Certainly," Chandra declared. "The man insulted me by assuming I'd go to bed with him a few hours after meeting him."

Marsh gave her a wry smile. "Yes, of course," he agreed. "I don't blame you in the least." He almost added "the cad" but thought that might be a bit over the top.

"Ah, here's dinner now," she said, satisfaction curving her lips as the server placed their meals before them.

After dinner, Marsh drove Chandra straight home to her condo on the outskirts of the city. "You don't need to get out," she said, even though he hadn't made a move to do so. "It's perfectly safe."

"Yes, I see the doorman," he said, eyeing the burly uniformed man standing sentinel by the entrance.

"Thank you for a lovely dinner," she said, as the doorman strolled forward to open the door for her.

"Thank you for joining me," he answered, hoping his tone didn't reveal his relief. He politely added, "I'm glad you were free for the evening."

"And I." She smiled with a tinge of disappointment, and slid from the seat.

Marsh never liked disappointing a lady—even one who seemed to have given him a line about not going to bed with a man hours after meeting him—but his mind was clearly elsewhere this evening. He'd put the Jag he kept in Houston into Drive before she'd reached the doorway, and Jen was back on his mind by the time he pulled into traffic.

Why the hell had he hired her?

Marsh sighed. He had hired Jen because he was getting desperate. She was intelligent, personable, fully qualified, friendly and willing to do the cooking.

Yet, he had to admit, she was the reason he had come to Houston. After meeting her, when the touch of her hand made his palm—and parts south—itch, and when that itch had swiftly turned into a familiar warmth that spread through his body, he knew he was in trouble.

He wanted her. He had wanted her within minutes of meeting her, and it had played hell with his normally sound judgment. So, afraid he'd do or say something unacceptable, he manufactured a business trip to put some distance between them, calling his friend Scott to set up a meeting in Houston. To his confused embarrassment, after sitting across the breakfast table from Jen that morning, he couldn't get to the airstrip soon enough. He had arrived forty-five minutes earlier than he had asked his pilot to be there.

Marsh kept the plane primarily to get from his house in Dallas to the ranch in Colorado in a hurry if he needed to, but used it himself for quick trips like this one. Except that this trip had been unnecessary. He felt like an idiot, getting all hot and sweaty over a woman he had just met. Sure he had been all hot and sweaty over women before, like his previous wife, but he had been a lot younger then. And look where that had gotten him.

Well, the heat was gone now and so was the sweat. Marsh was resolved to revert to form—cool and aloof. He just had to remember that Jen was an employee, nothing more.

Cool and aloof, that would be his mantra.

Marsh could only hope.

* * *

Satisfyingly tired from the day spent cleaning the house, Jen lay curled up in bed, floating in the in-between world of wakefulness and sleep.

The growling sound of a vehicle jerked her awake. She glanced at the clock on the nightstand—it read 1:30 a.m. She heard the automatic garage door open, then slide shut again. Moments later she heard the kitchen door. She rolled onto her back, listening.

Although she would never have admitted it, Jen had not slept easily the previous two nights. She had wakened often, listening. She told herself it was just her new surroundings, that she wasn't used to sleeping in the quiet hill country yet.

Yeah. Right.

A sigh whispered through her lips. Her eyelids grew heavy, slowly closing. *Marsh was home.* Too fuzzy-minded to question the comfort she drew from that thought, Jen drifted into a deep, restful sleep within seconds.

She woke the next morning feeling rested, and had breakfast ready when Marsh entered the kitchen at pre-cisely six-thirty. She had wondered if he would make it after returning to the house so late, but there he was, wide-awake, alert and handsome as the rugged devil.

"Good morning." She greeted him with a smile and a large plate in hand. He did not return her smile.

"Morning," he said as he sat down and drew his nap-kin over his jean-clad knees. "Smells good."

"Thanks," she said, setting the plate of eggs, pota-toes and a large steak in front of him. She turned back to the counter to get her own plate.

"Have a seat." It wasn't so much an invitation as an order.

But today, Jen didn't mind. He was the boss, after all. They ate in silence again. Marsh didn't say a word until after she had removed the plates and served the coffee.

"You cleaned the house." His tone was hard.

"Yes." She held his gaze, slowly arching one questioning brow.

"Why?"

Her other brow went up in surprise. "Because it needed cleaning."

"Yes, it did. But you weren't hired to clean."

"I cleaned the kitchen," Jen shot back at him. "You didn't object to that."

"I hired you to cook," he said, returning fire. "So of course I wouldn't object to you cleaning the kitchen. That has nothing to do with the rest of the house." He frowned, perplexed. "I don't get it. Why would a woman like you even consider cooking and cleaning in any house?"

"What do you mean, a woman like me?"

"You're from a rich family, dammit. And I didn't mean 'a woman like you' as a slur, if that's what you're thinking. You don't need to work at all, never mind cook and clean. It doesn't make sense."

Jen sighed, fully aware she should have expected this reaction from him. Before she could begin to explain, he tossed more at her.

"You come from a well-known, wealthy family, grew up in the lap of luxury in the highest social circles—"

"Hold it right there." Jen cut him off. She shoved her chair back, scraping it over the floor tiles as she slapped her hands on her hips. He opened his mouth. "First and foremost, Mr. Grainger, I am not a member of any social circle. I am not a social butterfly. My parents are the socialites. I was practically raised by my parents' housekeeper and chef, Ida and Tony."

She paused for breath but rushed on before he could get a word out.

"They gave me a sense of being loved for myself, and taught me the value of honest work. Ida taught me how to take care of a beautiful house. Tony taught me how to prepare delicious meals. *This* is a beautiful house," she continued. "It deserves to be kept that way. And yes, I'm used to well-prepared meals."

Marsh was quiet for a moment, as if waiting to see if she was finished. When she didn't speak, he said, "It will only get dusty again."

She rolled her eyes. "Then I'll clean it again."

"And what about the work you were hired to do?"

Jen made a quick study of his closed expression, trying to decide if he was about to fire her from a job she hadn't yet begun. At any other time in her life, she wouldn't have cared. Now, for some strange reason she didn't want to examine too closely, she *did* care. She wanted this job, cleaning and all.

She wanted to stay here with him.

"I'll clean on Saturdays." She again arched one brow. "Or were you thinking to have me work in the office on weekends, too?"

"No, of course not." He heaved a sigh. "I'll pay you for the cleaning."

"Thank you." She smiled at her victory. "I'll get the breakfast things away so I can get started in the office." To her surprise, he began clearing the table.

"I'll help here," he said, carrying dishes to the dishwasher. "The sooner we can get started, the better. I have a lot of work to do." His voice was rough, as if

he were embarrassed about helping with anything domestic.

Jen fought against a laugh. "Yes, sir."

He sighed again. "I asked you not to call me 'sir'."

She nodded. "I know."

She was really beginning to enjoy being with him.
Was she nuts? He had barely been civil to her since
she'd arrived at the house. How could she even think
she was beginning to like the man?

Maybe she had been fawned over for too long, by
her parents, and Ida and Tony.

Possibly, a man like Marshall Grainger was just what
she needed. A no-nonsense, straight-talking man with
a perfect smile and silver eyes.

No doubt about it, she thought. *I am nuts.*

Three

Marsh sat in front of the computer, a newer model than the one Jen had used at her previous job. She told him the machine was new to her, so he began with the basics. He had drawn another chair up to the desk next to him. They were so close that whenever he turned to explain something to her, or she leaned in to get a closer look at the data on the screen, their thighs briefly brushed against each other.

It was purely accidental and yet Jen felt a quiver of awareness when his hard thigh touched her soft one.

He smelled good, and not of the cologne she'd seen in his bedroom. Jen wished she had noticed the smell of his woodsy soap and his natural musky male scent earlier while they'd cleared away the breakfast things, so she could have been prepared. Now, here, sitting so close to him, his scent enveloped her. And it wasn't a bad thing—not at all.

Yanking her mind away from Marsh and back to the business at hand, she reached across him with her right arm to point at data on the screen she didn't understand. At the same time, he lifted his hand, his forearm brushing over her breast.

For an instant they both froze. She pulled her arm back, he dropped his hand. Jen tingled all the way down to her toenails.

"I—" he began.

"It's all right." She cut him off, her voice as cool and calm as she could manage. "I know it wasn't deliberate."

"That's right, it wasn't, but still—"

Again she interrupted him. "Let's just get back to work. Okay?"

"Yeah, sure," he agreed, his tone rough-edged. "What was your question?"

Instead of reaching across him, she read the part she wasn't sure of. The tension quivering between them still hovered as he explained.

They broke for lunch not much later. "I'm going to my office," he said, starting for the room opposite hers. "I'll be with you in a few minutes."

"I'll start lunch," she said. "Is a chef salad okay with you?"

His office door shut before he could give her an answer.

Jen went into the kitchen, threw the salad together and stood at the counter eating while getting the ingredients together for Yankee pot roast for dinner. She was peeling potatoes—trying to ignore the fact that her body was still tingling from Marsh's touch—when he entered.

"Aren't you going to sit down?" he asked, digging into his salad.

"I'm about finished," Jen answered, popping the last

forkful into her mouth as she slid the roast pan into the oven. The last thing she needed right now was to sit close to Marsh Grainger one second sooner than she had to.

They were back at her desk fifteen minutes later, both making sure to keep as much distance between them as possible. By midafternoon, Jen was up to speed.

"I think I can handle it now myself," she said, aware that his scent was making her overwarm.

Marsh nodded. He pushed back the chair and glanced at his watch. "You can quit for the day, you've got a lot of data to mentally process. I'll see you at dinner."

"Is six all right?"

"That'll be fine." His office door shut, but Jen stayed right where she was, needing a moment to gather herself together.

Working with Marsh Grainger was definitely going to be difficult if she couldn't even handle accidental physical contact with the man.

Some employee *she* was going to be.

That night, Jen's cell phone rang. She wasn't surprised to see that it was her mother calling, wondering what had taken her so long. Jen sighed as she answered. "Hello, Mother."

"Hello, Mother? *Hello, Mother?*" Celia Dunning came close to shouting, and Celia rarely shouted at anything. "You take off leaving only a note saying 'I'm off to see the wizard,' and all you say is 'Hello, Mother'?"

"What else am I supposed to say?" Jen answered, gritting her teeth to hold her temper. "I left you a note. You couldn't have been too perturbed—it's been almost a week since I left." Try as she might, Jen couldn't ignore the hurt she felt over the fact that it had taken her mother so long to call.

"I'm sorry." Celia now sounded contrite. "Your father decided on the spur of the moment Thursday evening that he felt lucky and wanted to fly to Las Vegas. He was right," she went on. "He hit a winning streak at the tables." She sighed. "We got back a little while ago. I just found your note."

"Okay." What else could she say?

"Where are you, Jennifer?" Celia's voice was now tight with concern.

"I'm working for Marshall Grainger," Jen said, warmth spreading over her as she said Marsh's name out loud. She tried to snap herself out of it. "As I also wrote on my note."

"Jennifer Dunning," her mother said, sounding panicked, "I want to know exactly where you are living."

Lifting the phone from her ear, Jen stared at it in astonishment. The sound of her mother's obvious nervousness was shocking. Very little rattled her mother. She hesitated to reveal that she was living in Marsh's home, afraid her mother would really freak out.

"I'm living in Mr. Grainger's house," she said as calmly as she could, steeling herself for the explosion.

There was a quiet pause, then Celia went off like a rocket. "In his *house?* What house—here in Dallas? Are you out of your mind? Good heavens, Jennifer, have you any idea of that man's reputation?"

"I may not be socially inclined, Mother, but I'm not unconscious. Of course I'm aware of his reputation." Jen answered with hard-fought calm. "But I am here in the capacity of his assistant, not his mistress. And I'm staying in the housekeeper's quarters, in the back of the house," she tacked on reassuringly.

"But you already have a position here in Dallas."

Ignoring the sting of injured tears in her eyes, Jen said, "Mother, I quit my job over two weeks ago." She didn't add, *And you never noticed.*

"You did?"

Jen closed her eyes. "Yes, I did."

"But why didn't you tell me?" Celia demanded, her tone impatient.

"You were…busy, and I didn't want to interrupt." She cringed at the memory of discovering her parents' secret.

"But still, Jennifer, you could have told me."

Tears trickled down Jen's face but she was damned if she would allow her distress to show in her voice. "Well, I'm here now and enjoying the work."

"But where is here exactly?"

"Mr. Grainger's home is near Fredericksburg." There was no way Jen would reveal the location of the house, certain that if she did her mother would show up within a day or two.

"Jennifer." Impatience was strong in Celia's voice. "Where precisely—"

"Oh, I'm sorry," Jen interrupted her. "Mr. Grainger is calling. I have to go. We're very busy."

"But—"

Again Jen interrupted. "Mother, please, I must hang up now. You can call me again, or email me. Goodbye." She gently pressed the off button.

Jen wiped the tears from her eyes, realizing in that moment just how deeply it affected her that it had taken her parents so long to realize she was gone. She had indeed shocked them with her actions, but at this point, her mother's reaction felt like too little too late.

At some point, she would have to talk to them about

what had happened. But she wasn't going to be ready for that conversation anytime soon.

The rest of the week played out much the same as the first day in her office, except for one difference—and it was a big one.

On Tuesday, after serving dinner, Jen was about to take her meal up to her apartment when Marsh again asked her to join him. But this time, he actually started talking to her moments after she seated herself opposite him.

Of course, it was mainly talk about the ranch business, but that beat silence hands-down. She did have one problem, though—the quiet sound of his voice caused a quivery sensation inside her, and as if that wasn't enough, there seemed to be a constant hum of energy flowing between them, not only at the table but whenever they were in the same room. But based on his attitude, it obviously didn't mean a thing to him.

All in all, she'd become uneasy whenever he was around.

On the weekend, Jen barely saw anything of Marsh as she was busy cleaning and doing her laundry. A few times, when she was overheated, she had a swim before making a meal. She fell into a pattern of curling up with a book in the evening and ignoring her mother's phone calls. Jen had nothing to say for now.

The time seemed to fly by. After several more weeks of work during which Jen saw very little of Marsh, it came as a surprise one Saturday morning when, after clearing away the breakfast things, he stopped her as she headed for the laundry room.

"Jen," he said. "Do you ride?"

Blinking, Jen turned, laundry basket held in front of her. "What?"

"I asked if you ride," he said. "Horses."

"Oh, yes. Why?" She noticed a small smile twitching at the corners of his mouth.

"I'm going for a ride, to give the horses a run while getting some fresh air. I was wondering if you'd care to join me," he said. "Other than a few laps in the pool, we've both been inside all week."

Stunned by the sudden invitation, Jen could barely speak. She simply stared at him, trying not to be affected by the snug fit of his jeans clinging to his flat belly and his tight butt, the width of his shoulders beneath a chambray shirt, the sprinkling of hair on his forearms below the turned-back sleeves. She cautioned herself against accepting his invitation.

And then she accepted.

"I'd love to go," she said, ignoring for the moment how simply being near him affected her.

"Good." Marsh gave a quick nod and started for the kitchen door. "Leave the laundry until later."

"I need to change," Jen said, glancing down at the faded, torn clam-diggers she had put on to clean. "It'll only take a minute."

"I'll go saddle the horses." He stepped outside, hesitating before closing the door to say, "Take your time, I'm in no hurry."

As Jen headed to her apartment, her heart beating quickly from more than just the exercise of climbing the stairs, she wondered exactly what she'd just gotten herself into with Marsh Grainger.

Now, why in hell did I do that? Marsh thought, striding to the stables. Wasn't it hard enough merely sitting across the table from Jen, watching the smooth suppleness of her body as she moved around the kitchen?

He started saddling the mare he had chosen for her. When had he become a masochist? Marsh shook his head. He hadn't been with a woman in several months. Hell, he hadn't been off the property in weeks, not since he'd been to Houston. And he had come home from there frustrated and dissatisfied.

Finished saddling the mare, he turned to his mount. *What is it about Jen that is different from any other woman? And how many times have I asked myself that question since she moved in?* Marsh mused, throwing the saddle blanket over the back of his horse. Okay, she was beautiful—traffic-stopping beautiful—but he had met many beautiful women, a lot of them deeply in love…with themselves.

On the other hand, Jen didn't appear at all narcissistic or even impressed by her beauty. That was okay, he was impressed enough for both of them. She had a mouth made for kissing. The thought made him warm. Warm, hell, it made him hot. Mentally tamping down his sudden need, he directed his thoughts away from her lips to a more comfortable direction.

On reflection, Jen appeared down-to-earth and easygoing with a good sense of humor and an excellent work ethic, and her cooking could put most professional chefs' offerings to shame.

But the thing that really got to him was she sang while she worked. Even though her tone was soft it had filtered under his office door a few times. The sound had the power to cause a strange sensation inside him, bringing back old memories he hadn't thought about in years.

He was just a kid, a kid whose mother had left him

wondering what he had done to make her go. His father was so desolate he barely spoke to his son.

Fortunately, Marsh had had a friend from school. His name was Ben, a good kid whose mother, Marie, invited Marsh to come to their home whenever he wanted to go. And, with the constant gloom and doom in the house, Marsh was always ready to go.

Marie had a beautiful laugh, and she laughed a lot. It was a feel-good sound that touched something in him… just like Jen's singing.

Marsh had a startling realization. Practically every-thing Jen did evoked those warm sensations he had en-joyed in Ben's home. He knew Jen would make a good wife and an excellent mother—without straining he could almost hear her crooning to a baby.

This was what he was thinking when he looked down and realized Jen was standing next to him. All he could do was hope she wasn't a mind reader.

Jen had obviously caught Marsh deep in thought— she could tell from the faraway look on his face that he hadn't known she was there. She'd been pretty lost in thought herself the whole time she'd been changing into jeans, a pullover cotton sweater and low-heeled ankle boots. She'd grabbed a straw cowboy hat from a hook on the wall in the laundry room, and strode out into the beautiful October day, aware that her breath was com-ing a trifle quickly the closer she got to the stables—or rather, to Marsh.

He hadn't heard her come in, and for a moment, she'd just watched him standing by the horses, reins in one hand as he stroked the neck of the nearest animal with the other, an expression of deep contemplation on his face shadowed by the brim of his hat.

For an instant, Jen had wondered how it would feel to have his hand stroking her. She'd had that image in her head as she came to stand next to him. And when he turned to look at her, the expression on his face sent a sizzle up her spine, leaving her breathless.

"Ready to go?" he asked, handing a set of reins to her.

"Yes," she said, forcing her gaze from him to the horses. "They are beautiful animals," she murmured, moving forward to stroke the white star on the long head of her horse. She laughed as the shiny roan nuzzled her hand. "Morgan horses?"

"Yes," he answered, offering her a smile that set off the sizzle again. "Do you need help mounting?"

Jen shook her head, certain that if he touched her, however lightly, the sizzle would consume her. "Is she gentle?" Her voice was barely there. She cleared her throat.

Marsh frowned. "Yes. Is something wrong?"

"No…no." Feeling like a fool, she again shook her head. "I'm fine."

"Her name is Star." He shrugged. "Applicable, if not very original."

"I think it's perfect." Smiling, Jen moved to the left side of the horse, slipped her boot into the stirrup and swung her leg over into the saddle. She didn't realize until she settled into the leather that Marsh had mounted at exactly the same time.

He glanced over at her. His steely eyes held a silvery gleam. "Ready?"

"Yes." Jen nodded, suspicious of the meaning behind that gleam.

They moved off at a walk, which became a jog.

Marsh turned to look at her. "Are you up for a good run?"

"I'd love it," she said.

He took off.

Laughing, she was beside him within seconds. He flashed a grin, she returned it. The flat-out gallop was invigorating and ended much too soon. Marsh pulled his mount up beside a narrow stream and dismounted.

Jen did likewise, following as he led his horse to the water. "What's your horse's name?" she asked, looking over the sleek, dark brown gelding.

"Cocoa," he said, his tone serious.

"You're kidding." She couldn't help the laugh that escaped. "Cocoa?"

"Isn't that what his color looks like?" he said, "Dark, rich cocoa?"

"Yes, delicious dark chocolate, like your hair."

The words were out before she could catch herself. She had been looking at the horse, but her eyes instinctively found his. "I...uh..."

"Yours is golden-honey and looks like silk." His voice was low, almost a growl.

Jen was suddenly hot, an ache settling in the pit of her stomach. She stared at him in silence a moment, searching for something to say. "Th...thank..." Her throat went dry as he stepped close to her.

"You're beautiful." A wry smile played at the corners of his mouth. "But then you know that." He moved to within a breath of her. "Don't you?"

If only she could breathe. She managed to inhale. "Thank you." Surprise, she had managed that, too. "And you're right. I do know." She swallowed, quickly licking her lips. It didn't help—they dried again as his gaze followed the movement of her tongue. "I've been hearing it from the day I was born." He was standing too close, much too close. "But no one has said it quite like you."

"I want to kiss you."

"Wh…what?" Her chest felt tight. Her heart was thumping. The ache in her stomach swirled down to the core of her body. "Why?" *Dumb, Jen,* she thought.

"I want to taste you." His breath misted her lips. "I want to find out if you taste like honey."

Yes, yes, a murmur inside her head whispered as she trembled…and parted her lips.

Marsh didn't hesitate. Lowering his head, he touched his mouth to hers with gentle care. Then he slightly, tentatively deepened the kiss as he pulled her into a tight embrace. She made a soft sound in her throat. His mouth went hard to devour hers.

Oh, he is delicious, Jen mused fuzzily, curling her arms around his taut neck and spearing her fingers through the thick strands of his silky hair.

Releasing his hold on her, he stepped back, causing her arms to drop, her fingers to slide from his hair. He stared hard at her. "You taste good."

"You need a haircut." It was true, but Jen could have kicked herself for saying it. Still, that was better, she felt sure, than admitting his taste outdid anything she ever could have imagined.

"You're right." He laughed and raked his fingers through the wavy dark strands.

Jen loved the sound of his laughter, delighted she had been the cause of it, wanting to make him do it again, especially knowing how seldom he laughed.

They stood staring at each other for several long seconds. She wanted to fling herself back into his arms, take another taste of him, this time with her tongue.

She took a hesitant step toward him. Star chose that

moment to nudge her. She laughed and turned to pet the animal just as Cocoa gave a whinny.

"At the risk of sounding corny and cliché," she said, "I think the horses are getting restless. I guess we'd better head back."

Marsh nodded as he moved to Cocoa. "I have a few phone calls to make."

Jen mounted, and glanced back at Marsh. *Heavens*, she thought, *he looks magnificent on a horse.*

"Who do you think enjoys it more?" He raised an eyebrow. "You or the horse?"

Jen laughed, then, clicking her tongue to get Star moving, she called back to him, "Me."

As they galloped back to the stable, Jen could barely think of anything besides that kiss. But once they dismounted, everything went back to the status quo. Marsh handed the horses over to a man who suddenly appeared at his side, without another word strode off to his office. Jen smiled at the man, assuming he was one of the security guards. Confused by the tumble of emotions inside her, Jen headed inside, started the laundry and went to her apartment to change before cleaning.

She undressed and put on the raggedy clam-diggers and shirt she'd had on earlier. She still planned on giving a quick brush-up to the first floor, but first, she needed a cup of coffee.

Marsh beat her to it.

When she walked into the kitchen the aroma of brewing coffee wafted to her. Marsh was standing at the stove, stirring something in a pot. Jen knew without looking that the pot held soup.

"I hope you don't mind me taking over your kitchen," he said, "and that you like vegetable soup." He slid a quick glance at her, his eyebrows arched.

"I don't mind you taking care of lunch at all," Jen replied, trying to sound as normal as possible though being close to him was making her body vibrate with the need to kiss him again. "I think I'll have a grilled cheese sandwich with my soup. Would you like one, too?"

"Sure." He gave a shadow of a smile. "Thanks." Marsh seemed as cool as could be. Obviously that kiss hadn't had half the effect on him that it had had on her.

Concentrating on the job at hand, she removed the bread from the cabinet. The faint sizzle that was still running laps up and down her spine slowly began to ease as she got to work—until she couldn't help but look over at Marsh, and found him looking right back at her with that impenetrable silver gaze.

Jen felt it all the way down to her toes.

She was in deep, deep trouble.

Four

"How many horses do you have?" *Oh, how brilliant,* she thought.

"Six," he answered.

"Do…er…you take care of them yourself?" *Again, brilliant,* she chastised herself.

Was the slight smile he gave her holding a tinge of ridicule or was it pity?

"No," he said. "Ted, a retired wrangler, cares for them. If you want to ride, see him. Whenever you're free."

"Oh, I see, thank you."

"Any other questions of the equine variety?" he asked, that smile twitching his lips.

Of course the twitch drew her attention to his mouth, which made her suddenly warm with memories of his kiss.

She wet her lips.

His gaze zeroed in on her mouth.

She grew warmer.

"No." Her voice was subdued.

They ate the rest of their meal in absolute silence.

"Coffee?" Marsh finally said.

"I'll get it." Jumping up, Jen went to fill two mugs with the steaming aromatic brew. He chuckled at her, that attractive masculine sound making her ache all over even as it annoyed her—he clearly felt he had the upper hand. She decided to throw him a curveball, just to see how he'd react.

"My mother called me last evening."

"That's nice."

"Well, actually it wasn't very pleasant," she admitted.

"Problems on the home front?"

"Yes," she said, eyeing him carefully. "My parents are having a problem with my living alone in this house with you."

He laughed outright.

Jen's insides went all soft at the sound. "You find that amusing?" Well, it was pretty funny. Her mother and father, of all people. Of course, he was unaware of that nasty situation.

"My reputation precedes me," he said, his laughter fading. "I hope you assured her you're safe here."

Without pausing to think, Jen said, "Am I?"

"I assume you're referring to that kiss earlier." His tone was dry.

"Yes," she answered, meeting his steady gaze with a challenging stare.

"There was a reason for it," he said, suddenly all business.

"What reason?" Jen couldn't imagine what he was referring to.

"It was a test." His silvery gaze held her in confused thrall.

She frowned. "I don't understand."

"I want a child, an heir—better yet two."

He spoke so calmly, Jen was stumped for a moment. When his meaning sunk in, she actually yelped. *"What?"*

"Oh, don't be alarmed, you passed."

"What do you mean, I passed?"

"The kiss test," he said. "You passed with flying colors."

"I still don't get it. What is a 'kiss test,' and what does it have to do with heirs?"

"I've decided you'd make not only a good lover but a good wife and mother," he explained casually. "Of course there's more to good sex than a great kiss."

Jen was flabbergasted. Her throat had gone so dry she had to pause to swallow. "Are you proposing to me...or propositioning me?"

He gave her a wicked smile, his silver eyes shimmering. "Both."

Jen glanced around the room as if seeking help. Finding none, she picked up her mug, unsure whether she wanted to drink from it or throw it at him. "This is insane."

"What's insane about wanting a child?" He stood, and came to lean against her side of the table. He was close—too close.

Jen had to raise her head to look at him. "Nothing," she said. "It's your way of going about it that's strange. Now back up."

"What?" He frowned.

"I said back up." Jen's tone was more order than request. "I want to stand up." He obliged, and she stood and turned but he caught her arm, bringing her to a halt.

"I'd much rather we go upstairs and test our physical compatibility."

Jen stared at him a moment as she would a being from another planet, torn between wanting to shut him down—and wanting to go upstairs with him so she could have his mouth on hers again. Finally she asked, "Are you nuts?"

Rather than the anger she expected, Marsh treated her to his insides-melting laugh.

"I like you," he said. "You're as prickly as I am. I believe we could make a go of it."

"Of what? A marriage of convenience?" Jen somehow managed to keep her voice calm.

"Yes." He nodded.

"Whose?"

"What do you mean, whose?" He appeared perplexed.

"My convenience…or yours?" She lost the battle for control of her voice. "Are you looking for a 'me Tarzan, you Jane' kind of arrangement?" She gave a quick, firm shake of her head. "No, thank you."

She pulled her arm from his to walk away. He grabbed her again.

"Damn you, let me go." She yanked her arm only to almost fall as he released her at the same instant. Reacting at once, he caught and steadied her.

"I'm sorry, was I hurting you?" His expression held genuine concern.

Jen drew a deep breath before answering. "No, but you're ticking me off big-time." She took another quick breath. "Now, like it or not, I am going to do some work." She glared at him. "Got that?"

She could tell he held back another laugh. "Yes, I think I've got that."

"Good." She studied him for a second. Damn, why did those lips, that mouth, those hands make her so crazy? And why did those very attributes tempt her to agree to his outrageous suggestion? "Please," she said, cringing at the near plea in her voice, "go somewhere, anywhere but here. I don't need an audience to clean."

With that, she strode to the laundry room, dumped the first load of wash from the washer into the dryer and got her cleaning supplies from the storage closet. A combined sigh of relief and regret whispered through her lips as she walked back into the kitchen to find he wasn't there.

She came to a dead stop when she found him waiting for her in the living room.

Eyeing him warily, she arched one brow.

"First, I am not looking for a 'me Tarzan, you Jane' relationship." He took a step closer to her and stared down at her. She felt her face flush against her will. "What I'm looking for—"

Jen knew she couldn't let him finish that sentence.

Dropping the cleaning products where she stood, she headed for the stairs.

"Where are you going?" he asked, sounding genuinely confused.

"Out," she called back, taking the stairs two at a time to get away from Marsh Grainger and his too-tempting proposition as fast as she could.

Five

"The hell with it," Marsh muttered as he strode through the house, seeking refuge in his office.

Dammit, the woman was driving him crazy. Was she coming back for dinner? Was she coming back at all? For an instant Marsh felt his stomach tighten at the idea of her leaving for good.

She was great at her job—all her jobs. He couldn't afford to lose her.

What had he done?

He sighed. He had spooked her by jumping the gun with his "test kiss" business. Well, in all honesty, he had startled himself, as well. He had never been the impulsive type. But ever since she'd walked into his life, he'd been doing nothing but acting on impulse. The idea of the two of them getting together on a permanent basis had been brewing at the back of his mind for days—and getting stronger with every touch, every conversation.

Why not? he had asked himself. She obviously wasn't involved with any other man, seeing as how she never mentioned anyone and hadn't left the house except to go shopping since she had started working for him.

Still, he probably should have given the idea more thought, given her more time to get to know him, which was his reason for inviting her to ride with him that morning in the first place.

And why was he beating himself up like this? It was so…so not like him.

Facing the bare truth, Marsh admitted he was burning to be with her, to make love to her. He had been observing her from the very beginning. Along with a growing respect for her, along with the feelings he experienced listening to her sing softly while she was working… He had entered the house from the stable one very warm Saturday afternoon and stopped in his tracks as he passed through the dining room. Hot and sweaty, he had stood there, transfixed by the sight of Jen getting out of the pool, water sluicing the length of her slender body barely covered by a string bikini.

In that instant he was not only hot and sweaty, he was rock hard and hurting. He wanted her so badly his back teeth ached…along with the rest of him.

It was during the days following that encounter that Marsh began thinking about bargaining with Jen, offering her his name, his home, his bed in exchange for a child. Finally, he had decided to take a chance—and for him to take a chance with a woman, even a woman such as Jen, was a huge step for him.

Had he botched his chances with his abrupt actions and suggestions? A "test kiss"? Another "test" to see if they would be good together in bed? He grimaced.

Not the most romantic approach. But he had never had any trouble romancing a woman before.

Of course, Jen wasn't just any woman. She was different, special.

Dammit.

He couldn't blame her if she had left for good.

Had she taken all her things? She had had ample time as she hadn't brought very many with her. Hell, she wouldn't need to take anything but herself—she could send for her belongings, or have someone else come for them.

He'd really made a mess of things.

Sighing, he picked up the phone and made a few work calls. Then he sat in front of his computer, watching the cursor blink, as if impatient for him to decide what he was going to do. He put it to sleep.

Just then, the phone on his desk rang. He slid a glance at the caller ID, and eased back into his chair.

"Yes, Jen?" Marsh was pleased at the casual note he had managed.

"Can you handle dinner on your own?"

"Why?" he asked, heaving a put-upon sigh.

"I'm going to run into San Antonio and have dinner there, along the River Walk," she explained.

"Why don't I join you for dinner?" Marsh said. "I think maybe I need to explain a few things to you." He actually held his breath while waiting for her answer—that had *never* before happened to him with any woman.

"Well…"

Before she had a chance to say no he rushed on. "We could have dinner and then stroll along the River Walk or take a boat ride." The moments crawled by. He was holding his breath again.

"Okay," she said. "What time should I meet you?"

"Would six-thirty or seven work?"

"Seven would be fine. I'll see you then." Her voice came over the line hurried, a bit rough. "Bye."

Marsh's breathing slowly returned to normal. Could their having dinner together away from the house be considered a date? Marsh thought about it for a moment. He supposed it definitely could—if he hadn't just scared her out of the house with his proposition.

Hell, he mused, what was he getting all worked up about? He knew how to go about charming a woman— he had charmed his share, maybe more than his share. So why sweat it? He could begin over dinner, and probably have Jen eating from his hand by...

No. He couldn't, wouldn't approach Jen as if she were any other woman. She wasn't.

So no seduction, unless it happened completely naturally, he told himself. This date was simply a way for him to back up and make amends to the employee he was so desperate to hold on to.

Of course it was.

Jen slipped the cell phone into the side pocket of her shoulder bag as she walked out into the golden sunlight from the cool, soothing interior of the Mission Alamo.

No matter how many times she visited San Antonio, the first thing she did was head for the old mission. Although traffic was busy on the broad street so close to the complex, inside it was always quiet, and on the hottest days, it seemed cool. There was a sense of peace and calm inside the Alamo Jen had never experienced anywhere else. And she had always thought how lovely it would be to be married inside that quiet and serene old shrine.

It could happen if she agreed to Marsh's proposal.

Jen shook her head. The thought of wearing his ring, sharing his bed, bearing his child—it was so very tempting. But she couldn't stand the idea of living with him knowing he didn't love her, and not knowing if she could love him.

It was absurd to even be thinking about Marsh in that way.

Wasn't it?

Waiting for the light to change so she could cross the street, she glanced down, frowning slightly at the tremor in her hands. Speaking to Marsh, agreeing to meet him for dinner had shaken that inner peace, ruffled her sense of calm.

Why had she called him in the first place?

Wait a minute, she thought, trying to get control of her thoughts. *Why in the world should I feel nervous about having agreed to meet Marsh for dinner? We not only have dinner but every meal together in the house—his house—three times a day, every day.*

But this wasn't the house, she mused. And there was the small matter of the fact that he had proposed to her.

This was a date. A Saturday-night date. And on this particular Saturday he had kissed her, and asked her to go to his bed…and have his child!

All of it gave Jen pause. A date with Marsh? A marriage with him? A *life* with him? She'd barely let herself want him, or imagine a future beyond right now. Was a long-term relationship something she wanted?

Maybe.

She couldn't suppress the thrill of anticipation that skidded the length of her spine just thinking about the possibilities.

Oh, yes, he was what she wanted, she finally conceded, and *he wanted her*. The thought lodged in her mind as she crossed the bridge to the River Walk.

He had admitted as much, she thought, ambling along, unconscious of the throngs of people around her. Well, he didn't actually say he wanted *her*. He said he wanted a child—an heir, maybe two.

Not quite the words a woman wants to hear when receiving a marriage proposal. Hell, she mused, she had once received a fervent proposal from a young man who had actually dropped onto one knee to pledge his undying love for her.

Marsh's proposal was a far cry from that.

Jen strolled into the Rivercenter Mall and headed straight for Victoria's Secret without even realizing what she was doing. She was looking through the sales tables when she glanced up, her gaze caught by a mannequin. The nightgown was barely there and what *was* there was flame-red.

On the spot, Jen motioned to a nearby smiling sales clerk and bought the sinful-looking gown.

She wouldn't admit that she was thinking about Marsh as she did so.

Jen left the mall and made her way to the restaurant. She started when a hand touched hers, taking her bag from her.

"Hey—" she began, turning to glare at the person.

"You're late," Marsh drawled.

Jen somehow managed to keep from rolling her eyes. "I was shopping and lost sight of the time."

"Obviously," he said.

"Oh, lighten up," Jen retorted.

While imperiously arching a brow he gave way to a smile. He shot a cuff to look at his watch. "We're five minutes late."

"How very sophisticated of us," she murmured. "I hope they are duly impressed."

"Nah," Marsh said, shaking his head. "They probably expect us to be late."

Surprised and amused by his casual tone, Jen gave a soft laugh. "What if we aren't late enough and we have to wait for a table?"

Marsh slanted a positively wicked look at her. "It ain't gonna happen, kid. The name's Grainger, remember?" He opened the door for her. "Besides, I know the owner and chef."

The place was medium-size, the décor blending with the River Walk theme. The food was superb, the service outstanding.

Jen barely noticed.

It occurred to her that it was strikingly different being out with Marsh than sitting opposite him at his kitchen table. Here, tonight, Marsh captivated her. He was…everything she had ever thought a man should be.

Handsome, urbane, but most importantly, intelligent. His intelligence shone from his silvery eyes, along with a keen sense of humor she had never heard mentioned about him before. Had most people missed it? Jen didn't see how it was possible for anyone to miss what was right there in front of them. At times, his eyes fairly danced with the light of devilish humor.

Why did he have to turn out to be a womanizer? Or was he? If the gossipmongers had missed Marsh's sense of humor, had they misread other things about him, as well?

Beware of wishful thinking, she told herself.

"What are you thinking?" he asked.

Marsh was sitting with his forearms on the table, cradling his after-dinner brandy. His hands moved slowly, warming the potent liquid. She wondered if this was the moment when he was going to explain himself to her.

"About you," she admitted.

One dark eyebrow arched. "What about me?"

He lowered his head. His lips parted to sip the brandy. Jen felt she could actually taste his lips, the tang of the brandy on them.

"Oh," she said with a delicate shrug, "I'm just wondering exactly what it is you wanted to talk about tonight."

He chuckled and the sound seemed to go right through her.

He took another sip, keeping his eyes on her. "I feel I might have offended you with my…business proposal."

Jen nearly spit out her wine. "Is that what that was?"

He nodded. "It was. I'm a businessman, Jen. When I see something that looks like a good, smart opportunity, I take it."

Her heart skittered a little at the idea of being "taken" by Marsh. By the glint in his eye, she could tell that was exactly what he wanted her to be thinking.

"But like I said, I'm sorry if I offended you."

Jen couldn't help but wonder, as she sat there looking at the gorgeous Marsh Grainger, how many other women he had presented with his "business" proposal. But then, how many women could a man possibly meet if he spent all his time at home, in his house?

"Why do you hide out in your home instead of working in your office in Dallas?"

For a moment—a long moment—she was certain he had no intention of answering her. In fact, she was steeling herself for a rebuke.

"I get more done that way."

Jen was a little startled at his blunt admittance. A

tiny frown tugging her brows together, she asked, "You can get more work done alone than you can surrounded by people to assist you?"

He nodded, tipping the glass to finish off his drink. "I do have people—too many people—around me to assist. I prefer the quiet of my office at the house. On the other hand—"

He was interrupted by their server asking if he could get something else for them.

"No, thank you, just the check," Marsh said, his gaze steady on Jen's face. "Are you going to finish your wine?"

"No." Jen shook her head, a small smile playing on her lips. "I'm driving."

Turning from her, he took care of the check. Then he circled the table to hold her chair for her.

"You were saying," Jen prompted him as soon as they were back outside. As they walked, the crowds had to go around them—it didn't hurt that Marsh was such an imposing, intimidating man.

"On the other hand," he said, strolling beside her, unaware of the impatient looks of some of the people having to skirt around them. "There are times I have to go into Dallas or Houston for important meetings."

"As you did the weekend I started working for you," she recalled aloud.

He hesitated, a half smile shadowing his lips for an instant. "Yes," he said, his tone wry.

Now, what was that all about? The man was certainly an enigma. If she thought about everything that had happened between them in one day, it practically made her head spin. First a kiss, then…a proposal.

A proposal was serious business. Was she seriously considering it?

"Hello, Jennifer." Marsh's softened voice drew her from introspection. "We're here."

Here? Where? Blinking herself back from the realm of Marsh's hot kiss and the proposal to the present, Jen was startled to find herself standing next to her car. Now, how in the world had he known where she had parked?

"How did you…"

"I looked."

"You looked?" She stared at him in amazement. "All the places to park around here, and you not only looked for my car, you spotted it?"

Marsh shrugged. "It's pretty hard to miss an old, dusty white Caddy, even at dusk."

Although Jen took offense at his description of the vehicle she loved, she let it slide for the moment. "Okay, so where did you park?"

"Back there a few blocks. You wait here while I go get it and I'll follow you home."

"I know the way home, Marsh," she said.

"I know you do," he replied. "But I'm still following you back to the ranch, so you wait here. That's an order, Jennifer. I can't have you disappearing on me— we're not quite done talking yet. And we need some privacy to do it."

And with that, he just turned and walked away.

Six

Jen was fuming. Certain smoke was rising from her ears, she stared after Marsh. Who the hell did he think he was?

Well, yeah, he was her boss—he was boss to a lot of people, she reluctantly conceded—but that didn't give him the right to issue orders to her on a date. Sighing, she nevertheless slid behind the wheel of the Caddy like a good and obedient employee.

Anger seared through her.

Her day had been a whirlwind, starting with their ride. There was the kiss, and the perplexing and—if she was being totally honest with herself—rather flattering proposal. She had enjoyed their ride to the stream. She had enjoyed the horses. She had even enjoyed Marsh's kiss.

Who was she kidding? She hadn't just enjoyed his

kiss, she had melted into it, and wanted more when it was over…only to hear him tell her it had been a test.

A test! As if that were not bad enough, he proceeded to ask her to have sex with him to make certain they would be good together in bed. And if it so happened they *were* compatible as lovers, he then would marry her, simply because he considered her good wife and mother material, mother being the most important role as he needed an heir to inherit his vast wealth and would prefer two children. Like royalty, she supposed—an heir and a spare.

She'd been thinking about that proposal all day. But damned if now, after their first date, she wasn't quite sure how she felt.

Especially since he'd just ordered her around.

Jen didn't realize she was gritting her teeth until she heard the sound of a horn and glanced at the side mirror to see Marsh pulled up alongside the car parked behind her. Starting the engine, she eased out onto the street and drove ahead of him.

He stayed on her tail, as if their bumpers were locked, all the way back to the ranch. Jen had the whole drive to work up a full head of angry steam at the way he had again managed to confuse, excite and befuddle her all in one day.

She tried to untangle the emotions in her head. How did she feel about Marsh? She had enjoyed having dinner with him—he had been good company. The conversation they had engaged in had been amusing.

So, what was she *really* fuming about?

Jen knew full well what she was really fuming about—her growing attraction to a man who wanted to give her a compatibility test. But it was so much easier to tell herself she was annoyed by his arrogant demand that she wait for him to follow her back to the ranch.

It was as good an excuse as anything else she could come up with on the spur of the moment.

As Jen drove past the two stone pillars on either side of the road to the house, she thrust her arm out the window in a wave and gave a quick honk of the horn in greeting to the guard, as she had been doing every time she left or returned to the ranch. The guard gave a honk and flashed his lights in response.

Watching for it, she noticed neither Marsh nor the guard acknowledged one another.

She was not surprised; she imagined he saw no reason to greet his employees every time he left or returned to the property. He paid his people very well—Jen knew because she cut the checks, her own included. She presumed he figured that was acknowledgement enough. And it had been, for her. Until he'd broken their delicate truce with that kiss.

And that proposal.

Suddenly tired, Jen pulled into the space Marsh had allotted her in the garage and killed the engine. Marsh pulled into the slot next to her. A deflated sigh whispered through her lips as she got out of the car and walked to the trunk to retrieve her shopping bag.

"Let me help you with that," he said, plucking the Victoria's Secret bag from her fingers. *If he only knew what's in that bag,* she thought.

He trailed her through the doors and up the stairs to her apartment. As she never locked the door, she walked right inside and turned to relieve him of the bag.

Marsh was right behind her and closed the door with a quiet but definite click.

Jen arched her brows in question.

"Aren't you going to offer me a reward for carrying your bag?" he asked.

"Reward?" Her brows lowered while her eyes narrowed. "What sort of reward?"

He almost smiled.

He'd been smiling all day. She wondered if it had hurt his lips, then chided herself for the snide thought.

"Coffee, wine, something stronger?"

"Something stronger, huh?" Jen asked in a wry tone. "You wouldn't be thinking of getting me tipsy, would you?"

Marsh made it all the way to a real smile this time. "Not at all, coffee will be fine. The last thing I want is for your mind to be cloudy when I take you to bed."

His response stopped her cold. Well, not exactly—while it gave her chills on the surface of her skin, it ignited a blaze inside her.

She was silent for a moment, staring into the heat burning in the depths of his eyes. Coming to her senses, she said, "Excuse me?"

"I think you heard me."

"I thought we had more 'talking' to do, Mr. Grainger."

"We do. But it's a very special kind of talking," he said, giving her a smile so charming she felt it all the way down to her toes.

She broke eye contact and hurried away, into the kitchen.

"Coffee will take only a few minutes. Make yourself comfortable." Jen was amazed at how calm and composed she sounded, when what she was feeling was confused and, yes, so turned on she could hardly breathe.

She spilled coffee grounds from the measuring spoon as her trembling fingers dumped them into the basket.

She also spilled a few drops of water as she poured the water into the well.

Damn, she thought, what was it about Marsh that could rattle her so easily? Okay, he was handsome in a rough-hewn, chiseled way. But he was too arrogant and full of himself. His reputation with women was less than sterling, a living, breathing bad boy.

Except in his case he was most definitely a man.

She had read somewhere that every woman wanted to be the one to tame a bad boy. At the time, Jen had expelled a very unladylike snort of derision.

Yeah, she had thought at the time, that was what she lived for—being one of whatever number of eager females in line to tame a bad boy.

Why would any woman think that—after who knew how many a womanizer had been with before—*she* would be the one to bring him to heel and keep him there? More to the point, Jen mused, why would she want to?

If he's as hot as Marsh... said a little voice in her head.

Had Marsh Grainger managed to change her stance on bad boys?

"Coffee ready?"

Jen jumped but managed to swallow the yelp of surprise that sprang to her lips.

Marsh was standing behind her, close, too close. She gathered her composure as she drew a quick breath.

"Yes." Jen was satisfied with the even tone she had managed. "It only takes a few minutes for—" She stiffened, her voice cutting off completely. He had lifted her long hair away from her shoulder.

"What are you doing?"

Brilliant. She knew exactly what he was doing.

"Smelling you," he murmured, slowly inhaling her scent. "You smell good."

The tip of his tongue touched the sensitive skin near the back of her ear. She grew cold, and then hot. "M... Marsh?"

"You taste good, too." His tongue slid the length of her neck to the curve of her shoulder.

Jen gasped as suddenly he turned her around to face him. "Marsh...you... I..."

"I want you, Jennifer. I've wanted you since I set eyes on you and that kiss only made me want you more." Lowering his head he brushed her mouth with his, gliding his tongue along her bottom lip. "And I think you want me, too."

"I...I don't... Oh!" She trembled as he moved, pressing his body to hers. "You shouldn't..."

He did. Cradling her face with his hands, he again touched his mouth to hers. His kiss was gentle, sweet, soft.

Knowing she should resist, push him back, away from her overheating body, Jen instead surrendered to the neediness gnawing inside her. Curling her arms around his taut shoulders, she gave up her mouth to him.

Marsh took her mouth, owned it, claimed it with the thrust of his tongue, and in that instant she was his. Bad boy or not.

So much for her brave words about resisting a womanizer. Too late...she was lost.

Later, Jen would wonder how they had managed to leave a trail of clothing from the kitchen to her bedroom without once breaking that kiss.

When at last he lifted his mouth from hers, they were both naked, heaving in deep breaths of air. Shivering, tiny hitches of breath still catching in her throat, Jen stared into his eyes, fascinated by the blaze of desire she found in their depths.

Without a word, Marsh tossed back the top sheet and puffy white comforter she had bought for her bed. Then he reached for her, gently settling her on the smooth white sheet in the center of the mattress, stretching his long, hard body next to her.

"I was going to ask you to put on that pretty little red nightgown you bought for tonight, but I think I like you better like this," he growled.

Jen felt herself turning bright red at the image of Marsh looking in that bag while she'd been in the kitchen making coffee. She wanted to insist that she hadn't bought the nightgown for tonight, but she wasn't sure if that was true or not. And it certainly didn't matter now.

Marsh caressed her jawline, outlined her lips with his fingers. His touch was so very gentle yet so very arousing. Jen lifted her head, inviting his kiss.

"Yes," he murmured, lowering his head to glide his tongue over her lips, then fusing his mouth to hers.

Jen loved the taste of him. His long, deepening kiss made her ache for more. She slid her free arm around his neck and thrust her fingers into his hair.

A low sound of pleasure whispered from her mouth into his when his left hand slowly moved from the curve of her neck to the curve of her breast. Leaving her mouth, his lips followed the path of his hand.

Jen was on fire inside. She moaned and arched her back when his tongue gently lashed the now hard tip of her breast. A moment later she arched her hips as his hand moved down her body to cup her mound before inserting one finger inside her. In the next instant, a soft cry spilled from her throat as he brushed his thumb over the most sensitive spot there.

In her mind, Jen saw herself as a flame, burning higher and higher just for him. She arched again, harder against his hand, into his teasing fingers.

Straightening his arm resting against the bed, Marsh moved his long body to cover hers, cradling himself between her thighs.

She could feel him, the length of him, the hardness of him nudging the entrance to her body. She moved in silent invitation for him to enter.

With one swift, deep thrust he was inside her, tightly, uncomfortably filling her.

Jen expelled an involuntary cry of pain as her body tensed and stiffened.

He froze in place, shock in his silvery eyes.

"What is it? Have I hurt you?" His voice was strained.

Before she could respond, he said in a tone of near disbelief, "Are you…a virgin?"

Jen's harsh breaths were beginning to ease. "No… no, I'm not a virgin." She drew a deep, calm breath. He began to withdraw. She grasped his hips with her hands, holding him in place. "No," she repeated, the tension now easing from her body.

"If I'm too big for you…" Concern colored his voice, not quite hiding a hint of disappointment.

"It's okay." She offered him a small smile. "I'm adjusting. It'll be all right." She curled her legs around his waist, holding him to her. "Just give me a moment."

"Okay," he agreed, his expression puzzled, his voice a little breathless. "You want to tell me what happened there?"

"It's been a while since I've been with a man, that's

all," she said, adding with a little laugh, "and you're big."

"And you're tight," he said, desire flaring in his eyes.

Jen maintained his gaze, watching it change as she started to move her hips slowly, seductively against him. The flame inside her was quickly flaring to life again as her body relaxed, adjusting to the new sensation of the fullness of him.

Fleetingly, she recalled her painful though limited experience while still in college. In comparison to Marsh… In truth, there was no comparison. Wanting more, Jen moved against him, letting him know she was ready.

Exhaling a long sigh, Marsh began to move with her, his expression still wary but his body eager for hers. He began slow and easy, but with the urgent feel of her fingernails digging into his hips, he increased his tempo.

Faster. Deeper. More, more, Jen demanded with her body, claiming him as he claimed her. Tension tightened inside her, driving her wild. "Faster. Deeper." She didn't even realize she had cried aloud.

Marsh was with her, every literal inch of the way. It was building inside his body. Jen could feel him keeping pace with her, getting closer and closer to the edge. Her strained breaths were keeping time with his.

Gazing up at him—at the tautness of his face, at the tendons standing out in his arched neck—excited her, gave her the will to wait for him.

The world exploded for both of them. They cried out as if with one voice. Never in her life had Jen experienced anything so all-consuming, so carnal and beautiful, so completely fulfilling.

Easing his body down to hers, Marsh buried his face in the curve of her neck. Jen circled her arms around his sweat-slicked shoulders. Ever since that fumbling, inept jock in college, she had been afraid she could never experience the sheer pleasure she had heard about, read about in books. Her fears were the main reason she had tried so hard to keep her distance from men— from Marsh.

Foolish woman.

"That was wonderful." Jen was so satiated and content she was barely aware of speaking the words aloud.

Marsh lifted his head to look at her, his eyes now a soft gray. "That was way more than wonderful," he said between slowly leveling breaths. "That, lady mine, was absolutely mind-blowing."

Lady mine. Jen shivered, wondering if he called all the women he had been with "lady mine."

"You're cold." Easing himself from her, he sat up and pulled the comforter over them. Curling his arm around her, he drew her body to him. "Better?"

"Yes." Jen sighed. It was true, it was better. In spite of all the rumors, the chattered gossip about him, she felt warm, safe and at home in his arms. She knew it was temporary—*she* was probably temporary, unless she accepted his crazy proposal. But she didn't want to think about that.

For now, she was content.

But her contentment lasted all of a few moments.

"Okay, let's hear it." His voice, though quiet, was demanding.

Jen lifted her head from his chest to frown at him. "Hear what?"

"You said it had been a while since you'd been with a man. Exactly how long is a while?"

Jen wet her lips, thinking *Dammit*. And she had been so comfortable. "I don't think that is really any of your business," she said, dredging up her most haughty tone of voice.

Marsh appeared less than impressed. "It is now. So tell me."

"And if I choose not to?"

His arm tightened around her. "I'll keep you right here in the bed until you do."

Jen blinked. "You wouldn't."

He smiled. "Try me."

Standoff. Jen knew he meant what he said. Still it bugged her to give in to him, even though she had obviously given in to him in a much bigger way mere minutes ago. Of course, that was different—her body had made that decision for her.

She heaved a dramatic sigh.

"Oh, brother," he drawled. "What's the big deal? Tell me and get it over with, then we can both get some sleep."

He hesitated, adding with a wicked grin, "Maybe."

Maybe? Jen felt a twinge of excitement zinging through her. Did he mean…? Of course that was what he meant, she chided herself.

"The big deal is," she began, trying and failing to ignore the flame that was very quickly coming back to life inside her, "I hadn't been with a man since my senior year in college."

Marsh jackknifed to sit up, staring down at her in shock. "That would be how many years ago?"

"It doesn't matter anymore," she said, impatiently. "Do you want to hear about it or sit there staring open-mouthed at me in disbelief?"

"I didn't say I didn't believe you," he shot back at her. "Even though you must admit that is hardly the norm for a woman like you."

It was Jen's turn to sit up and glare at him eye to eye. "What do you mean, a 'woman like me'? What kind of woman would that be?" she demanded, completely unaware of her exposed breasts.

"A gorgeous, sexy, incredibly responsive woman." He was glaring right back at her. Even his glare was turning her on.

She lowered her eyes. "You think I'm gorgeous and sexy?" Jen knew full well she was beautiful, but hearing it from Marsh…well…the flame inside her burned even hotter.

"You know damn well you are both those," he retorted. "You're also exciting and good company and have a great sense of humor." His brows shot up. "Okay?"

"Yes," she murmured, glancing up at him. The comforter had dropped to their waists but the shiver that coursed through Jen's body had more to do with his compliments than the chill in the air. "You're not bad yourself," she said, daring to hold his bold stare.

Marsh actually laughed. "Thanks." Taking her with him, he lay down again, pulling her to him before tucking the comforter around them again.

"Okay, Jennifer," he said, tilting her face up to plant a kiss on her lips. "Talk to me."

"It's almost funny now, but at the time it was anything but," she began. "He was a jock…of course," she continued. "I had been curious about sex, as all my friends seemed to talk about it exclusively. Yet up until that point I hadn't felt attracted to any man." She wasn't about to elaborate—she had worked too hard to forget that incident in the school parking lot to dredge it up now, here, with Marsh.

Expecting some sort of wry remark from him, possibly concerning her sexual proclivities, she raised her gaze to his. His expression was attentive, free of either ridicule or disbelief.

Encouraged, she rushed on to relay the whole stupid incident to him and have it over with. "What had attracted me to him was that he was not only athletic, he was very nice as well as intelligent." She paused, wincing as the memory played in her mind.

"Go on." His voice was soft, kind. Jen was aware that she was seeing a side of Marsh she hadn't seen before, and it touched her.

"I agreed to go out with him," she said. "It wasn't a big deal, just to the Pizza and Beer Joint—which, by the way, is the actual name of the place. I had one glass of beer with my pizza, and he had five. He wasn't drunk," she added, "only a little tipsy and talkative."

She paused, the memory uncomfortably vivid. "At least I thought he wasn't drunk." She closed her eyes. "How's that saying go…he holds his booze well?"

Again Marsh tilted her head up to gaze into her eyes. "Jennifer, I have a distinct feeling you have never told another person about this encounter. Am I right?"

She answered with a quick nod of her head.

"Figured." His voice actually held a note of compassion. "You know," he continued softly, "I'm convinced you'll feel better if you get it out in the open once and for all. And I promise I won't alert the media immediately after you've finished," he teased.

She smiled, chiding herself for feeling stupid over an error in judgment years ago. Knowing Marsh was right she drew a deep breath and went on.

"Walking back to my off-campus room he put his arm around my waist and drew me against him. Although he was still talking away, his steps were steady, even. When we got to my room, he just walked in as if it were his own. I opened my mouth to protest, he silenced me with his lips pressing hard against mine."

Jen grabbed another breath before rushing on. "I really didn't mind the kiss—I rather liked it. But within seconds he had me flat on my back on the bed. His hands were everywhere, his tongue was scouring the inside of my mouth."

She paused for a moment.

"I tried to push him away, if only to breathe. When I began to struggle he lifted his head. His breathing was short and raspy, his voice raw as he said how badly he wanted me beneath him. Yanking my pullover up, he opened the front clasp of my bra and took my breast into his mouth. While shocked, I must admit the feel of his wet mouth on my breast sent an exciting sensation through me."

Jen halted once more to catch her breath.

"Jen, you don't have to—" Marsh began. She could hear anger in his tone, anger at the guy who had taken advantage of her.

"No—" she cut him off "—let me finish now or I might never finish."

He stayed quiet.

She continued. "He didn't rape me, if that's what you were thinking. I was willing, almost eager to experience the incredible pleasure every female I knew had raved about incessantly. He was eager, too—overeager. He yanked my jeans off and merely dropped his to his ankles. Then, well, it wasn't good." She closed her eyes. "Can we leave it at that?"

Marsh tightened his arm around her and held her, rocking her slightly side to side while smoothing her hair.

"It's over, Jennifer." His voice was soft, soothing, with underlying concern. "Did I hurt you like that?"

Jen pushed back against his hold so she could look up at him. "No." She shook her head. "After that initial discomfort and adjustment to you, I…I…"

"You what?" Marsh murmured, gliding his hand from her hair to her back.

Gathering herself, Jen boldly met his intent gaze. "I enjoyed it. I more than enjoyed it. It was…" She hesitated before admitting, "It was incredibly fantastic."

"Yeaaah," he said softly, drawing the word out. "Wanna do it again?"

Laughing softly, Jen freed her arms, clasped them around his neck and drew his mouth to hers. "Yes, please."

The second time was even better.

They fell asleep locked in each other's arms.

Seven

Jen woke a little after five in the morning. It was pitch-black in the room. Not wanting to wake Marsh, she refrained from lighting the bedside lamp, but to no avail. He woke while she was carefully disentangling herself from him.

"What are you doin'?" he mumbled, reaching for her.

Tossing back the covers she escaped his reach by slipping from the bed. "I'm going to the bathroom. I'll only be a moment. Go back to sleep."

Once inside the bathroom, Jen knew she would be in there longer than a moment—the shower looked so inviting, and she felt so pleasantly achy.

After cleaning off what was left of her makeup and brushing her teeth, she stepped into the shower, sighing with pleasure as the warm water cascaded over her body.

While she was drying off, Jen noticed a shirt of

Marsh's hanging on the back of the door. Now feeling a little awkward walking around nude, she pulled on the shirt before leaving the room. She stopped dead at the sight that met her eyes on her first step into her bedroom.

Stark naked, Marsh was leaning back against the headboard amidst the tangle of bedsheets and covers that had slid out of place during their rather hectic bout of sensual exercise.

"What are you doing?"

One browed arched. "Waiting for you." His voice was both wry and dry. "More to the point, why are you dressed?"

"I'm not fully dressed," she returned, every bit as wryly and dryly. "I'm only wearing a shirt."

"Not for long," he retorted, a sly smile crossing his face as his gaze traveled up and down her body.

"Indeed?" Jen said, trying and failing to ignore the tingle along her spine.

"Yes, indeed." He clasped his hands behind his head.

"Aren't you going to shower?" she asked the first thought that swam into her squishy brain.

"I think there's plenty of time for that later." He offered her a blatantly sexy smile. "Lose the shirt, lady mine, and come back to bed."

Jen was surprised to discover just how happy she was to toss off the shirt and crawl into the bed next to him.

As before, Marsh pulled her tightly against him. Then, to her surprise, he gave her a soft, sweet kiss, settled into his comfort place and whispered, "Sleep in tomorrow."

She felt a moment of disappointment, and then suddenly felt as if she couldn't keep her eyes open. Resting her head on his chest, she was asleep within seconds.

Jen woke later to discover she was alone in the bed and it was past ten in the morning. It was Sunday, a perfect day for sleeping in. For a moment, she considered snuggling deeper into the comforter but a rumble in her stomach made the decision for her. She was hungry.

Yawning and luxuriously stretching, she was quickly reminded of the exercise she and Marsh had indulged in during the night. She ached in very delicate places.

It felt amazing.

Pushing herself up, groaning at the pull in her thigh muscles as she slid her legs off the bed and stood up, Jen winced as she took a slow step.

Wow, she thought, moving slowly to the bathroom. She'd had no idea she'd hurt like this after reveling in so much unbelievable pleasure.

Can anyone say ecstasy?

Jen laughed softly at the wayward thought that swirled through her mind. But, in truth she had achieved ecstasy, or at least that was how she'd describe the shattering, mind-bending sensation Marsh had given her.

So she ached here and there…especially *there!* But oh, it was so worth it. Heaving a sigh of longing, Jen filled the tub with hot water.

She caught her breath as she slid into the tub, releasing it in relief when the heat of the water slowly began to ease the soreness from between her legs. Leaning back against the end of the tub Jen luxuriated until the heat dissipated. Then, draining the water, she stood and had a quick sluice down with warm water.

Forgoing makeup, she stepped into lacy panties and a matching bra. Wincing from a twinge of pain, she pulled on well-worn jeans, a cotton knit top and beaded-strap flip-flops.

Glancing around, Jen considered cleaning the apartment even though she had cleaned it Friday evening. She knew what she was doing, of course—marking time, looking for an excuse, *any* excuse, to stay inside the apartment and hide out.

Because Jen didn't want to face Marsh. What could she say to him? *Hey, you're a terrific lover, let's do it again sometime.* No, she most certainly couldn't say that, although that was the way of it. Even with her very limited knowledge she could tell he was an excellent and talented lover.

He apparently had plenty of experience.

She wondered if she'd passed the "compatibility test."

Jen sighed. Here she was, standing in the middle of her bedroom, dying for a cup of coffee and a big breakfast and afraid to go down the stairs and face him.

It was then that a shocking thought slammed into her mind.

Marsh hadn't used protection…and she had never had a reason to go on the pill.

What if…? Was it possible he had deliberately tried to impregnate her?

Jen mentally blocked the very idea, telling herself she wouldn't think of the possibility. Nevertheless, she did some quick mental tallying, relieved at the realization that it wasn't the right time of the month for conception.

Still, she knew the timing wasn't always reliable. She began to tremble. Should she run to a pharmacy for a morning-after pill?

Jen didn't run—she didn't even walk. She vacillated, uncertain, gnawing on her lip.

Oh, for pity's sake, move, she chided herself. *You're an adult woman, intelligent and strong. You can handle whatever fate throws at you. Now go get yourself a cup of coffee and something substantial to eat.*

But what if Marsh brought up the subject of marriage and babies again? What if that's all last night had been about for him?

Don't go looking for trouble, she told herself. *Deal with it if it comes looking for you.*

Squaring her shoulders, Jen left the room.

So her breathing was a trifle uneven, her heart rate a bit fast.

She'd live.

Marsh was in his office, sprawled lazily in his large butter-soft leather desk chair, the back of the seat facing the computer. His long legs were stretched out in front of him, crossed at the ankles, his feet bare. He had left the door open a few inches, waiting.

After the singular intensity of his release both times at the shattering climax with Jen, Marsh had almost immediately fallen into a deep sleep. Yet he had awakened less than four hours later, wanting more of her. She had been so tight and warm and…

Marsh felt certain Jen must be sore and aching. Only a brute would demand more, and he was no brute. His own body full, hurting with need, he'd slid her off his chest, chilled by the loss of her warmth, and settled her onto the mattress, tucking the comforter around her.

Scooping up his clothing he'd quietly left the apartment.

He had shaved, dressed, then went straight to his office, where he had been ever since. He hadn't eaten. His stomach was empty. He needed a gallon of coffee. He waited.

It was while he waited, aroused and ready, wanting her so bad it hurt, that memory stirred.

He had not protected her. Damn…and he had had

a package in his pocket, just in case he got lucky. And he had gotten very, very lucky. She was magnificent... and he hadn't protected her.

Marsh was unconcerned for himself. Truth to tell, he would love to have a child with her. But he hadn't deliberately left the condom in his pocket, not even subconsciously. He had too much pride to stoop to impregnating a woman in an attempt to bind her to him.

If it happened again—and he sure as hell hoped it did—he'd be sure to use protection.

Marsh didn't hear a sound, but he caught the scent of Jen when she reached the bottom of the stairs and headed for the kitchen. Exhaling a soft sigh of relief, he pushed himself out of the chair and followed her. Jennifer and coffee...what more could any man want?

"Coffee ready?"

Startled, Jen flipped the coffee scoop, sending the grounds flying to the floor.

"Good grief, Marsh!" she cried out, spinning around to glare at him, gasping for breath. "Are you trying to give me a heart attack?"

"I'm sorry." His lips twitched, making a lie of his apology. "I'll clean up the mess."

"You're damned right you will." She slammed her hands to her waist. "Meanwhile, can you be quiet long enough for me to make the coffee?"

"My lips are sealed," he said, turning away but not quickly enough to hide his smile from her.

Jen refilled the basket with fresh grounds and poured water into the pot. "Okay, the coffee will be ready in a few minutes." She turned back to him, raising her voice over the sound of the vacuum he was using to clean up the grounds. "Have you eaten?"

"No," he answered, shaking his head. "And I'm starving."

"Right," she drawled. "But then, when aren't you?"

Flipping the switch on the vacuum, he flashed a grin at her that caused a hitch in her breathing and a warm, exciting sensation in every cell and nerve in her body. "I can't deny it, I do love to eat."

"So do I," Jen admitted, proud of the steadiness of her voice when she was feeling overwhelmed with desire for Marsh—again. How much of this could she take? "So, what are you hungry for?"

Marsh ran a slow glance over her body. "Do you want the polite answer or the truth?" His voice was low, sensuous, suggestive.

"The polite answer," she quickly replied, fighting an urge to ask for the truth.

Marsh grinned. "Okay, then I'd like toast and a ham, cheese and tomato omelet, if you have the ingredients."

"I do." Telling herself to grow up and calm down, Jen headed for the fridge. "You can pour the coffee. I'm dying for a cup."

"Can't have that," he said, sounding amused. Opening the door on a cabinet he removed two large mugs and poured the coffee before the water had completely run through.

Ten minutes later they sat down to eat. Fifteen minutes after that they were both finished, not a crumb on their plates. Collecting the dishes, Jen stashed them in the dishwasher. She felt wonderfully full and nervous as hell. She had calmed down somewhat as she cooked and ate, but sitting back down at the table across from Marsh with nothing to occupy herself with but the coffee mug, the queasiness in her stomach started up all over again.

"So, what do you want to do today?"

The sensitized area between her thighs kept Jen from admitting to her desire to crawl back into bed with him and spend the rest of the day there. Instead, she said, "I'm going to finish the wash I started yesterday and then—"

"Don't even think about cleaning the house." Marsh cut her off in a warning tone.

Jen leveled a look at him. "If I had planned to clean the house, Mr. Grainger, I would clean the house," she retorted succinctly. "That's what I get paid to do."

"But I'm the boss, Ms. Dunning, and—"

"After the laundry," Jen said, figuring it was her turn to cut him off, "I'm going to curl up with the romance novel I started the night before last." Jen drew herself up, raised her chin and challenged his authority. "You got a problem with that?"

Marsh shrugged. "No," he said, his tone unconcerned. "It *is* your day off."

"Damn straight." She walked out of the kitchen and into the laundry room. The sound of his chuckle stalked her across the room, causing a hot shiver up her back to the nape of her neck.

"I'll be in my office," he said, then paused, his voice lowering to a sensual growl. "If you should need me for anything."

Oh, that's so not fair, Jen thought, digging out damp clothing and transferring it into the dryer.

Need him for anything? Jen's body began to heat up in very tender spots. Hell, she needed him for everything.

The very thought brought her to an absolute standstill. What on earth was she thinking? She didn't need anyone, least of all a man who was notorious for his disdain for women.

But Marsh really didn't seem like a man who disdained women. Did he? Or had he just worked his magic on her so completely that she couldn't tell what was real anymore?

Get a grip, she told herself.

Oh, sure, she had enjoyed her romp in bed with him—more than enjoyed it. She had reveled in it. It had been great sex. Well, she assumed it was great because it made her feel great. But that was no reason to lose her sense of reality.

Oh, hell, maybe it was time to take a hike, look for another job, maybe in another state, or even country, because she feared she was way out of her depth with Marshall Grainger.

But…she didn't want to leave. She loved her job. She loved—

No! Her stomach muscles twisted. It felt as if all her muscles twisted. Jen took off at a near run for her apartment.

"Jen?"

She stopped short on the fourth step, her breath catching in her throat at his soft call. "Yes?"

"Is something wrong?" He sounded concerned.

She half turned to look at him, immediately sorry she did so. He stood in the doorway to his office looking so blasted sexy. Somehow, Jen managed a reassuring smile.

"No, what could be wrong?" she asked, thinking, *Everything—everything could be wrong.*

He frowned. "Where are you going in such a hurry?"

How was it that even frowning he looked good enough to eat? She shook her head, trying to shake loose both the highly sexual image that flashed into her mind and the errant thought that went with it.

She inched backward and up one step. "I'm going to get my book. I decided to sit and read in the kitchen while waiting for the laundry to finish." *Liar, liar, pants on fire,* the tiny voice chided inside her head.

He smiled. She melted inside.

"The romance novel, right?"

"Yes."

"Is it good....the romance story?"

Jen grew stiff. Was there a note of mockery hidden inside his even tone?

"Yes, it is." She slid honey into her voice. "I wouldn't be reading it if it weren't." She raised one eyebrow. "What genre do you read?"

"I don't read fiction," he answered.

"Too bad, you don't know what you're missing."

"I'm a busy man, Jennifer. I have enough to read with business papers and periodicals."

"And what do you do to relax?" she asked, annoyed by his condescension.

This time his smile was slow, sexy, his eyes revealing his thoughts. "I was completely relaxed with you last night."

Jen froze, while the flame roared to life deep inside her. She didn't know what to say, how to respond to him. She certainly wasn't about to admit to the shimmering satisfaction he had given her. The last thing he needed was a booster shot to his ego.

He simply stood there, leaning against the door frame, his hands in his jeans pockets, his eyes hooded, his smile cool, for all appearances totally at ease.

Yeah, thought Jen, *like a tiger crouched and ready to spring.* Slowly, she backed up another step.

"I think we should get married." His remark startled Jen, even as something sprang to life inside her. She shouldn't have been surprised, of course—a part of her had known this was coming.

For a long moment the silence was complete. Then Jennifer erupted.

"You can't be serious, Marsh!"

"I am. You know I am."

Damn him. How could he be so calm when she felt about ready to fly into pieces? She stood there, shocked speechless, afraid that if she opened her mouth she'd admit the idea of spending every day and night with him for the rest of her life was very tempting.

Lazily, he straightened, moving away from the door, taking a step toward her.

Jen backed up another step.

He kept moving. "Getting married is the perfect solution."

"To what problem?" she asked, taking another step back, grasping the banister when she nearly stumbled.

She never saw him move but suddenly he was there, steadying her by drawing her into the safety of his arms.

"Are you okay?"

"Yes." She gulped air into her body. "I'm fine. You can let me go now."

"I'd rather not."

"Marsh, please." Jen drew another quick breath, which didn't help a bit in slowing her rapid heartbeat. "I need some time, some thinking space. We barely know each other, and certainly not well enough to get married."

"We have the rest of our lives to get to know each other," he said, his arms tightening possessively.

"Marsh, please, you're hurting me." It was a blatant

lie. While she *was* afraid, she wasn't afraid of him. What he was really doing was exciting her to the point where she feared she'd give him anything he asked of her.

"I've never deliberately hurt a woman in my life." His voice was now cold, his expression colder. His arms dropped away from her as he backed down the stairs to the foyer.

Reflexively, Jen reached out a hand, as if to stop his retreat. "Marsh, please." She wet her lips, shivering as she saw his narrowed eyes follow the path of her tongue. "It's too soon. I need time. As I told you before, it's been a long time since I've… Well, I've never experienced anything like what happened last night. It's a lot to process."

His cold expression shifted, giving way to warmth. "We do very well together, Jennifer." He smiled. "During the day *and* at night."

Jen bit her lip to keep from returning his smile. She was raking her mind for something coherent to say when he saved her from herself.

"Do you want to be courted?"

"Courted?" Jen blinked.

"Yes," he said, dead seriously. "You know, do things together besides sit across the table from each other at mealtimes."

"You mean like going riding and having dinner dates?" she asked.

"Sure, why not?" He smiled. "What do you enjoy doing in your free time besides reading?"

"You already know I like to ride." He nodded. "Well, I also like to play tennis and swim, and…" She grinned. "I like going shopping."

He gave her a wry look. "I'll ride with you. I'll play

tennis with you. I'll swim with you. We can go out to dinner, maybe even a movie now and again, but I draw the line at shopping."

She laughed. "Okay." She arched one brow. "But you'll still be the boss."

Smiling, he arched a brow right back at her. "During working hours, of course."

Jen nodded agreement. "Of course."

"But understand one thing, Jennifer," he went on, his voice now serious. "I fully intend to continue asking you to marry me until you say yes."

Jen froze. She should have known he was being too easy to get along with. Her silence must have warned him she was about to protest because he went still, too, his gaze hard on hers.

"I promise I won't force the issue."

"Okay," she said uncertainly.

"Now, promise you won't bolt to your car the minute I go into my office?" His voice was now a combination of suspicion and amusement.

Deciding the man was capable of driving a woman to drink—or dive straight into his arms—Jen nodded, lifted her hand to cross her heart with her forefinger and said, "I promise." She let a moment pass before adding, "I couldn't anyway. Most of my clothes are in your washer and dryer. But," she said as he turned to go, forcing him to turn back around, "I won't sleep with you at your beck and call." She hesitated a brief moment then added, "But I might, if I'm in the mood."

For a moment Marsh simply stared at her, then, surprising her, he agreed. "In that regard, you're the boss, and you'll call the shots."

Staring at him in wonder, Jen said, "Okay. Thank you."

"You're welcome. You know what?" He didn't wait for an answer. "You're cute when you're confused." Shaking his head he turned and walked back into his office, laughing. The echo of his bone-melting laughter lingered in her mind long after he had closed the door to his office.

Jennifer heaved a deep sigh. It simply wasn't fair for one man to be so damn attractive in so damn many ways. Of course, she knew she couldn't accept his proposal, such as it was. But it should be interesting to be "courted" by him.

Temptation whispered in the back of her mind: *grab him while his offer stands.*

Was she nuts? Possibly sharing his bed on occasion was one thing, but marriage? Shaking the very idea out of her head, Jen resumed climbing the stairs, and decided she'd stay upstairs—away from Marsh—for a while. Her heart was still pounding wildly and she wasn't quite sure she trusted herself around the man. She grabbed her book and sat, determined to keep any and all thoughts of Marsh from her mind by losing herself in the trials and tribulations of someone else's life for a while.

The story, a contemporary romance written by one of her favorite authors, immediately grabbed her attention. Within a few minutes, Jen's imagination slipped her into the role of heroine. It didn't take many pages, which Jen turned with increasing speed, before it became obvious the author was adeptly maneuvering the protagonists into a love scene.

What had started out with ever-increasing sensual banter quickly became heated. Without realizing it, Jen's body had grown taut, her breathing quick and shallow.

She turned a page and—

Her cell phone rang. Startled out of the hot and heavy scene, Jen muttered a curse and turned the book page down before answering the call.

"Jennifer, why haven't you come home for a visit, or at least called me?" Celia demanded imperiously.

At the sound of her mother's voice, an image flashed into Jen's mind of her mother in the throes of sex with a man who was not her husband. Would that awful image haunt her for the rest of her life? She dreaded the very idea.

Drawing a deep breath, she pushed the image aside. "I've been busy, Mother," she said, her voice a hair above a tremor. Her mother didn't seem to notice her distress. Of course, she thought, that was exactly like her mother.

"Surely you get weekends off," Celia snapped back. "He can't work you seven days a week."

He might try. Jen smiled at the very idea. "Of course not," she said. "This past weekend I drove to San Antonio to do some shopping."

"And last weekend and the weekend before that?" Celia's tone held a pout.

"Mother," she began, smothering an impatient sigh. That's as far as she got.

"Well, you absolutely must come home next weekend." Not a request, a command.

Indeed? Jen's eyebrows arched. "Why?" she asked, too politely.

"Don't you dare take that tone with me, Jennifer." Celia sounded on the verge of losing it. "The Terrells' Halloween masked ball is next Saturday, and as you are well aware, we always attend."

Oh, well then, why didn't you tell me at once? I

wouldn't dream of missing the Terrells' annual Hal-
loween romp, Jen thought, her lips curling into a gri-
mace. William Terrell—not Bill, never Bill, but always
William—was the man in bed with her mother that
awful night. His wife, Annette, was the woman with
Jen's father.

"Mother, you know I have never cared for that
party," she said, forcing herself to remain calm. "And
I wasn't planning to attend this year. I'm not sure if I
can make—"

"You will be here," her mother insisted. "For heaven's
sake, Jen, all your friends will be there. They will be
expecting to see you there, as well."

"Mother, I have been corresponding with my friends
ever since I arrived here. I know for a fact that none of
my gang is attending the party—they haven't in years,"
she said. "As a matter of fact, they feel as I do about it."

"And that is?" Celia asked.

"That we're past it. Our lives have gone in different directions. If you'll recall, the girls who always attend are no longer my friends. And they're still into the
social scene. I've attended the Terrells' party because
they are *your* closest friends." She nearly choked on
the word *friends.*

"But—"

Jen quickly cut her off. "My true friends were never
part of the social scene. All of us are into a different
lifestyle." She gave a soft chuckle. "We work. We enjoy
working."

"But if you come home, you would still be able to see
them," Celia said. "I could arrange something."

Celia could be very convincing when she wanted to
be. Even though Jen had kept in touch with her friends
online, it was never the same as being in their com-

pany. It would be fun to see them. Until that moment, she didn't realize how very much she had been missing them.

And getting away from Marsh right now couldn't hurt, given the way he was making her feel. Which was, basically, turned on. Constantly. Which led her to think about dangerous things, like marrying him.

Going home for a visit would give her some serious thinking time.

"Okay," she capitulated, "but I won't stay long."

"Come for lunch," Celia said, adding before Jen could refuse, "I'll invite your 'gang,' as you insist on referring to them, to join us."

Jen made a face at the condescending inflection her mother had used with the word *gang*. Though she knew her mother held no animosity toward her friends, Celia still considered them beneath Jen. "What time?" she asked, suddenly tired and wanting the conversation to be over.

"Well," Celia now said with brisk satisfaction, "come early, but I'll invite the girls for one. Will that be all right with your schedule?"

"Yes, Mother." Jen gritted her teeth.

"Oh, and don't forget a costume." With that, her mother disconnected.

Great, Jen thought, resisting an urge to throw the phone across the room. A costume. She had forgotten the costume part of the stupid gala. She'd have to run into Dallas early, or possibly Friday evening, to pick up something suitable.

Maybe she'd go as a sexy vampire with long pointed teeth. That ought to make an impression.

The only question now was, how would Marsh react when she told him she was going home for a visit?

Or maybe the *real* question was, how would she feel being away from him for a few days?

She didn't like the answer she came up with...not one little bit.

Eight

Marsh began his courting campaign first thing on Monday morning, making Jen nervous before she'd even had her coffee.

Even at that early hour it was already warm outside and the weather forecast was for the temperature to rise into the eighties by the afternoon. After breakfast he said, "How about a game of tennis followed by a swim?"

Jen was struck dumb for an instant. Marsh always went directly to work after breakfast. She had never dreamed that this whole courting thing meant he'd actually take time out of his workday to spend with her.

"I'd love it," she said. "But we've got to—" That's as far as she got before he cut her off.

"We can work after we've had some exercise." Taking her hand, he led her away from the table. "Let's get changed." Releasing her, he sprinted up the stairs. "Last one on the court's a slowpoke."

"Hey, no fair," Jen protested as she chased after him.

To Jen's surprise, Marsh played a mean game of tennis. He won, but she made him work for it. "You're good," she said, bent over with her hands on her knees, drawing in deep breaths of air. "Where did you learn to play like that?"

Marsh was breathing every bit as heavily but he remained upright. "I was on the tennis team in college. You're good, too." He smiled at her. "For a few minutes there, I was afraid you'd beat me at my best sport."

Jen arched her brows in surprise. "You didn't play football?"

"Yeah, I did. But, after the first time I had my bell rung with a concussion I decided I liked tennis better." He flashed a killer grin at her. "My daddy didn't raise no fool."

From the court they went to the pool. Marsh stripped off his shirt and dove right in. Jen had pulled on a T-shirt and shorts over her bikini. Stepping out of the shorts and yanking the shirt off her sweaty body, she dove in after him.

There was no contest this time—they simply swam together. Jen was reveling in the sensation of the water rippling over her heated flesh when suddenly she let out a yelped, "Wha—!"

Marsh had dunked her.

Sputtering, Jen came up from the water to the sound of Marsh's laughter. She immediately retaliated. Jackknifing into a deep dive, she grasped his ankles and pulled his legs out from under him.

When he surfaced, Jen was laughing. For a moment, she watched him warily, but relaxed when he grinned at her.

"I deserved that," he admitted.

"Yes, you did," she said, grinning back at him.

"But I'll get you back for it," he teased. "Maybe not today, maybe not tomorrow, but I will get you back for it."

That night, to her surprise, Jen slept alone. As much as she told herself she was glad Marsh hadn't made as much as a suggestion that they share his bed, she didn't sleep well.

Dammit. Having decided she wouldn't sleep with him again until she was certain of his true feelings for her, she expected she'd feel relieved that he hadn't tried to seduce her. But all she felt was disappointment.

On Tuesday afternoon, Marsh left his office two hours earlier than usual and, rapping on Jen's door, ordered, "Pack it in, Jen, and go change into jeans and boots. We're going to ride into the sunset together."

Opening her office door, Jen gave him a wry look. "Ride into the sunset together?"

"Yeah, you've been buried every night in that romance novel," he said, grinning. "I thought asking you to ride into the sunset with me would sound romantic to you."

"You are a complete nut," she said, laughing at him.

"Maybe so," he drawled. "But I'm still the boss."

They actually did ride into the sunset. Standing side by side on the crest of a small hill, their mounts nibbling on the short grass nearby, Jen and Marsh watched the sun set the sky ablaze in breathtaking splashes of pink and streaks of lavender as it slowly disappeared in the distance.

"Romantic?"

Jen smiled at his hopeful tone. "Beautiful," she answered.

He took her hand, drawing her closer to him so he

could wrap his arm around her shoulders. "What about now?"

"Getting there," she murmured, drawing in the scent of him, the very essence of him.

Releasing her hand, he touched her cheek, drawing the tips of his fingers along her soft skin. She hitched a breath. At the soft sound, he lowered his head to brush his lips over her now trembling mouth.

"And now?" His breath teased her lips.

"Oh, yes." Raising her hand to the back of his head she brought his mouth to hers.

His kiss was sweet, gentle, wonderful for a full minute. Then, with a growl low in his throat, his desire took over.

Jen clung to him, owning him with her fierce embrace. Her feelings were running rampant. It was so good, so exciting, it was almost scary. Jen half expected Marsh to lower her to the grassy knoll, take her right there with the rainbow of colors arching across the twilight sky.

And she couldn't have stopped him.

But Cocoa and Star could.

Jen pulled away from Marsh when Star gave her a strong nudge against her shoulder. At the same time she heard Marsh curse as he was nudged by Cocoa.

"Unromantic beasts," he muttered, giving the horses a gentle shove away from them.

Jen couldn't control the burst of laughter that poured from her throat.

"Think it's funny, do you?" Marsh made a good attempt at a scowl, then lost it to his own roar of laughter.

"Yes, and so do you. And you were trying so hard, too."

"Trying?" One dark brow arched. *"Trying?"*

Leaning into him, Jen kissed his whisker-roughened cheek. "Actually, you were doing very well."

He reached for her. She danced away to grab up Star's reins. "Sunset's over. I think it's time to head back before it's dark."

"You don't need to be afraid of the dark," Marsh said, swinging up and into Cocoa's saddle as she mounted Star. "I'll protect you."

"I'll bet," she answered. "If I let you, you'll protect me right out of my jeans."

"Boy," Marsh said, in mock despair. "You are one very smart lady."

Jen laughed.

Marsh laughed with her.

By midweek, Jen could feel the changes occurring in their relationship. She was no longer wary of him, and she felt a closeness growing between them, a camaraderie.

And now he was approaching her about spending the night together, yet Jen held him off. No matter how often he complained of being lonely in that big bed of his, she stuck to her determination and slept in her own bed…alone, missing his closeness, his warmth.

As the days of the week slipped by, Jen knew she had to tell Marsh of her plans to drive to her parents' home in Dallas on Friday night. She had put it off, somehow knowing he wasn't going to be happy about her leaving. Thursday evening, Jen broached the subject after they had just finished a meal of salad and perfectly cooked steaks Marsh had made on the grill on the patio.

"Why?" he asked, when she had finished.

Why? Jen thought. "Why not?" she asked. They had spent most of the week together exclusively. Why shouldn't she spend one weekend away from him?

Marsh was getting to her—she was weakening toward his idea of them being together on a permanent basis. The realization was making her a bit edgy. Now, if he was going to start being possessive as well, she thought again that a little distance from him was a good idea.

Oh, who was she kidding? Jen was afraid she was falling for him, getting in too deep. So she took refuge in a show of independence.

She didn't even try to soften the impatience in her tone. "My weekends are free, aren't they?"

"Yes, of course." Marsh shook his head. "It just seems this came out of the blue. I was expecting to spend the weekend with you." His voice took on an edge, one she didn't particularly like. "Do you have plans or something?"

"Yes, I have plans," she said, surprised and annoyed by his manner. "On Saturday, I'm having lunch with several of my friends at my parents' home. And I'm attending the Terrells' party Saturday evening."

"Ah, the famous Terrells' Halloween masked ball, costumes required," he said in a ridiculing drawl, "and bedrooms available for couples for…private conversation."

That stopped Jen cold. "You're kidding," she said, raising an eyebrow. "Aren't you?"

Marsh smiled in superiority. "No, innocent one, I assure you, I am not kidding."

Jen wasn't sure what she resented more—his haughty smile or him calling her "innocent one." "But…"

"Have you been to the gala before?"

"Yes, I have, several times." Jen raised her chin in defiance. "Why do you ask?"

His silver eyes suddenly looked dark and stormy. "I

would have believed once would have been more than enough to turn you off the debauchery."

Debauchery? At the Terrells' party? She could believe it about the Terrells—she had seen them in action. Still, surely her old friends, who had also attended the gala for years, would have mentioned it. She was considering not attending the affair after all when Marsh decided the issue.

"I think you'd do better staying right here," he said, not quite an order but close enough.

"Then you can think again," she said, none too sweetly. "I'm going."

And that's when the cold front moved in.

They didn't speak to each other for the rest of the night. The next morning, while clearing away the dishes after a silent breakfast, Jen felt as if she was about to scream. Why was he acting like this? What did he expect she would do over the weekend—have a mad, wild fling with some mysterious man at the party? Is that why he had felt compelled to inform her—no, warn her—about the availability of bedrooms at the Terrells'?

Jen was building up a head of angry steam merely thinking about his manner. Without a word, she started walking out of the kitchen toward her office.

"Jennifer."

The snap in his tone stopped her cold. At the end of her patience, she whirled around to glare at him. "What?" Her tone had a decided bite.

"Go now," he said. "If you work the day, you'll have to drive to Dallas in the dark."

As if she hadn't known that, Jen thought. It was the end of October. Was he that eager to get her out of his sight? A pang zinged in her chest. *Fine,* she thought. *I'll give the man what he wants.*

She changed course from her office to the stairway.

Marsh came after her, coming to a stop one step below her. "Jen, wait," he said, his long fingers circling her wrist, his voice softening. "You are coming back, aren't you?"

Slowly turning, she gave him an arch look. "Well, I was planning on doing so, but if you keep snarling at me, I'll come back just to collect my stuff."

"Was I snarling?" While Marsh spoke, he was gently tugging on her wrist, slowly drawing her closer to him. "I realize I might have been a bit brusque, but snarling?"

His distinctive scent, his sheer maleness sent shivers rushing up her spine. Her heart began to thump, her breathing catch in her throat.

"Marsh," she managed to whisper when he raised her hand close to his face.

"I'm not going to hurt you," he murmured, lowering his head to touch his warm lips to her pounding pulse. "The last thing in this world I want to do is hurt you."

Jen's heartbeat seemed to stop altogether as his lips moved to the center of her palm. A warm sensation fluttered deep inside her. She had to get out of there, she thought, fighting an impulse to thread her fingers through his dark hair, lift his mouth to hers. If she didn't go now, at once, she'd be melting all over him, curling her arms around him, begging him to take her to his bed.

No, no, no. The word rang through her mind as she backed up a step, pulling her hands away from the temptation of his mouth, his body.

"Marsh, I'm going." Jen continued to back away, fighting her need for him every step of the way. To her relief—and also chagrin—he didn't follow her. But his gaze, a blaze of silvery-blue desire, tracked her every move.

"Have a good visit with your parents and your friends, Jennifer." His sensually soft voice stroked every nerve in her body. "And behave yourself."

Behave herself? Jen was suddenly fuming again. The man could make her crazy in an instant—it was amazing. Fortunately she had reached the landing as she spun to glare down at him, her nerves jangling now for an altogether different reason.

"I am not a child, Mr. Grainger," she said distinctly through gritted teeth. "And you will not speak to me as if I were. That is, if you would like me to come back."

He offered not an apology, as she had expected, but a blatantly sexy smile. "Oh, you'll come back, sweet Jen, because I know you want me as much as I want you."

Oh, hell, Jen thought. She did want him, dammit, here, now, right on the stairs. Shocked by how weak she was, how weak and needy he could so easily make her, she spun around and strode down the hallway to her apartment.

"Yes, you may go," he said, sounding more like a stern parent than an employer, never mind a lover.

"And you can go to hell, Marshall," she called back at him, slamming the door shut behind her.

Jen grabbed the carry-on she had packed that morning and turned to take a quick look at herself in the mirror. She hardly recognized the person looking back at her, a woman whose face was flushed with anger, frustration and more desire than she knew what to do with.

It was a good thing she was leaving for the weekend.

Opening the door just enough to peek out, Jen sighed her relief that Marsh was gone and dashed down to the garage. Tossing her stuff into the trunk, she jumped into the driver's seat and took off as though the devil himself was after her.

* * *

Why didn't I even say goodbye to her?

The question nagged at Marsh long after Jen's car had disappeared from view. Hell, it was less than an hour since she had driven away and already he was missing her. He was missing everything about her.

If he was honest with himself, Marsh knew damn well why he hadn't carried her bag and walked her to her car like a gentleman. He was sulking like a spoiled kid because he hadn't had his own way.

Still, he admired her for defying him. He admired her for everything she was—tough, unafraid and soft and sweet…at times.

This was the second time he'd managed to drive her away. What was he doing wrong? Marsh wasn't used to getting things wrong with women. He was used to his words and actions always having the desired effect, and to getting exactly what he wanted. But with Jen, it was completely different. There was something about her, something about the way she saw him—she didn't automatically do or say what he wanted. She thought for herself, and wasn't instantly swayed by whatever charm he was laying on.

As annoying as that was, it was also hotter than hell.

The days they had spent together "courting" were some of the best of his entire life. Besides her ability to stand on her own two feet, what was it about her that had so captured his interest and imagination?

She intrigued him. She was *more* than any other woman he had ever met—he didn't know how else to say it. And since Marsh couldn't explain it to himself, he'd never consider even trying to explain his feelings to anyone else.

Especially not to her.

He wanted her, wanted her more than any other woman he had ever met. He wanted her until he ached with the wanting, ached in his body and mind. But it was about more than that. It wasn't just the mind-blowing sex, it was…what?

It was nuts. That's what it was. It was totally and completely nuts. But there it was. As badly as he wanted to be a father, to have an heir, he *needed* more. He wanted her—and only her—to be the mother of his children.

The realization shocked him. It wasn't just that he wanted her to accept his business proposition so he could have what he wanted. It was that he wanted to build something with her, he wanted her by his side, he wanted her to be his partner in life.

He wanted…a life. With her. Period.

So what the hell was he supposed to do now?

At lunchtime, Jen stopped at a roadside pizza shop. Sitting in a booth at the window, she sipped iced tea as she glanced at the strip mall on the other side of the highway. Checking out the stores, her glance passed, then returned, to the second to last of them.

Holidays, Holidays, Holidays arched across the display window, which was decorated with everything Halloween.

Less than a half hour later, Jen parked the car in the lot close to the store. She was pleased to discover that the merchandise was of a much better quality than usually found in discount stores. After all, she couldn't show up at the gala in a cheap costume—her mother wouldn't hear of it.

"Need help?" a smiling woman asked from behind a cash register. "Or just browsing?"

Jen returned her smile. "I don't think I need help, just directions to the costumes."

The woman waved her arm. "They're along the back wall. That's what's left of them."

"Thanks," Jen said. "I'll have a look."

The woman hadn't been kidding—what was left on the wall was slim pickings. Still, one costume hanging near the end caught her eye at once.

"Perfect," she murmured, coming to a halt in front of a gypsy-girl outfit. She touched the full black skirt shot through with golden thread. *Velvet?* Jen thought, surprised. Her hand moved from the skirt to the off-the-shoulder loose blouse. *Silk?* Amazing. The garment was a deep red, the neckline and long sleeves trimmed with a wide ruffle.

Carmen. The name jumped into her head along with an image of the outfit worn by the sultry soprano who had performed the role of the lusty Carmen when Jen had attended the opera at the Met the last time she had visited New York City.

She called out to the clerk to join her at the back.

"Find something, did you?" the woman asked, coming to a stop next to Jen, her gaze drifting to the costume. "Beautiful, isn't it."

Jen nodded. "Gorgeous."

"A bit pricey," the woman added, as if in warning.

"That's all right," Jen said. "I'm going to need a few accessories."

"I've got it covered. Come with me."

When Jen left the store, she was carrying a shopping bag in each hand, a small smile of satisfaction curving her lips. The skirt, blouse and accessories had cost her a bundle but she didn't care. Since learning the truth about her parents' indiscretions with the Terrells, she had decided this was the last Terrell Halloween bash she would ever attend. This was the last time she was ever going to appease her mother in this regard, so she might as well go all the way.

When she got home, she was struck by a strange sensation. After only a few weeks away, the word *home* didn't seem to fit anymore. When, she wondered, had she begun thinking of Marsh's place as home?

Jen realized she had started to consider his place her home after the incredible night they had spent together. The fact that the atmosphere around the house had felt strained since their argument didn't matter—it still felt like home. And that fact alone was kind of scary.

After parking her car in the slot that had been hers ever since she got her driver's license when she was seventeen, Jen entered the house by the kitchen door.

She had spent many hours in the kitchen while she was growing up, warmly welcomed there by Tony. She had learned her cooking skills from him in that kitchen…the skills Marsh so vocally appreciated.

Marsh.

Jen sighed. She had been gone less than a day and she was homesick. She scolded herself, heading for the elevator in the hallway right off the kitchen. The elevator rose to her apartment, which took up the entire second floor of the wing attached to the house. Her father had built the wing to house Jen's grandmother when the elderly woman's arthritis put her in a wheelchair.

Jen had adored her grandmother, who died while Jen was in her junior year of college. After graduation Jen had moved into the apartment, and even though she had replaced the Victorian-style furniture and decorations the older woman favored with more modern things, she still felt close to her grandmother there.

That was before she went to live in Marshall Grainger's sprawling house. Stepping inside the living room Jen had once felt so comfortable in, she set her shopping bags on the floor and sighed as she dropped into her favorite chair.

The roomy place now seemed no more welcoming than an expensive hotel suite.

It wasn't the house in the hill country she was missing, Jen reluctantly admitted to herself. It was the man living in it, waiting for her return.

Oh, Lord, I am in trouble, Jen thought. *Willingly or not, I have fallen in love with Marshall Grainger.*

The man who had not so much proposed to her as decided all on his own that they should get married.

For business reasons, essentially.

This was the man she'd decided to fall in love with?

She heaved a heavy sigh. If only he had indicated some genuine feelings for her. Oh, he enjoyed her company, liked teasing her, kissing her, touching her and pursuing more intimate, sensual, exciting endeavors. And while she reveled in his attention, and couldn't believe the extreme pleasure he was able to give her over and over again, she still longed for him to confess deeper feelings for her. But he never did, and she feared he never would.

Arrogant jerk.

Calling him names in silent frustration didn't help at all, she found.

She was still in love with him.

Sighing, Jen shook her head, as if shaking thoughts of Marsh from her mind—yeah, right—and rose to scoop up the bags to carry to her bedroom.

Before getting settled, she decided she had better let her mother know she was back. Lifting the phone from her nightstand, Jen hit the button for the interior of the house. Ida, the housekeeper for as long as Jen could remember, answered with the first buzz.

"Yes?"

"Hi, Ida," Jen greeted the woman warmly. "It's Jen. Is Mother there?"

"Hi, honey," the older woman replied, still using the same endearment she had always used with Jen. "No, your mother had a dental appointment this afternoon. Are you hungry?"

Jen laughed. Those words had always been the first thing Ida had asked her whenever she walked into the house. "Well, come to think of it, I could eat a snack. I haven't eaten since lunch and all I had was a slice of pizza. What are you offering?" Frowning she tacked on, "Where is Tony? I came in through the kitchen and it was empty."

"He went grocery shopping," Ida said, amusement in her voice. "He wanted some special goodies to serve you and your friends for lunch tomorrow."

"Oh, I can hardly wait," Jen said.

Ida laughed again. "Well, would you settle for a cold roast beef and cheese sandwich now?"

"Hmm, sounds good. Give me a few minutes and I'll be down."

"Take your time."

It took only minutes to hang up the skirt and blouse Jen had purchased. Leaving the apartment, she strode to the end of the hallway and clattered down the back stairs.

"Jennifer's home," Ida said, laughing as Jen entered the room. "Do you ever *walk* down a flight of stairs, honey?"

"Only when I'm being a lady, which isn't too often,"

Jen answered, walking to the woman and right into her arms. "It's good to see you, Ida."

"Oh, Jennifer," Ida said, "I miss you—your laughter, your bounding up and down stairs."

"I miss you, too." Stepping back, she sighed. "I had to go. I needed new…scenery."

Ida nodded. "I understand."

Jen suspected Ida knew and understood everything that ever happened in this house. "I know you do," she replied, lowering her gaze.

"Now, then," Ida said briskly. "Your sandwich is ready and I have a fresh pot of coffee brewing."

"You know me so well." Crossing the room to the large solid wood table, Jen seated herself in front of the plated sandwich with a pickle slice next to it.

Tony came in the back door toting two canvas grocery bags just as she was finishing the sandwich. Without much coaxing, she soon had him and Ida at the table with her, the three of them drinking coffee and chatting away, catching up with one another.

Ida had left the kitchen to go finish up what she had been doing when Jen buzzed her, Tony was in the pantry and Jen was nursing her second cup of coffee when her mother swept into the room.

"There you are," she said with a note of censure, as if Jen had no business in the kitchen.

"Yes, here I am," Jen said, rising to accept the brief hug and air-kiss her mother brushed over her cheek. "How are you, Mother?"

"I'm fine now that the dentist has taken care of the tooth that was bothering me." Her gaze touched on the cup on the table. "Is there any coffee left?"

"Yes, I'll get some for you." Scooping up her cup,

Jen went to the cabinet, took out another cup, then filled both with the aromatic brew. Tony bought only the best.

Sitting close to her mother while they sipped their coffee was a novel experience for Jen—they had never done it before. *Why now, after all this time?* Jen wondered as she glanced at her mother, struck by how odd it was to sit with her in the kitchen.

"I wasn't expecting you until tomorrow." Her mother's eyebrows rose in question.

"I left this morning. Mr. Grainger gave me the day off."

Her mother nodded but didn't say anything about Marsh, even though Jen had expected she would. "Did you get a costume or must you still go shopping?"

"I got one. I stopped for lunch and noticed a holiday shop in a strip mall across the highway. There wasn't a large selection left but I found one."

"Are you going to tell me what it is?" her mother asked.

Jen shrugged. "It's only a gypsy outfit," she answered. "But as I said, the selection was small."

"I think a gypsy outfit will do fine."

Jen hid the smile tickling her lips. Her mother was in for a shock when she saw what Jen was going to do with the outfit. "What's your costume?"

"I'm going as a Southern lady in an antebellum costume."

What else? Jen thought. "I bet it's gorgeous. I can't wait to see it. I presume Dad's wearing the costume of the Southern gentleman?"

"Yes, of course," she answered.

Rhett Butler, of course. Jen smiled. Her parents would be a spectacular couple. Jen enjoyed the thought for a moment, until she heard Marsh's words ringing in her ears about the bedrooms at the masked ball. She looked away from her mother for a moment, trying to bring herself back to the present.

Her mother finished her coffee and walked to the sink to rinse her cup. "I'm afraid you'll be alone for dinner, Jennifer," she said. "As we weren't expecting you until tomorrow, your father and I accepted a dinner engagement for this evening."

"That's all right, Mother," Jen said. "I'm sure I can find a crust of bread and a bit of cheese to eat."

"I beg your pardon?" Tony scowled at her from the doorway to the pantry.

Jen laughed. Her mother even managed a chuckle. "I'm off to have a short nap." She again brushed Jen's cheek, this time with a real and surprising kiss. Celia hesitated a moment then murmured, "If you'll follow me, I'd like for us to have a talk before I take my nap."

Jen blinked before nodding her head. "I'll be up in a minute."

Without another word, her mother swept from the room.

"She certainly knows how to make an entrance and exit," Tony drawled as he strolled into the room. "And you, young lady, you will enjoy a delicious dinner right here in the kitchen." He tried to look angry, which was pretty funny.

"On one condition." Jen scowled back at him.

"Name it." He cocked an eyebrow.

"You and Ida join me at the table."

He smirked. "I was planning on it."

Curious about her mother's startling request for a discussion—and it was a request, not an order—Jen went straight to her mother's lavishly decorated bedroom. And it *was* her mother's bedroom. Celia and John had slept in separate bedrooms for as long as Jen could remember.

She lightly knocked on the wood panel, softly calling, "Mother?"

The door immediately swung inward, almost as if her mother had been hovering on the other side, anxiously waiting for her daughter.

"Come in, dear," she said, indicating a small table flanked by two chairs. "Have a seat."

"Thank you," Jen said, inwardly frowning at the puzzling invitation as she sat.

"Jennifer," Celia said, seating herself in the other chair, "I think it's time for you and I to have a mother-and-daughter, heart-to-heart talk."

Stunned, Jen stared at her mother. "A heart to heart?" she repeated. "Mother, isn't it a little late for that? I'm crowding thirty. I know all about the birds and the bees. Men and women, too," she said, attempting to make a joke to break the tension. What on earth was her mother about to say?

"I know, dear." Celia's smile was sad. "I wasn't referring to you. I was referring to me." She paused, and swallowed. "To me, and William Terrell."

"Mother, I…" Her voice came out raw. Not wanting to hear whatever her mother had to tell her, Jen put her hands on the arms of the chair to stand. She practically wanted to run from the room.

"Jennifer, listen." Celia placed a hand on Jen's arm, keeping her seated. "I need to explain the situation."

Jen tried once again to rise. This time her mother stopped her with the desperate plea in her voice.

"Jennifer, please."

Cringing inside, Jen sank back into the chair, half-sick about what she feared she was going to hear. "Okay, Mother, I'll listen."

Celia drew a deep breath before saying, "You saw us together at some point, didn't you?" She asked the question as if certain Jen would know what she meant by "together."

"Yes." It was barely a whisper from Jen's trembling lips. "And Dad with Annette." She drew a quick breath. "I left my car out front and came up the stairs heading for my place." Tears were trembling on the edges of her eyelids. "The doors were open and…"

"That's enough." Celia sounded choked, her elegant fingers squeezing her daughter's arm.

Jen sent a quick glance at her mother, a pang twisting in her chest at the sight of tears running down her mother's beautiful face. She wanted to run, yet she couldn't move, her knees weak, her body trembling.

"Will you listen as I explain?" The strain in Celia's voice caused another pang in Jen's chest.

Afraid to trust her own voice, Jen nodded her assent.

"I love your father but I'm not in love with him." She sighed. "I've known him all my life. Our families were neighbors. He and I grew up together. I was always trailing after him. For some time, he tried to chase me away," she said, a smile touching her lips, "but eventually he gave in and let me follow him around. We were companions, pals." Here, her voice hardened. "We were never romantically interested in each other."

"But then—" Jen was silenced by her mother's raised hand.

She drew another deep breath before continuing. "Unknown to either your father or me, soon after my birth, our parents decided it would be a perfect idea to betroth the two of us, thereby keeping the wealth of the families together."

Jen simply could no longer be quiet. Eyes widening in disbelief, she said, "That is absolutely ridiculous."

"Yes, of course it is," Celia agreed, shaking her head. "Let me finish the entire stupidity of it all, then you can say anything you wish." She raised her brows. "Okay?"

"Okay." Jen sank back into the padded chair. But she managed to add, "I suppose we should have just had our coffee up here."

Celia gave a soft laugh. "I suppose we should have, but we can do that another time."

Realizing her mother was offering a sort of olive branch, Jen felt another sting of tears in her eyes. Indelicately sniffing, she said, "I'd like that."

"And I." Her smile wider now, Celia brushed the tears from her cheeks before continuing. "At the time our respective parents informed us we were getting married, neither your father nor I had met anyone we were romantically interested in, although we had both dated others. Of course, there was one holdout—your grandmother. She adored her son, and she liked me. She didn't think it was fair to either of us."

"She was right," Jen said.

"Yes—" Celia nodded "—but she was overruled. Both of us caved in to their demands." She closed her eyes as if in pain. "Praying we could come to fall in love, we really tried. We were both delighted when I realized I was pregnant with you, and thrilled when you were born."

Sniffling, Jen nodded.

Celia handed her a small box of tissues, taking one herself. After mopping up, she went on with her story.

"Then I met William." She briefly closed her eyes.

When she opened them she stared straight into Jen's. "I fell in love with him at first sight, and he with me." She paused to give Jen time to respond if she wanted to do so.

Jen remained quiet, waiting until her mother finished.

"I give you my word of honor, Jennifer, nothing happened between William and me until two years later." She shook her head as tears started once more. "That was when your father and Annette told William and me that they were in love." She shook her head in despair. "Sorry tale, isn't it."

Jen couldn't remain seated—she jumped to her feet. "Why didn't you get divorced?" she cried. "Hasn't it been hell living like this?"

"Of course it has, and we did discuss the possibility of divorce," Celia said, getting up to face Jen. "But by then your father's family's finances were so entwined with my family's, and there was you and the Terrells' son, Bill Jr., to consider." She dropped back onto the chair as if exhausted. "We decided to go on as we have been." She swiped at the tears with a delicate hand.

Trembling, shoulders shaking, not knowing exactly what she was feeling about the whole mess, Jen sat back down on the edge of the chair and covered her eyes with her hand.

"Jennifer, please try to understand. I love your father. We are still companions and pals. He feels the same, but there's William and Annette…" Sighing, she let her voice trail away.

"Mother," Jen began, anxious about the defeated look on Celia's face.

"I've wanted to talk to you so often, to bare my soul, but you seemed to always be running away, if only to

hide inside yourself." Her soft voice was tinged with
pain, her eyes wet again. "Can you ever forgive us,
Jennifer?"

"There is nothing to forgive, Mother," she said, walking the few steps needed to wrap her arms around her
mother. "This is your life—yours and Dad's." Stepping
back, she gave her mother an understanding smile.

Now Celia was sniffling. She laughed as Jen handed
her a tissue before taking one herself.

"Will you talk to Dad, tell him I'm not angry or re-
sentful? I'm not, you know. I'm just glad you explained
it to me."

Celia sniffed once more. "We do love you very much,
you know. We always have. And we are very proud of
you."

"Thank you." Jen echoed her mother's sniff. "I love
you, too." Jen smiled and turned to leave the room.
"Now I'm going to get out of here and let you get your
nap. It wouldn't do to have you go out tonight looking
tired and puffy-eyed, and not like your usual lovely
self."

As she opened the door Celia said softly, "Thank
you, Jennifer. Have a nice dinner with the help."

Startled, Jen glanced back in time to see her elegant
mother give her a wink. Laughter bubbling up inside
her, she closed the door.

But when she was back in her apartment, Jen had to
sit down and take a moment for herself. An arranged
marriage. Her parents had an arranged marriage. She
could barely wrap her mind around it. While it helped
her to understand what was going on between them,
it was strange to know that she was the product of a
union between two people who were not in love, and
never had been.

Jen moved to the queen bed in her bedroom, intending only to rest for a while, to give her mind the time to process all that she had learned. Suddenly, an image of Marsh came to mind, and she shivered, realizing the similarity between Marsh's proposal and the marriage her parents shared. She closed her eyes against the sudden sting of hot tears. She couldn't—absolutely could not stand it if, having agreed to marry him, Marsh later met and fell deeply in love with another woman. She didn't think her heart could take that. But wasn't that what would happen, if she entered into an arranged marriage of sorts with Marsh? If he wasn't in love with her, he certainly wouldn't stay with her if he fell in love with someone else. A man like Marsh had opportunities all the time—it wouldn't take much for him to accept one.

Jen knew right then and there that she couldn't continue to work for Marsh, to live with him…to be with him. It was too dangerous for her heart. She would go back to the house after the Terrells' party and hand him her notice in answer to his proposal.

Running away again? The thought drifted through her tired mind. She didn't run from life—did she?

Actually feeling sick to her stomach, she banished the thought for a few moments of calming meditation. She created a beach scene in her mind, wavelets rippling upon the sand. And a woman, hands jammed into the pockets of a jacket, head down, walking down the beach…alone. Tears streaming, Jen finally drifted off to sleep.

Leaving his workout room on the second level of the garage, Marsh was covered with sweat. Frustrated by what he thought of as Jennifer's defection after the incredible times they had shared the previous few days, he had tried to work out his simmering anger by punching the hell out of the big bag hanging from the ceiling.

When that didn't work, he followed up by running like a fighter in training on the treadmill.

That didn't work, either.

In fact, it hadn't helped much at all except to make him sweaty and tired. After a shower, Marsh pulled on jeans and a T-shirt and walked barefoot down the stairs to his office, only to stare sightlessly at the cursor on his computer screen.

She hadn't called since she'd left. He couldn't believe that he'd been waiting to hear from her, but he had. Marsh had never, ever in his entire life "sat by the phone," so to speak, waiting for a woman to call him. He just wasn't that type of man.

Or at least, he hadn't been…until he'd met Jen.

He missed her, more than he had believed himself capable of missing any woman. *I want a life with her* kept ringing through his head. He had never had that thought about anyone before, not even the woman he had married.

Damn, why had he let Jen go to Dallas?

Marsh snorted aloud at himself. How could he have stopped her? By taking her to bed? While the idea held appeal—a lot of appeal—Marsh knew that Jen would have resented him for using sex to keep her there. And she probably would have left afterward anyway.

Just the thought of sex with Jen made Marsh crazy with longing. He shifted on his leather desk chair to relieve the ache in the lower part of his body. Images of her beautiful naked body ran through his head and he was powerless to stop them. Her incredible eyes, her perfect breasts, her flat stomach, the sweetness between her long legs…

He needed her. It was a very difficult admission for him to make, even to himself. But he wanted her. And despite the fact that he'd gotten hard just thinking about her, he didn't just want her naked in his bed. He wanted her here in the house, in the swimming pool, riding horses over his land, cooking with him on the patio grill, softly singing while she went about her work. A shadow of a smile feathered his lips as he wondered if she hummed while working in her office.

"Oh, hell." Marsh gave up and, bending to the trash basket beside his desk, picked out a silver-trimmed black card. The printing on the card was bloodred, requesting his company at the Terrells' Annual Halloween Ball. He had, as usual, received the invitation weeks ago, even though he not only never attended, he didn't even bother to respond.

Sighing in defeat, Marsh put his computer to sleep, pushed back his chair and strode from his office to the stairs.

If you can't fight 'em, join 'em, he thought.

Hell, he'd have to find a costume. The very idea of him, Marshall Grainger, putting on a stupid costume for a woman, was a hard truth to swallow.

But then an idea struck him in a flash. It was easy enough to pull off. And the best part was, he had almost everything he needed right in his apartment in Dallas.

A few hours later, Marsh was exceeding the speed limit as he headed for the city. He caught sight of the perfect shop only because he had to stop for a red light—Holidays, Holidays, Holidays, it was called. Making a quick turn when the light turned green, he parked and strode into the shop and found what he needed to complete his outfit.

Marsh grimaced as he tossed his store bag into the

car. He detested getting dressed in a stupid costume, even if it was the simplest disguise he could come up with. He shook his head and slipped behind the wheel.

The lengths a man will go to just to get a woman into his bed...permanently.

Nine

The phone on Jen's bedside cabinet buzzed, waking her from her nap. Yawning, she picked up the receiver. "Yes?" she asked, still only half-awake.

"Good morning, glory, did you see the rain…dear?" Tony's chipper voice sang in her ear.

Jen laughed. "You're a goof, and it's not morning and it's not raining."

"I know, but her majesty has left the building and supper is ready, so rustle your tush down here."

"Give me five minutes," she said.

"Okay, princess, see you in five." He disconnected.

Jen didn't move for a moment, as the conversation she had had with her mother came rushing back to her. She pondered the situation for a minute, reminding herself that her parents' lives were their business. And Celia's heartfelt avowal of their love for her eased a hurt that Jen had buried deep inside herself.

But she still couldn't help thinking about how her parents' situation compared to her situation with Marsh. She knew what she had to do. She hated it, but she knew it.

She set the phone aside and went to her bathroom to splash water on her face before brushing her teeth. Exactly four and a half minutes later she ran into the kitchen announcing, "I'm here and I'm starving. What's for supper?"

"One of your favorites," Tony announced. "Cheeseburgers and Greek salad," he finished.

"Oh, heavenly," she said, running around the table to hug him. "You whip up the best Greek salad in the whole world."

"I know." Tony grinned back at her.

Ida stood patiently behind her chair at the table, smiling indulgently. "If you two are done with your comedy act?" she said dryly.

Tony gave Jen a quick hug before stepping back from her embrace. "You see, Jennifer, that's the reason I don't marry her. I hear nothing but nag, nag, nag."

"Oh, I see," Ida shot back, primly seating herself at the table. "I'm good enough to sleep with but not to marry."

"Ida!" Tony glanced at Jen in alarm. "Cover your ears."

"I'm a big girl, Tony, and I've known about you and Ida for years now."

Tony appeared half-sick. "How did you find out?"

"For heaven's sake, Tony," Ida chided him. "I told her."

Tony brought a hand up to his chest as if in pain. "I can't stand it," he cried dramatically as he set a luncheon plate in front of Jen. "Anyway," he groused, "I did ask her to marry me, at least a hundred times. She said no."

Jen shot a startled look at Ida.

The older woman shrugged. "Why ruin a great relationship?"

Curious and surprised by the older woman's attitude, Jen decided to keep her opinion to herself.

Later, back in her room, Jen pondered the exchange between Tony and Ida. They were close to the same age, somewhere in their late fifties, Jen figured. They made an odd couple. Ida was of medium height, a bit plump and still very pretty, her face unlined. She had lost her husband to cancer after only a few years of marriage and apparently didn't feel the need to marry again. So she had made a home with Jen's parents.

Tony was flat-out handsome, tall and lean with gleaming dark eyes and a ready smile. And he was one terrific cook. Jen had often wondered why he had never opened his own restaurant. Now she wondered if he stayed with her parents to be with Ida.

While they both had their own quarters in the huge house, Jen knew they slept together in Tony's bed.

Is that what Marsh had in mind for her? The thought wormed its way into her mind, making her restless. Getting out of her chair, Jen began to pace the apartment as if by walking she could find the answers to her dilemma.

Marsh had said he wanted marriage and children.

Without love.

Jen shivered at the chill that snaked down her spine. Whereas Ida and Tony had love without marriage, Jen found herself facing the idea of marriage without love, just like her parents. She couldn't help thinking that Ida had the best deal.

Like other young women, Jen had wanted marriage and children. But she had always dreamed that love would come first. And while she admittedly was head-over-heels in love with Marsh, he was admittedly hot for her body.

Although he did consider her good wife and mother material. But so what? What good was any of that without love?

Sighing, Jen looked around, finding herself in her bedroom. She plopped onto the bed to be comfortable while ruminating.

Fat chance of being comfortable while thinking about Marshall Grainger.

What to do? Was it enough that she loved him? Should she take a gamble and marry Marsh even though she knew he didn't love her? Should she accept his offer—be his wife, keep his books, take care of his home, cook his meals and share his bed and someday, hopefully, bear his children?

Jen felt a twist of longing inside. She so wanted to bear his children…their children.

She was already keeping his home and his books and cooking his meals. Why not take the next leap of faith and pray they could make a go of marriage, even if he didn't love her? They would have the intimacy of the bedroom, and in truth Jen craved his body as much as he seemed to crave hers.

Was that enough for her? Could she make it enough? Was she strong enough to live out her life under those conditions? Jen bit her lower lip. Like a greedy child she wanted it all—all of Marsh, including his love.

But, she reminded herself, Marsh didn't believe in love.

Square one.

This was real life, Jen told herself, heaving a deep sigh. She loved him, and was beginning to doubt that she would ever love any other man. In real life one played the hand that was dealt—it was pointless to wish for it all. That was the stuff of romantic fairy tales, dreamed by teenagers.

She was a woman, a woman in love with a man who wasn't going to love her back.

And it sucked.

Jen woke the next morning still balanced on the sword of indecision, so to speak. Although she had gone to bed early, she had lain awake most of the night mentally replaying the pros and cons of her present situation.

All things considered, Jen simply could not decide what to do about her relationship with Marsh. She had changed her mind several times already, going from vowing never to see him again to agreeing to marry him. Teetering on the edge was not her style, as a rule. For just about as long as she could recall, Jen had thought through a problem then quickly made a decision, as she had when deciding to accept Marsh's terms of employment.

On reflection, Jen thought what she should have done at the time was jump back into her car and run. Then, having only just met him, she could have gone on her way, personally unaffected by him…except for that strange sizzling sensation that zinged up her arm when they first shook hands.

It had started right away. She should have fled when she still had the strength.

She replayed her conversation with her mother, in which her mother said she was always running away in some way, shape or form. She frowned. Had she been running away her whole life, first from the guy in the school parking lot? Had she run to the hill country after finding her parents in compromising positions with their best friends?

Had she run back to Dallas to escape her feelings for Marsh?

Jen shook her head to dispel the vision in her mind, only to find herself with her thoughts of Marsh again. In time, the memory of his touch would pass, wouldn't it? Gazing at her hand, Jen had an eerie sensation she could still feel him. Maybe the sensation wouldn't have passed.

Somehow she knew she would very likely never forget those delicious sensations.

She got out of bed and headed into the bathroom for a shower. She had to shove thoughts of Marsh aside and pull her act together. Her friends were due to arrive for lunch in less than an hour.

She set the shower at full blast hoping the cold water would clear her thoughts. Maybe time with her "gang" could help her decide what to do about the new man in her life.

It was time to come clean with them about where she'd been all this time—and who she'd been with.

Her friends were right on time, all five—Kathie, Marcie, Karen, Leslie and Mary—pulling their cars into the driveway one after the other. Jen ran to meet them.

After hugs all around, they made their way into the house. The grilling started almost immediately.

"All right, Jen, where did you run off to?" Kathie demanded, giving Jen a mock stern look.

"I missed you!" Marcie said, putting on a pout.

"Yeah, you sneak, it's time to come clean," Karen added.

"If you'll recall," Jen chided, herding them into the house, "I kept in touch online."

"But you said absolutely nothing," Mary replied.

"There's a man, isn't there?" Leslie asked.

Jen ushered them through the dining room and onto the shaded patio where Tony had laid an elegant setting for seven on the round garden table. Glasses of iced tea were waiting for them.

It was a perfect day for lunch outside. The temperature was in the high seventies with a lovely fall breeze. "Isn't it gorgeous out?" Jen asked.

"Come clean, Jen, *now.*" It was an order from Kathie in her sternest drill-sergeant tones.

"Who are you working for? More to the point, what kind of work are you doing? And why did you leave so mysteriously?" Marcie asked.

"I'm getting suspicious," Mary said, giving her a narrow-eyed look.

"And I'm getting impatient," Karen added.

Jen held her hand up to get them to stop. "I'll tell you all about him—about everything. Let's just sit down first, okay?"

"Is he deliciously handsome and sexy?" The salacious note Leslie had managed to achieve had all of them laughing as they settled at the table. It was like old times, the six of them laughing together as they so often had in college. It was wonderful—just the tonic Jen had been needing.

The laughter came to an abrupt stop when Jen's mother joined them at the table. Seating herself, she glanced around the table, one eyebrow arched.

"Having fun, ladies?"

"Actually, we were, Mother," Jen said. "It was as if we were back in the dorm again."

"We're trying to get your daughter to tell us who she's working for," Karen asked.

"For whom, dear," her mother corrected. "You don't know about Jennifer and Marshall Grainger?" Now both eyebrows were raised.

Jen nearly spit out her drink.

"Marshall Grainger?" Kathie repeated in awed tones.

"Holy…shoot," a wide-eyed Marcie said, catching herself to clean up her language just in time.

All the women at the table looked at Jen, waiting for her to offer some sort of explanation.

"Yummy," Leslie said. "But Marsh Grainger isn't exactly—"

"How did you even—" began Kathie.

"It's a long story. I swear, I'll tell you everything. Later," Jen added.

"Well, this is a happy group, isn't it?" Tony drawled, coming to a halt at the table. "Shall I wait a few minutes to serve?"

"Heck no, I'm starving," Marcie said.

Only Marcie, Jen thought fondly. "No, you can serve now, please," Jen said.

"May," her mother corrected again. "You *may* serve now, Tony, thank you."

Who, whom, can, may—what the hell difference did it make? She was among friends, her very best friends. Though Jen was sorely tempted to say something very impolite to her mother, she held it back, not wanting to spoil her friends' good humor and lunch. Besides, she didn't want to endanger the accord she and her mother had reached yesterday afternoon.

Tony had prepared a wonderful warm day luncheon.

In the center of the table he set a large pitcher of freshly brewed iced tea with mint. "There's more of everything, ladies," he said as he turned away, "including the tea. Just give me a call for refills."

"I swear," Celia muttered, "that man grows more familiar every day."

"Maybe," Jen agreed dryly. "But, keep in mind, he is one of the best chefs in the city."

Her mother surprised Jen by smiling at her. "Well," she conceded, "there is that," she added, continuing to peck daintily at her meal.

The rest of the women, including Jen, set to devouring every morsel on their plates. Before they had reached the fruit salad, her mother patted her lips with her linen napkin and set back her chair.

"I have a bridge date this afternoon, Jennifer." She sent a friendly smile around the table. "Enjoy the rest of your time together, girls. It was nice seeing you all again." She hesitated in the doorway. "We'll be leaving for the Terrells' at nine o'clock, Jennifer."

"I'll be ready," Jen replied.

With the stature of a queen, she walked away, a chorus of goodbyes following her.

"The Terrells'?" Marcie said the minute the door closed behind Celia. "Are you actually going to that old people's party?"

"I am," Jen said on a sigh. "But this is the last year. It really isn't just old people who go. There are still some younger ones there."

"And every one of the young lions hell-bent on kissing butt to get to the top." Kathie's voice held an acid tint.

"That's the name of the game, isn't it?" Leslie observed. "Wasn't that the reason we all decided to get our degrees and concentrate on breaking through the glass ceiling?"

Marcie grinned. "I opted out by grabbing my delicious husband and immediately having his babies."

Jen felt a funny pang in her chest at her friend's innocent mention of marriage and babies.

"Speaking of delicious, Jennifer, it's time you told us what in the hell is going on with you and Marsh Grainger," Leslie said.

"Yes," said Mary. "Let's get down to discussing something way more interesting than a fusty old party or our careers."

Jen took a deep breath, and launched into her story. She decided not to tell her friends exactly what had sent her fleeing from her parents' house—she did truly believe that what her parents did was their own business. All she said was that there had been an issue, and she'd decided it was time to strike out on her own and get some distance.

And that was how she ended up working for—and living with—Marshall Grainger.

Her friends were all ears—until they were all questions. This time, their questions were serious.

Jen launched into a recitation of her activities since accepting Marsh's offer of employment. She told them everything having to do with the job. But for reasons she couldn't quite explain, she left out the personal side of the story.

They wanted to know what he was like to work for, and whether he was as tough and aloof as gossip described him.

And they also wanted to know how she kept from jumping his bones.

"I've got strong principles, and he has a bad rep," she

said, and they believed her. It was the truth, to some degree. Jen stood by her principles, and Marsh did have a reputation for using women…but, she had fallen for him. And, after all, he had asked her to marry him.

But for reasons she couldn't entirely explain, she didn't tell her friends about that. She could tell by the expressions on their faces that they weren't buying her story, but they knew when to quit, and didn't press her. When her story came to an end, too much time had passed and her friends needed to go. With hugs and promises to stay in touch, they went their separate ways.

Jen went back to the patio to begin clearing the table. Tony was beside her as she reached for a second plate.

"I'll take care of that," he said, moving her out of the way with a nudge. "You ladies sounded like you were having a good time."

Jen's smile was soft. "Yes, we did have a lovely time. Your lunch was superb."

He flashed a bright smile at her. "Thank you, ma'am, that's what I like to hear." His eyes teased her. "Now go away and let me do my job."

"Yes, sir, master chef," Jen said. "But never say I didn't offer to help."

He waved a hand as she walked into the dining room from the patio.

Back in her room, Jen glanced at the bedside clock. It was a little after three and her mother had said they'd be leaving at nine. Six hours. Time enough to do the ranch books before she needed to get ready.

Clicking on to her laptop, Jen logged in to the ranch accounts and got to work untangling the facts and figures the technology-challenged foreman tossed into the PC at the ranch. It didn't take her long to straighten out the mess, pay the couple of bills due and cut the checks for the employees.

After logging off the ranch server, she decided she might as well wrap up the end-of-week with the home books.

Home. The word filled her mind and brought a wave of longing so intense Jen gave a soft gasp. Marsh.

Oh, Lord, she wanted to go home. To Marsh.

Damn. Damn, damn. What in the world was she going to do? He had proposed to her. But he didn't want *her,* the person. He wanted her body, and she readily admitted, at least to herself if not to her friends, that she wanted him as badly.

But he didn't really want *her.*

He wanted an assistant, a cook, a housekeeper, a wife, a mother to his children. And she, Jennifer Dunning, would do. It didn't hurt that she was bright as well as beautiful.

Big flipping deal.

Feeling her eyes begin to sting with threatening tears, Jen closed the computer, set it aside and curled into a ball on her bed. Impatiently, she brushed her fingers over her eyes. She wouldn't cry. Not over the high and mighty Marshall Grainger. She damn well would not cry.

Jen sobbed into her pillow.

She woke to darkness. Reaching out her arm, she flicked on the lamp on the bedside table and stared bleary-eyed at the clock set next to it. It read 7:10 p.m.

Time to get it together, she told herself, dragging her listless body from the bed.

Her face was a mess. Shoulders slumped, Jen stared at the sorry excuse for a woman reflected back at her

from the wide bathroom mirror above the sink. Salty
tracks of dried tears lay stiff on her cheeks.

Pathetic.

With an impatient shake of her head, Jen set to work
on making herself presentable. It wasn't easy. She still
felt tired. That in itself was annoying as she rarely felt
tired, especially not emotionally tired. The last thing
she wanted was to put on that stupid costume and pile
makeup on her face. Heaving a sigh, she adjusted the
water temperature and stepped into the shower.

Fifteen minutes later, her body glowing from the hot
shower and her hair hanging in dripping tendrils down
her back, she stood shivering as she wrapped herself
into a long fluffy bath sheet.

As soon as her body was dry, she went to work on
her hair. Drying her hair was always a project—there
was so much of it, a veritable mass of blond locks that
became tumbled waves and curls as it dried. But, at
last, she turned off the appliance and pulled on her lacy
panties before facing the next challenge.

Standing before the dresser mirror, Jen set about
piling her hair on top of her head, fastening it there so
she could slip on a net cap. The cap would contain her
hair beneath the wig of long, riotous black curls she had
bought on impulse.

After more than a few *damns* and some stronger
words, Jen had the wig securely fastened in place.

Deciding it didn't look half-bad, she shook her head.
The wig stayed in place and long black curls went flying
wildly around her head and down over her shoulders.

Offering her image a smile of satisfaction, she went
to work on the makeup. Being a blonde, Jen was naturally fair. Opening a container of makeup a shade darker
than her usual shade, she applied it smoothly. Blush

next, high on her cheekbones. She darkened her eye-brows with a black brow powder, and swept black mas-cara on her lashes. She finished with a generous coating of scarlet lipstick.

"Jenny, I hardly know you!" she said to the stranger in the mirror. She shook her head. "No, not Jenny, not even Jen." She needed a sexy, sultry name to go with this getup. She mulled it over as she stepped into the costume. Carmen? Nah, too obvious. Rosa? Nope. "Margarita." She drew the name out in a throaty voice. Yeah! Perfect. Now, a big spray of perfume, a pair of black soft leather ballet flats and—

Stepping back, she perused her reflection. Damn if she didn't look terrific—and nearly unrecognizable. She inched the top of the full-sleeved blouse to the edge of her left shoulder, leaving it there. On the right, she nudged the thin material off the shoulder. Tucking the blouse into the skirt, she wrapped a chain belt around her waist, attaching an empty jewelry pouch into which she then slipped her cell phone, a key to her parents' house and some money. She gave the skirt a shake. The folds swirled around her ankles.

Jen topped the outfit off with large gold hoop ear-rings, a four-strand gold jangle necklace and a shawl in blending shades of black, sand, dark green and a splash of magenta.

Lifting her arms she swept the shawl in an arc and settled it over her shoulders.

Now she was ready.

Her parents were waiting for her in the foyer. "Oh, I'm sorry, am I late?" She hadn't bothered to look at the clock.

"Not at all, we just came down," her father answered.

"And may I say you look fantastic, Jennifer." He always called her by her full name.

"Yes, you do," her mother agreed. "Very effective."

Jen gave them a brilliant smile, giving silent thanks for the candid explanation her mother had offered her concerning the situation with the Terrells. "Thank you," she replied, shifting a glance from one to the other. "And you two look absolutely fantastic."

Her father opened the door to usher them out. "The car's right out front. Off we go to the Halloween gala."

For the last time, Jen thought to herself. She was never going to the Terrells' party again. It was time to make some changes in her life. She was going to figure out what she wanted to do about Marsh, about her living situation, about everything.

After tonight, her life was going to be totally different. One way or another.

Ten

The dance, the last of more than she could recall, finally ended. Her breathing a bit heavy from the fast-paced number, Jen smiled at her surprisingly spry elderly partner as he thanked her before walking away.

It was hot in the room. The place was jammed. Jen was sweaty and tired of the party. She was tired of dancing, too. It was time to get out of there.

Lifting a corner of the shawl she had tied around her waist, she dabbed at perspiration dampening her neck. She was smoothing the shawl back into place when she felt a long-fingered hand curve around her waist.

"You've danced with just about every man here tonight."

His voice was a rough whisper close to her ear. "I think this one is mine."

A chill chased the heat from her neck all the way down to the base of her spine.

Marsh.

"Not talking to me?" He nipped gently at her ear.

Jen had to swallow. He was pressed against her back. Talk to him? She could barely breathe. "Why…why didn't you tell me you were going to be here?"

"It was a last-minute decision." His arm moved, turning her to face him.

He looked dangerous, and delicious. He had dressed as a gentleman of years past, out for a night at the opera or theater. He was wearing what she'd wager was his own hand-tailored tuxedo, black tie and pleated, blazing white shirt. He also had on a silk top hat, a long black cape with a stand-up collar, and held a silver-handled black walking stick.

Breathtaking.

He started moving against her sensuously, suggestively, enticing her to dance with him. She raised her gaze to his. His eyes glimmered with intent like sun-struck silver.

"I watched you dancing." He lowered his head to murmur against her ear. "You dance very well. Will you dance with me?"

Dance? She could barely move. His hard body pressed against hers was sapping all the strength from her. She felt light-headed. She had to get out before she made a fool of herself by collapsing at his feet.

"No, I don't want to dance." Jen hardly recognized her own voice it was so dry and shaky. "I want to get some air."

Marsh moved back a bit to look into her face. The smile he gave her was positively wicked. "With me?"

"I just want to leave, please."

"I can't resist a lady who says please."

Keeping his arm around her waist, Marsh turned and

headed for the front entrance, sweeping her along with him as he strode toward the door.

"Wait." Jen halted abruptly as she came to her senses. "I must tell my parents I'm leaving." She turned out of his embrace only to feel his arms slide around her waist as he turned with her.

"I'll come with you," he said.

"Marsh," she began.

He set his brows into an arrogant arch. "You're ashamed to be seen with me?"

"No, no." Jen shook her head. She wasn't ashamed, just terrified of what he might say to her parents. "I just, well, I believe they are having a conversation with friends."

He didn't bother to respond as he piloted her toward the pair standing near the long buffet table.

Jen braced herself as he came to a stop before her parents. "Mother," she managed, pausing to wet her lips. "I'm leaving now."

"I see," her mother responded, a suspicious gleam in her eyes. "Aren't you going to introduce your friend?"

"No need," her father said, a friendly smile on his face. He extended his hand. "Marsh, I'd like you to meet my wife, Celia."

"A pleasure," Marsh said.

Celia arched a brow. "Are you escorting Jennifer, Mr. Grainger?"

"Yes, ma'am," he responded in a tone of respect.

"Mmm," she murmured again, eyeing Marsh up and down.

Jen's stomach clenched in apprehension.

Her father laughed. "Celia, I think you need a glass of champagne. Run along, Jennifer." He turned a stern look on Marsh. "You will take care of her." It was not even close to a question.

"Yes, sir," Marsh answered at once.

Nodding, her father murmured good-night and, taking Celia's hand, led her away.

Marsh was chuckling as he took a stunned Jen to the door. "Do you have your car?"

They were outside. Jen drew a deep breath. The air had turned cold. It hit her flushed skin like an Arctic blast chilling her exposed flesh. Loosening the filmy shawl from around her waist she drew it around her shoulders. "No, I came with my parents."

"Good." Taking her hand, he led her to his car, a sleek black Lincoln parked right in front of the large house.

"You left your car here?" Jen said, sliding into the passenger seat when he opened the door for her.

He slid behind the wheel and slanted a look at her. "I wasn't planning on staying."

"Then why bother to come at all?"

"I came to collect you…and you know it."

The grin he flashed created a shudder in her lower regions. Now, even with the chill air, Jen felt hotter than she had in the house, and it had nothing to do with the thin shawl.

"Where are we going?" she said, turning to look out the window. "My parents live in the other direction."

"I know where your parents live, Jen," he said. "We're going to my place here in town. We'll be there in a few minutes."

"I didn't know you had a place in town." The thought that she and Marsh would be alone soon, at his place, a place that presumably had a bedroom, was almost more than Jen could bear. She simultaneously wanted to flee from him and tell him to drive faster.

Jen glanced out the window. They were in the heart of the city, tall office buildings looming over the car. Marsh turned onto a ramp leading to the private underground parking lot of one of the tallest buildings. Inserting a card into a pad on the chain-link gate, the gate silently slid open, and silently closed again after he drove through.

She knew at once where they were. This parking lot, the building towering overhead, contained the corporate headquarters of his business. *Grainger Building* in bold brass letters arched over the double front doors at the main entrance. She had passed it many times.

"You live here?" she asked as he pulled the car into a spot marked Private.

"No." Marsh shook his head as he swung open his door. "I keep this place for when I have to be in town for business reasons."

Although he circled the car, Jen was out before he got to her. "Convenient."

"Come along," he said, lifting the cape to swirl it around her shoulders. "You're shivering."

Warmth from his body intensifying the shiver, Jen moved with him to the door. He inserted another computerized key card into a barely noticeable slot. Shiny brass elevator doors parted with a soft swish.

Inside he pushed an unmarked button. The door swished shut and the car began to rise…quickly.

The penthouse, Jen thought. The car came to a smooth stop and the doors again softly swished apart.

Marsh's arm still firmly around her waist, he took her with him when he stepped from the car.

To Jen's surprise they didn't step directly into the

penthouse but into a spacious lobby. Still moving her
with him, he crossed the lobby to the only door visible.
He drew out another card to open the door.

Pushing the door open, Marsh swept out his arm,
inviting her inside.

"Step into my parlor," Jen murmured, catching her
breath as she entered. What she could see of the place
was absolutely elegant.

"You consider yourself the fly?" Marsh said in reference to her quote, amusement woven through his voice.

"And you the spider," Jen said, shrugging out from
beneath his cloak and handing it to him.

"Is that the way you think of me?" Although his
voice was even, she caught the slight edge to it.

Jen turned to meet his steely gaze.

"No, not at all," she answered without hesitation. "I
was being a smart-mouth."

Some of the glitter faded from his eyes. "Are you
afraid of me, Jen?"

"Of course not." She protested the very idea. "Why
should…" She paused, holding his steady gaze, changing her tune. "Do I have reason to be afraid, Marsh?"

Smiling, he shook his head. "No, Jennifer, you don't.
If you'll recall, I asked you to marry me."

She glanced away. "I do remember."

"I'm still waiting for an answer."

Jen moved into the room, over to the floor-to-ceiling
windows. The view of the city lights from the top of the
building gave her an altogether different perception of
it than from the street.

"It's beautiful," she murmured, speaking more to
herself than to him.

"Yes." He came up behind her, sliding one arm
around her waist. "And I'm still waiting for an answer."

She closed her eyes. "Marsh, I just don't know. I...I..."

"Don't," he murmured. This time his lips brushed her ear, bringing a flutter to her chest and heat flooding to parts south. "I can wait for your answer, at least to that question. But I need to know if you'll stay with me here tonight, Jennifer." His voice was warm, rich, deep—she could feel it vibrating through her down to her toes.

"Yes, Marsh," she answered against her will. "I will stay with you tonight."

Applying light pressure to her waist, he drew her closer. "Now, for the price of one kiss—a scorcher, mind you—I'll give you the guided tour of the apartment. Deal?" He grinned.

"Deal," she echoed, leaning into him and bringing her hands up to cradle his face, drawing him to her.

His mouth gently touched hers. But Jen was having none of it. He had said a scorcher, and that was what he was going to get.

She nipped at his bottom lip before taking his mouth with her own in a silent demand. Marsh was quick to comply, taking over the kiss with the expertise of experienced mastery.

A low groan deep in her throat, Jen melted into him, returning his kiss with all the passion she'd been unable to express since she'd left Marsh a day ago. His tongue invaded. She met the attack with a thrust of her own. It was wonderful, exciting, nearly overwhelming.

But it was not enough. She wanted more, much more, and from the sensation of him pressing against her belly, she had no doubt he felt the same.

Finally, needing more air, she eased back a few inches to gaze into his eyes.

"Can we put off the grand tour until tomorrow?"

she asked between quickly drawn breaths. "I need to be naked and in bed with you."

"Now you're talking." Sweeping her up into his arms, Marsh strode from the living room into his bedroom. It was dimly lit by the lights in buildings outside. All Jen noticed was that the room was large…and his bed took up the majority of space.

She began working on the buttons of his shirt. He already had her blouse on the floor. Within moments their clothing lay scattered around the bed, decorating the carpet. Marsh had his teeth clamped on the corner of a silver package he had removed from his trouser pocket before dropping his pants to the floor. She could see he wanted to be inside her as much as she wanted him there.

Tossing back the bedcovers, and once again lifting her, he settled her in the center of the bed and stretched his long length beside her. His skin felt like warm silk over long tight muscles.

Jen already felt hot and desperate with need for him. The feel of him moving over her, on top of her, shattered the last of her swiftly fading inhibitions. Moaning, she moved restlessly against him, parting her legs in invitation.

His reaction was swift. Grasping her hips, he dragged her into full contact with his steel-hard erection.

She shuddered in anticipation.

Jen braced her hands on his chest but suddenly he was gone. She murmured a protest but swallowed it when she opened her eyes to see him applying the condom.

"Let's be smart this time," he said.

Jen was surprised but too desperate to have him inside

her to say anything. Lifting her hips again, he moved into her, sheathing himself deeply within her heat.

"Yes," she whispered, closing her eyes again. Then, "Oh, yes," as he began to rotate his hips, delving deeper, deeper into her body.

Jen had never believed the stories told by women about crying out when reaching climax. She became a believer moments later, calling his name in a hoarse voice she barely recognized as her own as her body appeared to shatter into a million pieces.

Marsh's cry echoed her own. Head thrown back, tendons straining in his neck, he stiffened an instant before wrapping his arms around her. Jen was drawing shaky breaths into her depleted body when Marsh, still buried deep inside her, gently lowered his tension-taut body against hers, his indrawn breath as raw as her own.

"Marsh?" Jen forced out his name between gulps for oxygen. "Are you all right?"

"Yeah," he answered, his warm breath tickling her ear. "But for a moment there, I felt certain I had died."

"Yeah," she echoed. "Me, too."

"Wanna try it again?"

Jen expelled a breath in a burst of laughter. "Are you kidding? I can barely breathe." She hesitated a mere instant before adding, "Give me a second."

"Okay," he said, nipping at the soft skin beneath her chin.

Jen slid from under him and made her way to the bathroom. Finding a light switch, she flipped it, stifling a gasp of appreciation at the opulence of the room. There was a lot of marble, swirls of dark chocolate and white, and a huge tub with all kinds of gadgets she was tempted to play with. A long wooden-slatted bench sat next to a walk-in shower stall along one wall. On the facing wall, an even longer vanity cabinet with two sinks and an array of interesting-looking bottles and jars and candles was set below a mirror in exact proportion to the cabinet.

For a moment, Jen was sorely tempted to jump into the shower stall for a quick sluice over her sweaty skin. But she decided she'd much rather get back to Marsh as fast as she could.

Her eyes widened as she came back to the bed and saw one of the most beautiful sights she'd ever seen in her life. Marsh, buck naked and rock hard…again.

She took advantage of the moment to admire his fantastic body as he opened another package and put the condom on.

Ready for him, Jen curled her arms around his neck, sighing with contentment as he settled himself in the cradle between her thighs.

"How could you have…" She didn't know how to finish asking how he had revived so quickly.

Marsh just smiled at her and said, "Maybe it has something to do with the fact that you are the sexiest thing I've ever seen, Jen."

Jen would have thought that the second time the pace would be slower, easier. And it might have been, if she had allowed Marsh to set the pace. But Jen shocked herself with her need, her hunger, touching him, tasting him everywhere. Within moments he was inside her again, taking, giving, demanding, pleading. It was too fast, too intense, too hot and over much too soon.

Marsh barely grunted before collapsing on top of her, harsh breaths bathing the curve of her neck, sending delicious shivers up her spine. And though his voice was little more than a whisper, she heard what he said.

"Jennifer, Jennifer…you are one amazing woman."

"I know," she said in the best demure tone she could manage, a satisfied smile curving her well-kissed mouth.

Lifting his body onto his forearms, Marsh threw back his head and roared with laughter. He was still laughing when his mouth came crashing down again on hers, his tongue diving deep, claiming her as his own.

"I adore you," he said, when he was forced to break away to breathe. "Marry me."

Jen ached at his words. She wanted to confess that she couldn't marry him, because he *adored* her but didn't love her. But something stopped her from telling Marsh the truth—she simply couldn't do it. "I told you, Marsh. I must have more time to think about it."

He heaved a heavy sigh of frustration. "Dammit, Jen, what's to think about? We're compatible. We work well together. More importantly, we have fun together. And you wouldn't dare tell me we're not great together in bed." A tiny shudder rippled through him. "I swear to you that never before in my life have I experienced anything even close to what I've just shared with you."

Jen opened her mouth to respond, to say it was more about sex than any deep, meaningful affection but he wasn't finished.

"And damned if I'm not getting hard again."

This time Jen bypassed demure and went straight for wanton. "So please shut up and do the same thing to me again."

Marsh did…again and again throughout the rest of the night and into the early morning hours.

Jen opened her eyes to bright sunlight pouring through the wall of windows onto her face. Groaning a protest, she immediately shut them again.

"Hit the white button on the nightstand." Marsh's breath fluttered the hair at her temple.

Squinting, Jen reached out, her hand groping for the button. Her fingers barely brushed it. With a soft swish filmy curtains slid from the ends of the windows to join together in the center, defusing the brightness of the midday sunlight.

"Oh, lovely," Jen murmured, daring to open her eyes again. She turned her head to find Marsh's silver eyes watching her. She smiled. "Good morning."

"Morning." He smiled back at her. "God, you're beautiful."

"I'm sure." Jen laughed as an image of what she must look like in the light of day after the night they had spent practically devouring each other. She dreaded looking at what all that activity had done to her gypsy-girl makeup.

"Oh, you are, Jen. You look all tousled and heavy-lidded, like a woman well loved."

Well screwed, Jen thought, a bitter taste at the back of her throat. He didn't mean *loved.* Not the way she wanted him to mean it. In that instant, she wanted to go. She had to go. She felt queasy. Tossing back the covers, she slipped from the bed and dashed into the bathroom, locking the door behind her. She could barely hear Marsh calling to her.

"Hey, Jen, what the hell?"

After cleaning the makeup from her face the best she could, Jen stood in the shower, her tears mingling with the drumming water splashing over her head. *He doesn't believe in love. He doesn't believe in love.* The phrase repeated inside her head, keeping time with the spill of shower water. She cried harder than she imagined possible, trying to be silent so Marsh wouldn't hear. She felt as if her heart were breaking in two.

Later, standing dripping on the shower mat, Jen didn't remember bathing or shampooing her hair, yet her body was wet, her hair soaked. Picking up one of the bath sheets folded and piled on the slatted bench, she slowly dried her body, trying not to think about all the amazing things Marsh had done to her the night before.

Her hair was still dripping water down her back. There were two round stiff-bristled men's hair brushes set to one side of the vanity top. Picking up the nearest to her, she worked at brushing the tangles from her mass of thick hair, perhaps harder than she needed to. When she finished, the hair lay smooth against her shoulders and the brush was matted with her blond hair. She looked closer and saw that her hair was tangled in the brush with his.

She left it there.

Jen was about to wrap her shivering body in the wet towel she had discarded when she turned and noticed a dark brown terry robe hanging from a hook on the door. Dropping the towel into a large open basket, she shrugged into the robe. It was the softest, warmest robe she had ever touched. Clutching the robe close, she drew a deep, courage-gathering breath and, opening the door, strode back into the lion's den.

The particular lion waiting there for her looked relaxed stretched out in all his naked glory on the bed, his long, lean body bathed in sunlight. But the relaxed look was deceiving. The glitter in his narrowed silver eyes gave him away.

"Jennifer, what's going on?" His voice was low, but edged with concern.

"Nothing." Unable to bear looking at the sheer masculine beauty of him, Jen turned away, grimacing at the sight of her discarded clothing littering the floor, the costume seeming so silly and forced in the morning light.

"Nothing, huh?" The concern in his voice hardened. "Then what the hell are you doing?"

Scooping up her panties and the now crumpled skirt she had worn, Jen slowly turned to look at him. Although she hadn't heard him move, Marsh was now sitting on the side of the bed, the sheet pulled up to his waist.

Jen swallowed to moisten her parched throat. "I'm picking up my clothes to get dressed."

"Why?" His tone was flat, his expression passive.

"Why?" She shook her head as if in disbelief he had asked the question. "It's after noon. It's time I get home." A pure bald-faced lie if Jen had ever told one, especially given the fact that the only place she now considered home was next to Marsh. She fought as hard as she could not to cry.

"Are you concerned about getting home, or do you have a case of morning-after remorse?"

"No remorse," she said as calmly as she could, thinking that she would never regret a moment of the time she had spent with Marsh. Not a moment. Straightening her spine she met his silvery gaze with a hard stare of her own.

"No?" He arched a brow. "Then why have you dumped me into the deep freeze?"

"You keep at me," she said, scrambling for a way to protect herself against him, a way to keep herself from telling him the truth. "I told you I need more time." She paused, seeing something new in Marsh's eyes for a moment, something she couldn't quite identify yet. She relented a little—she couldn't help herself. "I haven't dumped you into the deep freeze."

He arched a brow at her. "Feels damn chilly to me."

"I'm sorry." That was the truth, she suddenly realized. She *was* sorry. Why blame him for the fact that she foolishly fell in love with him? It wasn't his fault her heart was choosing him even though her head was saying no. "I just don't like being pressured."

"Okay, I'll back off...for a while." His piercing gaze softened as a small smile crept across his mouth.

Oh, heavens, his mouth. Jen could feel his talented mouth, could taste him. He looked good enough to eat. The thought abruptly brought her to her senses, reminding her that she needed to get out, to get away from Marsh before she fell back into bed with him, and then found herself crying in the bathroom again, her heart breaking into pieces.

"Thank you." Bending again, she scooped the now crushed blouse from the floor. "But I still want to go home." As she retrieved the black wig, she wrinkled her nose with distaste at the thought of putting the costume back on in order to go home. What had she been thinking last night?

She hadn't been thinking at all, clearly.

"You don't have to wear those clothes to go, even though you did look sexy as hell in your costume. Turned me on something awful," he said, rising to stroll to the bathroom. "We'll find you something to wear."

In an effort to conceal a shiver of response to his admitted sensual reaction to her gypsy attire, Jen held the robe's two sides together, snuggling into the soft terry warmth. "Thanks."

"I'm going to grab a shower, then I'll drive you home." The bathroom door closed quietly behind him.

Recalling the night they had spent together in his king-size bed, her wanton surrender to him, Jen sank, weak-kneed, into a deeply cushioned chair. Biting her lip, her bravado show of spirit deflated, she glanced around for her small string bag. It lay on the floor, next to the chair she had sunk into.

A sigh whispered through her slightly parted lips.

She loved him, more with each passing day. The time she'd spent without him had seemed interminable from the time she'd left the house until he had slipped his arm around her at the party. She longed to be with him every day, sleep beside him every night…

Jen heard the shower running full force. Her imagination instantly produced an image of Marsh, the water falling over his perfectly formed, magnificent body. Heat rushed to the most sensitive part of her body.

Closing her eyes, she leaned back against the chair. His sexy, masculine scent clung to his robe, increasing the heat now radiating throughout her body.

She wanted to be with him, ached for him so badly she had to resist a compulsion to shrug out of the robe and join him in the shower, join with him under the pounding spray.

No. Think, she railed at herself. *Back away. Now.*

While you still have a modicum of resistance in your mind, if not your body.

The sound of the rushing water ceased. Jen went stiff. In the moments it took him to towel off and walk back into the bedroom, she had made her decision and closed her eyes, as if closing him out of her life as well as her view.

She could not go on this way, loving him heart and soul, knowing all the while he did not love her. Eventually, it would kill something inside of her, something that made up who she was.

"Ready?"

Jen opened her eyes. Marsh was smiling at her. His smile went through her like a knife. Dragging up an ounce of fortitude from deep inside, she managed to return his smile without breaking down.

"Yes." The mere whisper was all she could manage.

They left the penthouse together after Marsh found her a shirt and a pair of shorts that practically came down to her knees. Fortunately, he didn't touch her as they walked to his car. Had he so much as touched her elbow, she was afraid she'd fall apart.

They rode in silence to her parents' home some miles out of the city. The ride seemed to take forever. Jen already had her door key in hand when Marsh steered the car up the driveway and to a smooth stop next to the broad sweep of steps to the porch.

She was ready with her hand on the door release, prepared to bolt and run. But Marsh touched her arm. It was a light touch that felt to Jen as though it scorched her arm to the bone.

"I'm going straight back to the house from here," he said, a slight frown drawing his eyebrows together. "Are you driving back today or waiting until tomorrow morning?"

Jen wet her lips. She had to tell him she wouldn't be going back to his house, that she couldn't bear being with him, loving him and knowing he didn't love her. She should have told him before they left the condo, but she simply couldn't, not then. And she didn't think she could now, either.

"Probably tomorrow morning," she said, lying through her teeth. "Less traffic then."

His silvery gaze probed hers for a moment. Then he removed his hand from her arm. "Okay."

"Goodbye, Marsh." The words hurt like fire in her mouth. She pushed the door open, slammed it shut and took off running, unable to look back for fear that she'd go straight back to him and tell him that yes, she would spend the rest of her life with him.

Even if he didn't love her.

Eleven

Where the hell is she?

Marsh frowned at the recurring question stabbing at his mind, unconscious of his fingertips smoothing the silky material of the shawl Jennifer had left in his car when he had dropped her off on Sunday afternoon.

Or more accurately, when she had practically run away from him after he had dropped her off Sunday afternoon.

There was something going on with her, something she wasn't telling him. But the more pressing issue at the moment was, where the hell was she?

If she had left her parents' home Monday morning, or even later in the day, she would have been back at the house before dark. It was now Wednesday evening, and there had been no sight or sound of Jen.

If something had happened to her—an accident, or illness—Marsh was certain he would have heard about it by now. He had called her cell phone only to receive a request to leave a message. Cursing, he had disconnected. He didn't want to talk to voice mail, he wanted to talk to Jen. Swallowing his pride, he had called her parents' phone, only to be informed by the housekeeper that the family was not at home.

Marsh got that message loud and clear. The family, including Jen, would not be accepting calls from him. So, no, there had been no accident, nor was she ill. And she didn't wish to speak to him.

Maybe it was time to face the fact that Jen was not coming back.

You damn dumb ass, Marsh condemned himself. He had pushed her too hard in his bid to convince her to marry him. And now he ached for her like he had never ached for anyone, ever—not just for the nearly unbelievable pleasure he had achieved with her, but for simply being with her, being near her, conversing, laughing, even arguing.

He began to pace the length of his large office, memories swirling of their time together.

Jen humming as she went about her work.

Jen laughing as they raced the horses.

Jen deftly cooking up a meal fit for a king…for him.

Coming to a dead stop, Marsh closed his eyes. Because he had wrapped himself in bitterness and convinced himself he didn't believe in love, he had carelessly thrown away the most precious gift ever offered to him.

Suddenly, as if he had been smacked upside his head, Marsh leapt from his chair.

He was in love with her.

He was *in love* with her.

What was wrong with him? How could it have taken him so damn long to come to that conclusion?

He had to talk to her, tell her, beg if necessary. She had to know how he felt. That would change everything.

Wouldn't it?

But what if she hadn't come back because she didn't—or couldn't—love him?

He suddenly remembered why he didn't believe in love. Or rather, why he didn't actually want anything to do with love. Because it made people crazy. It made them do weird things. And people who claimed to love other people didn't necessarily treat them the way they should be treated. He knew about that firsthand.

Get over it, he told himself. This was his chance. Jen was his opportunity. She was the one. If he blew this, then it wouldn't matter one way or the other whether he believed in loved because he would never get a chance to try ever again.

He had to tell her. And he had do it as soon as possible.

A soft tearing sound caught Marsh's attention. Frowning, he glanced down at his hand, his long fingers tangled in her shawl. He had ripped the fine fabric.

Cursing himself, Marsh set the shawl aside before he could do more damage to it. There was an elderly woman in San Antonio he knew who was sheer magic with a needle. She would mend it so perfectly, Jen would never see the tear.

Glad for something positive to do—as he sure as hell hadn't accomplished much by mentally beating himself up for being an unconscious moron—Marsh picked up his phone and dialed the woman's number.

Minutes later, Marsh roared through the gates of the

property heading for San Antonio, the carefully folded shawl on the seat next to him.

He was going to fix it. He was going to fix everything.

Jen drove through the gates to Marsh's house. As always, she hit the horn and waved to greet the security guard parked in the all-wheel vehicle nearly hidden beneath the lone tree at the top of the knoll.

Jen was nervous. Although throughout the past couple of days she had repeatedly vowed to herself, and aloud to her empty room, that she would not return to Marsh, here she was, feeling much too at home for her mental comfort.

Pulling to a stop at the garage, Jen knew at once Marsh wasn't home because his truck was gone.

What if he had driven to Dallas to coax her back to the house—and to him?

Jen stopped dead in her tracks, caught between a burst of laughter and a cry of despair. As if the confident and arrogant Marshall Grainger would ever conceive of crawling, or even boldly striding, to any woman to beg her to return to him.

The mere thought was ludicrous. At any rate, it didn't matter. She had no intention of remaining at the house. She had returned only to turn down Marsh's offer, then immediately head back to Dallas as soon as she had collected her personal belongings. She had planned to tell him face-to-face, and even admit to him that the reason she couldn't marry him was because she loved him, and knew that he'd never love her.

Maybe it was better that he wasn't there. It was definitely safer for her. In truth, she ached to see him, but she feared what she would do if she did. Whatever it was, it would probably lead to her being in a loveless marriage, and that would tear her apart inside. No, it was better this way.

Heaving a sigh, Jen went straight to the apartment. As the temperature had again climbed into the sixties after dropping into the low fifties for two days, the apartment smelled stale and felt stuffy.

Crossing to a living room window, she flipped back the lock and opened it just as Marsh's truck growled to a stop next to her once-again-dusty Cadillac.

A thrill went through her as she saw his long legs stretch out from the cab and reach to the ground. A frown creased his brow as he stared at her car.

Jen stepped back from the window as he turned to glance up before striding to the garage entrance. Knowing he was headed for her apartment, she stood, quivering inside, gathering her composure to project a show of confidence.

He knocked on the door. Jen was stunned for a moment. Fully expecting him to walk in as if he owned the place—which in fact he did—she stared at the door, her mind frozen.

"Jennifer?"

For a second, she had a crazy urge to hide so that if he did walk in, he wouldn't see her. And she wouldn't have to tell him what she came to say. But she'd put it off too long. It was time to come clean. That promise she'd made herself before the gala about her life being different one way or the other? Now was the time to make that a reality.

"I'm coming," she answered, wetting her dry lips as she crossed to the door. She swung it wide as she stepped back.

A jumble of all sorts of emotions welled up inside

her at the sight of him. Dressed in a soft chambray shirt tucked into the slim waistband of his well-worn jeans that covered the tops of his scuffed boots, his hair tousled as if from his fingers raking through the silky strands, he looked…

He looked like the man she was so desperately in love with. Damn him.

"Is it Monday already?" he drawled, running a slow glance over the length of her body and back again to settle on her eyes. He took a step toward her.

Jen stepped back. "Marsh, please don't." She raised a palm to halt his progress.

As if she could.

Walking to her, he pulled her into his arms, bent his head and crushed her mouth with his.

Jen was a goner and she knew it…but she had to try, didn't she? She had to stop him long enough to state her position.

"Marsh…I can't," she began.

"Yes, you can," he murmured, barely moving his lips from hers. "And very well, too."

To prove his point, he proceded to show her his idea of her position, which was flat on her back, him on top of her, right there in the middle of the living room floor.

Within moments boots, jeans and underwear were gone. Although she protested, her protests were weak, and so was she—weak with her need for him.

His mouth devoured hers, his hands gripping her hips—she fully expected him to ram into her. Then, something incredible happened. Instead of taking her with the passionate force she'd become accustomed to, Marsh entered her body with exquisite gentleness, slowly, as if savoring every movement until he was fully, deeply inside her, filling the emptiness she'd been denying she felt.

"Home."

His voice was so low, Jen wasn't certain she'd heard him correctly.

He began to move and within seconds she was moaning, moving with his increased thrusts, craving more and more of him, enough to last her a lifetime.

It was more intense than ever before, her release wildly shattering. Tears filling her eyes, she drew deep breaths, reminding herself of what she had to do.

They lay side by side, naked from the waist down. As her breathing returned to normal, Jen steeled herself to speak.

Marsh beat her to it. "I really didn't think it was possible to reach such intense sexual pleasure, the absolute zenith of orgasms."

The tears, stinging hot, overflowed Jen's eyes to roll down her temples into her hair. "Marsh." Her nails dug into the plush nap of the carpet. "I came here today to get my stuff…to tell you I can't stay with you, that I…"

Feeling him grow still beside her, she broke off.

"What?" His voice was soft but rough-edged. "Say it, Jennifer. Say whatever it is you have to say."

Ignoring the spill of tears on her face, she turned her head to look at him, and immediately wished she hadn't.

His silvery eyes glittering, he held her misty gaze. Were there tears in his eyes? She couldn't tell, because he got to his feet fast, in one fluid movement. Scooping his clothes and boots from the floor, he turned and strode to the door.

"I'm going to clean up," he said, his voice tight. "We'll talk about this when I get back." Not bothering to wait for a reply, he walked out, leaving the door wide-open behind him.

Rising, Jen was not nearly as fluid as Marsh had been.

She was still shaking with the aftershocks of the intensity of pleasure rippling through her body, and the pain in her heart.

She had come here determined to break off the untenable relationship she had been sharing with Marsh. Instead, she had betrayed herself by surrendering at his first kiss.

Gathering her clothing and boots while trying to pull her composure together, Jen headed for the bathroom. Positive Marsh would not be gone for long, she pulled her clothes back on and tried to get herself together.

Jen was brushing her hair when Marsh strolled back into the apartment and without hesitation opened the bathroom door and stood there, simply watching her.

Jen considered a protest then rejected the idea…it would simply be a waste of her breath. Setting aside the brush, she walked past him into the living room. Turning, she stood tall, placed her hands on her hips and stared back at him in open defiance.

"So. You're going to run, from me and what we've got together?" His voice roughened. "What we've just shared together?"

"Sex," Jen retorted, wincing inside at his accusation that she was going to run. Again. But this was different, she insisted in silent despair. This was for the rest of her life, not just to escape an uncomfortable situation. She wanted to stay so much, too much, but…

The sound of his voice scattered her jumbled thoughts.

"Fantastic sex," he corrected her, his voice beginning to sound strained. "But we've got more than that and you know it."

Jen was shaking her head before he'd finished. "It's not enough, Marsh."

"What the hell more do you want?" he said. "We enjoy the same things. We enjoy each other. You said you love it here at the house. What else is there?"

Jen sighed and drew a quick breath before calmly answering. "Love."

She watched Marsh take in what she'd said, and she saw something cross his face. For a moment, she allowed herself to hope, but his words made it clear that she was foolish to do so.

"We could make it work," he said, his tone strange, unfamiliar. "It's been done before, a marriage without love."

Jen's spine stiffened. So she was right. He didn't love her. He didn't love her at all.

"I don't believe I could do it," she said, forcing herself to continue on. "When I marry, I want to spend my days and nights working and sleeping beside a man I'm in love with, knowing he loves me, too."

She waited, hoping against hope that she'd been wrong, that he would tell her that he loved her more than she could know. But that's not what he said.

"I see." Shaking his head, his expression blank, he turned and walked to the door, pausing to glance back at her. "If you change your mind, you know where to find me." That said, he pulled open the door and walked out of the room.

And out of her life.

The realization was crushing. Standing rigidly still, afraid if she moved she would fall apart, Jen gasped for air, hurting so badly she wanted to drop to the floor and sob until the pain eased.

But she didn't drop to the floor, nor issue one sob. She brushed away tears with an impatient swipe of her hand.

She loved him, deeply, passionately, but she had no intentions of falling apart for him. She wasn't the type for drama—she was the type that carried on under difficult conditions.

She'd survive, Jen assured herself, beginning to gather her things together. A large shopping bag she had brought with her from home contained the shirt belonging to Marsh. Sighing, she reached into the bag to stroke the material. Tempted to take it with her, she pulled her hand back.

"You're a fool, Marshall Grainger," she muttered. "We could have built a wonderful, loving relationship and made beautiful children together."

Though soft, the sound of her own voice startled her. The word *children* rang in her mind. Once again she felt the sting of tears in her eyes. She shook her head. *It's over,* she told herself. *Get on with your life.*

The explanation Jen offered her parents for her return home was that she missed her friends and the activities in Dallas. Of course, it was far from the truth. Although Jen dearly loved her friends, they were often in touch, and Jen had never wanted to be involved with any activity in the city.

To her mother's vocal dismay, Jen was at heart a homebody. She stayed in, spending her time with Tony and Ida, cooking and keeping the house neat. A pang twisted in her chest as she recalled working in Marsh's beautiful home.

Jen spent time on her computer perusing help-wanted sites. But she wasn't looking for work. She was looking for possible postings by Marsh.

None appeared, which Jen found rather strange. Perhaps he had decided to advertise in local newspapers, she thought.

Thanksgiving came and went. Her parents went, too, setting out on a monthlong cruise. Jen threw herself into her long-held tradition of decorating the large house for Christmas with Tony and Ida. Only at weak moments did she wonder if Marsh ever bothered to decorate his house for the coming holiday.

When the house was finished, sparkling with gold and silver decorations, Jen set about shopping. She started with gifts for Tony and Ida. Then she shopped for her parents—never an easy chore as both were very particular. Yet all the while as she browsed the stores, Jen caught herself pausing to inspect an item she just knew would be perfect for Marsh.

So much for putting him out of her mind.

The most fun Jen had shopping was when she was buying gifts for her gang. They had a rule about price—no expensive gifts allowed. The idea was to find tokens of affection, not ostentatious things to impress or display.

The week before Christmas the six of them got together for lunch, and to exchange the presents. There were a lot of oohs and aahs. But as soon as the gift giving was over, and the wineglasses refilled, the interrogation began.

"What made you quit your job with Marshall Grainger?"

Jen sat quietly a moment, wondering what to say, what excuse to make up. Glancing around the table and seeing concern in each one of their faces, Jen knew only the truth would do.

"I love him," she whispered, tears welling in her eyes.

There was a collective gasp, and then her friends all reached out to her at once. The love and support she felt from them was overwhelming.

"What's the problem?" Kathie asked.

"He doesn't love me."

Everyone started to protest at once.

"Please." Jen held up a palm, blinking away the tears. "I really don't want to talk about it." Up until her blurted confession the atmosphere had been festive, happy. "This isn't the time or place."

"You never want to talk about it when you have strong feelings," Mary said.

"Which is fine," Karen insisted. "But just know that you deserve happiness, and you deserve love, and if you think Marsh is the one for you, then you have to get over your fear and tell him."

Jen was stunned into silence by her friend's speech. As a favor to her, they agreed to change the subject. But when they parted company a short time later, exchanging good wishes for the holidays and thanks for the gifts, they reminded her of what they had said.

More than a bit depressed, and feeling guilty for putting a damper on their holiday lunch, Jen drove straight home. Pulling into the driveway, she was startled to see Marsh's black Lincoln in front of the house. She could see he was in the car and felt a thrill when he turned to look at her.

She drove past him to the garage at the back of the house. She heard the purr of the Lincoln pull up next to where she'd stopped.

She got out of the car, turning to face him when he came to a halt beside her car. He was holding a plastic grocery bag in one hand and he held it aloft.

"I brought you something."

Considering the season, she naturally assumed it was a gift. "I wish you wouldn't have," she said. "I have nothing to give you—"

"It's not a Christmas gift," he said, setting her mind at ease. "It belongs to you."

"Oh."

"You might invite me inside."

Jen hesitated.

"For a few minutes?" His voice held a strange note. Was it a hint of pleading? Jen dismissed the very idea.

"All right, come in." Her key card at the ready, Jen slid it along the slot. The elevator glided open and she stepped inside the car, Marsh at her heels.

"Convenient," he said, teasing her. She couldn't help but smile at his use of the very word she'd used to describe the entrance to his apartment after the gala that night. She loved how Marsh remembered everything she said, down to the last detail.

"It goes to my late grandmother's apartment." The door slid open and Jen stepped inside, Marsh beside her.

"Yours now?" he asked, glancing around the room.

"Yes." Seeing him, being so close to him, made Jen feel teary again. The last thing she wanted was to have him see her crying. "You have something of mine?"

"Yes." He handed her the bag.

Frowning, Jen reached inside and withdrew a tissue-wrapped bundle. She unwrapped it to find the shawl she had worn to the Halloween ball. She hadn't even missed it.

"Thank you," she said, unconsciously stroking the soft material.

"You left it in my car after the gala."

Reminded of the night they had spent together, she suddenly wanted him to leave as she could feel her composure crumbling. Being around Marsh was nearly impossible.

Her friends' words rang in her ears. Should she— *could she*—tell him the truth?

He hesitated, drew a breath as if unsure of himself, then quickly said, "I do have a gift for you, if you'll accept it."

Jen didn't understand. He held nothing in his hands. "What is it?"

He took a hesitant step toward her. "It's my heart. And it's wrapped in my love for you, if you'll have it." He took another step and then another until he was mere inches from her seemingly frozen body.

Jen stared at him, unable to believe he had said what she had heard. "Marsh…"

"I know you don't love me." He swallowed as if it caused him pain. "And I know I declared years ago that I didn't believe in love." Raising his hands, he cradled her face with his palms. "I've been such an ass. I knew from the beginning that I wanted you." To her amazement, his eyes grew misty, only this time it wasn't her imagination. There were real tears there. "I just didn't realize why I wanted you so very much."

Tears now flowing from her eyes, Jen could barely speak. "Marsh, wait—"

"No." He cut her off with a shake of his head. "Let me finish. The simple truth of the answer hit me like a fist. I am so much in love with you and I don't know how to tell you. I wanted it to be romantic for you, hoping you'd begin to return my love. But I've been emotionally dead for so long, I don't know how—"

This time Jen cut him off. "Marshall Grainger, where on earth did you get the idea that I don't love you?"

He looked at her hard for a few moments. His mouth opened, but no words came out at first. "You...you do love me?"

Jen nodded, tears spilling down her cheeks. "If you don't kiss me right now, I won't be responsible for my actions."

His intense, silvery stare turned soft and warm. "What actions?" His voice was low, almost desperate with the sound of hope.

Jen smiled. "I was thinking about showing you how very much I love you. I love you, Marsh. I have for a while now."

Claiming her mouth with his, he swept her up into his arms. When they finally came up for air, he whispered, "Which way to the bedroom?"

Several hours later, Marsh stowed Jen's suitcase in his car, slid behind the wheel and started the motor. Glancing at her, he asked, "Ready to go home?"

Jen smiled. "I'm ready to go anywhere with you."

He set the car into motion, satisfied that they would soon be putting his ideas for their future into motion.

Settling into the warmed butter-soft leather seat, Jen pondered the past several hours. She still could barely believe Marsh had come to her, baring his soul while confessing his love for her.

She wanted to kick herself for all the time she had wasted being miserable away from him. All that misery could have been avoided had she just told him the truth the last time she had been to the house.

Well, the misery was now over. Marsh loved her, and Jen luxuriated in the very thought of his love.

Even so, she had remembered to take care of business, so to speak. Buzzing the kitchen phone, she had told Tony not to fuss for dinner as she would be leaving for Marsh's house within a few hours.

"I figured," the unflappable Tony replied. "I saw his car in the driveway. What about your parents?" he asked. "You remember they'll be home on the twenty-second for the holidays?"

"Yes, I remember," Jen said. "I'll be calling them with the news."

"News?" Ida, obviously listening in on one of the other extensions, asked. "There will be news?"

"Wonderful news," Jen said. "And that's all I'm saying at this time."

It was late when they arrived at Marsh's place. Stepping from the car, Jen gazed at the house, emotion tightening her throat. Home. Her glance at the tall man lifting her case from the car sent a wave of sheer contentment through her. No, she thought, as much as she loved the house, Marsh was home to her.

Not aware of him watching her, Jen started when he asked, "What are you thinking about?"

"How very much I love you," she answered without hesitation. A teasing smile feathered her lips. "And that I'd happily live in an empty refrigerator box under a bridge somewhere as long as you were there with me."

Though Marsh laughed, he dropped her case with a thud and strode to draw her into his arms. "While I seriously doubt that will ever be necessary, I'm both humbled and grateful to hear you say it."

If there had been so much as a tiny question in Jen's

mind about Marsh's declaration of love for her, hearing him admit to being humbled erased it forever.

Spearing her fingers into his hair, she thanked him with a searing kiss. Naturally, one kiss led to another, and then another, all the way into the house and up the stairs to his bedroom.

Physically and emotionally exhausted, they fell asleep still wrapped in each other's arms to sleep most of the next day away.

Over breakfast at seven that evening, dressed in Marsh's luxurious robe at his request, Jen listened to his suggestions for the holidays—and for planning their wedding.

First on his list was shopping for Jen. Then calling a friend of his...who just happened to be a judge.

They left early the next morning for San Antonio. Once in the city, they went their separate ways, agreeing to meet for lunch at the same restaurant along the River Walk where they had dined the previous time they had been there.

Excited about her venture, Jen went looking for the perfect wedding dress. Two hours into her search she found it. In what the saleslady referred to as "barely white," the dress was dressy but not formal. The filmy material clung to her upper body while the slightly flared skirt swirled around her legs just below her knees.

Her major purchase made, Jen set about looking for the perfect accessories. She decided on black pumps with three-inch heels along with a black clutch purse with a gold tone clasp. She chose a black pearl necklace with a matching bracelet and teardrop earrings.

The last—and to Jen the most important—purchase she made was a Christmas gift for Marsh. Delighted with her choices, she strolled along the River Walk to the restaurant. Marsh was waiting for her next to the entrance, a bemused smile on his face in response to her self-satisfied expression.

"You look very pleased with yourself, my love," he murmured, sweeping her into his arms right there in front of the world.

"I am," Jen said, giving him a quick kiss on the mouth. "I'm only a few minutes late."

His laughter ringing with the sound of happiness, Marsh ushered her into the restaurant.

"You spoke with the judge?" Jen asked anxiously the minute she was seated.

Marsh smiled. "Yes, he will be delighted to marry us at city hall the day before Christmas."

Jen sighed with satisfaction. "Good."

"Yes," he agreed. "Very good."

Later, over an after-dinner liqueur, Marsh reached for Jen's left hand. "I have a Christmas gift for you, but I can't wait. I want to give it to you now."

Jen began to tremble, almost certain she knew what it was—he *was* holding her left hand, after all.

She was right.

Reaching into his jacket pocket, Marsh drew out a small dark blue jeweler's box, opened it, then slid a large, many-faceted diamond solitaire engagement ring onto her finger.

"Oh, Marsh," she whispered. Without words, she let her misted eyes speak for her as, taking his hand, she brought it to her mouth to place a soft kiss on his palm.

"I guess that means you like it." His voice was rough with emotion.

"I love it," she said, "almost as much as I love you."

Jen waited until they were getting ready for bed that night before she presented him with the large boxed gift she had purchased. "I can't wait till Christmas, either."

Upon tearing away the festive wrap and whipping off the box lid, Marsh laughed as he pulled out an exact match to the terry robe he had given to her.

The last few remaining days before the holiday flew by. Jen and Marsh worked together during the day as they had before, he in his office, she in hers. She tidied the house and cooked the meals. He worked outside with the horses.

Although unchanged, the house looked barren to Jen. She longed for bright, glittering decorations. Marsh promised her he would help her deck every room of the house next Christmas…then surprised her with a small but fully decorated tree that he set in the center of the table.

Throughout those few days, being together was the same, yet different. There was a new depth of feeling, a sense of utter rightness and contentment that had been missing before. This time, they belonged together.

Jen called her mother on the day she and her father returned from their cruise. She offered a brief explanation of the situation between her and Marsh, and promised they would both be there for her mother's traditional family Christmas noontime brunch.

Christmas Eve day dawned bright and sunny. By midafternoon the weather was mild. Marsh was awed by the way she looked in her beautiful wedding dress, and she complimented him, for her husband-to-be looked devastatingly handsome in a charcoal-gray suit, white shirt and pearl-gray striped tie.

"One would think we were going to do something special," he remarked dryly as he helped her into the freshly washed and gleaming car.

"One would be correct," Jen agreed, her voice uneven due to the excited flutter of her heart.

"Then let's do it," he said, leaning in to kiss her cheek before starting the car.

At four-thirty in the afternoon the day before Christmas, it was quiet inside the Mission Alamo as two people stood, alone, together. As always, Jen was filled with a sensation of peace inside the structure. The very air they breathed held a sense of holiness. It was the perfect setting for their intentions.

They stood facing each other, arms at their sides, their hands tightly clasped.

"First off," Marsh began, "I swear to love you with every beat of my heart and every part of my body."

"And I," Jen replied, "I swear to love you with every beat of my heart and every part of my body."

He smiled before going on. "I, Marshall David Grainger, take thee, Jennifer Louise Dunning, for my lawfully wedded wife."

"I, Jennifer Louise Dunning, take you, Marshall David Grainger, for my lawfully wedded husband."

They were silent a moment. Both had wet eyes. Then Marsh drew Jen into his arms to hold her as if she were the most precious person in the world. Crying softly with joy, Jen wrapped her arms around his neck and clung as if she would never let him go.

Hand in hand, Marsh and Jen walked from the mission into the twilight of Christmas Eve.

Tugging gently on her hand, Marsh slanted a grin at her and said, "Now let's go see that judge."

"Yes, let's," she said, grinning back at him.

* * * * *

MILLS & BOON®

Why shop at millsandboon.co.uk?

Each year, thousands of romance readers find their perfect read at millsandboon.co.uk. That's because we're passionate about bringing you the very best romantic fiction. Here are some of the advantages of shopping at www.millsandboon.co.uk:

* **Get new books first**—you'll be able to buy your favourite books one month before they hit the shops

* **Get exclusive discounts**—you'll also be able to buy our specially created monthly collections, with up to 50% off the RRP

* **Find your favourite authors**—latest news, interviews and new releases for all your favourite authors and series on our website, plus ideas for what to try next

* **Join in**—once you've bought your favourite books, don't forget to register with us to rate, review and join in the discussions

Visit **www.millsandboon.co.uk**
for all this and more today!

MILLS & BOON®

Why not subscribe?
Never miss a title and save money too!

Here's what's available to you if you join the
exclusive **Mills & Boon® Book Club** today:

- ✦ *Titles up to a month ahead of the shops*
- ✦ *Amazing discounts*
- ✦ *Free P&P*
- ✦ *Earn Bonus Book points that can be redeemed
  against other titles and gifts*
- ✦ *Choose from monthly or pre-paid plans*

Still want more?
Well, if you join today, we'll even give you
50% OFF your first parcel!

So visit **www.millsandboon.co.uk/subs**
to be a part of this exclusive Book Club!

SUBS_2015

MILLS & BOON®

Helen Bianchin v Regency Collection!

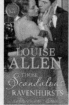